翻译研究论丛

Literary Stylistics and Fictional Translation

申丹（SHEN Dan） 著

文学
文体学与
小说翻译

北京大学出版社
PEKING UNIVERSITY PRESS

图书在版编目 (CIP) 数据

文学文体学与小说翻译 / 申丹著. —北京：北京大学出版社，2017.7
（翻译研究论丛）
ISBN 978-7-301-27936-6

Ⅰ. ①文… Ⅱ. ①申… Ⅲ. ①文学 – 文体论 ②小说 – 文学翻译　Ⅳ. ①I04

中国版本图书馆 CIP 数据核字 (2017) 第 012624 号

书　　名	文学文体学与小说翻译 WENXUE WENTIXUE YU XIAOSHUO FANYI
著作责任者	申　丹　著
责任编辑	张　冰　郝妮娜
标准书号	ISBN 978-7-301-27936-6
出版发行	北京大学出版社
地　　址	北京市海淀区成府路 205 号　100871
网　　址	http://www.pup.cn　新浪微博：@ 北京大学出版社
电子信箱	zpup@ pup.cn
电　　话	邮购部 62752015　发行部 62750672　编辑部 62759634
印　刷　者	三河市博文印刷有限公司
经　销　者	新华书店
	650 毫米 × 980 毫米　16 开本　18.25 印张　360 千字 2017 年 7 月第 1 版　2017 年 7 月第 1 次印刷
定　　价	48.00 元

未经许可，不得以任何方式复制或抄袭本书之部分或全部内容。
版权所有，侵权必究
举报电话：010-62752024　电子信箱：fd@pup.pku.edu.cn
图书如有印装质量问题，请与出版部联系，电话：010-62756370

Preface

This book is based on my Ph. D. dissertation completed at the University of Edinburghin 1987. By that time, few scholars had tried to relate literary stylistics to translation studies, especially in terms of fictional translation. Even at present, efforts are still not often made to apply stylistics to the translation of prose fiction. The second decade of the new century has seen some unprecedented publications in the field of stylistics, with 2014 witnessing the appearance of *The Routledge Handbook of Stylistics* (Burke; see Shen 2015a) and *The Cambridge Handbook of Stylistics* (Stockwell and Whiteley; see Shen 2015b), and 2016 the publication of *The Bloomsbury Companion to Stylistics* (Sotirova; see Shen 2017), which join forces in marking a new stage in the development of stylistics. All the three volumes contain a chapter on the relation between stylistics and translation, in contrast with previous collections of essays in the field which are not concerned with translation (Weber 1996; Lambrou and Stockwell 2007; McIntyre and Busse 2010). In the former case, however, the chapters in question invariably focus on the translation of poetry. The same is true for the chapter "Stylistics and Translation" (by Boase-Beier) in *The Oxford Handbook of Translation Studies* published in 2011. Only occasionally, there appear essays with the analytical focus set on prose fiction (see, for instance, Malmkjær 2004; Horton 2010).

Not surprisingly, book-length studies devoted to the relation between stylistics and fictional translation are rarely found. 2015 saw the publication of *Style in Translation: A Corpus-Based Perspective* (Huang), which examines the translator's style in fictional translation with the statistics provided by corpus analysis. This approach has the advantage of scientifically and objectively revealing the habitual or consistent stylistic choices of the translator, but is hard put to explore subtle relations between local stylistic choices and literary significance in the source and the target texts. As the present study indicates, the field of fictional translation presents various subtle issues calling for in-depth stylistic investigation, a kind of investigation that can feed back into stylistics itself and may also help enrich literary criticism. The meeting and clash between two different linguistic, literary and cultural systems in translation may shed fresh light on the thematic functions of the stylistic devices involved as well as on the relevant literary and cultural conventions which condition the writer's and the translator's choices and which tend to remain opaque within the boundary of a single language.

Since the cultural turn in the 1980s, the focus of critical attention has shifted to various contextual factors constraining the translator's choices, and to the reception and functioning of the translated texts in the target culture. This has redressed previous neglect of the cultural context but, at the same time, has led to the neglect of the stylistic features of the text to a certain extent, especially in terms of the source texts. The influence of deconstructionism, feminism and postcolonialism on translation studies has more or less lent to this kind of neglect. Fortunately, the new century witnesses an increasingly balanced concern between the context and the text in various fields, including translation studies. This book, which reveals various subtle stylistic features in the original and explores how to transfer them into the target language and culture, may help to achieve more balance between the text and the context.

Twenty years after its first publication, this book, which has been reprinted five times, is still much in demand. It has been out of stock for quite some time and Peking University Press has decided to republish the book in a new format. I believe that it will continue to be helpful to academics, researchers and students both in the field of translation studies and in the fields of stylistics and literary criticism.

Upon the reprinting of this book, I would like to express my gratitude to those at Edinburgh who introduced me to linguistics or stylistics: Keith Mitchell, Jean Ure, Gillian Brown, Professor J. Hurford, and, in particular, Elizabeth Black. I am especially grateful to my doctoral supervisors the late Professor James P. Thorne and Mr. Norman Macleod for their insightful criticisms and suggestions. Special thanks are also due to Dr. A. W. E. Dolby, Professor Jonathan Culler and Professor Henry Widdowson, who read part or whole of different manuscript versions and offered helpful comments. In addition, I deeply appreciate the contribution to this book made in various ways by my family, especially my husband Xing Li, and my friends and colleagues.

A version of chapter 4, titled "Stylistics, Objectivity, and Convention," was published in *Poetics* vol. 17, no. 3, 221 — 238 (Copyright 1988 by Elsevier Science B. V., Amsterdam, The Netherlands). A fragment of chapter 5 and a large part of chapter 7 appeared in the article "Syntax and Literary Significance in the Translation of Realistic Fiction" in *Babel* vol. 38, no. 3, 149 — 167 (Copyright 1992 by The International Federation of Translators). A major part of 6.1 appeared in the article "On the Aesthetic Function of Intentional 'Illogicality' in English-Chinese Translation of Fiction" in *Style* vol. 22, no. 4 (winter 1988). A version of 6.2, titled "Objectivity in the Translation of Narrative Fiction," was published in *Babel* vol. 34, no. 3, 131—140 (1988). A version of 6.3, titled "Unreliability and Characterization," was published in *Style* vol. 23, no. 2, 300 — 311 (Summer, 1989). Fragments of chapters 6 — 8 appeared in the article "The Distorting Medium: Discourse in the Realistic Novel" in *The Journal of Narrative Technique* vol. 21, no. 3, 231—249 (fall, 1991). A large part of chapter 8 appeared in the article "On the Transference of Modes of Speech (or Thought) from Chinese Narrative Fiction into English" in *Comparative Literature Studies* vol. 28, no. 4, 395 — 414 (Copyright 1991 by The Pennsylvania State University). I am grateful to the editors and publishers for permission to reprint.

CONTENTS

CHAPTER 1　INTRODUCTION ··· 1
  1.1 BASIC AIMS ·· 1
  1.2 LITERARY STYLISTICS ··· 2
  1.3 APPLYING STYLISTICS TO LITERARY
      TRANSLATION ··· 7

PART ONE
LITERARY STYLISTICS AS A DISCIPLINE

**CHAPTER 2　THE CONCERN OF STYLISTICS AS AN
               INTERMEDIARY DISCIPLINE** ······················· 15
  2.1 SOME DIFFERENT CONCEPTIONS OF STYLE ········· 15
  2.2 OBJECTS OF INVESTIGATION OF LITERARY
      STYLISTICS ··· 22
**CHAPTER 3　LINGUISTIC FORM AND LITERARY
               SIGNIFICANCE** ··· 34
**CHAPTER 4　THE LINGUISTIC BASIS: OBJECTIVE OR
               SUBJECTIVE?** ·· 60
  4.1 LINGUISTIC OBJECTIVITY: A MATTER OF
      CONVENTION ·· 61
  4.2 STRUCTURAL FEATURE, PSYCHOLOGICAL
      VALUE AND LITERARY SIGNIFICANCE ················· 62
  4.3 DOES INTERPRETATION PRODUCE LINGUISTIC
      FACTS? ··· 75

4.4 A CONSIDERATION OF "WHAT IS STYLISTICS? PART Ⅱ" ……………………………………… 84

PART TWO
APPLYING STYLISTICS TO THE TRANSLATION OF FICTION

CHAPTER 5 THE PLACE OF LITERARY STYLISTICS IN THE TRANSLATION OF FICTION ………… 91
  5.1 THE INSUFFICIENCY OF GENERAL TRANSLATION STUDIES ………………… 91
  5.2 CHARACTERISTICS OF FICTIONAL (VS. POETIC) TRANSLATION ………………… 95
  5.3 LITERARY STYLISTICS AND DECEPTIVE EQUIVALENCE ………………………… 107
CHAPTER 6 ASPECTS OF LEXICAL EXPRESSION ………… 110
  6.1 DEVIATION IN THE FORM OF "ILLOGICALITY" ……… 110
  6.2 OBJECTIVITY ………………………………………… 137
  6.3 UNRELIABILITY AND CHARACTERIZATION ……… 151
  6.4 "REDUNDANT" ENCODING ……………………… 167
CHAPTER 7 ASPECTS OF SYNTAX …………………………… 174
  7.1 SYNTAX AND PACE ………………………………… 175
  7.2 SYNTAX AND PROMINENCE ……………………… 184
  7.3 SYNTAX AND THE IMITATION OF PROCESS ……… 196
  7.4 THE TRANSFERENCE OF PARALLELISM ………… 205
  7.5 JUXTAPOSITION AND PSEUDO-SIMULTANEITY … 212
  7.6 LINGUISTIC FORM AND FICTIONAL REALITY …… 215
CHAPTER 8 SPEECH AND THOUGHT PRESENTATION … 221
  8.1 BASIC MODES IN ENGLISH ……………………… 222
  8.2 BASIC MODES IN CHINESE ……………………… 224
  8.3 THE TRANSFERENCE OF BLEND ………………… 226
  8.4 THE TRANSFERENCE OF DIRECT SPEECH ……… 234

8.5 THE FUNCTIONS OF FIS AND THE NEED
FOR ITS PRESERVATION 247
8.6 THE TRANSFERENCE OF SLIPPING 252
8.7 CONCLUSION 260
NOTES 263
BIBLIOGRAPHY 269

CHAPTER 1

INTRODUCTION

1.1 BASIC AIMS

Literary stylistics and literary translation have rarely been considered in relation to each other. Despite the fact that the literary translator's choice of words, syntax etc. frequently raises stylistic issues and that literary translation therefore constitutes a congenial area of stylistic investigation, attempts at applying stylistics to literary translation have so far, in relation to English and Chinese at any rate, been scarcely made. Thus, in contrast with the more or less sophisticated stylistic analysis widely undertaken in Anglo-American intralingual literary studies for the past thirty years or so (stylistics, it must be noted, was not introduced into mainland China until around 1980), criticism of literary translation, particularly of the translation of prose fiction, has remained remarkably traditional, characterized by general and impressionistic comments on style or by an intuitive analysis with a notable lack of sensitivity to subtle stylistic devices. To bring studies of literary translation up to date and to improve, as a result, the quality and standard of literary translating, there is surely an urgent need to replace traditional impressionistic approaches by more precise and more penetrating stylistic models and methods. The first aim of the present book is therefore to argue, mainly by way of practical analysis, for the usefulness and necessity of a stylistic approach to the study of literary translation in general and of the translation of prose fiction in particular.

Stylistics, however, is not here taken for granted. And this brings us to another basic aim of the present book, which is to explicate the nature, function and validity of literary stylistics as a discipline (with reference to English only). The stimulus for this explication came from two contrastive sources: the vagueness of the claims made by some proponents on the one hand and the fallaciousness of the attacks made by some opponents on the other. While issues such as the objects of investigation and, more significantly, the characteristic mode of argumentation of stylistics will be discussed in considerable detail, no attempt is made to summarize its historical development, or to study and compare the linguistic models employed by stylisticians, for such a study lies beyond the scope of the present book.

In accordance with the two basic aims, this book is divided into two major parts, with the first part examining stylistics as a discipline and with the second arguing and demonstrating the application of stylistics to the translation of prose fiction. It need hardly be said, though, that the contribution to stylistics which this study seeks to make is not confined to the first part. The problems and solutions that emerge in interlingual fictional transfer, as will be extensively analysed in the second part, help to reveal certain of the essential aspects of novelistic technique, offering fresh insights into the functions or values of stylistic devices as well as into the relevant literary conventions which condition the writer/translator's choices and which tend to remain opaque within the boundary of a single language.

1.2 LITERARY STYLISTICS

Anglo-American literary stylistics originated and developed under the combined influence of developments in modern linguistics, Anglo-American practical criticism, French structuralism, the Russian Formalist School and the Prague Linguistic Circle. Marked by the use of linguistic models in the interpretation of literary texts, this is a discipline mediating between literary criticism and linguistics of different levels and in various forms.

This intermediary discipline is referred to, apart from the unqualified title "stylistics," either as "literary stylistics" or as "linguistic stylistics."[1] The epithet "literary" stresses its difference from a descriptively-oriented approach to literary texts, an approach which treats literary texts as data or as formal linguistic objects; and an approach where the main thrust is directed towards the possibility or necessity of applying linguistic theory to the description of literary texts, and/or towards the exemplification of the linguistic system with the textual features concerned, and/or towards the explication of a linguistic model adopted in the analysis (see, for instance, Halliday 1966 & 1967:217—223; Sinclair 1966 & 1968; Thorne 1965 & 1969; Levin 1967; Carter 1982). With the aim of supporting or promoting literary interpretation and taking literary texts as communicative acts, literary stylisticians operate along the lines of traditional common-sense based interpretative strategies of literary significance, focusing on linguistic choices which are thematically or artistically motivated.

The epithet "linguistic" emphasizes on the other hand the difference between this intermediary discipline (which is based on or informed by modern linguistics) and the more traditional approaches to literary style. If the discipline in question can be treated, at least in part, as an extension of practical criticism, the extension mainly lies in linguistic observations and insights, in the analytic and systematic knowledge of communicative and linguistic norms (cf. Carter 1982:4—7). In this discipline, that is to say, the emphasis falls both on the explicitness or precision of the linguistic description and on the resultant literary effects. Analysts are often eclectic in approach, drawing on whatever different linguistic models are called for in the analysis.

By now, stylistic investigation has been extended to all levels of linguistic structure and to all the three major literary genres of poetry, prose fiction, and drama. During the past twenty years or so, there has emerged an increasing interest in fictional prose but on the whole poetry, because of its higher frequency of foregrounding and the shorter length of the text as a thematic unity, has been given more attention. Thus, although the second part of this work will focus on the translation of prose fiction, in discussing stylistics as a discipline, I shall quite often touch on stylistic analysis of poetry. It is true that the two genres differ considerably in terms of stylistic properties (the phonological property, for instance, does not feature in the novel while modes of speech are hardly found in poetry). But the conventions which underlie the literary significance of linguistic form are essentially the same in both genres; and this in turn determines that stylistic analyses of both, as will be discussed in Chapters Three and Four, share fundamentally the same mode of argumentation.

The discussion of stylistics as a discipline will start, in the following chapter, from a scrutiny of its characteristic concern. A basic distinction between linguistic habits and aesthetically motivated choices will be drawn as a prelude to a consideration of two contrasting levels of stylistic investigation, viz., linguistic form and, with reference to traditional realistic fiction in particular, fictional 'facts'. Insofar as realistic fiction is concerned, the aesthetic function of linguistic form can usually be located at the level of narrative discourse in contradistinction to the level of fictional reality. This distinction, which comes from the French structuralists' distinction between histoire (the narrated story) and discours (narrative discourse), lends perspective to the traditional distinction between "what" and "how" or "content" and "expression" (see Fowler 1977; Chatman 1978). While narrative discourse (or narrative style) is the direct object of linguistic analysis, fictional 'facts' are essentially extralinguistic (with the exception of the verbal reality composed of a character's speech, thought or mind-style), an area where linguistic models, leaving aside the analogous or quasi-models employed by structuralist critics, usually do not apply. Such a distinction is not only helpful but also necessary in view of some rather extravagant claims made by linguists or stylisticians, such as the following:

> as no science can go beyond mathematics, no criticism can go beyond its linguistics (Whitehall 1951:713)

Surely one may call all textual facts "linguistic" in a loose sense. But the distinction between truly linguistic facts and, strictly speaking, extralinguistic facts usually holds, in relation to realistic fiction at any rate. If the purpose of a stylistician is to explicate how textual facts give rise to the total meaning of the work, the analyst must take account of both. The analysis of the latter, however, would depend, instead of on a linguistic knowledge of the workings of (or effects in) language, primarily on common-sense based close observation of the relation between the fictional 'facts' involved and their aesthetic function (see the discussion in 2.2.2).

The consideration of the objects of investigation of stylistics naturally leads us to a discussion in Chapter Three of the stylistician's characteristic mode of argumentation. The stylistician's typical progression in argument from one frame of reference, that of linguistic form, to another, that of literary significance, has been subjected to a series of criticisms. I have singled out and shall argue against two contrasting attacks: one made by Roger Pearce from the perspective of a linguist and the other by Stanley Fish from the viewpoint of a critic. While Pearce's charge is seen to be based on a misunderstanding about the purposes of literary stylistics and about the conventional nature of signification, the influential paper written by Fish "What is stylistics and why are they saying such terrible things about it?" (1973) also displays a notable lack of understanding of the nature, function and validity of stylistics as an intermediary discipline. By analysing various charges made by Pearce and Fish and by exposing a number of intentionally or unintentionally misleading devices involved in their argument, I hope to help reveal the true nature of the typical mode of argumentation used by literary stylisticians, providing a reliable, though not necessarily comprehensive, picture of its theoretical foundation, its analytic procedure and its main characteristics. The picture may gain further clarity not only from a comparison made between this stylistic mode and two others (i. reading from linguistic form to personality and ii. a study of the relation between impressionistic terms like "terse" or "complex" and identifiable structural properties), but also from a discussion of the essential similarity and contrast between the present stylistic mode and Fish's own "affective stylistics."

In Chapter Four, which is largely complementary to Chapter Three, we shall come to a consideration of the objectivity of the stylistician's primary frame of reference, i. e. the linguistic basis, an objectivity which, though taken for granted by stylisticians, is seriously challenged by Stanley Fish in "What is stylistics and why are they saying such terrible things about it? Part II" (1980). I shall argue, as a major premise, that the distinction between "objective" and "subjective" as usually drawn does not apply to a phenomenon such as language and, further, that, in the social reality of language, objectivity is, in effect, a matter of conventionality: in more specific terms, what is conventional is objective and what is personal is subjective. Starting from this basic premise, an explication and evaluation will be taken up in terms of the different degrees of objectivity of the three correlated levels involved in the stylistician's characteristic mode of argumentation: structural feature, psychological value and literary significance. This is followed by a discussion of Fish's challenge to the objectivity of the stylistician's linguistic basis, a challenge which is wrongly based on a failure to discriminate between convention and interpretation. By way of the explication and the discussion as such, I hope to throw some further light on the nature, function and validity of the stylistician's characteristic mode of argument in particular and of stylistics as an intermediary discipline in general.

1.3 APPLYING STYLISTICS TO LITERARY TRANSLATION

Literary translation, particularly the translation of prose fiction, has benefited very little from recent developments in linguistics. "In the typical linguistics-oriented study of translation," as Lefevere observes, "some lip service is usually (almost ritualistically) paid to literary translation, but this serves more often than not as an excuse to skip the problems connected with the particular type of translation and to move on to what are considered the 'real' issues" (1981:52). Indeed, just as a purely linguistic description of literary text does not have much to offer to literary criticism, translation studies with only a linguistic concern have little or no bearing on problems characteristic of literary translation. I shall discuss in some detail, at the beginning of the second part, the inadequacy of linguistics-oriented general translation studies when applied to literary discourse. The remedy, though, may be readily sought in literary stylistics, which, not only informed by modern linguistics but also taking literary competence or sensitivity as a prerequisite, can provide interesting insights into the aesthetic functions of the verbal choices, particularly the subtle stylistic or rhetorical choices, made by the author and by the translator.

It is understood that literary translating is a complex process subjected to the influence of numerous variable factors, such as whether the translation should be source-language-oriented or target-language-oriented, or whether a given original should be adapted for certain pragmatic purposes. The dimension to which stylistics has the potential of making most contribution is chiefly formal or structural. By sharpening one's sensitivity to the workings of the language system, by improving one's understanding of the function of stylistic norms, and by enhancing one's awareness of how literary conventions and the writer's creative acts combine to make linguistic form take on aesthetic significance, stylistics operates to help the literary translator to achieve functional equivalence or expressive identity. What is involved is of course not only the aesthetic function of linguistic features in the respective languages but also the stylistic correspondence, which is often not contemporary, between the two languages involved.

Now, the fact that I have chosen to concentrate on the translation of prose fiction—more specifically, of the traditional realistic kind—is not due to a belief that prose fiction should be placed at the centre of poetic discourse. Rather, it is to be accounted for by the fact that problems associated with the translation of realistic fiction as a literary genre have been most neglected and, further, that many of those problems, which may be subsumed under the heading "deceptive equivalence," can be quite effectively dealt with by stylistic analysis. As shall be discussed in 5.2.2, "deceptive equivalence" is found in both of the two contrasting dimensions of narrative structure: the narrative discourse and the narrated story.

Generally speaking, in traditional realistic fiction, the writer's manipulation of linguistic form at the level of narrative discourse functions not as an end in itself but rather as means for various thematic effects, such as efficient characterization, or for making the fictional reality operate more effectively in the work's thematic design. At this level, the occurrence of "deceptive equivalence," which conveys approximately the same fictional 'facts' but fails to capture the aesthetic effects generated by stylistic or rhetorical devices in the original, is primarily ascribable to the fact that, in translating realistic fiction, the translator is inclined to establish equivalence at the level of "paraphrasable material content" (Bassnett-McGuire 1980:115), focusing on the represented fictional reality and overlooking the novelist's formal operations over and above the experience depicted. Such an inclination is attributable not only to the usually isomorphous relation between the fictional world and the real world (allied to the resultant suspension of disbelief) but also to the translator's lack of awareness of the novelist's verbal artistry which is much less obtrusive than that of the poet's. Responsible for the translator's stylistic non-discrimination is the backwardness of fictional translation studies which have on the whole remained impressionistic and which often go no further than "referential equivalence" (it should be clear that "deceptive equivalence" at the level of narrative discourse typically constitutes referential equivalence). There is surely an urgent need to introduce stylistic analysis as a means of exposing "deceptive equivalence" as such, and as a means of enhancing the translator's stylistic competence, one that is essential to achieving functional equivalence in literary translation.

In realistic fiction, a large part of the aesthetic significance resides in the created fictional reality which is "expressed through, rather than inherent in, language" (Leech & Short 1981:2). At this level, "deceptive equivalence" takes the shape of distortion of fictional 'facts' which is mistaken by the translator as some form of equivalence. What concern me here are not errors caused by inadequate linguistic competence (which is the concern of general translation studies) but distortions resulting from, among other things, translators' failure to take account of the structural or thematic functions of the fictional 'facts' involved. As a matter over and beyond linguistic competence, the cases here tend to pass off as reasonable correspondence to the original, whose distorting nature becomes detectable probably only in the light of the surrounding literary context, in terms of the function of the expressions in the larger thematic unity. This level has received relatively little attention in intra-lingual stylistic analysis; a fact which is not surprising since, as distinct from linguistic form where one can pinpoint a set of alternatives (like direct speech, indirect speech, free indirect speech etc.), in the case of fictional 'facts,' it is difficult to determine the potential choices or alternatives (one needs to bear in mind that stylistics is always comparative in nature). Because of the translator's distortions which constitute actual alternatives to the original and which help highlight the aesthetic effects obtaining in the source-language text, this level seems to present great stylistic interest in the analysis of fictional translation.

Of the three chapters—six to eight—of illustrative analysis in the second part, Chapter Six is concerned, to a great extent, with the level of fictional reality, forming a contrast to the following two chapters which focus on the aesthetic function of narrative discourse. These three chapters deal with lexical expression, syntax, and speech and thought presentation respectively. It is understood that, in terms of either encoding or effect, lexical choice is often inseparable from other linguistic choices, particularly that of syntax; and that the boundaries between those choices are in themselves frequently problematic. Despite this, I choose to discuss them separately, for such a division helps to highlight some specific problems peculiar to each category. In discussing one category, if other linguistic features are seen to be relevant, they are also freely discussed. Although the limitation of space only permits me to investigate some aspects of lexical expression, syntax and speech/thought presentation, the discussion should have implications for literary translation in general.

Most of the data analysed in the second part are drawn from English translations of Chinese prose fiction, more specifically, translations of Cao Xueqin's *Honglou Meng* (written in the middle of the eighteenth century and regarded, by consensus, as the greatest Chinese novel), and of works by some well-know modern Chinese writers, such as Lao She, Lu Xun and Mao Dun.[2] Now, Chinese and English, which not only belong to different language families but also represent quite different cultures, differ greatly in terms of linguistic and literary conventions. We shall pay special attention to certain of the peculiar ways in which language generates aesthetic effects in Chinese and to the methods used by the translators to achieve expressive identity in English. But in order for the analysis to proceed from an immediately relevant point of departure, implicit allowances are sometimes made both for the basic linguistic differences between Chinese and English and, if the translation is not contemporary with the original, for the diachronic changes involved.

The data invariably take the shape of selected passages. Indeed, with more than one text (the original plus its translations) to deal with simultaneously, one may have to adopt some convenient mode of analysis. Although the effects are often locally identifiable, it is understood that the textual features concerned do not function in isolation, but interact with all the other related elements in an integrated pattern or in the work's thematic design. In the analysis, I am eclectic in approach, drawing primarily, but by no means exclusively, on Halliday's systemic functional grammar. With the definite practical purpose of helping improve literary translation, linguistic models are treated only as subservient tools. As linguistic technicality is, generally speaking, kept to a minimum (in order to be adequate to the purpose), the analysis should be easily accessible to literary translators.

PART ONE

LITERARY STYLISTICS AS A DISCIPLINE

CHAPTER 2
THE CONCERN OF STYLISTICS AS AN INTERMEDIARY DISCIPLINE

A literary text, as a construct of language, is a multi-level and multi-dimensional entity, to which different analytic models, each with its given assumptions and interests, may apply. Not surprisingly, the conceptions of and the approaches to literary style are marked by proliferation, diversity and one-sidedness. The present chapter seeks to define the typical objects of investigation of stylistics as an intermediary discipline in relation to the concerns of some other approaches to literary style.

2.1 SOME DIFFERENT CONCEPTIONS OF STYLE

The difference in the conception of style first has to do with the domain of style: genre or period style differs, not only in scope but also fundamentally, from the style of a particular author or text. I shall now touch briefly on genre or period style, then proceed to a discussion of two contrasting concepts of authorial or textual style.

2.1.1 Style as Genre or Period Characteristics

The characteristics of the use of language found in a particular genre (or school) or period of literary writing have frequently attracted the attention of investigators of style. Significantly, genre or period style differs from authorial or textual style in the sense that, rather than a writer's personal choices, it involves a set of given conventions or rules with which a writer operating in that particular genre or period complies or is expected to comply. If the style of a given author or text is determined primarily by contrast with the styles of other authors or texts found in the *same* genre (and/or period), the style of a genre or period is on the other hand defined in relation to the styles of *other* genres or periods. Now, given that genre or period style is theoretically fairly uncontroversial (like the investigation of registers in non-literary language), there seems no need to go further.

2.1.2 Style as Habitual Traits of the Author

Many analysts, particularly author-detection stylisticians, have focused on the linguistic habits of the writer. Traditionally, the measurement of style as such rests on intuitive impression or statistics. Starting from the 1960's, some transformational grammarians such as Hayes and Ohmann have resorted to transformational analysis to make explicit the author's characteristic preference for surface syntactic choices, one aspect of style which is taken by Ohmann as "a central determinant" (1964:438).

As habitual traits in contrast with thematic devices, this aspect may be treated as the "unconscious pole" of the writer's use of language (Milic 1971). Not surprisingly, the critic in this vein is typically concerned with the association between style as such and the writer's personality rather than the literary significance of the text(s). Now, leaving aside the true intent of the widely cited aphorism of Buffon's "The style is the man" (cf. Gray 1969:39; Milic 1971), if one claims that style reflects the personality of the author, one may mean by "personality" either behavioural/mental characteristics or distinctive ways of perceiving and organizing experience or perhaps both.[1] In terms of the former, a notable critical attempt is made by Henri Morier who postulates a one-to-one correspondence between eight classes of style as such and eight kinds of temperament and mental makeup: weak, delicate, balanced, positive, strong, hybrid, subtle, and defective (see

Ullmann 1965:25—26; cf. Milic 1971:77). But such associations can be, and often are, far-fetched in that "some peculiarities of style need have no psychological background: they may be mere mannerisms or tics" (Ullmann 1965:24). Or it may even throw a false scent, that is, suggest some personality quite contrary to that of the author (see Ullmann 1965:30—31). Now some points need to be noticed here. First, the view that a writer's personality determines the quiddity of his or her style implies that the writer can exert no control over the style at all, all of it being determined by habits, associations, and conditioning (Milic 1971:80). It follows that if the writer consciously controls his or her linguistic choice for this or that purpose, as in the case of techniques or rhetorical choices, his or her 'style,' if we may still call it so, most probably no longer reflects his or her personality. Secondly, as Milic observes, a rhetorical choice may shade into a linguistic habit. In such a case, the change may be due to personal predilection and, therefore, possibly personality but it may be due to factors that do not have to do with personality. Furthermore, when searching for personality in linguistic habits, one needs to be on guard against attributing choices that are more or less determined by subject matter or genre to the writer's own predilection or personality (see Leech & Short 1981:12; Lutwack 1960:211; Milic 1971:82—83).

When it comes to the correlation between the author's linguistic habits and his or her distinctive ways of perceiving and organizing experience, the picture seems to be less problematic. This kind of association has received much attention from Ohmann, who holds that:

> each writer tends to exploit deep linguistic resources in characteristic ways—that his style, in other words, rests on syntactic options within sentences ... —and that these syntactic preferences correlate with habits of meaning that tell us something about his mode of conceiving experience. (1966)

It seems worth mentioning that, while the reflection of the author's behavioural/mental characteristics is more or less confined to linguistic habits, the reflection of the author's cognitive process may be found both in the habitual and in the rhetorical, or thematically-motivated, choices. But of course the habitual and the rhetorical/motivated differ from each other in the sense that what the former reveals is, as Ohmann puts it, "a habit of meaning … a persistent way of sorting out the phenomena of experience" (1967), whereas what the latter brings out is on the other hand the author's specific vision or viewpoint concerning particular fictional event(s) (Ohmann seems to regard such cases as "temporary epistemologies"). Perhaps precisely because the habitual and the rhetorical/motivated can both correlate with the author's cognitive processes, one finds here frequent overlap between the two kinds of choices. It has been observed that in some experimental writers like Donald Barthelme, there is a consistent use of highly simple language, a linguistic "habit" that is however motivated by a desire "to support, even establish, a particular point of view—that the world is meaningless, disjointed, and doomed by poverty of experience" (Traugott & Pratt 1980:168—169). Similarly, Henry James's preference for complexity and for placing causes after effects is in a sense motivated by his particular concern with psychological realism (see Leech & Short 1981:102).

Now, in terms of literary/thematic interpretation, one needs to be aware that a "distinctive frequency distribution is in itself no guarantee of stylistic relevance, as can be seen from authorship studies, where the diagnostic features are often, from a literary standpoint, very trivial ones" (Halliday 1971:344). Nevertheless, some critics who focus on the author's habitual and recurrent linguistic choices may well take the author's linguistic habits and literary significance as necessary correlates. Ohmann (1964), for instance, after offering a description of Faulkner's syntactic traits based on a typically Faulknerian passage, declares:

The move from formal description of styles to critical and semantic interpretation should be the ultimate goal of stylistics, but in this article I am concerned only with the first step: description.

However, once literary interpretation is actually brought in, attention tends to shift from the author's linguistic habits to rhetorical or thematically-motivated choices. This seems to be the case even when it comes to writers like Conrad, Hemingway or James whose habitual traits are closely tied up with the subject matter. To take Ohmann's own analysis for example: in his evaluatively-oriented analysis (1966) of the final sentence of Conrad's "The Secret Sharer," much attention is directed towards the particular syntactic organization (e.g. the rhetorical movement) of *that* sentence, which is very much motivated by the immediate thesis of that sentence and the underlying theme of the story. In effect, only by treating the syntax as so motivated, rather than as habitually preferred, can one make full sense of Ohmann's observations such as "The syntax of the last sentence schematizes the relationships [the narrator] has achieved, in identifying with Leggatt's heroic defection, and in fixing on a point of reference—the hat—that connects him to the darker powers of nature" (ibid.). It is true that the syntax concerned exemplifies some of Conrad's habitual traits such as the use of chaining in syntactic expansion. But the stylistic significance comes largely from syntactic devices that are motivated in that particular context and that are more subtle than, say, a mere chaining effect. The sentence in question points to the fact that a linguistic form, while being on a general level representative of its author's habitual choice, may contain a subtle internal organization motivated in its given context, the analysis of which, as distinct from that of the habitual, cannot be divorced from the immediate thesis and/or the underlying theme. And this brings us to a different conception of style.

2.1.3 Style as Artistically or Thematically Motivated Choices

Investigators of style, if concerned with literary interpretation or evaluation, tend to focus on artistically or thematically motivated choices. Such a concentration is unequivocally displayed in Halliday's definition of foregrounding:

> Foregrounding, as I understand it, is *prominence that is motivated*. It is not difficult to find patterns of prominence in a poem or prose text, regularities in the sounds or words or structures that stand out in some way, or may be brought out by careful reading; and one may often be led in this way towards a new insight, through finding that such prominence contributes to the writer's total meaning. *But unless it does, it will seem to lack motivation*; a feature that is brought into prominence will be "foregrounded" *only if* it relates to the meaning of the text as a whole. (1971:339; my emphasis)

A similar exclusion is found in the French structuralist Todorov's statement:

> Every utterance will ... have a multitude of stylistic characteristics. But only a part of them will normally be "actualized." In other words, the structural description of a particular text *will not consider a property stylistic* if it cannot show that this property is found in relationship with others, at other levels, or, to put it in other terms, that it is meaningful. (1971:36)

Stylisticians in this vein are interested in that part of a writer's style which displays conscious or quasi-conscious artistry or craftsmanship (cf. Milic 1971; Mukarovsky 1964:19); a part that contains various kinds of stylistic or rhetorical devices functioning as semantic reinforcement or modification, including "technique" both in Ohmann's narrow sense (1964:425) and in a broader sense as used by Schorer who regards "the resources of language" as "part of the technique of fiction":

> language as used to create a certain texture and tone which in themselves state and define themes and meanings; or language, the

counters of our ordinary speech, as forced, through conscious manipulation, into all those larger meanings which our ordinary speech almost never intends. (1967:66—67)

Stylisticians operating along these lines do take the author's linguistic habits as part of the author's style but they establish a clear criterion of relevance, namely, sematic/thematic or artistic function, dismissing thematically or artistically irrelevant linguistic choices as being trivial. This position is arrived at via different paths. A most common route that leads to such a position is a concern with the subject matter, with the object and purpose of artistic creation or literary communication, treating style as expressive or affective elements operating to heighten the aesthetic effect. Such a concentration by stylisticians on the aesthetic purpose, function and value associated with the use of language in literature may find an interesting expression in Cluysenaar's observation that "stylistic exploration can be the equivalent, for literature, of the painter's or sculptor's workshop" (1976:9). Style is thus identified with various linguistic features, devices and patterns which function to produce artistically or thematically related effects; and language is naturally examined in the context of literary interpretation.

Now, because of the limitation of space, I shall not go into other different, though possibly overlapping, conceptions of style, such as style as deviation from a norm (see Enkvist 1964:23ff. ; Todorov 1971: 30; Mukarovsky 1964; Leech & Short 1981:43ff.) or style as textual characteristics: a concept of style as shown in Halliday's earlier descriptively-oriented analyses of literary texts. With the distinction drawn above between habitual traits and motivated choice, we now come to a consideration of some specific objects of investigation of stylistics as an intermediary discipline.

2.2 OBJECTS OF INVESTIGATION OF LITERARY STYLISTICS

The concern of stylistics as a discipline mediating between linguistics and literary criticism can be simply and broadly defined as thematically and artistically motivated verbal choices. This title, however, involves different layers or dimensions of the text. Which dimension or dimensions are brought under focus in one particular analysis depends on factors such as the linguistic model(s) used, the stylistic properties of the text (e. g. in which aspect(s) foregrounding or defamiliarization occurs) or the analyst's own interest. Attention will be directed here to two contrastive dimensions of the text: i) linguistic form and ii) fictional 'facts.' The former constitutes the most prominent and characteristic object of investigation of literary stylistics; and the latter has been singled out mainly because of its relevance to the analysis in the second part.

2.2.1 Linguistic Form

Linguistic form as a title covers many specific categories such as surface syntactic choice, lexical choice (e. g. from different registers), figurative expression, metre, alliteration, or modes of speech presentation (e. g. direct vs. indirect speech). The aesthetic significance of linguistic form varies a great deal in literature—not only from poetry (which often works by elegant concentration) to the novel (which often works by exhaustive presentation [see Watt 1957:33]), but also within the genre of prose fiction. Anthony Burgess observes:

> Novelists, like poets, work in the medium of human language, but some may be said to work in it more than others. There is a kind of novelist (conveniently designed Class 1), usually popular, sometimes wealthy, in whose work language is a zero quantity, transparent,

unseductive, the overtones of connotation and ambiguity totally damped ... Such work is closer to film than to poetry, and it invariably films better than it reads. ... To the other kind of novelist (Class 2) it is important that the opacity of language be exploited, so that ambiguities, puns and centrifugal connotations are to be enjoyed rather than regretted, and whose books, made out of words as much as characters and incidents, lose a great deal when adapted to a visual medium. ... Needless to say, there are stylistic areas where the two classes of fiction overlap. ... (1979:15)

What interests me here is not so much the distinction itself as the point that different types of prose fiction present different degrees of aesthetic significance of linguistic form. Modern experimental novels of Woolf, James, Joyce and their like, which figure at the very heart of opaque writing and which have a close affinity with modern poetry, are a type where "form is accorded maximum importance" (Lodge 1977:44) and where aesthetic significance is inseparable from the novelist's exploitation of the possibilities of language. Indeed, that "[Joyce's] language demands our central attention as critics, is a proposition that no one is likely to challenge" (Lodge 1966:30).

But a quite different picture emerges from traditional realistic fiction where language is much more referential or informative and where aesthetic effects tend to reside more in the created fictional reality which is expressed through, rather than inherent in, language. If, in modern poetry or experimental fiction, foregrounding may be taken as forming the primary coherence, in the present type of novel, primary coherence is normally constituted by the represented fictional reality. Here one can usually postulate a distinction between the narrative discourse and the narrated story, locating aesthetic function of linguistic form at the level of narrative discourse. This point is reflected in the following comment by Wayne Booth:

"style" is sometimes broadly used to cover whatever it is that gives us a sense, from word to word and line to line, that the author sees more deeply and judges more profoundly than his presented characters. But, though style is one of our main sources of insight into the author's norms, in carrying such strong overtones of the merely verbal the word *style* excludes our sense of the author's skill in his choice of character and episode and scene and idea. "Tone" is similarly used to refer to the implicit evaluation which the author manages to convey behind his explicit presentation, but it almost inevitably suggests again something limited to the merely verbal; some aspects of the implied author may be inferred through tonal variations, but his major qualities will depend also on the hard facts of action and character in the tale that is told. (1961:74)

Fictional reality does not, of course, exist apart from the sequence of words symbolizing it, yet it constitutes "a more abstract level of existence, which in principle is partly independent of the language through which it is represented, and may be realized, for example, through the visual medium of film" (Leech & Short 1981: 37) Essentially, one infers fictional 'facts' in the same way as one infers facts from news reports or historical documents (see Fowler 1981:169). In reading a realistic fiction, then, the reader tries to reconstruct the experience the novelist has represented and then evaluates the writer's formal operations made on it as regards, say, whether the author is manipulating linguistic form to imitate or "shape" the experience involved (see 7.5).

Such a distinction between fictional reality and narrative discourse or narrative style is often found problematic in poetry. To look at a short poem by Roethke:

CHILD ON TOP OF A GREENHOUSE

The wind billowing out the seat of my britches,
My feet crackling splinters of glass and dried putty,
The half-grown chrysanthemums staring up like accusers,

Up through the streaked glass, flashing with sunlight,
A few white clouds all rushing eastward,
A line of elms plunging and tossing like horses,
And everyone, everyone pointing up and shouting.

Like many others, this poem is marked by absence of temporal references and, as Widdowson observes (see 1975: 54 — 57), the nominal groups which constitute this poem are characterized by the progressive aspect without tense—"billowing," "crackling," "staring," "flashing," "rushing," "plunging," "tossing," "pointing" and "shouting":

> The effect of isolating aspect here is to make a statement about a sensation of ongoing movement which has no attachment to time. The boy is perched on top of a greenhouse, physically aloof from the world below and at the same time removed from the reality which it represents, detached from real time and aware only of a kind of timeless movement. (57)

The point is that the subjective impression as such which the poem records constitutes the very reality conveyed by the poem. Here, the reader is unlikely to draw a line between the fictional 'facts' which are necessarily transient and the narrative discourse; but rather, he or she would tend to take the fictional reality as one of ongoing movement with no attachment to time. Generally speaking, what matters in poetry is, as indicated here, the poet's personal vision or, in other words, a reality as perceived by the poet, whereas what counts in realistic fiction are both "the hard facts of action and character" and the author's vision of, or attitude towards, those facts. This distinction is of course not absolute, since in both cases fictional reality is derived from the conventional model of reality; and since in both cases reality is dissociated from an immediate social context, not being truth-conditional. Yet the difference remains. It is quite inconceivable that a novelist would put down "I am the enemy you liked, my friend ... " as Owen does in poetry. And if the lines quoted above were to appear as a description in a novel (where, however, the writer would have to provide more context of particularity), the reader would surely try to identify the fictional 'facts' in contradistinction to the I-narrator's subjective impression.

In effect, I see in this difference one of the fundamental reasons which account for the fact that monism is happier with poetry and dualism with the novel.[2] Given that linguistic form is typically used both in poetry and in the novel to convey the author's vision, in poetry, where the poet's personal vision of the reality tends to be or become the reality, the values generated by linguistic form, particularly in the case of figure of speech, tend to be inseparable from the reality conveyed. In the novel, however, the values generated by linguistic form, if operating at the level of narrative discourse, are normally distinguishable from fictional reality. But of course the explanation lies also in the obvious difference between the two genres in terms of verbal intensity or opacity: poetry as a genre often works by elegant concentration with foregrounding achieving "maximum intensity to the extent of pushing communication into the background ... in order to place in the foreground the act of expression, the act of speech itself" (Mukarovsky 1964:19); whereas the novel as a whole often works by exhaustive presentation, attracting much less attention to the linguistic medium. In the context of the novel, we can usually assume:

> The fiction remains the invariant element: the element which, from the point of view of stylistic variation, must be taken for granted. But of course it is only invariant in a special sense: the author is free to order his universe as he wants, but for the purposes of stylistic variation we are only interested in those choices of language which do not involve changes in the fictional universe. (Leech & Short 1981:37; cf. the discussion of fictional reality in 2.2.2)

Although such a distinction between fictional reality and narrative discourse or narrative style is often found untenable in poetry, in terms of some kinds of linguistic form like poetic rhythm, alliteration, register, or certain surface syntactic choices, it is still plausible to draw a distinction between the values generated by linguistic form and "cognitive meaning" or "propositional content" (see chapters 3 & 4). If "stylistic value" is used to refer to the value attached to linguistic form and "content" used to stand for cognitive meaning or fictional reality, the total significance of a given sentence or text may be formalized with the following equation:

CONTENT + STYLISTIC VALUE = (total) SIGNIFICANCE

The plus sign, though, is potentially misleading since stylistic values function not only as semantic reinforcement but also as semantic modification (see 7.5.2 Shaping the fictional reality; also Widdowson 1975:39ff.). In the latter case, (total) significance typically comes from the paradoxical tension or interaction between content and stylistic value, in a form such as:

CONTENT↔STYLISTIC VALUE = (total) SIGNIFICANCE

In fact, we may need some other formulations to formalize the relation between content and stylistic value as such. The two formulations above do not, for instance, apply to the first case analysed in Chapter Six, a case where Jane Austen manipulates linguistic form to create multiple ironic oppositions or contrasts between narrative style and fictional reality, with the narrative style embodying the author's viewpoint and strengthening the comic effect. Yet, in this case, the narrative style, instead of positively superimposing a meaning on fictional reality, is only to be rejected as being deceptive by the reader in his or her reconstruction of the experience conveyed.

Now, if the referent of "content" is fairly clear, what "stylistic value" stands for may be rather vague. As the object of investigation of literary stylistics, it refers to thematic and aesthetic values generated by linguistic form, values which convey the author's vision, tone and attitude; which embody the mingling or shifting of points of view (e. g. through changes in register); which add to the affective or emotive force of the message; which contribute to characterization and make fictional reality function more effectively in the thematic unity. Although the effects can be locally identifiable, it is understood that linguistic features never function in isolation but in relation to each other, all contributing to the total meaning of the work. In fact, the individual choices of words, syntax etc., which are selected from their paradigmatically-related alternatives in the linguistic system, are very often combined by the verbal artist into foregrounded or unique patterns which generate extra values or meanings by virtue of similarity (e. g. parallelism) or contrast (e. g. that between direct and indirect speech). In literary discourse, stylistic values may simply reside in appropriate choices from the conventional norm or take the shape of violation of conventional usages or rules, to the extent of changing the code itself. In either case, the aesthetic values are seen to embody the possibilities or advantages of the linguistic medium in contrast with other media such as film, painting or photographing.

Before turning to the level of fictional reality, it seems worthwhile to mention a prominent object of stylistic investigation of modern English fiction, namely, character's mind-style (see Fowler 1977) which, if occurring at the level of primary narration in a third-person novel, presents an area where the distinction between narrative discourse and fictional reality is, I think, untenable. Conventionally or traditionally, the primary narration in a third-person novel conveys the view of the authorial narrator in contradistinction to the views of fictional characters, hence the distinction between narrative discourse or narrative style and fictional reality (including characters' cognition or consciousness).[3] In some modern English novels, however, primary narration is used, for shorter or longer stretches of the text, to dramatize the viewpoint of a character (or some characters), to the extent of totally suppressing the style of the authorial narrator. A most telling case is the well-known "Lok's language" found in primary narration in William Golding's *The Inheritors*, a language which embodies the primitive world-view of the prehistoric character Lok in stark contrast with that of the modern authorial narrator (see Halliday 1971). I see in such cases an effort to defamiliarize or to deautomatize the narrative discourse. As primary narration in a third-person novel conventionally contains the reliable representation by the authorial narrator, the occurrence at this level of a character's idiosyncratic or uncanonical view surprises the reader into a fresh awareness of this narrative dimension which intervenes between what is represented and the reader. Further, by virtue of the fact that a third-person character's cognition or conceptualization is directly revealed at this primary narrative level, the character's mind-style as such generates a striking effect of immediacy, vividness and authenticity (much of the effect would be lost if the narration were to appear, where applicable, in first-person).

Now, the point to notice is that here the "narrative discourse," being composed of the cognition or conceptualization of a character as distinct from that of the authorial narrator, forms part of fictional reality. It is true that the "narrative discourse" as such shares with authorial narration the quality of being distinguishable from the fictional events it represents: we infer, for instance, from Lok's "The stick began to grow shorter at both ends. Then it shot out to full length again" the fictional event that "The man drew the bow and released it," with Lok's conceptualization standing in ironic contrast with the represented event. Yet both the character's perception and the perceived event form part of fictional reality. Nevertheless, while the perceived event is by nature not linguistic (see below), a character's conceptualization, being one possible expression (of the same event), is in itself verbal, with its aesthetic significance residing in the author's choices of linguistic form: in his choosing, for instance, "The stick began to grow shorter at both ends" instead of "The man drew his bow."[4] Not surprisingly, different conceptualizations of the same event are taken by Leech and Short as a form of stylistic variation (1981: 36). Following the same line of thought, one may even go so far as to treat different types of character's speech or thought (e. g. formal vs. informal) as stylistic variation (see 5.2.2).

2.2.2 Fictional 'Facts'

Except for that aspect of fictional reality which is in itself verbal (e. g. character's speech, thought or mind-style), fictional 'facts' are "extralinguistic… which are essentially independent of language, even though for their communication we must and do require the medium of language" (Hasan 1971:303). As far as the 'non-verbal' facts are concerned, aesthetic effects do not, generally speaking, reside in the author's manipulation of language. In a stylistic analysis of a passage from Joseph Conrad's *The Secret Agent*, Chris Kennedy observes that:

> the second group of verbs of perception are interesting in that the phenomena emphasize Verloc's role as a passive observer of an act he can do nothing to prevent. Mrs. Verloc's actions and her husband's perception of them are described only indirectly (Mr. Verloc never sees his wife, but makes connections between certain sounds and sights and her physical presence). He hears a plank creak and infers that she is coming towards him. He does not see the knife, the hand and the arm, but sees a shadow which he recognises as a limb and a weapon which he further identifies as an arm and a knife. (1982:88)

Apparently, the stylistician is not talking here about the effects generated by the author's linguistic choices but by the author's creation of fictional 'facts.' Indeed, insofar as those extralinguistic facts are concerned, linguistic models are usually quite irrelevant (functional grammar seems to form an obvious exception, whose ideational aspect, though, has been serviceable to stylisticians typically in describing mind-styles or viewpoints). The difference between the following two translations cannot, like the contrast between the actual and hypothetical 'facts' in the quotation above, be accounted for by linguistic terms:

> (A) ... But Old Tung Pao didn't dare let himself think of such a possibility. To entertain a thought like that, even in the most secret recesses of the mind, would only be inviting bad luck!
> (B) The more he thought the more he became afraid, afraid that the thoughts might come true. (see the analysis in 6.1.3)

Literary stylisticians differ radically in their concern with those extralinguistic facts. Many stylisticians firmly exclude them from their investigation. Ruqaiya Hasan, for instance, declares that "not any other element but *only* the linguistic element of literature concerns stylistics" (1971:299—300). This exclusion is surely understandable. But some stylisticians do take exception. Traugott and Pratt, for example, state that:

> Stylistic choice is usually regarded as a matter of form or expression, that is, as choice among different ways of expressing an invariant or predetermined content. But this view is mis-leading, for writers obviously choose content too. In our grammar, with its semantic and pragmatic components, both content and expression can be viewed as matters of choice. (1980:29)

While agreeing that both content and expression are matters of choice, I do not think the confinement of stylistic choice to form or expression is misleading. In the light of the preceding discussion, it should be clear that, given the distinction between content and expression, only the latter embodies the writer's style in the sense of his way of using language. However, the confinement as such does lead to difficulties. As aesthetic effect pertaining to language *per se* is just one aspect of the total significance of the text (though it can be a most essential aspect), limiting one's attention to this single aspect deprives one of the opportunity to explicate the overall impact of the work (I think here lies a root cause of the subservient role of stylistics—see Fowler 1971:39—40). If one has the intention, as many stylisticians do, of showing how textual facts give rise to the total meaning, one has to take account of both expression and content. Obvious as the point may seem to he, it is not to be taken for granted. Cluysenaar, for instance, finds it necessary to assert:

> Each text, whether a whole work or a passage, is treated here as an act of communication to which all features of language, *including meaning*, contribute. (1976:15; my emphasis)

Quite similarly, David Lodge sees a need to stress that the novelist's selection and ordering of fictional "surrogates" for actual experience "must have an aesthetic motive and an aesthetic effect" (1966:46), or put another way, that the author's "denotative use of words is of aesthetic significance" (61).

Interestingly, while stylisticians or critics concerned with language have to make clear why they should pay attention to "content" or "denotative use of words" at all, fictional reality has long been the concern, or, with reference to realistic novels, a central concern of traditional critics. The latter, of course, characteristically operate at a high level of abstraction, depending heavily on subjective impression and providing remarkably little textual substantiation. The stylistician's analysis of this textual dimension is, by contrast, marked by close attention to the relevant fictional 'facts' (most importantly to their relation with the surrounding textual features), concretely pointing out, say, what symbolic meaning a given object is seen to take on or what function a particular act serves in characterization. Naturally, in stylistic investigation, those 'facts' are often, if not always, analysed in relation to the writer's artistic manipulation of linguistic form, both of which, or the interaction of which, contribute(s) to the total aesthetic significance of the work.

To avoid diversion, I shall not go into other more peripheral concerns of stylistics, such as textual surface or deep structure (see Fowler 1977). In the following two chapters, I shall focus sharply on the aesthetic function of linguistic form, that is, focus on the characteristic object of investigation of stylistics.

CHAPTER 3
LINGUISTIC FORM AND LITERARY SIGNIFICANCE
—in defence of literary stylistics in terms of
its characteristic mode of argumentation

In the preceding chapter, a distinction was drawn between linguistic habits and aesthetically-motivated choices. And, as already observed, it is the motivated choice that concerns stylistics as an intermediary discipline. This discipline, which typically studies the relation between linguistic form and literary significance, has on the one hand a large number of practitioners and on the other no lack of attackers. The presence of the latter is, to a large extent, attributable to the fact that the theoretical foundation and the characteristics of this discipline have not yet been fully spelt out.

The major concern in this chapter is to make explicit, by way of defence, the theoretical foundation, the analytic procedure and the main characteristics of stylistics as such. My basic claim is that, being intermediary, the existence of stylistics is justifiable both in terms of a pragmatic need (primarily to account for phenomena marked by a progression from linguistic form to literary significance) and in terms of theoretical legitimacy (i. e. backed up by a set of underlying conventions). In this chapter, however, attention will be directed only to the matter of theoretical legitimacy, while the pragmatic need in question will be frequently touched on and extensively exemplified in other parts of this book. As regards theoretical legitimacy, we shall first consider the charge from Roger Pearce who, commenting on existing work in stylistics, says:

> there appear to be only two conceivable disciplines or modes of

> argument. One of these, producing the characteristic statements of literary significance or interpretation allegedly based on linguistic fact is, in essentials, *without theoretical foundation*; the mimetic fallacy is the most common way in which this deficiency is obscured. We are left with the *purely* grammatical statements, which, I have argued, are more open to objective discussion and investigation. (1977:28; my emphasis)

Our present concern is of course limited to the former kind of statement which relates linguistic form to literary significance and which constitutes, in Pearce's words, the "characteristic or typical mode of assertion in linguistic stylistics as opposed to linguistics or criticism" (20). The target that bears the brunt of Pearce's criticism is an analysis made by Cluysenaar (1976), who, commenting on the syntax of a short poem translated from the Chinese by Arthur Wally:

Swiftly the years, beyond recall.
Solemn the stillness of this spring morning.

says,

> what we have is a skillful use of syntax to mine the meaning. Line 1 is "incomplete" in a sense not applicable to line 2. The adverb *swiftly* leads us to expect a verb, a verb which could still appear after *beyond recall* (read aloud, the intonation should preserve that possibility). The second line therefore breaks in upon line 1, as if line 1 were short of time, and in its completeness it represents time stilled instead of snatched away. ...

Pearce admits,

> It is clear that in some sense there is a parallel: we know from experience in the world that if we are short of time we may have to leave tasks uncompleted. If we have time snatched away, are interrupted, we may break off what we are doing in the middle of it. We can see, then, the possibility that the experience of this

relationship in the world, between lack of time and incompleteness, may lead to an association producing the psychological sensation of being short of time when something appears incomplete (or, of course, the other way round). (21)

Nevertheless, according to Pearce,

> It is clear that there can be no progression in argument from one frame of reference, that of the linguistic facts of the poem, to the other, that of a literary interpretation. The link between the two is undemonstrable; we could as justifiably claim that an incomplete line represented eagerness to rush on to what was next, excitement and energy, or, equally, somnolence, boredom and dropping to sleep. ... The mistake ... is to construct or accept two frames of reference in the first place. ... in the absence of some testable theory to establish a strong link independently attested the claim is merely a juxtaposition of two facts; it has just as much validity as those statistical jokes which attribute the rise in deaths due to cancer to the rise in the number of multi-storey buildings or the like, since there is a perfect correlation between the two. (21—22; my emphasis)

It should first be made clear that my intention is not to defend any individual stylistician. I am in fact well aware that some existing stylistic analyses are inadequate in terms of either linguistic description or interpretation, or both. But, as indicated above, the burden of Pearce's charge is, in essence, not the inadequacy of the individual analyses but the illegitimacy of the progression in argument from one frame of reference, that of linguistic form, to the other, that of literary interpretation. In fact, a firm belief in this illegitimacy has led Pearce to suggest, as a primary task, the disposal of "a distinct third discipline of stylistics between linguistics and criticism" (27). In what follows, I shall start by analysing Pearce's analogy, an analysis that may serve to bring out the extent to which the progression in question is misunderstood, then proceed to a discussion of the theoretical foundation of the stylisticians' typical mode of argumentation. Finally, we shall consider the matter of the acceptance of two frames of reference.

Now, it is in my view fallacious to invalidate the "parallel" between linguistic form and literary interpretation with the "parallel" between the rise in deaths due to cancer and the rise in multi-storey buildings. The two parallels in effect do not belong to the same paradigm: the latter concerns two objective phenomena (and in this sense, they belong to the same frame of reference), the former concerns, by contrast, an objective phenomenon and a subjective response. In the case where what is involved are two objective facts, intuition or psychological sensation has, as a third party, no role to play: it goes nowhere to claim "We all feel that the rise in deaths due to cancer is caused by the rise in the number of multi-storey buildings." The causal relation between the two objective facts can only be established on scientific grounds. Nevertheless, in the case of the parallel between linguistic form and interpretation, intuition constitutes one of the two directly involved factors. Thus it makes perfect sense to claim, "In the context of the poem, the incompleteness of predication in line 1 makes us feel as if line 1 were short of time." Clearly the fact and the response are causally related so long as the speaker and his informants are not lying. Here the potentiality of the objective fact to arouse the subjective response cannot be tested by scientific means but may however be proved, at least hypothetically, on statistical grounds. As a matter of fact, statistics forms a means commonly used to investigate the potentiality of an objective phenomenon in terms of arousing a certain subjective response in a human being of a given community. If, say, 95% of the beings concerned have the given response, the causal relation between the fact and the response can be established on the scale of the community. But obviously even if 100% of human beings all feel that the rise in deaths due to cancer is caused by the rise in multi-storey buildings, the causal relation cannot (given, of course, the existing power of human intuition) be established.

However, as distinct from such a case as, say, the sight of a tiger causing a sense of horror, the subjective impression prompted by a linguistic form/pattern is not a matter of simply instinctive response. Like many subjective responses that are conditioned by convention, underlying the stylistician's response there exist certain literary conventions that constitute, I think, the theoretical foundation of the stylistician's argumentation (a foundation that 1 shall come to shortly). So far as Pearce is concerned, he does not seem to be aware of the existence of the underlying conventions which "guide the interpretive process and impose severe limitations on the set of acceptable or plausible readings" (Culler 1975:127). As quoted above, in the case concerned, Pearce has got a set of contradictory interpretations, each of which is to him equally justifiable:

> we could as justifiably claim that an incomplete line represented eagerness to rush on to what was next, excitement and energy, or equally, somnolence, boredom and dropping to sleep. ...

I very much doubt that Pearce really finds all the alternatives equally plausible—in the context of the poem. And I hope that he is not suggesting that the mind is a *tabula rasa* in approaching a literary text. If he is, I would like to refer to the chapter "literary competence" in Culler *Structuralist Poetics* (1975) where Culler argues at length about literature as an institution, about (the implied) readers as readers equipped with literary competence (that is, a set of conventions for reading literary texts), and the reading activity as a rule-governed process of producing meanings. Thus Culler:

> To read a text as literature is not to ... approach it without preconceptions; one must bring to it an implicit understanding of the operations of literary discourse which tells one what to look for. (113—114)

CHAPTER 3   LINGUISTIC FORM ... SIGNIFICANCE

And regarding the critic in particular:

> He must show his readers that the effects he notices fall within the compass of an implicit logic which they are presumed to accept. (125)

In the present case, the principle convention expected to be at work is clearly the convention of thematic unity of form and content, or put another way, the implicit logic of form reinforcing meaning or contributing to the theme. This implicit logic or convention is well followed by Cluysenaar and seems to be taken for granted by Pearce himself; both points can be inferred from Pearce's criticism:

> Here, because line 1 is incomplete, and because part of an interpretation of the poem involves the comparison of time stilled and time snatched away, the parallel is asserted. ... it is clear that it is only the details of the interpretation of the poem that have led to the imposition of this significance on a syntactically incomplete line. (20)

In my view, the thematic unity of form and content is an essential convention or implicit logic by which Pearce's alternative interpretations can be tested. On a more basic level, given that, say, "being short of time" is in itself an interpretation derived from the incompleteness of the syntax, some other conventions are involved, to wit, i) the rule of significance, i. e. it is *possible* for linguistic form to take on literary significance, and ii) there is some analogy or parallel that serves to correlate the linguistic form with the response elicited. The parallel in Cluysenaar's claim is, as quoted above, conceded and well spelt out by Pearce.

In my view, the set of conventions—(a) the rule of significance, (b) there being some analogy or parallel (see the detailed discussion about the nature of the parallel in the following chapter) and, (c) thematic unity of form and content—together (probably among others) constitute the basic theoretical foundation both of the stylistician's claim and of the reader's acceptance of such a claim. Without convention (a), the stylistician would not look for significance in linguistic form and the reader would be in no position to accept any claim that a certain linguistic form/pattern gives rise to a certain sensation or mood or the like. That is to say, a syntactically incomplete line would in any context have no more significance than that it was a syntactically incomplete line. Surely, but for this convention, Pearce would not have offered alternatives to Cluysenaar's interpretation. Indeed, without this convention, a writer would not, in the first place, manipulate linguistic form in order to achieve certain effects. Without convention (b), Pearce would not have considered a "parallel" in Cluysenaar's claim necessary, let alone taken the trouble to spell it out. And with the (b) convention, if one claimed that the incompleteness of the syntax represented fulfillment or happiness, the claim would, I believe, be found unacceptable by competent readers, even though a reader's own personal experience might well lead to such associations. The point to notice is that "To be an experienced reader of literature is, after all, to have gained a sense of what can be done with literary works and thus to have assimilated a system which is largely *interpersonal*" (Culler 1975:128; my emphasis).

As regards the convention of thematic unity of form and content, I take it to be a fundamental principle that directs the interpretative process and imposes severe limitations on the set of acceptable or plausible readings (there does, of course, exist a certain degree of indeterminacy since literary meanings are often ambiguous and are typically encoded in an unconventional way). By virtue of this convention, the stylistician always takes into account the features which surround the linguistic form/pattern concerned in context. This means that the literary significance with which the linguistic form/pattern is associated is context-bound, a point which is reflected in Pearce's comment:

There are, though, in all of these claims, the possibilities of empirical significance. It may be possible to set the constrains in such a way that the claims become: *in this context* such and such an effect is produced. (22)

Even if the mind is not aware of it, these conventions, probably among others, are at work in the stylistician's interpretative process. They constitute the theoretical foundation of the stylistician's mode of argumentation and form the criteria by which the plausibility of a claim that a certain linguistic form/pattern generates a certain literary meaning can be tested.

Now, despite the considerable lengths gone to above to show that the stylistician's claim is not a juxtaposition of two facts (the linguistic fact and the interpretation are causally related) and is not "without theoretical foundation" (so long as one does not deny the existence of the underlying conventions), the argument will get nowhere if we do not falsify Pearce's basic premise:

the only feasible interpretation of such a claim is, anyway, one which reverts to reliance on intuitive acceptance of psychological rather than linguistic phenomena. It is clear that there can be no progression in argument from one frame of reference, that of the linguistic facts of the poem, to the other, that of a literary interpretation. The link between the two is undemonstrable ... (21).

Given this premise, even if a stylistician's claim were accepted by all competent readers who presumably share a set of underlying conventions, the claim could still be regarded as a fallacy in that its very acceptance of two frames of reference would, "in the first place," be a "mistake." What I see in this premise (plus relevant contextual information) is inconsistency in Pearce's position concerning i) himself and stylisticians and ii) stylistics and traditional criticism. Pearce on the one hand criticizes stylisticians in terms of accepting two frames of reference, but he on the other hand concerns himself with the interpretation of literary texts, which necessarily involves an acceptance of two frames of reference. Furthermore, while Pearce proposes, primarily because of the stylistician's acceptance of two frames of reference, "to dispose of a distinct third discipline of stylistics between linguistics and criticism," he subscribes to criticism as well as linguistics (27—28). Pearce does not seem to be aware that criticism of literary texts also entails an acceptance of two frames of reference unless the critic were purely imagining, i. e. imaginings not elicited by the signs in the text. As far as I can see, in terms of accepting two frames of reference, criticism differs from stylistics only in the sense that in the case of criticism, one frame—that of the textual fact—is not specifically spelt out let alone linguistically analysed. Thus, while a stylistician may put down a detailed description of certain linguistic patterns in the text (and the interpretation elicited), a critic may put down no more than, say, "this novel" or "Wordsworth's 'Tintern Abbey'" (and the interpretation elicited). Indeed, if the critic's interpretation forms, say, a thematic synthesis of the text as a whole, the only thing that the critic can do to concretize the textual frame is to put down, instead of "this novel" or "Wordsworth's 'Tintern Abbey'," all the signs in the text.

It will have become clear that to rule out the acceptance of two frames of reference (linguistic or textual facts and subjective responses elicited) is in effect to rule out literary interpretation in general. And if one does accept literary interpretation, one has to accept two frames of reference, an acceptance that is, in my view, neither a mistake nor a fallacy. Now having reached this conclusion, the conclusion of my overall argument will be clear, in short, Pearce's criticism of the mode of argumentation characteristic of stylistics is a criticism that is unjustifiable and fallacious.

Pearce's criticism is however far from being original. After his own attack on "numerous examples" from stylisticians "of equations between linguistic forms and literary meanings" (Carter 1982:16, fn4), Pearce says:

> Fish (1973), in a comprehensive and polemical attack on stylistics, its procedures and principles, makes many of the points embodied here.

Despite the common ground between Fish and Pearce, their respective criticisms are made from two distinct perspectives: Pearce's from the point of view of a linguist, Fish's from that of a critic. To gain a fuller picture, we now turn to a consideration of Fish's charges.

Basically, Fish's charges fall under the following headings: (1) circularity, (2) arbitrariness, (3) decontextualization and (4) failing to take into account the reader's reading activity, with (2) (3) (4) closely related to each other. In terms of "circularity," Fish offers three examples, the first is taken from Milic (1966):

> The low frequency of initial determiners, taken together with the high frequency of initial connectives, makes [Swift] a writer who likes transitions and made much of connectives.

This statement is circular but one can dismiss this 'example' on the grounds that other stylisticians seldom, if ever, make such a statement (like "The large amount of adjectives in the text indicates that the writer likes to use adjectives") and, further, that such a statement has nothing to do with stylisticians' characteristic mode of argumentation which is, significantly, marked by a *progression* from linguistic form to literary significance. Another example is taken from Halliday (1971) who, commenting on a sentence from *Through the Looking Glass*: "It's a poor sort of memory that only works backwards," says,

> The word poor is a "modifier," and thus expresses a subclass of its head word *memory* (ideational); while at the same time it is an "epithet," expressing the Queen's attitude (interpersonal), and the choice of this word in this environment (as opposed to, say,

useful) indicates more specifically that the attitude is one of disapproval. ...

And here is Fish's charge:

> When a text is run through Halliday's machine, its parts are first disassembled, then labeled, and finally recombined into their original form. The procedure is a complicated one, and it requires a great many operations, but the critic who performs them has finally done nothing at all.

Now, it might be superfluous to point out that the analysis in question is a linguistic description (used by Halliday to illustrate the fact that a sentence embodies different language functions—see 1971:331－337); and it might be truistic to assert that descriptive linguistics is distinct from stylistics (though the two may, up to a point, overlap). What a linguistic description tries to achieve is to formalize and, possibly, to enhance one's intuitive awareness of language, either in terms of its grammatical function, e. g.

| John | loves | music. |
| Subject | Verb | Object |

or in terms of the more general language functions (as in the present case) or of the like. Clearly, to accuse Halliday's description above of being circular is, by extension, to accuse all linguistic or grammatical statements of being circular (Indeed, describing "John" as "subject," "loves" as "verb," "music" as "object" seems to involve more 'circularity'—in Fish's sense). And to say that "the critic who performs them has finally done nothing at all" is by extension to nullify all efforts made by linguists or grammarians. Now, it goes beyond the present concern to explicate further the goals or principles of inquiry of linguists or grammarians. Suffice it to say that this example does not apply to stylistics as an intermediary discipline. Its being brought in may be attributable either to a lack of awareness of the distinction between linguistic description and stylistic analysis, or, if not, to a purposeful attempt to make a characteristic of one discipline (a perfectly understandable and justifiable characteristic indeed) pass off as that of another discipline. The remaining example is the only one that has to do with stylistics but which, as will soon become apparent, is unrepresentative of this discipline. It is taken from Thorne (1970) who, after an analysis of some linguistic features in Donne's "A Nocturnal Upon St Lucie's Day," observes in passing:

> It seems likely that these linguistic facts underlie the sense of chaos and breakdown of natural order which many literary critics have associated with the poem.

And here is Fish's charge of "circularity":

> That sense ... has obviously been preselected by Thorne and the critics he cites, and is, in effect, responsible for its own discovery.

It should be mentioned in the first place that Thorne, in this part of his essay, is concerned with linguistic structures characteristic of poetry and with how to give them an adequate grammatical description. As a matter of fact, except for the passing note quoted above, hardly any attention is paid to the relation between syntax and literary significance as such. Apparently being preoccupied with other concerns, Thorne happens to refrain here from mentioning his own interpretation and refers instead to the interpretation of some critics. Now, need it be asserted that such a case is rarely seen in stylistic analysis? Indeed, one needs only to read the preceding part of this same essay by Thorne (190—191) for exemplification of the fact that stylisticians usually state their own responses to the linguistic facts concerned, in which case, Fish's charge of circularity no longer holds good. Given such a statement: "These linguistic facts underlie my feeling/sense of chaos," the feeling/sense is clearly not "responsible for its own discovery" but is, instead, elicited by the linguistic facts.

It is not surprising that none of these 'examples' really supports the charge of circularity. As an intermediary discipline, stylistics is marked by a progression, versus circularity, in argument from linguistic form to literary significance. It is this progression that, as will be recalled, bears the burden of Pearce's criticism. And this progression now brings us to Fish's second charge, i.e. "arbitrariness" or "illegitimacy."

In its broad sense, stylistics comprises several analytic modes, among which is reading from syntax to personality. This reading is treated by Fish, due to a lack of discrimination perhaps, as on a par with the reading from syntax to literary significance, both modes being seen as equally arbitrary or illegitimate. Here is Fish's comment:

> While Ohmann and Milic are interested in reading from syntax to *personality*, Thorne would like to move in the other direction, from syntax to either *content* or *effect*, but his procedures are *similarly* illegitimate. (my emphasis)

It will be recalled that at the beginning of this chapter, I pointed out the fallacious nature of an analogy drawn by Pearce between two "parallels": one concerns two objective phenomena while the other concerns an objective phenomenon and a subjective response. Now as we shall presently see, Fish's analogy here is just as fallacious as that of Pearce. Given the following two kinds of statement:

(i) "[Swift's] use of series argues a fertile and well stocked mind."
　　　　　　　　　　　　　　　　　　—by Milic

(or: "Swift's use of series argues an unwillingness to finish his sentences"
　　　　　　　　　　　　　　　　　—Fish's alternative)

(ii) "This highly repetitive style plays a major part in creating the mood of aimless, nervous agitation the passage conveys."
　　　　　　　　　　　　　　　　　　—by Thorne

to argue that type (ii) is not as illegitimate as type (i) is largely to repeat what I said when analysing Pearce's analogy. In (i) what is directly involved are two phenomena (the latter may not be existent) that actually lie outside the critic's mind; the critic's intuition forms a third element. Given the existing power of human intuition, the assumption that one can read directly from linguistic form to the quality of an author's mind is—and here I agree with Fish—"unexamined and highly suspect": hence the arbitrariness or illegitimacy. By contrast, in (ii) the critic's intuition forms one of the two directly involved factors. The "mood" in question is, as a matter of fact, the critic's own intuitive response elicited by "this highly repetitive style" among other things. The "style" and the "mood" (generated in the critic's mind) are causally related: the former giving rise to the latter. In sharp contrast with (i), the assumption here that one can read directly from linguistic form to literary significance is, given the existing power of human intuition, widely if not universally accepted-and undoubtedly by Fish himself. If enough competent readers share Thorne's interpretation, the causal relation between the style and the mood (in the reader's own mind) can be established on the scale of the implied readership. But even if competent readers, who obviously cannot penetrate into the author's mind, all share Milic's interpretation or Fish's alternative, the causal relation between the two phenomena concerned cannot be established on any scale. What makes the case interesting is that, in order to make the fallacious analogy appear reasonable, Fish uses Thorne's passing note (see above) to represent, as the only example given, Thorne's or stylisticians' reading from syntax to literary significance. Fish writes,

> Thorne discovers, for example, that in Donne's "A Nocturnal Upon St Lucie's Day" selectional rules are regularly broken. "The poem has sentences which have inanimate nouns where one would usually expect to find animate nouns, and animate nouns... where one would expect to find inanimate nouns." "It seems likely," he concludes, "that these linguistic facts underlie the sense of chaos

and the breakdown of order which many literary critics have associated with the poem."

As already noted, such a case rarely occurs in stylistic analysis. As a matter of plain fact, in a reading from syntax to literary significance, Thorne and other stylisticians usually state their own interpretations of the linguistic facts involved. This is exemplified by the second part of this same essay of Thorne's from which (ii) is quoted but which is, completely and unjustifiably, left out by Fish. The reason for this 'editing' may emerge by way of comparing the following four kinds of statement:

(a) these linguistic facts underlie my feeling/sense of chaos
(b) these linguistic facts underlie their feeling/sense of chaos
(c) Swift's use of series argues a fertile and well stocked mind
(d) these linguistic facts (underlie my sense of chaos and) seem likely to underlie their sense of chaos

Type (a) is, as analysed above, legitimate. Type (b), however, is open to Fish's criticism. Unless the speaker "I" is informed by "they," "I," as a *third* party, is in no position to know whether the linguistic facts and their feeling/sense are actually correlated or not. Thus (b) is an illegitimate assertion (unless ...) in that their sense of chaos may have little or nothing to do with the linguistic facts observed by "I" (the case is therefore as illegitimate as reading from syntax to personality [c]). Indeed, by now the reason why Fish leaves out Thorne's second part and chooses instead the 'example' concerned should have become apparent. In effect, Thorne's claim "It seems likely ..." does not belong to (b) but to (d) which is, instead of an assertion, a conjecture. According to Fish, Thorne's claim

is at once arbitrary and purposeful. The "breakdown of order" exists only within his grammar's system of rules (and strange rules they are, since there is no penalty for breaking them); it is a formal, not a semantic fact (even though the rules are semantic), and there is no warrant at all for equating it with the "sense" the poem supposedly conveys.

Obviously, Thorne's speculation is treated here as an illegitimate assertion (compare (d) with (b)). The point to notice is that, as a speculation, Thorne's claim is legitimate. It is true that the linguistic fact is formal not semantic. But in my view, the remark "it is a formal, not a semantic fact" serves merely to blur the picture. The relationship under discussion is one between linguistic form and literary significance or, in Fish's own words, "between structure and sense." The linguistic fact is certainly no other than formal or structural. The "warrant" for having such a speculation lies, as in the case of a stylistician's own reading from "structure" to "sense," in a set of conventions: (a) the rule of significance, i. e. it is possible for linguistic form to take on literary significance, (b) there being a 'parallel' (see chapter 4), (c) the thematic unity of form and content (see the discussion above). These underlying conventions, at least (a) and (c), are taken for granted by Fish himself who should therefore be aware that there is, in effect, warrant for Thorne to speculate about the possible correlation between the structure and the sense concerned.

As distinct from Pearce, Fish's charge of arbitrariness also bears on the descriptive apparatus used by stylisticians. Part of the reason for Thorne's being chosen as a target lies in Thorne's being a linguist of "the generative persuasion." Fish asserts that transformational devices "operate independently of semantic and psychological processes" and that it is therefore unjustifiable to read from those devices to literary significance. Thus, while acknowledging the possible relation between structure and sense, Fish regards Thorne's claim above as illegitimate for, among other things, "the 'breakdown of order' exists only within his grammar's system of rules." Prior to this, in a criticism of another transformational linguist, Richard Ohmann, Fish writes,

... in order to turn the description into a statement about

Faulkner's conceptual orientation, Ohmann would have to do what Noam Chomsky so pointedly refrains from doing, assign a semantic value to the devices of his descriptive mechanism, so that rather than being neutral between the processes of production and reception, they are made directly to reflect them. In the course of this and other essays, Ohmann does just that, finding, for example, that Lawrence's heavy use of deletion transformation is responsible for the "driving insistence one feels in reading" him …

It should be noted in the first place that descriptive apparatus or formal terms, which belong to a metalanguage (though taken from the object language), do not have any signification unless used in connection with their referents; the relationship between the two, as that between sign and meaning, is arbitrary. In stylistic analysis, formal terms are used quite literally to 'symbolize' structural choices which occur in actual language events. In the present cases, the breaking of "selectional rules" (in a Donne poem) or the heavy use of "deletion transformations" (in Lawrence's work) refers to particular structural choices found in the text. Given Fish's acknowledgment of the possible correlation between "structure" and "sense," he apparently does not take structural choice as being independent of semantic and psychological processes or as being neutral between the processes of production and reception. So on the one hand, Fish takes the following correlation to be possible:

Structural Choice　　　and　　　Significance

while on the other, he denies the possible correlation between

Structural Choice　　　and　　　Significance
(as symbolized by
formal terms)

And he glosses over the inconsistency by substituting a tripartite relation:

(1) Structural Choice→Formal Description→Significance

by a binary relation:

(2) (—)—Formal Description→Significance

Thus, in Thorne's case, the correlation is made to appear as one between something existing "within his grammar's system of rules" and the "sense" concerned; similarly, in Ohmann's case, as one between "the devices of his descriptive mechanism" and "a semantic value." I would like to stress that, no matter in what terms the structural choice is formalized, the stylistician is not talking about the correlation between significance and the formal terms as such but about the correlation between significance and the structural choice as symbolized by the formal terms. If one does not deny the possible correlation between structure and sense, there is surely no reason for one to deny the possible correlation between structure (expressed in formal terms) and sense.

Now, we have seen that Fish's Charge of arbitrariness, directed against reading from linguistic form to literary significance, rests on a number of misleading devices, namely, (1) equation: that which makes the analytic mode appear as illegitimate as reading from linguistic form to personality; (2) surrogation: as if the mode comprised the stylistician's description on the one hand and the literary critic's interpretation on the other; and (3) substitution: making what is actually a correlation between linguistic choice and significance appear as a correlation between formal categories and significance. All these devices are, not surprisingly, used by Fish in his criticism of what he sees as arbitrariness in Halliday's analysis of Golding's *The Inheritors* (1971).[1]

Closely related to the charge of "arbitrariness" is Fish's charge of "decontextualization." According to Fish, lack of contextual constraint partly underlies the "arbitrariness" or "illegitimacy" of stylistic analyses. In terms of the characteristic mode of argumentation, Thorne and Halliday bear the brunt of the attack. In Thorne's case, Fish's charge is in effect based on an equation imposed on two different modes of analysis. Fish writes:

Thorne begins in the obligatory way, by deploring the presence in literary studies of "impressionistic terms."... the task of stylistics is to construct a typology that would match up grammatical structures with the effects they invariably produce: "If terms like 'loose,' or 'terse' or 'emphatic' have any significance... it must be because they relate to certain identifiable structural properties" (188—189). What follows is a series of analyses in which "identifiable structural properties" are correlated with impressions and impressionistic terms. Thorne discovers, for example, that in Donne's "A Nocturnal Upon St Lucie's Day" selectional rules are regularly broken. ... "It seems likely," he concludes, "that these linguistic facts underlie the sense of chaos and the breakdown of order which many literary critics have associated with the poem."... It is not my intention flatly to deny any relationship between structure and sense, but to argue that if there is one, it is not to be explained by attributing an independent meaning to the linguistic facts, which will, in any case, mean differently in different circumstances. ...

The analysis of the Donne poem is taken from the third part of Thorne's essay which is made by Fish to serve as an example of "a series of analyses in which 'identifiable structural properties' are correlated with impressions and impressionistic terms" (the concern of Thorne's first part).[2] Thus the correlation between structure and sense is equated with the correlation between identifiable structural properties and impressionistic terms like "terse," "complex" and "emphatic." This imposed equation is at once misleading and purposeful. The two correlations in effect differ fundamentally from each other in that the correlation between structure and impressionistic terms is marked by invariability while the correlation between structure and sense is context-bound. This may be accounted for by the fact that the two actually do not belong to the same level. The point will be clearer if we have another look at the following observation by Thorne:

> This highly repetitive style plays a major part in creating the mood of aimless, nervous agitation the passage conveys.

Clearly, this sentence contains two levels: the more basic level "style" and the higher level "mood": the former generating the latter. As a matter of fact, the correlation between "identifiable structural properties" and "impressionistic terms" goes no further than the basic level (while the other correlation is one between the basic and the higher level). Broadly speaking, the basic level in itself contains two levels: one basic (identifiable structural properties), one higher (impressions or impressionistic terms like "repetitive," "complex" and "terse"). Significantly, this higher level consists of judgements that are, in essence, structural or linguistic. The point may become clearer if we replace the term "style" by "structure": "these highly repetitive structures" or "these complex structures." It is therefore not surprising that the correlation is invariable, irrespective of changes in context.

As distinct from this correlation (between structure and structural judgement), the other correlation is one between linguistic fact and literary significance (compare: "these structures are complex" with "these complex structures help to convey the sense or mood of ... "). Thus, over and above linguistic competence, what underlies a stylistician's claim of the latter correlation is literary competence, i. e. a set of literary conventions, the most fundamental of which is the convention of thematic unity of form and content (see above). By this is meant that such a claim is necessarily contextualized. This is a fact that is, as we have seen, acknowledged by Pearce:

> There are, though, in all of these claims, the possibilities of empirical significance. It may be possible to set the constraints in such a way that the claims become: *in this context* such and such an effect is produced.

And directed against Cluysenaar's claim in particular, Pearce says,

> It is clear that it is only the details of the interpretation of the poem that have led to the imposition of this significance on a syntactically incomplete line. Cluysenaar would obviously not want to claim that incomplete lines always represent time snatched away, or them always being short of time.

Given the fundamental difference between the two kinds of correlations (one context-free, one context-bound), it is highly misleading for Fish to use the analysis of the Donne poem as an example of "analyses in which 'identifiable structural properties' are correlated with impressions and impressionistic terms." As a result, reading from structure to sense is equated with reading from structure to impressionistic terms, the former consequently being made to appear as unbound by context as the latter. Thus, Fish gains a chance to criticize Thorne in terms of "attributing an independent meaning to the linguistic facts" and, furthermore, a chance to make himself a saviour of the stylistician's characteristic mode of argumentation:

> It is possible, I suppose, to salvage the game, at least temporarily, by making it more sophisticated, by contextualizing it.

To this, one can simply reply that there is no such a need since the game is already contextualized.

Closely related to the charge of decontextualization is the heart of Fish's attack, to the effect that stylisticians do not take account of the reader's reading activity. In Fish's opinion, stylisticians

> acknowledge no constraint on their interpretations of the data. The shape of the reader's experience is the constraint they decline to acknowledge. Were they to make that shape the focus of their analyses, it would lead them to the value conferred by its events. Instead they proceed in accordance with the rule laid down by Martin Joos: "Text signals its own structure," treating the deposit

of an activity as if it were the activity itself, as if meaning arose independently of human transactions.

Whatever the denotation or connotation of "the reader," in a literal sense, "the reader" can only refer to the analyst. It follows that Fish is actually criticizing stylisticians in terms of not taking into account their own reading activities. Considering literary stylistics as a whole, I think this charge is also unreasonable (some individual stylisticians, though, do neglect the actual reading experience—see the discussion in 4.4). I have been stressing the fact that the literary conclusions in stylistic analysis are usually no other than the analysts' intuitive responses (to the data) which are elicited in the reading process. That is to say, the literary significance is precisely a "value conferred by its events," i.e. "acquired" by stylisticians in the context of the reading activity. Nevertheless, what Fish means by focusing on the shape of the reader's experience is much more than what stylisticians practise. In Fish's view, the legitimate analytical method is one that should

> *slow down* the reading experience so that "events" one does not notice in normal time, but which do occur, are brought before our analytical attentions. It is as if a slow motion camera with an automatic stop action effect were recording our linguistic experiences and presenting them to us for viewing. (1970:128)

Stylisticians usually do not, so to speak, bother to slow down the reading experience which comprises, in Fish's words (1970:140), "all the precise mental operations involved in reading, including the formation of complete thoughts, the performing (and regretting) of acts of judgement, the following and making of logical sequences." What underlies this approach is Fish's belief of "meaning as an event." He writes,

> It [the sentence] is no longer an object, a thing-in-itself, but an *event*, something that *happens* to, and with the participation of,

the reader. And it is this event, this happening—all of it and not anything that could be said about it or any information one might take away from it—that is, I would argue, the *meaning* of the sentence (1970:125).

In my opinion, it is much more helpful to regard a word, phrase, sentence etc. as an object and the interpretative process as an event, an event in which the object (this word, or these words in this order) affects the mind or the mind responds to the words as they succeed one another. Fish's object of investigation is the interpretative process which actualizes meaning but which should not be equated with the meaning of the date. Given the opening sentence of Fielding's *Tom Jones*: "An author ought to consider himself, not as a gentleman who ... ," in the process of interpretation, when the reader has taken in "an author ought to," he or she may have a number of (preconscious) projections of what follows: "write" (?), "say" (?), "act" (?) etc. Similarly, when the reader has taken in "an author ought to consider himself not as," he or she may (unconsciously) predict what follows as "a character" (?), "a peasant" (?), "a professor" (?) etc. In my view, these predictions or hypothesizing acts are mental operations involved in interpreting the sentence, but these predictions ("write"/"say"/"act" (?) or "a character"/"a peasant"/"a professor" (?)) are not part of the meaning of "an author ought to consider himself, not as a gentleman. ... " The hypothesizing or preliminary interpretative acts do often, but not always, take on significance. While it is surely arbitrary to dismiss such acts as being one and all inconsequential, it is no less arbitrary to regard them one and all as being significant.

The analytical mode proposed by Fish is, in my view, legitimate, although it might be a laborious, if not an inapplicable, approach when the text contains more than a few sentences. The point to notice is that the literary stylistician's analytical mode is also legitimate. Given that the reading experience, whether put down on paper or not, remains the same and that the interpretations, in either case, are intuitive responses acquired by the analyst in the reading activity, the difference between the two approaches seems to me to be not much more than a difference in the level of abstraction at which the analysis operates. This may be backed up by the fact that once Fish's analysis begins to operate at an abstract level, (i.e. in a summary fashion, as opposed to recording chronologically every moment of the raw—possibly preconscious—interpretative process), it begins to sound very much like a stylistician's production, for example:

> there are two vocabularies in the sentence; one holds out the promise of a clarification—"place," "affirm," "place," "punctual," "overthrow"—while the other continually defaults on that promise—"Though," "doubtful," "yet," "impossible," "seems"; ... The indeterminateness of this experience is compounded by a superfluity of pronouns. ... (1970:125)

Whether aware of it or not, Fish's analysis at such moments deviates, to a certain extent, from his basic principles. First, the lexical choices, which are singled out with a certain degree of generality, are in a sense considered in relation to each other. What is focused on here is in effect some relevant semantic similarity within, or contrast between, the two vocabularies (or the interaction between the pronouns). Closely related to this is the deviation from the consideration of the temporal flow of the reading experience which forms the basis of the mode proposed by Fish who assumes that

> the reader responds in terms of that flow and not to the whole utterance. That is, in an utterance of any length, there is a point at which the reader has taken in only the first word, and then the second, and then the third, and so on, and the report of what happens to the reader is always a report of what has happened *to that point*. (1970:127)

This obviously does not apply to the analysis quoted above where the temporal or chronological order is, as it were, broken and where the analyst (who I suspect has gone through the whole utterance more than once) is apparently taking account of the whole utterance. As a result, one's precise responses to each individual word are obscured (the response to "place" is presumably different from that to "affirm") and the responses to the words in between overlooked. But this 'loss' is accompanied by a perceptible 'gain': the relevant aspect of the linguistic experience is systematized or organized in terms of similarity or contrast and is thereby refined as well as highlighted (which is an advantage of investigating formal patterns). Interestingly but not surprisingly, in dealing with units larger than the sentence, Fish's analysis operates at an even higher level of generality. In his analysis of Plato's the *Phaedrus* (1970:135—138), one is given, instead of "the basic data of the reading experience," general summaries or impressionistic conclusions, such as

> The *Phaedrus* is a radical criticism of the idea of internal coherence from a moral point of view; by identifying the appeal of well-put-together artifacts with the sense of order in the perceiving (i.e. receiving) mind, it provides a strong argument for the banishing of the good poet who is potentially the good deceiver.

In order to reach such general conclusions, i.e. to answer the question "What does the *Phaedrus* as a whole do?", the mind needs to operate at a considerably high level of generality. The reader/critic simply has to 'slight' what each individual word does (possibly whole sentences or even larger units are slighted) in a consistent and progressive effort of summarizing or generalizing. These deviations or inconsistencies in Fish's practice point to the fact that the analyst's task is, at least potentially, not only to (1) duplicate or record "moment by moment" the interpretative process (i.e. to play the function of a "slow motion camera") but also to (2) systematize or organize some moments of responses or 'cues' of responses (formal patterns) in terms of similarity or contrast, and to (3) summarize or generalize the whole experience. Each approach has its own advantages and limitations. Approach (1) has the virtue of bringing to light "all the precise mental operations involved in reading" but it leaves no room for organizing or generalizing (some aspects of) the reading experience. The second approach highlights the interaction between the relevant (cues of) responses but necessarily involves overlooking the intermediate ones. The third approach synthesizes the whole only at the expense of the "basic data" of reading.

If the three approaches are taken as three mental proceses, they are, I think, actually parallel in the reading activity. While responding to the text "bit by bit, moment by moment," the mind is, perhaps unconsciously, responding to the interaction between the elements (normally not in succession) of a formal patten; similarly, while interpreting one word, phrase etc. after another, the mind is trying to reach such general conclusions as the one quoted above. The point to notice is that as far as the analyst is concerned, he or she is able to focus, at least at any given moment, only on one approach or process and, moreover, that one approach cannot take the place of another, each having its own concern, its own principles of inquiry, as well its own limitations.

CHAPTER 4

THE LINGUISTIC BASIS: OBJECTIVE OR SUBJECTIVE?

Having discussed, in the preceding chapter, the progression from linguistic form to literary significance, we now come to a consideration of the linguistic basis itself. To a stylistician, linguistic facts constitute the objective basis of literary interpretation. This assumption, however, is seriously challenged by Stanley Fish who concludes his "What is stylistics and why are they saying such terrible things about it? Part II " with the following statement:

> formal patterns are themselves the products of interpretation and ... therefore there is no such thing as a formal pattern, at least in the sense necessary for the practice of stylistics: that is, no pattern that one can observe before interpretation is hazarded and which therefore can be used to prefer one interpretation to another. The conclusion, however, is not that there are no formal patterns but that there are always formal patterns; it is just that the formal patterns there always are will always be the product of a prior interpretive act, and therefore will be available for discerning only so long as that act is in force. Or, to end with an aphorism: there always is a formal pattern, but it isn't always the same one.
> (1980:267)

I see in Fish's contention some misunderstanding about the nature of formal patterns in stylistic analysis, a misunderstanding that makes necessary an explication of the linguistic basis. This chapter is devoted primarily to such an explication, seeking to elucidate what the linguistic basis really involves and, further, to examine to what extent it is objective. To make clearer the relationship between linguistic form and literary interpretation, an explication and evaluation will be taken up in terms of the different degrees of objectivity of the three correlated levels involved in the stylistician's characteristic mode of argumentation: structural feature, psychological value and literary significance, paying special attention to the nature of the psychological value which serves as a link or "parallel" between the linguistic basis and the interpretation concerned.

4.1 LINGUISTIC OBJECTIVITY: A MATTER OF CONVENTION

"Objective" and "subjective" in the modern sense is a distinction drawn between what exists independently of the perceiving or thinking self and what is constituted by mental operations. This distinction, however, does not apply very pertinently to a phenomenon such as language. By language, one does not mean a sequence of sounds (or letters) in their own right but a conventionalized system of sounds or sound symbols used for communication. The term "word" involves two concepts: the linguistic sign and the symbolized meaning; the relationship between the two is usually not natural but arbitrary, imposed by the perceiving or thinking self and established through convention. Syntactic relationships and other linguistic structures are no less arbitrary. Seen in this light, language, though consisting of real sounds or concrete signs (whose formation is in itself arbitrary), is a subjective system of arbitrary relationships which no longer obtain when the relevant convention changes and which do not obtain outside the given speech community.

Within the linguistic domain, then, the distinction between "objective" and "subjective" as usually drawn does not apply, since language is in its very nature a subjectively-produced, arbitrary entity.

But, as things are, the distinction between "objective" and "subjective" is still drawn in this domain. So far as the modern English speaking community is concerned, the sign "table" having the capacity of standing for the physical object involved is seen as an objective fact which a member of the community has to take for granted. Similarly, however arbitrary the syntactic or phonological rules, they constitute social facts which individual speakers have to acknowledge and abide by.

Clearly, "objectivity" has here taken on a new sense which is "conventionality." The distinction here between "objective" and "subjective" is in effect one between what is conventional and what is personal. This change in criterion is inevitable when we move from the natural reality of the world into the social reality of language where there is not any natural but conventional fact and where therefore the only criterion of objectivity is and can only be conventionality.

Bearing in mind that language is a social or conventional reality and that objectivity in the linguistic domain is a matter of conventionality, we now proceed to a tripartite distinction: structural feature, psychological value and literary significance.

4.2 STRUCTURAL FEATURE, PSYCHOLOGICAL VALUE AND LITERARY SIGNIFICANCE

4.2.1 A Basic Distinction

Language is, to repeat a truism, a patterned system. In the numerous, diversified language events, there are found a limited number of conventionalized structural elements. In terms of the English clause type, there exists a hierarchic structure, ranging from (what is called) a rankshifted clause to a main clause. As regards speech presentation, five basic modes are found in use, such as direct speech and indirect speech (see chapter 8).

These linguistic features are constituted by virtue of, or classified according to, the relation or contrast of these structures to their paradigmatically or syntagmatically related structural elements. Such relations or contrasts, which are established through convention and are therefore regular in language events, often, if not always, give rise to quite constant psychological values. In the conventionalized syntactic hierarchy, a subordinate clause is seen to be psychologically less prominent than a 'corresponding' main clause ('corresponding' in the sense that it could have been chosen instead). Similarly, the mode of direct speech is seen to have more immediacy or impact by contrast to indirect speech.

The different psychological values taken on by linguistic features are frequently exploited in literary contexts as a means of achieving various thematic significance. The following is a case in point:

> Curley's fist was swinging when Lennie reached for it.
> (John Steinbeck, *Of Mice and Men*, Ch. 3)

This sentence has been discussed by Leech and Short:

> The second clause of this sentence describes the turning point in the fight between Lennie and Curley, and yet Lennie's action is backgrounded by its subordinate status. On the face of it, Steinbeck would have done better to write something like: "As Curley's fist was swinging, Lennie reached for it." But what he did write fits in very well with his overall strategy in the novel, that of absolving Lennie of responsibility for his actions. By downgrading Lennie's part in the fight, he makes it seem an inadvertent and blameless reaction to Curley's onslaught. (1981:221)

The relative psychological obscurity of the subordinate clause is purposefully used here to downgrade the protagonist's action.

The capacity of the passive voice to make obscure the agent role is found exploited by quite a few writers for achieving various thematic effects. In Joseph Conrad's *The Secret Agent*, for example, in depicting Mrs Verloc's killing of her husband, the writer uses "the knife was... planted" and "the blow [was] delivered" (rather than "she planted the knife," "she delivered the blow") as a means of strengthening the "impression of detachment, of someone who is not responsible for her actions" (see Kennedy 1981:86—89). In terms of modes of speech, an area in fiction that has been intensively studied by stylisticians, the contrast in impact between the direct and the indirect form is used by many novelists to reflect or underline the contrast in role or attitude of characters (see 8.4.2.1). Such a use is found in that same novel of Conrad's as a means of emphasizing the contrast between one interlocutor's dominant role and the other interlocutor's submissiveness (see Jones 1968).

4.2.2 Degrees of Objectivity

Of the three entities involved (structural feature, psychological value and literary significance), structural feature, as conventional fact obtaining within a conventional system, has a strong claim to objectivity in the sense defined above. In modern English, the contrast between, say, (what is called) main and subordinate clause or between direct and indirect speech exists independently of individual speaker's mental operations.

When it comes to psychological value, however, one is on much less sure ground as a whole set of psychological assumptions are brought in. The claim that a main clause is psychologically more prominent than a corresponding subordinate clause may rest largely on two assumptions: that an independent entity is psychologically more prominent than a dependent one (other things being equal), and/or that what is mainly conveyed appears to be more prominent than what is circumstantial (cf. Dillon 1981:129—134). The objectivity of the claim, then, is determined on the one hand by the truth of the presumed perceptual characteristics, and, on the other hand, by the truth of the presumed linguistic convention: whether the (what is called) subordinate clause is truly dependent on the main one and/or whether the former is circumstantial in relation to the latter. If the truth of both aspects obtains (exceptional cases are, of course, always expected in such a social reality), the claim can be regarded as objective.

The same applies to other correlations between linguistic features and psychological value. Take, for example, the claim that "Y was done" has, by contrast to "X did Y" or "Y was done by X," the effect of making implicit and therefore of obscuring the agent "X." The objectivity of this claim rests partly on the truth of the perceptual assumption that what is explicitly stated is psychologically more prominent than what is merely implied and partly on the linguistic convention that the agent is usually spelt out, against which assumption the judgement "making implicit" alone makes sense.

The contrast in immediacy or impact between direct and indirect speech again rests on the linguistic convention on the one hand (i. e. the contrast between the presence and absence of quotation marks as well as the contrast in person, tense and deictics) and on the other hand on human perceptual characteristics (the difference in psychological distance or impingement between perceiving what is actually occurring and perceiving what is indirectly reported).

Two points should be noted here. First, as a simple matter of this feature producing this psychological effect, such a correlation is characterized by directness and specificity. Secondly, due to the fact that the linguistic contrasts are conventionally regular and the perceptual characteristics involved are communal, if not universal, the correlation in question is stable, unaffected by changes in context. These factors contribute to the testability or determinacy of the correlation involved.

Indeterminacy arises much more when we proceed to the correlation between structural feature and literary significance (via, importantly, the more basic correlation between structural feature and psychological value). Broadly defined, the literary significance in question is the thematic value taken on by a structural feature in a particular literary context. In the preceding section, I mentioned several examples of the correlation between structural feature and literary significance, such as Steinbeck's use of a subordinate clause to downgrade Lennie's action, making it seem "an inadvertent and blameless reaction to Curley's onslaught" or Conrad's use of passive transformation in depicting Mrs Verloc's action as a means of strengthening "the impression of detachment, of someone who is not responsible for her actions." Essentially, two determining factors are found operating here. One is the linguistic form (or formal pattern) and its basic psychological effect, e. g. syntactic subordination and the resultant psychological obscurity; the other takes the shape of the context in which the linguistic form is found.

It should be noted that, in discussing the correlation between a linguistic form/pattern and its literary significance, the more basic correlation between the linguistic form/pattern and its (basic) psychological value is sometimes not spelt out. But whether stated or not, this more basic correlation always exists, serving as, so to speak, an indispensable bridge that links the linguistic form with the significance involved. In my opinion, the objectivity of the correlation between linguistic form and literary significance is very much contingent upon the distance between the basic psychological value (which is unaffected by changes in context) and the contextualized literary significance. To return to Cluysenaar's analysis of

Swiftly the years, beyond recall.
Solemn the stillness of this spring morning.

discussed in the preceding chapter. In this case, the basic psychological effect produced by the syntax of line 1 seems no more than the feeling of "its being incomplete or unfinished," which is quite some distance from, though associated with, the thematic value of "being short of time." Of the two determining factors which operate here: (a) the linguistic form and its basic context-free psychological effect and (b) the particular literary context, the latter seems to have a large part to play, which means that a greater role is played by subjective association than by objective linguistic fact.

For a reason that I shall come to shortly, the structural feature itself forms a stronger determining force in the cases referred to in the last section. Another such case is found in Joseph Heller's *Catch-22* where, in depicting a brisk sequence of events, the writer uses a long "run on" sentence to generate an effect of everything happening at once. There is here a shorter distance between the basic psychological effect of "the syntax being interconnected" and the contextual significance of "the events being interconnected, to the point of a pseudo-simultaneity" (see the analysis by Turner 1975:73).

It is important to note that the "distance" in question is not a matter of similarity in the superficial sense. It is, to a great extent, a matter of the conventional relation between the depicting means and what is depicted. In the conventional use, syntactic completeness or incompleteness has nothing to do with the significance of time. But syntactic connection does have to do with the connection between events. If two events are interconnected, they are likely to be put into the same sentence; if not, they are likely to be marked off from each other by a sentence boundary. That is to say, syntactic relation is conventionally used to reflect or underline the relation between events. The same applies to the three cases mentioned in the last section: syntactic subordination is conventionally used to foreground or background events; passive voice offers a conventional means of obscuring the agent role; similarly, indirect speech, by contrast to direct speech, provides a conventional means of toning down and distancing the speech. As distinct from Cluysenaar's case, there is here an intrinsic link between the basic psychological effect conventionally associated with the linguistic features and the thematic significance associated with the features in the given literary contexts.

At this point, it seems worthwhile to bring in Epstein's analysis of Milton's "Lycidas," line 167:

Sunk though he be beneath the watry floar

In pronouncing the stressed vowels, the movements of the tongue and lower jaw from "mid central" to "high front" to "back" are said to mime "the relationship low-high-low expressed in the lexis—the body of Edward King on the sea floor (low) and the surface of the sea (high). The high front vowels mime the notion 'the watery floor' far beneath which King has sunk" (see Epstein 1981:181).

This observation is highly subjective and arbitrary in that, according to convention, the movements of the tongue and lower jaw (which do not, strictly speaking, even belong to language proper) do not have anything to do with the movements of the represented phenomena. In reading, one responds to the words, the syntax, the phonological sounds or to the lay-out of the text, but not, at least not usually, to the movements of the tongue and lower jaw. One certainly does not feel any contradiction between the position of the tongue in pronouncing the stressed vowel of "above" (mid central) and the meaning of the word (on top of or higher than).

Unless the text brings in some way the imitative function of such physical movements into the reader's interpretative activity (cf. Attridge 1982:291 — 292), it is arbitrary to make associations between those movements and the meaning of the text. If in Cluysenaar's case above, the incomplete predication of line 1 constitutes a striking deviation from the norm, apparently forming a device thematically motivated and consciously chosen (rather than a mistake resulting from carelessness), in the present case, the text does not seem in any way to direct attention to the movements of the tongue and lower jaw involved. The analyst, however, does find something deviant: "The unusual number of high front vowels—four in a row ['he be beneath']—flanked by mid or back vowels suggest that this phonological mimesis is deliberate" (181). But as far as I can see, the "unusual" frequency of the high front vowels, upon which Epstein's claim for the writer's conscious choice is based, is not really unusual. The point will be clear if we compare "he be beneath" with "he is beneath" or "it is beneath his dignity." In both cases, the frequency of high front vowels seems to be at once normal and accidental.

Interestingly, Epstein's case, which relies on the fact that the same term "low" or "high" can be used to describe both the position of the jaw or tongue and the spatial situation of what is being described in the poem, seems to form a telling example of "metaphorical slippage" or of. "fancied resemblances" which arise merely from the ambiguity of words, such as the fancied connection "between a soft line and soft couch, or between hard syllables and hard fortune" (see Attridge 1982: 289).

Epstein's analysis has in fact been criticized by Stanley Fish in "What is stylistics? Part II." But Fish's criticism is somewhat off the point. The burden of Fish's first charge is the incomparability between the two kinds of motion concerned:

> the two patterns—one phonological, the other lexical—are not parallel in a way that would allow the first to be mimetic of the second. The movement low-high-low occurs on a vertical plane, while the movement mid central-high front-back occurs on the horizontal or curvilinear plane of the roof of the mouth. (1980:249—250)

A logical conclusion that one can draw from this comment is that, if the lexical movement (i.e. the movement of the represented phenomenon) were curvilinear, Epstein's analysis would hold water. Or, conversely, if the movement of the tongue were (more) vertical, say, were from "low front" to "high front" to "low front," Epstein's analysis would be (more) valid. This is a point that Fish apparently would not want to make.

Fish then shifts to a consideration of Epstein's interpretation, saying:

> It is by no means obvious that the line expresses the relationship low-high-low; indeed it would make equal and better sense (and one in accord with Milton's practice elsewhere) to say that the movement described is from low (sunk) to lower (beneath) to lower still. (1980:250)

But the question is: if Epstein's interpretation were accurate, would his analysis hold water? It should be clear that the crux of the matter does not lie in the relevant comparability or interpretative accuracy but resides, instead, in the conventional relation between the form and the content involved.

The point that I have been driving at so far is that linguistic form takes on literary function only through its basic psychological effect on the reader and, more importantly, that the objectivity of the correlation between linguistic form and literary significance is contingent upon the essential (vs. superficial) distance or similarity between the linguistic form's basic psychological value and the thematic value taken on by the linguistic form in a given literary context.

In fact, the two types of similarity examined above—one as shown in Cluysenaar's analysis, the other as displayed in all the other analyses referred to—can be generalized to subsume most, if not all, such relations in stylistic analysis. I have already touched on the basic difference between the two types: in the former type, there is no essential or conventional link between the two kinds of value involved, since the linguistic form does not, according to convention, have to do with the thematic value. In this type, while the basic psychological value serves, by virtue of some form of resemblance or association, to correlate the linguistic form with its thematic value, the thematic value is largely to be accounted for by the developing interpretation in the light of which the linguistic form is viewed.

In the latter type, by contrast, there exists an essential or conventional link between the two kinds of value involved in that the linguistic form is associated through convention with the thematic value. Of the two determining factors which operate here: (a) the linguistic form and its basic psychological value and (b) the literary context, the former has a greater role to play than its counterpart in the preceding type. As a rule, the shorter the (essential) distance between the basic psychological value and the contextual thematic value, the greater the determining force comes from the linguistic fact as opposed to the given literary context.

Now, let us consider one further case, taken from Widdowson (1975) who, commenting on the following verse from Tennyson's *In Memoriam*:

> He is not here; but far away
> The noise of life begins again,
> And ghastly thro' the drizzling rain
> On the bald streets breaks the blank day.

says:

> the monosyllabic structure of the words in the last line and the alliterative pattern they form reinforce the semantic import of the words as lexical items. The desolation that Tennyson feels is conveyed by the sound of the last line as well as by what the words themselves mean. (36—37)

The relation here between the phonological pattern's basic psychological value and its thematic value belongs to what I have classified as the "former" type. According to convention, the monosyllabic nature of a line of words does not have anything to do with "desolation," though it does give, by relation to a line of disyllabic or polysyllabic words, the feeling that each syllable stands on its own, unconnected with each other. In the present case, the analyst's intuitive leap from the basic psychological value to the thematic value rests, apart from the perceptible "parallel" between the two, entirely on the literary context; it is not in any way determined by the conventional use of the linguistic form.

It will be recalled that, in the last chapter, attention was directed to the underlying convention that there is expected to be a "parallel" which serves to correlate the linguistic form (or formal pattern) with the significance involved. By now, it should be clear that the "parallel" in question is in effect a quite variant entity. In what I have classified as the former type (which occurs most frequently in poetic analysis, particularly in the area of phonology), the "parallel" is a matter of superficial resemblance (like the resemblance in form between the monosyllabic nature of a line of words and the feeling of desolation) or a matter of an unconventional "cue" for subjective association (like syntactic incompleteness leading to the feeling of "being short of time"). Here the two elements involved—the form of language and the significance—are conventionally irrelevant to each other and, therefore, might not, despite the "parallel," be related in the given literary context (the resemblance might be, as in conventional use, merely accidental; the "cue" might be only private). The lack of conventional grounds points to the relatively great indeterminacy as well as subjectivity of the correlation involved. Without any conventional ground (what is in question is of course merely linguistic convention), the analyst can only base his or her claim on the contextual prominence of the linguistic form or formal pattern, on the contextual impact of its psychological effect, and on the shared intuitive response to the form or pattern in the particular context (cf. Attridge 1982:287ff.).

In what has been referred to as "the latter type" (which occurs more frequently in the analysis of prose-fiction or in the area of lexis, syntax, modes of speech), the "parallel" is, by contrast, a link based on convention. In Leech and Short's analysis of the sentence by Steinbeck quoted above, the correlation between the subordinate clause and its literary significance is based, to a certain extent, on the conventional value of the linguistic form as opposed to superficial similarity. The basic psychological value here (i.e. psychological obscurity) through which the linguistic form functions can be regarded as a conventional value basis for contextual association or extension. Indeed, one can treat the literary Significance as a contextual extension of the form's conventional value. The case will be even more apparent if we come to the area of lexical expression. To quote a few lines from Kennedy's analysis of a passage in Joseph Conrad's *The Secret Agent*:

> ... we are not told "Mrs Verloc took the knife," nor even "her hand took the knife," but "her hand skimmed ... the table ... the knife had vanished...." The reader is left to make the connection between the two actions, and this has the effect of "distancing" Mrs Verloc from her own actions. It is as though her hand has a force of its own, detached from Mrs Verloc's mental processes. We are told the fact that the knife vanished but not the cause of its disappearance. (1982:89)

Clearly, the effect of "distancing" Mrs Verloc from her own actions is a contextual extension of the conventional value associated with the chosen linguistic form. It is clear that in this type, the correlation between linguistic form and literary significance is, on the whole, more objectively based than that in the preceding type. And since greater determining force stems from the linguistic fact itself, the correlation is more likely to hold true, up to a point, for similar linguistic features in other literary contexts.

Now, while having the intention to explicate what was in the last chapter left vague in terms of the correlation between linguistic form and literary significance, I do have in mind the fact that the present chapter is meant primarily for a consideration of the objectivity of the linguistic basis, I started my argument in this chapter by defining linguistic objectivity as conventionality and claimed that conventional linguistic elements are objective. But given the fact that, in stylistic analysis, the linguistic basis frequently consists of deviant rather than normal entities, we must (before coming to a central question "Does interpretation produce linguistic facts?") opposed consider the relation between deviation and objectivity.

4.2.3 Deviation and Objectivity

In English, that the symbol "sun" refers to the burning star which the earth goes round is, by virtue of its conventionality, an objective linguistic fact. Against this norm, the deviant chain that "nus" stands for the same object is seen to be subjective and is to be ruled out as a linguistic fact. But the impossibility of this case's becoming a linguistic fact does not in effect reside in its unconventionality but lies instead in our inability to locate this deviant case within the conventional semiotic system.

No one would, I believe, deny that the incomplete predication involved in Cluysenaar's analysis forms a linguistic fact, although it is a deviation from the norm. The deviant case here is given a place in the conventional system by being defined in relation to the relevant element (i.e. what is conventionally a complete predication) in the system. Indeed, the whole set of categories used to describe deviation, such as "the breaking of selectional rules," all present attempts to define or determine deviant elements in relation to conventional elements upon which communication is based and upon which the deviant entities depend, significantly, for their own communicative function.

In effect, if a deviant entity is determined (or is determinable) in terms of in what sense and to what extent it deviates from the conventional element(s), it is located (or locatable) in the conventional system and forms, paradoxically, an objective linguistic fact. Now, having made clear what constitutes objective linguistic facts and, further, what is truly involved in the correlation between linguistic fact and literary significance, we proceed to a consideration of the following question.

4.3 DOES INTERPRETATION PRODUCE LINGUISTIC FACTS?

That linguistic facts are themselves the products of interpretation is, as quoted at the beginning of this chapter, the thesis of Fish's "What is stylistics? Part II" as well as a major argument of his "Interpreting the *Variorum*" and some other essays (see Fish 1980). The concern of the present section is firstly to point out a theoretical deficiency underlying Fish's argument, namely, a failure to realize that language is a social/conventional reality. This deficiency has led Fish to take linguistic convention as interpretation, so that conventionally objective linguistic facts are wrongly treated as entities subjectively produced by interpretation. Secondly, along the same line of reasoning, it will be argued that the properties that formal patterns take on in literature are produced by literary conventions as opposed to interpretation.

4.3.1 Linguistic Convention vs. Interpretation

In 4.1 attention was directed to the fact that language, though a subjective system of arbitrary relationships, constitutes, significantly, a social reality which, as distinct from the natural reality of the world, consists of conventional facts which members of the given speech community have to take for granted. Indeed, there is no reason why English should be made up of those forty-four phonemes; the existing phonetic system is no doubt an entity imposed by the perceiving or thinking self. But once established through convention, it becomes part of the social reality and exists independently of interpretation. Most certainly, the mental operations involved in establishing the social reality *per se* are to be distinguished from the mental operations involved in the interpretation of language events.

This basic distinction has, however, escaped the attention of Fish. After discussing the interpretation of some lines from *Lycidas* as an exemplification of how interpretative strategies "produce" formal features in an interpretative event, Fish turns to a discussion of conventional linguistic fact *per se*. Quite unintentionally (I believe), the interpretation of language events is equated by Fish with the convention involved in establishing the social reality itself, or vice versa. Here is some of Fish's discussion (see 162—167):

> in the analysis of these lines from *Lycidas* I did what critics always do: I "saw" what my interpretive principles permitted or directed me to see, and then I turned around and attributed what I had "seen" to a text and an intention. What my principles direct me to "see" are readers' performing acts; the points at which I find (or, to be more precise, declare) those acts to have been performed become (by a sleight of hand) demarcations *in* the text; those demarcations are then available for the designation "formal features," and as formal features they can be (illegitimately) assigned the responsibility for producing the interpretation which in fact produced them. (163)

> This may be hard to see when the [interpretive] strategy has become so habitual that the forms it yields seem *part of the world*. We find it easy to assume that alliteration as an effect depends on a "fact" that exists independently of any interpretive "use" one might make of it, the fact that words in proximity begin with the same letter. But it takes only a moment's reflection to realize that the sameness, far from being *natural*, is enforced by an orthographic

convention; that is to say, it is the product of *an interpretation*. Were we to substitute phonetic conventions for orthographic ones ... the supposedly "objective" basis for alliteration would disappear because a phonetic transcription would require that we distinguish between the initial sounds of those very words that enter into alliterative relationships; rather than conforming to those relationships, the rules of spelling make them. One might reply that, since alliteration is an aural rather than a visual phenomenon when poetry is heard, we have unmediated access to the physical sounds themselves and hear "real" similarities. But phonological "facts" are *no more uninterpreted* or *less conventional* than the "facts" of orthography; the distinctive features that make articulation and reception possible are the product of a system of differences that must be *imposed* before it can be recognized; the patterns the ear hears (like the patterns the eye sees) are the patterns its perceptual habits make available. (166, my emphasis except for "in" and "imposed")

It does not make sense to talk here about "part of the world" or "far from being natural." In the linguistic domain, there is, as distinct from the domain of physics or chemistry, no natural but conventional entity. The very talk here about being "natural" or "part of the world" points to an unawareness of the fundamental difference between the natural reality of the world and the social reality of language, an unawareness which is further borne out by the equating of linguistic convention with the act of interpretation.

If one is to be true to the social reality of language where there is no natural but conventional fact, one has to abandon the distinction between natural/objective fact and interpretation and to take up instead the distinction between conventional/objective fact and interpretation (see 4.1). Indeed, whatever mental operations are involved in its coming into being, the conventional English phonetic system forms an objective entity which exists independently of interpretation; similarly, however arbitrary are the conventional symbols, they constitute objective means of communication or, more to the point, objective objects of interpretation. The same applies to alliteration or other conventional linguistic facts.

Within this social reality, conventionality means rather than contradicts objectivity; and in this social reality, what conventionality contrasts with is nothing other than subjective (personal/idiosyncratic) interpretation. It is clear that the conventional acts of establishing the linguistic system *per se* are to be distinguished from the critic's interpretation of language events. The former is responsible for the establishment of the very "reality" as such, i. e. responsible for the production of the "objective objects" of interpretation. Quite contrary to Fish's thesis, I would assert that conventional linguistic facts are objective and that they are produced by convention as opposed to interpretation. What we have here is in fact a three-level model:

(i) Linguistic Convention/Linguistic System
(ii) Language Events
(iii) Interpretation

In simplest terms, linguistic convention establishes the linguistic system; cases of using this system form language events which in turn constitute the objects of interpretation.

Now, the language events that we are concerned with are actually literary texts or texts read/treated as literary works. The question arises: what produces the properties that linguistic facts take on in literature? Fish's answer is "interpretation" whereas my answer is literary convention as opposed to interpretation.

4.3.2 Literary Convention vs. Interpretation

It is, I believe, the system of literary conventions which are constitutive of the institution of literature that permit one "to convert linguistic sequences into literary structures and meanings" (Culler 1975: 114). Given that literary convention is much more easily mistaken as interpretation, it seems necessary, before we go any further, to make clear the basic distinction/relation between object and interpretation.

In the natural reality of the world, if one interprets a tree as a tree, it will not be claimed that one's interpretation has produced a tree but that one has recognized an external object (a tree) as a tree. Similarly, in the social reality of language, if one interprets the sign "tree" as referring to the physical object involved, it does not mean that one's interpretation has produced the arbitrary relation between the sign and the physical object but that one has recognized the conventional relation between the sign and the symbolized object.

In the former case, interpretation involves differentiation between different natural objects; in the latter case, interpretation involves, by contrast, not only differentiation between the different conventional signs but also assimilation of the various conventional/objective relations between sign and meaning. When one interprets the sign "tree" as referring to the physical object involved, one is merely having a mental representation of an assimilated conventional/objective relation, a relation which is produced by convention and which exists independently of one's interpretation. If, however, one interprets "tree" as referring to what is usually called "table," this relation between sign and meaning is, by contrast, a product of one's interpretation.

This distinction tends to blur when it comes to literary convention. Compared with linguistic conventions, literary conventions are much vaguer (in the sense of being much more general as well as implicit) and much more susceptible to change. As distinct from the fairly stable and specific conventional relations obtaining in the linguistic system, there are, in the institution of literature, no definite, specific conventional ways of converting linguistic sequences into literary structures and meanings.

But vague and general as they are, to the system of literary conventions are to be granted the (public) properties which texts take on in literature. Indeed, "when one reads the text as a poem new effects become possible because the conventions of the genre produce a new range of signs" (Culler 1975:162). The point to notice is that literary conventions contrast with the individual reader's interpretation. If one, in interpreting a text, abides by the set of relevant literary conventions (which one has assimilated), one is in a position to produce some acceptable interpretation. If, by contrast, one does not abide by them, the resultant interpretation is very probably idiosyncratic or unacceptable to other (competent) readers.

At this point, we may bring in Fish's notion of "interpretive communities." Fish writes,

> it is interpretive communities, rather than either the text or the reader, that produce meanings and are responsible for the emergence of formal features. Interpretive communities are made up of those who share interpretive strategies not for reading but for writing texts, for constituting their properties. (1980:14)

If Fish's notion of "interpretive strategy" involves confusion (its referents vary, as indicated above, from linguistic convention to the critic's interpretation), his notion of "interpretive community" is a no less mixed concept. On the largest scale, Fish's "interpretive community" refers to one critical approach (Fish's own "affective stylistics" or, by analogy, traditional criticism or stylistics); on the smallest scale, it refers to "two or more readers" who share the same interpretation (see 1980:171). That is to say, Fish's "interpretive communities" stands for different critical approaches or persuasions within one approach, or even smaller groups which operate within the same institution of literature. It seems to me that the interpretative communities as such differ from each other mainly in critical assumptions or procedures over and above literary conventions which obtain in the larger literary institution. This makes it possible for, say, stylisticians and literary critics, who approach the text from different perspectives, to agree on the same themes.

The point to notice is that, as parts of the same speech community, the different interpretative communities have to abide by the same linguistic conventions which produce objective linguistic facts. Moreover, as parts of the same literary institution, the different interpretative communities have to abide by the common literary conventions which obtain in the larger literary institution. Quite contrary to Fish's thesis, I contend that (public) textual properties are constituted by linguistic and literary conventions as opposed to the interpretative strategies *peculiar to* "two or more readers" or to a given critical approach.

In fact, the sequence of words which make up the text are usually chosen by the writer on the grounds of the conventional relations between words and meaning (as indicated earlier, the literary writer's creative exploitation of the conventional linguistic system frequently takes the shape of deviation from the norm). The text thus formed invites, or rather requests, the reader to bring into play the relevant conventions (specific or general) which the reader has assimilated. If one does not abide by the relevant conventions that obtain either at the time the text is written or at the time of the interpretative act, the result is very probably an idiosyncratic interpretation or a misinterpretation (as already noted, since literary conventions are vague and general and since literary, particularly poetic, meaning is often encoded in an unconventional way, a certain degree of indeterminacy is expected). It is clear that the text does exist independently of interpretation and that it forms an *object* rather than a product of interpretation.

Two things must be noted here. First, I do not mean to suggest that the reader has only a passive role to play. Given that literary conventions are vague and general and given that what those conventions involve is one's moral, psychological, artistic sensitivity or one's intuitive leap from linguistic sequences to literary structures and meanings, one is called upon to play the role of an *active* interpreter. This is particularly so in modern experimental works where the reader is called upon to fill in various gaps or to make sense of deviant elements frequently encountered in the text. Greater indeterminacy is expected here, but such processes of "filling in gaps" or of "making sense" are still governed, to different extent, by various conventions. Secondly, conflicting ideologies, rivalling religious beliefs, or different personal experiences are sure to bear, in varying degrees, on the interpretative act. But these variables serve to account for the distinction between readers or between groups of readers (see Culler 1982:68), who interpret the same text.

The distinction between convention and interpretation, once argued, may seem quite obvious, but it is not a distinction readily recognized. In the contemporary debate between the champions of the text and the champions of the reader, or in the various accounts of reading (see Culler 1982), one seems to have never come close to this basic distinction, which in my opinion is fundamental to such discussions. When E. D. Hirsch (1976) argues about the distinction between "meaning" (the author's intended meaning) and "significance" ("textual meaning in relation to a larger context, i. e., another mind, another area, a wider subject matter, an alien system of values, and so on"), what his arguments show is, as indicated by Culler:

> the need for dualism of this kind in our dealings with texts and the world, not the epistemological authority of a distinction between the meaning of a text and the significance interpreters give it, or even the possibility of determining in a principled way what belongs to the meaning and what to the significance. We employ such distinctions all the time because our stories require them, but they

are variable and ungrounded concepts. (1982:77)

The case is, however, not as hopeless as it appears. The theoretical or epistemological grounds for such a distinction can be sought in the distinction between convention and interpretation as discussed above: the "meaning" of a text lies in the relevant conventional relations (specific or general) between the signifier and the signified which obtain at the time of the writer's creative act (and which exist independently of an individual reader's interpretation), and the "significance" of the text resides in reader's interpretative acts.

Interestingly, in arguing that "linguistic and textual facts, rather than being the objects of interpretation, are its products," Fish comes to the point of nullifying the creative efforts made by authors. Fish writes,

> the answer to the question "Why do different texts give rise to different sequences of interpretive acts?" is that *they don't have to*, an answer which implies strongly that "they" don't exist. Indeed, it has always been possible to put into action interpretive strategies designed to make all texts one, or to put it more accurately, to be forever making the same text. Augustine urges just such a strategy, for example, in *On Christian Doctrine* where he delivers the "rule of faith" which is of course a rule of interpretation. It is dazzlingly simple: everything in the Scriptures, and indeed in the world when it is properly read, points to (bears the meaning of) God's love for us and our answering responsibility to love our fellow creatures for His sake. If only you should come upon something which does not at first seem to bear this meaning, that "does not literally pertain to virtuous behavior or to the truth of faith," you are then to take it "to be figurative" and proceed to scrutinize it "until an interpretation contributing to the reign of charity is produced." This then is both a stipulation of what meaning there is and a set of directions for finding it, which is of course a set of directions—of interpretive strategies—for making it,

that is, for the endless reproduction of the same text. (1980:170)

Fish's discussion here is apparently a play on abstraction. One can comfortably claim that most novels depict human life but this does not make the novels concerned the same novel: they differ in terms of the aspects of human life depicted, in terms of characters, plots, or in terms of choices of words, syntax. Indeed, if one is objective, one will surely acknowledge the existence of the different texts which are carefully wrought out by different writers and which embody those writer's creativity and artistic achievements.

4.4 A CONSIDERATION OF "WHAT IS STYLISTICS? PART II"

Having made clear the nature of the text and, prior to that, the correlation between structural feature and psychological value and literary significance, we now come to a consideration of Fish's "What is stylistics? Part II." As distinct from its predecessor considered in the last chapter, the focus of the charge here falls, as quoted at the beginning of this chapter, on the linguistic basis itself. Our discussion of this charge by Fish attempts to shed some further light on the degree of objectivity in stylistic analysis and, in a broader sense, on the nature of stylistic analysis as a whole. To avoid repetition and to save space, attention will be focused here on one most immediately relevant issue, namely, the relation between theme and formal patterns.

In "What is stylistics? Part II," an example that Fish singles out to criticize in terms of the correlation between theme and formal patterns is Keyser's analysis of "Anecdote of the Jar" by Wallace Stevens. As distinct from other stylisticians who try to identify thematically-motivated formal patterns, if any, *in the complex reading process* (see Macleod 1985:122; Widdowson 1972:29; Leech & Short 1981:13; Nash 1982:113; Fowler 1986:6—7), Keyser goes about analysing the structure of the poem first and only then tries to *find* an interpretation compatible with the established formal pattern, as reflected in the following observation:

> If ... there exists a relationship between form and meaning in this poem, it should be possible for us to find an interpretation congenial to the structure we have already established ... (1981: 110)

Such a procedure in which the linguistic analysis is done on its own is surely highly problematic. The structural property in question is phonological, principally, simple variation on the syllable round: "round," "surround," "around," "round" again, and "ground." Now, with the exception of onomatopoeia, phonological sound usually does not, according to convention, have to do with sense (see 4. 2. 2). The variation on the syllable "round" in the present case can, at least hypothetically, be merely accidental: these words chosen by the writer happen to have those sounds which happen to fall into a pattern. Keyser's conclusion that "The actual phonological shape of the property of the jar which, in English, takes the form of the word *round* imposes an order on the poem just as the semantic property ' round,' which the jar possesses, imposes an order on the wilderness" is one based on superficial similarity between the phonological pattern and the meaning concerned. Although in such a case, as made clear in 4. 2. 2, the formal ground available is no other than or no more than superficial similarity, it is problematic that one takes on trust such superficial similarity alone, since it can be accidental. To avoid arbitrariness, one has to ground the analysis on the contextual impact of the formal pattern's psychological effect, on the shared intuitive response to the pattern in the particular reading context. If, in reading a poem, a phonological pattern gives rise to a thematically-related response, it is probable that the pattern is encoded by the writer to reinforce or contribute to the theme; if, however, a phonological pattern does not in the reading process give rise to a thematically-related response, there is no reasonable ground to claim the correlation between the formal pattern and the theme concerned, even though there is some form of "parallel" between the two. Keyser's procedure, in which a phonological pattern is established on its own and only then is an effort made to *find* a theme congenial to the pattern can easily result in a false correlation based on accidental similarity.

Given that Keyser's procedure here is at once problematic and, in a sense, idiosyncratic, Fish's choosing it to represent stylistic analysis is clearly misleading. But some of Fish's criticism does bear on stylistic analysis in general. Fish writes,

> The phonological shape of "round" imposes an order on the poem only if you have already decided that the poem is about order. That is, the pattern emerges under the pressure of an interpretation and does not exist as independent evidence of it. In the event of a different interpretation, the pattern would be seen differently and be evidence in another direction. One might decide, for example, that the poem was about the many ways of viewing a jar (as in the thirteen ways of looking at a blackbird); it would then be a series of puns: the jar is round; it is also a round; it is a superround (*super* is the Latin for "sur" and means over, above, and on top of); and as the focus of attention it functions as a g-round. In the context of this reading, the pattern of sound would reflect difference and variation rather than similarity and order. (1980: 253)

Given what was said in 4.2.2, it will be clear that phonological pattern, which is conventionally irrelevant to sense or theme, is in no position to function as independent evidence of a literary interpretation. In the case of a correlation between the two, the determining force is expected to come, apart from some form of "parallel" between the two, largely from the particular literary context, from the developing literary interpretation in the light of which the linguistic form is viewed. But the important point to notice is that when we move into the area of syntax, modes of speech or, in particular, lexis, greater determining force is seen, often if not always, to come from the linguistic fact itself. In what I classified in 4.2.2 as "the latter type" of correlation between linguistic form and theme, the thematic value frequently takes the shape of a contextual extension of the linguistic form's conventional value. In such cases, the formal pattern functions more or less as independent evidence of the interpretation concerned. It will be recalled that at the beginning of this chapter, I quoted the following observation by Fish:

> formal patterns are themselves the products of interpretation and ... therefore there is no such thing as a formal pattern, at least in the sense necessary for the practice of stylistics: that is, no pattern that one can observe before interpretation is hazarded and which therefore can be used to prefer one interpretation to another. The conclusion, however, is not that there are no formal patterns but that there are always formal patterns; it is just that the formal patterns there always are will always be the product of a prior interpretive act, and therefore will be available for discerning only so long as that act is in force. Or, to end with an aphorism: there always is a formal pattern, but it isn't always the same one.

What I find misleading here is that the role of interpretation is emphasized and magnified to such an extent that the role of formal pattern or the determining force of language is completely and unexceptionally submerged. The picture that I have been trying to represent is one in which both entities—(a) the given context or the developing interpretation in the light of which the linguistic form is viewed and (b) the linguistic choices concerned—operate as determining forces, sometimes with the former dominating the latter, but not infrequently with the latter playing a decisive role. Indeed, but for the determining force of the linguistic basis as such, which embodies the writer's creativity and artistic achievements, the existence of stylistics, whose function is to account for how the writer's verbal choices give rise to or contribute to certain aesthetic or thematic significance, would not have been necessary. And but for the determining force as such, it would not be necessary for a literary translator to try to preserve the original effects with functionally equivalent means or devices in the target language. This points to the main task of the discussion in Part One: it seeks both to make a contribution to the understanding of certain aspects of stylistics as a discipline in itself and to pave the way for the application of stylistics to fictional translation. It need hardly be said that the study in Part One sheds light on the relevance (primarily in terms of the objects of investigation) and applicability (a quality based on validity) of stylistics to fictional translation, which is to be discussed in Part Two.

PART TWO

APPLYING STYLISTICS TO THE TRANSLATION OF FICTION

CHAPTER 5

THE PLACE OF LITERARY STYLISTICS IN THE TRANSLATION OF FICTION

The discussion in this chapter centres on the justification of and, particularly, the necessity for applying literary stylistics to the translation of prose fiction. Basically, three factors combine to make such an application necessary. The first is that general translation studies, which have received much impetus from recent developments in linguistics and some related disciplines, are seen to be insufficient when applied to the translation of literary discourse. The second, which is no less obvious, arises from within the theory and criticism of literary translation itself, where attention has been focused on poetry with little time spent studying the problems characteristic of the translation of fiction, particularly of the traditional realistic kind. The third factor, one that is more immediately relevant, is the fact that many specific problems posed by fictional translation, which may be subsumed under the heading "deceptive equivalence," can be, and at present can only be, quite effectively solved by the introduction of stylistic analysis.

5.1 THE INSUFFICIENCY OF GENERAL TRANSLATION STUDIES

By "general" translation studies I mean translation studies that operate on the level of ordinary or natural language. During the past two or three decades, developments in the fields of transformational grammar, general and contrastive linguistics, semantics, information theory, anthropology, semiotics, psychology, and discourse analysis etc. have exerted great influence on translation theory and criticism, enabling the discipline to broaden the areas of investigation and to offer fresh insights into correspondence or transference between linguistic and cultural systems (see, for instance, Rabin 1958; Nida 1964 & 1982; Nida & Taber 1969; Catford 1965; Newmark 1981; Duff 1981).

The traditionally-much-debated dichotomy between "literal" and "free" translation (see Steiner 1975:236ff. ; Kelly 1979:205ff.) has been replaced by various linguistically-informed modern distinctions, like Nida's "formal" versus "dynamic" correspondence, Catford's "formal correspondence" versus "textual equivalence," or Newmark's "semantic" as opposed to "communicative" translation. In general, more attention has been paid to the translating process and greater emphasis placed on "equal-response" of the target language reader (see Shen 1985). Such new perspectives on the theoretical front as well as the fairly extensive developments in specific interlingual contrastive studies have promoted considerably the understanding and mastery of the nature and skill of translation.

Given that literary translation primarily involves the transference of linguistic and cultural elements, developments in general translation studies are no doubt of relevance to a literary translator. But the point holds that this kind of study, which usually operates on the level of linguistic correspondence (including general stylistic norms), does not deal with problems intrinsic to or characteristic of literary discourse. One such problem, which is particularly significant in fictional translation, is how to make the appropriate choice(s) from grammatically correct "referential equivalents" or "stylistic variants" taking on different values or effects that tend to go unnoticed in ordinary discourse (see 5. 2. 2). If finding a grammatically-acceptable referential equivalent for the original is a matter of linguistic competence, the choice of a stylistically-optimal correspondent depends, by contrast, primarily on the understanding of the nature and function of literary texts.

It seems that some translation theorists have rather naive notions about what literary style involves. In Alan Duff's *The Third Language*, the problem of register in literature is put on a par with that in non-literary writing. Duff focuses on the necessity of achieving consistency in register in translation, illustrating this necessity by translations of both non-literary and fictional texts. Duff contends that:

> It would be a mistake, I think, to assume that only the literary translator is concerned with problems of style. Whatever discipline he may be working in ... he will have to decide on the *register* (formal—informal, official—unofficial) and to maintain this register consistently throughout. (1981:7)
>
> every text has a *register*, i. e. it is written at a level of formality or informality which is partly determined by the reader for whom the text is intended. (87)

However, it would also be a mistake to think of the treatment of register in fictional translation as merely a matter of achieving consistency. Register in fictional discourse has to be seen as being of a more complex nature, and as integrated within the structure of the work. In many novels, variations in register operate to characterize different mind styles, to generate effects of parody or comedy, to convey the implied author's sympathetic identification or ironic distance and, not least, to indicate the mingling of voices or subtle shifts in point of view between various participants involved (see Fowler 1977; Leech & Short 1981; Bakhtin 1981). Thus, rather than a superficial consistency in register (which a non-literary translator could be content with), a fictional translator would, or rather, should be concerned with thematically-motivated shifts in register, for it is in such deliberately-wrought variations that artistic significance inheres. In fact, many translation-critics are conscious of the essential difference in terms of style or expression between the translation of ordinary and literary discourse (see, for instance, Prochazka 1964; Popovic 1970; Brislin 1976; Cluysenaar 1976; Holmes 1978; Bassnett-McGuire 1980).

Indeed, in contrast with a non-literary translation,

> for a literary translation the criterion for the functional equivalence of its structural elements cannot lie in the linguistic system in its usual sense, as it will be determined by the specific regularities of structuring of the text as an artistic construct. If the textual element of a literary translation is to possess a literary value equivalent to that of the original, a decisive part will be played by the functional equivalence of such categories as, for instance, the thematic means, the means to build up characters, contextual procedures, the prosodic elements in lyric poetry—all of them categories implying the notion of a literary tradition and aesthetic conventions which depend largely on historical and socio-cultural circumstances. (Broeck 1978:39)

Apart from linguistic systems, in other words, literary translation also involves the encounter between literary polysystems and aesthetic conventions, including the conventions of artistic creation, of interpretation and criticism. In discussing problems concerning equivalence in translating poetry, Robert de Beaugrande justifiably draws a distinction between the general level (A) where one finds problems pertaining to "the relationships within or between language systems" (a level that "can be studied with the methods of linguistics and contrastive linguistics") and the more specific level (B) which "contains the more specific properties of poetic use of language and can be studied with the methods of poetics and literary analysis" (1978: 101). Now since linguistically-oriented general translation studies only deal with the basic level (A), they are apparently insufficient when applied to literary translation. It is true that there has been a substantial amount of research into the translation of literary discourse. But most attention has been focused on the translation of poetry with little time spent studying the problems characteristic of the translation of prose fiction.

5.2 CHARACTERISTICS OF FICTIONAL (VS. POETIC) TRANSLATION

This section directs attention to the fact that the problem of formal constraints, which has been much discussed in the criticism of poetic translation, does not, generally speaking, feature in fictional translation and, further, that the translation of fiction—particularly of the traditional realistic kind—presents its distinctive problems, many of which could be subsumed under the heading "deceptive equivalence."

5.2.1 Less Formal Constraints

In the large body of work discussing the translation of poetry, the weight of the argument often bears on the difficulties posed by the transference of such conventional poetic devices as verse form, stanzaic patterning, metre, line length, or rhyme scheme. The preservation of such formal features—either by "homologue" or "analogue" (see Holmes 1978:75)[1]—usually involves various losses or distortions of content (see Goodman 1954:227; Savory 1968:84; Nida 1964:157). In fact, the constraint is not limited to the relation between form and content and may be found acting upon the association between formal devices themselves. More specifically, the choice of a particular corresponding formal device could render, as observed by Holmes (1978:76), correspondence for certain further formal features in the source-text unfeasible or even unattainable.[2] Thus it is not surprising that the English translations of Catullus' Poem Sixty-Four display seven different modes of presentation, namely, (a) Phonemic translation, (b) Literal translation, (c) Metrical translation, (d) Poetry into prose, (e) Rhymed translation, (f) Blank verse translation, and (g) Interpretation (see Lefevere 1975); each mode is seen to overemphasize one or more elements of the poem at the expense of the whole (Bassnett-McGuire 1980:82;

cf. Goodman 1954:227). In connection with but distinct from this is the much-discussed formal constraint arising from the meaningful interaction between sound and sense, an element that features prominently in poetry as a genre and that significantly underlies the extreme difficulties of poetic translation (see Savory 1968:77 — 78; Widdowson 1975:36—37; Beaugrande 1978:102).

When it comes to the translation of prose fiction, not only is a constraint of the preceding kind nonexistent, but also the constraint resulting from the interaction between sound and sense is very much more limited (with some exceptions like Woolf or Joyce). It is obvious that rhythmic, phonetic, or phonological properties are much less essential to the genre of fiction. This is just another way of saying that a large part of the criticism of poetic translation does not apply to the translation of prose fiction, which-particularly the traditional realistic kind-poses its distinctive problems to the translator. Many of these problems could, I think, be subsumed under the heading "deceptive equivalence."

5.2.2 Deceptive Equivalence

While the distinction between scientific translation and poetic translation is undoubtedly clear, the distinction between scientific translation and narrative translation tends to be blurred by an inadequate awareness of the function of language in realistic fiction. If a translator is sure to take account of the aesthetic effects of language in a poem, when it comes to translating realistic fiction, the translator is inclined to establish equivalence at the level of "paraphrasable material content" (Bassnett-McGuire 1980:115). This is hardly surprising since the writer's artistic manipulation of language in realistic fiction is much less obtrusive than in poetry; and also since the isomorphic relation between the fictional world and the real world, allied to the resultant suspension of disbelief, can easily lead the translator to focus on the represented events or characters and to overlook the artistry involved in the use of the medium.

Such a neglect of the novelist's artistic manipulation of language is also found in some literary critics, as demonstrated by Philip Rahv's statement:

> All that we can legitimately ask of a novelist in the manner of language is that it be appropriate to the matter in hand. What is said must not stand in a contradictory relation to the way it is said, for that would be to dispel the illusion of life, and with it the credibility of fiction. (1956:297)

This view misleadingly confines aesthetic significance in the novel to the portrayed fictional reality and does injustice to many great realistic writers (like those referred to in the following analysis) who are distinguished not only "by a vital capacity for experience, a kind of reverent openness before life, and a marked moral intensity" (Leavis 1948:9) but also by their skillful manipulation of language for aesthetic effects or by their use of language to create a certain texture and tone which serve to reinforce or modify themes and meanings. In translating Jane Austen, for instance, if one fails to capture the impact of her voice as conveyed by her subtle linguistic choices, there is sure to occur the loss of a substantial part of her artistry (for exemplification, see 6.1.1).

It is worth noting that, as far as a reader is concerned, even if s/he does not pay special attention to the effects of the writer's style, s/he could still be affected, though perhaps only unconsciously, by the writer's stylistic or rhetorical devices during the process of extracting the fictional reality from the linguistic medium. But if a translator does not consciously take account of such devices, s/he is bound to fail to represent them in the target language. Thus various kinds of deceptive equivalence may emerge in narrative translation, which convey approximately the same fictional 'facts' but fail to capture the aesthetic effects generated by the original author's formal operations.

As already noted, "deceptive equivalence" in narrative translation also occurs at the level of fictional 'facts,' taking the shape of a distortion of fictional reality, which is mistaken by the translator as some form of equivalence. Theoretically, the boundary between the two kinds of deceptive equivalence in question is quite clear: one kind affects the represented fictional 'facts' while the other only bears on the formal operations over and above the experience depicted. But in actual cases, one may find ambiguity or indeterminacy concerning which of the two dimensions of narrative structure is involved (for exemplification, see the following chapter). Yet despite this tendency to overlap in practice, I would like to discuss the two kinds of deceptive equivalence separately, so as to see things in a clear theoretical perspective. (As this is only a preliminary theoretical discussion, some statements may be found rather vague, but they will be duly substantiated and clarified by the following practical analysis.)

At the Level of Fictional 'Facts'

Linguistically, this could be taken as the level of mere sense or the referential use of words. The stylistic interest here comes from the aesthetic motive underlying, or the aesthetic effect pertaining to, the novelist's creation of fictional reality *per se*.

The deceptive equivalence in some cases can be accounted for on the one hand by what I consider 'conceptual deviation' found in the original (i.e. violation of the relevant stereotypic conceptual frames in the translator's mind concerning human characteristics or behaviour under given circumstances) and, on the other, by the translator's failure to realize the larger structural or thematic functions of the fictional 'facts' involved (see 6.1 particularly 6.1.4). What frequently happens is that the translator alters the fictional 'fact(s)' according to his/her normal or conventional ways of conceiving things, probably with the assumption that his/her rendering, which appears to be more logical or sensible than the original in the immediate context, is what the author ought to have said, but failed to say, and so is therefore a reasonable form of correspondence to the source language text. Although strictly or locally speaking, this is a matter of the translator's falling short of the novelist's "capacity for experience," it is in effect, on a larger structural scale, frequently a matter of the translator's failure to realize the function of the narrator's withholding information, suppressing explanation or immediate contextual substantiation: factors which make for 'conceptual deviation' as such. As will be revealed by the analysis below, 'conceptual deviation' of this kind may have a significant role to play in characterization or plot construction, giving rise to desirable stylistic effects such as irony, intensity or suspense: effects which regrettably disappear in the process of the translator's 'normalization'.

In fictional translation, the translator's emotional involvement—typically with certain characters—may also lead to deceptive equivalence at this level. Interestingly, the alteration of fictional 'facts' here, which is characteristically motivated by "practical interests" coupled with "primacy effect" (6.2), is usually carried out quite unconsciously (hence *deceptive* equivalence). In such cases, while the translator's emotional involvement constitutes the primary factor, his/her inadequate literary competence (in terms of, say, the familiarity with the relevant novelistic conventions or the ability to perceive the larger structural or thematic functions of the fictional 'facts' involved) may also have a significant part to play. In 6.2, we shall examine in some detail the causes underlying, and the aesthetic losses resulting from, the translator's distortions as such.

Earlier, I made it clear that, in discussing deceptive equivalence, I do not concern myself with errors caused merely by inadequate linguistic competence (which is the concern of general translation studies) and I have been focusing on factors over and above that level: failure to realize the structural or thematic functions of the fictional 'facts' involved, normal or conventional ways of conceiving or perceiving things, and emotional involvement. But in some special circumstances, the issue may be complicated by 'traps' laid by differences in linguistic conventions between the source language and the target language. We shall see, in the last but one example in 6.3, how deceptive equivalence is caused by a joint function of the translator's lack of awareness of the intended dramatic irony and his failure to detect a trap associated with the frequent omission of subjects and determiners peculiar to Chinese.

Before turning to the level of the narrative discourse, I would like to bring in one aspect of fictional reality, namely, the speech and thought proper of characters, which differs fundamentally from the rest of the purported reality in that it is in itself verbal. In this area, deceptive equivalence may arise at two contrastive levels. One is the level of mere sense, where deceptive equivalence typically takes the shape of the translator's regrettable normalization of certain illogical or unreliable elements in the original speech or thought; elements deliberately encoded by the author for given purposes of characterization (see 6.1.3). But more often, deceptive equivalence in this verbal reality arises paradoxically at the level of linguistic form. Now, as far as monologic fiction is concerned, artistic significance in this verbal reality inheres very much in the novelist's successful differentiation between speech (or thought) types or idiolectal features (like the crude distinctions between formal and informal, vulgar and elevated, or simple and sophisticated) as a way of creating different objectivized and finalized images of people (Bakhtin 1973:150). Being a matter of linguistic differentiation in terms of, say, register or dialect, it is only natural that the artistic significance here lies in the choices of given linguistic forms as opposed to others which convey approximately the same cognitive meaning (but one needs to bear in mind that, in this verbal reality, the change from, say, a character's informal expression into a more formal one is an alteration of the experience depicted).

Basically, the translator's successful representation of this verbal reality in the target language depends on (i) the ability to differentiate the diversified speech or thought types in both the source language and the target language and to determine the general or specific correspondences between them; (ii) the understanding of the relation between the chosen speech or thought type and the given social or thematic role(s) of the character concerned; and (iii) the grasp on every single occasion of the relation between the characteristics, if any, of the character's speech or thought and the particular situation in which the linguistic expression is found. If the translator falls short in any aspect, s/he can easily produce cases of deceptive equivalence, which convey approximately the same cognitive meaning but fail to correspond to the particular speech or thought type chosen by the original author, leading as a consequence to various losses of the function of the original speech or thought in terms of characterization. In the following practical analysis, I shall only touch occasionally on this verbal reality but I shall devote a whole chapter to the formal operations carried out on it, i. e. to the different modes of speech and thought presentation, which pertain to the level of narrative discourse.

At the Level of Narrative Discourse

At this level, we are concerned with the authorial (and/or the dramatized) narrator's formal operations carried out on the purported fictional 'facts,' or, to put it another way, with the writer's exploitation of the resources or advantages of the linguistic medium in the representation of fictional reality. As far as the more or less "monologic" novel is concerned, the relation between fictional reality and formal operations as such is essentially a relation between fictional happening and the bearing brought on it by the all-encompassing authorial consciousness (in all types of narration). While fictional reality is in itself objectivized, represented by the implied author to fulfill certain thematic purposes, the way that linguistic form is manipulated to reinforce or modify that reality is a way of conveying the authorial vision of that reality (either directly or derivatively as in the case of first-person narration) and a way of making that reality function more effectively in the thematic unity constituted according to the author's artistic design (see 7.6). It is, however, understood that even in such authorial narrative discourse, there may be found a variety of characters' voices or social registers introduced typically through "speech allusion," i. e., "the selective imitation of a style of speech by the author" (Leech & Short 1981:349—350; see also Bakhtin 1981:298ff.).

In realistic fiction, deceptive equivalence at this level usually, as noted above, takes the form of cases which convey approximately the same fictional 'facts,' but fail to capture the aesthetic effects generated by stylistic or rhetorical devices in the original. The true equivalence that one should aim for here is functional equivalence (which conveys similar aesthetic effects of both content and form) or "expressive identity" (see Bassnett-McGuire 1980:25). But once we go beyond the solid ground of fictional 'facts', the problems of determining translation equivalence begin to emerge. Indeed, in the translation of realistic fiction, questions as to what constitutes a free variation on the original and what involves stylistic losses are more difficult to deal with than either in the translation of newspaper reports (where any version which conveys approximately the same amount of information with an acceptable style may be regarded as a translation equivalent) or in the rendering of poetry (where stylistic losses are often more detectable).

It seems to me that, in determining functional equivalence in somewhat monologic realistic fiction, the following two closely related aspects deserve particular attention: one is authorial vision, stance or point of view; the other is the function of the linguistic form in the thematic unity of the work. Now, in order to see things in perspective, we may make a comparison in terms of these two aspects between newspaper reports and such realistic fiction. In the case of a newspaper report, the reader, whose purpose is usually to extract information, does not purposefully seek the vision, stance or point of view of the reporters. In the case of a novel as a work of art and dominated by authorial consciousness, the reader is, by contrast, constantly seeking the authorial or narratorial vision or viewpoint which takes on aesthetic significance; which forms a crucial guide for the reader's interpretation[3]; and the search for which constitutes an essential part of the reading activity.

Since, in describing the same event, the difference in point of view between different encoders lies mainly in the different choices of linguistic form at the level of narrative discourse (as opposed to the narrated story), in the case of a newspaper report, where the encoder's point of view does not really count, the difference between, say, surface syntactic choices may well be overlooked. But precisely for the same reason, the differences in choice between linguistic forms matter a great deal in prose fiction. Thus, given the two different surface choices: "after doing X, he did Y" and "he did X and then did Y", one may find both forms equally acceptable in the translation of a newspaper report. In the translation of fiction, by contrast, one surface choice may be found more suitable than the other in that the difference between the two in terms of the narrator's viewpoint (emphasis; given vs. new; foregrounding vs. backgrounding) may bear on narratorial stance and on characterization, among other things.

Much more notable is the difference between a newspaper report and prose fiction in terms of the writer's irony or sympathy. In fictional discourse, the authorial irony or empathy, conveyable through choices, say, between words (6.1.1) or between modes of speech (8.5.2—3), constitutes an important dimension of the narrative structure, playing a positive role in shaping the characters concerned (who are in themselves a creation of the writer's imagination). Indeed, the fictional reader, whatever his/her political beliefs, is conventionally expected to share—

perhaps only in the process of reading—the author's irony or sympathy (cf. W. Booth 1961:137ff.). The translator's failure to use functionally-equivalent linguistic means to carry over the authorial stance may, as illustrated in 6.1.1, lead to significant aesthetic losses. By contrast, in the case of news reporting whose function is to communicate actual happenings (although, influenced or controlled by given ideologies, newspapers can distort facts), the reporter's irony or sympathy is not supposed to come into play; and if it is brought into play through certain choices of linguistic form, the translator will probably either overlook it or justifiably reject it. For, while such tonal property is undoubtedly significant in revealing the ideological stance of the reporter or newspaper concerned, it may not be of significance to the translator whose aim is usually to provide a piece of news for the general public in the target language rather than to demonstrate the ideological character of a given reporter/newspaper for some special purposes.

Interestingly, in fictional discourse, the authorial or narratorial vision as embodied by given choices of linguistic form tends to superimpose an additional meaning—either imitative or contrastive—on the fictional reality depicted (see 7.6). In the contrastive cases, there is usually found an attempt to use the value of the linguistic form(s) to 'shape' (vs. to imitate) fictional reality for certain thematic purposes (7.6.2). This additional meaning, or the imitating or 'shaping' effects as such, which pertain to the level of narrative discourse, may well be suppressed in the case of a newspaper report where the reader/translator's interest is usually limited to the narrated story and where the narrative discourse does not really count. In fact, underlying the aesthetic significance of the narrative discourse characteristic of fiction is, among other things, the convention of thematic unity of form and content, or more specifically, the convention of using linguistic form to reinforce or modify meanings and themes. With such conventions, it is natural for the writer to use the narrative discourse as semantic reinforcement or modification of the narrated story; and with such conventions, the reader is apt to look for thematic effects or values in the writer's choices of linguistic form. Thus, if a novelist uses the mode of direct speech instead of indirect speech, the fictional reader would consciously or unconsciously search for the underlying authorial intention in terms of characterization, for the possible connection between this choice of form and the role or attitude of the character concerned (see chapter 8). But if a news reporter uses the mode of direct speech instead of indirect speech, the reader is unlikely to try to find out the mode's thematic value or its function in characterization. What we have here is an essential difference in the function of linguistic form between literary and ordinary discourse. Given the same linguistic form or pattern, its stylistic values become functional in fictional discourse but tend to be dormant in nonfictional discourse.

Although focusing on the difference in the function of the writer's (or narrator's) point of view between newspaper reports and prose fiction, I have already touched on the difference between the two in terms of the structural or thematic function of linguistic form. As distinct from a newspaper report, a work of prose fiction is often marked by a thematic unity deliberately wrought according to the author's artistic design. The constituent parts form objectivized means used to generate thematically-related effects; that is to say, their functions are determinable only in relation to the total structure of the work (see Kroeber 1971:24 — 25). This forms a contrast to a newspaper report whose constituent part is responsible only to the specific event(s) involved. The thematically-unified structure characteristic of monologic fiction is surely a significant factor that conditions the author's ways of manipulating linguistic form. Given the thematic unity as such, it is not surprising to find in a novel a motif in the shape of the consistent use of a linguistic form or pattern over a long stretch of the text. In John

Fowles's *The Collector*, for instance, the contrast between the inferiority of the kidnapper and the dominance of the kidnapped girl is continuously reinforced by the contrast between the former's free direct speech and the latter's direct speech (the mode of direct speech, with the inverted commas serving as invitations to an auditory experience, functions to strengthen the auditory impact of the speech). More frequently found is the motif in the shape of the recurrent use of a given word or an expression. A case in point is the frequent references to "dark" or "darkness" in Lu Xun's "Remorse for the Past" ("Shang Shi"). As we shall see in 7.2, the failure to realize the significance of this thematic motif has led a translator to suppress unconsciously the symbolic meaning of "darkness." Clearly, to avoid such cases of deceptive equivalence in fictional translation, the translator needs to judge the function of the linguistic forms concerned in relation to the thematic unity of the work.

The necessity of taking account of the total structure of the fictional text in the translator's choices of linguistic form has been stressed by Bassnett-McGuire (1980:110—118) whose analysis reveals that, if the translator renders the opening passage of a novel without relating it to the overall structure, s/he runs the risk of producing what we consider deceptive equivalence, where the paraphrasable content is translated at the cost of everything else. It will have become clear that the implied author's, or dramatized narrator's, stance/viewpoint and the structural or thematic function of the linguistic form are two significant criteria for determining deceptive equivalence at the level of narrative discourse.

Now, because of the differences in linguistic and literary conventions, different languages have different stylistic norms or means; the same linguistic form, that is to say, may have different expressive values in different languages (see Broeck 1978; Popovic 1970). Further, the differences may be complicated by the fact that the source text is often not contemporary. When confronted with such differences, the translator's task is essentially to match the intended stylistic effects in the source language with functionally-equivalent, though formally-different, linguistic means in the target language. Failure to do so can easily make for deceptive equivalence with various stylistic losses. In terms of the translation between Chinese and English, the differences in stylistic norms or means feature prominently in the area of syntax and of speech and thought presentation, which will receive detailed examination in Chapters Seven and Eight.

5.3 LITERARY STYLISTICS AND DECEPTIVE EQUIVALENCE

For anyone who is familiar with literary stylistics and who knows the poor state of the criticism of narrative translation, the necessity of introducing the values and emphases of literary stylistics into the latter area—as an effective means of dealing with deceptive equivalence as such—would be fairly obvious. The deplorably small body of existing work on narrative translation is marked by general and impressionistic comments on style (showing little or no concern with its thematic relevance) or by intuitive analysis with a notable lack of sensitivity to the subtle stylistic devices.

At the level of fictional 'facts,' attention has been focused by and large on distortions caused by inadequate linguistic and/or cultural competence (typically in the shape of mistranslations of idiomatic expressions or syntactic errors). What I referred to as "deceptive equivalence" has hardly been discussed. As already noted, failure to realize the larger structural or thematic functions of the fictional 'facts' in the original constitutes a significant factor underlying deceptive equivalence at this level, a factor which could be effectively dealt with by stylistic analysis, characterized by close observation of the relation between the facts involved and the surrounding linguistic and textual features. The basic task of the analysis here is to elucidate those functions in the source language and the aesthetic losses in the target language, as a means of enhancing one's awareness of the aesthetic motive underlying, or aesthetic effects pertaining to, the author's choices of fictional 'facts.' Despite the obvious difference in the data, the analytical rationale or procedure here is in essence quite similar to the stylistic analysis operating at the level of narrative discourse where the issue is the relation between the author's choices of linguistic form and literary significance. Interestingly, because of the essential similarity between the analyses conducted at the two different levels, in intra-lingual stylistic analysis of narrative, the critic may also shift—probably quite unconsciously—from one level to the other (see, for instance, Kennedy 1982). But of course, most attention in intra-lingual stylistic analysis is devoted to the level of the narrative discourse (also the choices of linguistic form in the verbal reality composed of character's speech, thought or mind-style).

It is at the level of narrative discourse that literary stylistics may contribute most to the criticism of narrative translation (the same applies to the verbal reality as such). Existing work in intra-lingual stylistic analysis has shed much light on the aesthetic significance of narrative discourse, on the thematic functions or effects of various subtle stylistic devices. In the field of narrative translation, there have been some stylistically-informed analyses of the transference of narrative discourse (see Prochazka 1964; Lodge 1966:20—23; Bassnett-McGuire 1980:109ff.), which display a descriptive precision and stylistic sensitivity (concerning syntactic form in particular) not found in traditional translation criticism. But such attempts are rare; and some subtle stylistic areas like modes of speech or thought presentation, which have been extensively investigated in Anglo-American stylistic analysis, have remained completely untouched in the criticism of fictional translation. In view of the fact that deceptive equivalence is on the whole unexposed (and therefore not consciously guarded against), constituting a great threat to the literary effects generated by the novelist's manipulation of the linguistic medium, there is surely an urgent need to make extensive stylistic analysis of deceptive equivalence as such. The major role of stylistic analysis is to sharpen the translator's sensitivity to the aesthetic function of linguistic form in prose fiction, helping the translator to produce functional equivalence rather than referential correspondence with various stylistic losses.

Clearly, as distinct from a non-literary translator, a fictional translator needs to be equipped with adequate literary and stylistic competence. In the translating process, one must start with a detailed stylistic analysis of the original, trying to determine the aesthetic function of the individual component (be it a fictional fact or a choice of linguistic form) in the thematic unity of the work, otherwise deceptive equivalence may be unavoidable.

CHAPTER 6
ASPECTS OF LEXICAL EXPRESSION

In translating prose fiction, the translator's alteration of the original is, as a rule, most manifestly reflected in the area of lexical expression. In this area, what are most frequently subjected to change—a change that is often deliberate and almost invariably regrettable—take the shape of artistically or thematically motivated deviant choices of expression which undergo distortion primarily because they collide with the translator's normal or conventional way of conceiving, interpreting or presenting things. This chapter centres on the functioning of such deviant elements and on the losses or consequences brought about by the translator's alterations. The limitation of space permits me to deal with only a few aspects. Except for 6. 2 "Objectivity," the aspects discussed, which focus on "illogical," "unreliable," and "redundant" elements respectively, seek to high-light deviation in certain of its most notable forms.

6.1 DEVIATION IN THE FORM OF "ILLOGICALITY"

If, in literary discourse, "deviation" has become a favourable term, the word "ilogicality" remains unappealing in itself. But "deviation," with its typical violation of conventional grammatical rules or of normal expectations, would seem to be a form of "illogicality" in the broad sense of the word. This section is primarily concerned with "illogicality" in a relatively strict sense. What distinguishes the present concern from the usual referent of the term—as signalled by the inverted commas in the title, the term is used here for want of a better word—is its underlying intentionality. Even if the illogicality involved is ascribable to the mind of a character, it is deliberately encoded by the author for aesthetic purposes, not to mention antinomy or paradox found in authorial discourse (see Knox 1961; Cantrall 1972; W. Booth 1974). Given that illogicality forms an area in which the translator is most ready to make corrections, many cases of artistically-motivated "illogicality" are changed by the translator into some more coherent forms (the implication may be one of reading these cases as reflections against the original author), with the notable loss of stylistic or aesthetic values. Attention will be directed in this section to some such unfortunate transformations which may serve to highlight the point that, in order to avoid deceptive equivalence, a literary translator must be sensitive in detecting intentional "illogicality" and in reconstructing its true meanings or purposes. Of the multi-dimensional effects generated by deliberate "illogicality," we shall look into the effects of irony, authenticity, intensity and suspense.

6.1.1 "Illogicality" and Irony

"Illogicality" is often found in narrative fiction as a means of creating what is called "stable irony" (see Booth 1974). One way it effectively operates is shown by the following case taken from Jane Austen's *Pride and Prejudice*:

> Mrs Bennet was in fact too much overpowered to say a great deal while Sir William remained; but no sooner had he left them her feelings found a rapid vent. In the first place, she persisted in disbelieving the whole of the matter; secondly, she was very sure that Mr Collins had been taken in; thirdly, she trusted that they would never be happy together; and fourthly, that the match might be broken off. Two inferences, however, were plainly deduced from the whole; one, that Elizabeth was the real cause of all the

mischief; and the other, that she herself had been barbarously used by them all; and on these two points she principally dwelt during the rest of the day. (chapter 23)

What we have here is one of the innumerable ironic strokes found in *Pride and Prejudice*. The irony comes principally from the sharp contrast between the strictly logical progression (from "in the first place" to "fourthly") and the blatantly contradictory attitudes ("she persisted in disbelieving the whole of the matter" while "she was very sure that Mr Collins had been taken in"). The stable irony thus brought into being is heightened in part by the tension between the strongly affirmative "persisted" and the no less affirmative "was very sure" (compare: In the first place, she disbelieved ... secondly, she said that ...) and, further, by the quasi-logical expression "Two inferences, however, were plainly deduced from the whole," which is in turn set in contrast with the mundane conclusions that follow.

In fact, right at the beginning of the novel, it becomes apparent that logic is not a strong point of Mrs Bennet, "a woman of mean understanding, little information, and uncertain temper." The faulty logic displayed here, coupled with the beguiling logical appearance which amuses a superior reader, is well expected from such a comic character as Mrs Bennet. But the case is much subtler than it appears. What is, in effect, the status of the ordinal numbers? Are they taken from within the character's speech or are they simply imposed on the character by the mocking authorial narrator? The mode of presentation here can be regarded either as one alternating between narrative report of speech act and free indirect speech or as consistent narrative report of speech act (see chapter 8). In the former case, the ordinals are attributable to the character. The effect could be seen as one of unconsciously superimposing logicality upon illogicality (unconscious for the character's part, of course; still purposeful on the part of the author). But if, on the other hand, the mode of presentation is taken as consistent narrative report of speech act, the logical markers, which invariably occupy the initial, thematic position of the clause, may well be attributed to the summarizing narrator. Thus, what we have is a sober, logical reporting voice punctuating, so to speak, an incoherent reported content, with the logical markers, which ostensibly seek to tidy up the character's speech, bringing into comic relief the disorder or absurdity involved.

If the basic feature of an irony is a contrast between a reality and an appearance (see Muecke 1970:33), the contrast here is one between a beguiling logical appearance imposed by the narrator and an illogical reality produced by the character. In the subtle fusion and yet unmistakable conflict between the two lies the author's satirical humour and the source of the reader's mocking amusement. This is the way in which the monologic author ingeniously passes her implicit judgement on the character and the way to establish secret communication between the author and the reader at the expense of a deserving character.

The dominant note of irony which is struck in the contrast between beguiling logicality and blatant illogicality or mundaneness has completely disappeared in one of its Chinese translations:

Zai Weilian jueshi meiyou gaoci zhiqian, Beina taitai jieli
Before Sir William took leave, Mrs Bennet tried her hardest

yazhi zijide qingxu, keshi, dang ta zoule hou, ta liji dafa
to control her feelings, but, soon as he left, she immediately

leiting, qixian, ta jianshuo zhexiaoxi shi
flew into a rage, at the beginning, she said firmly that the

wanquanshi niezaode, gen zhe ta youshuo Gaolin
news had been completely made up, then she said that Mr

xiansheng shangle tamende dang, ta duzhou tamen yongyuan
Collins had been taken in, she swore that they would

buhui kuaile, zuihou ta you shuo tamende hunshi bijiang

never be happy, at last she said that their marriage would
poliewuyi.　　　　　　　Ta feichang fannao
certainly be broken off. She was very angry and annoyed,
yifangmian ta zebei Yilishabai,　　　ling yifangmian
on the one hand she blamed Elizabeth, on the other hand
ta aohui ziji bei ren liyongle.　　　　　　　Yushi,
she regretted that she herself had been used by others. Thus,
ta zhengtian xuxubuxiude sunma,　　wulunruhe ye
she kept on cursing for the whole day, there was simply no
buneng shi ta pingjing xialai.
way to appease her. (Trans. Dong Liu 107－108)

In this translation, the ordinal numbers are substituted by temporal adjuncts: "In the first place" by "at the beginning;" "secondly" by "then;" "thirdly" being simply omitted; and "fourthly" by "at last." The picture that emerges is one of Mrs Bennet changing her mind as time goes by, which is not abnormal and which does not amount to illogicality. Now, one may argue that the ordinals—"in the first place," "secondly," and so on—could function simply as indicators of time sequence (first, do this; second, do that, and so forth). But in this context, such a possibility seems to be very slight, since the processes involved appear to be durative in nature ("persisted in disbelieving…" "was very sure that…" "trusted that…") and since the following sentence—"Two inferences, however, were plainly deduced from the whole," where the processes are treated as components of an organic whole—also seems to suggest that Mrs Bennet does not change her mind. Notice that this quasi-logical expression, which considerably heightens the ironic contrast, is totally omitted by the translator (in its place is found the addition "she was very angry and annoyed," which is in perfect harmony with the mundane reality). It may be of interest to note that another Chinese translator Keyi Wang translated Austen's ordinals into "diyi" ("in the first place"), "di'er" ("secondly"), "disan" ("thirdly"), and "disi" ("fourthly"), which can only refer to "logical" progression as opposed to "temporal" sequence.

Behind the dominant contrast between a beguiling logical appearance and an illogical or mundane reality, there exist, in effect, some related sub-oppositions or contrasts, ingeniously worked out by Jane Austen but undermined in the translation. The first to be noted is the contrast between lack of self-control and calmness. The metaphorical "her feelings found a rapid vent," in which "feelings" are accorded the role of actor, clearly indicates the loss of self-control and leads one to predict such expressions as "shout" or "abuse barbarously." But what actually follows is the calm and volitional "she persisted in disbelieving ... she was very sure ... she trusted. ... " Without, notably, any explicit reference to the act of speaking, the processes involved, though contextually coming from externalised verbalisation, may well pass off, by virtue of their usual ideational function, as internalised cognitive processes. The impression is deepened by the apparently cognitive "Two inferences, however, were plainly deduced from the whole ... ," while the ambiguity between thinking and speaking potentially present in the term "dwell" also seems to lend support to the effect.

The ingenious transformation of inferrable speech into ostensibly calm thoughts brings us to yet another opposition: one between successiveness and simultaneity. While speech is marked by linearity, different thoughts can be held simultaneously in the mind. Austen's ingenious transformation, coupled with the use of the ordinals which normally refer to co-existing or parallel processes of reasoning, creates something of the impression that Mrs Bennet is holding the conflicting beliefs simultaneously (versus a matter of changing her mind), which contributes to the ironic effect. That the transformation in question helps generate simultaneity may be backed up by the fact that they are found incompatible with adjuncts which indicate change in time:

> At the beginning, she persisted in disbelieving the whole of the matter; then she was very sure that Mr Collins had been taken in; then she trusted that they would never be happy together; and at last she trusted that the match might be broken off.

Compare the translation:

> At the beginning, she said firmly that the news had been completely made up, then she said that Mr Collins had been taken in, she swore that they would never be happy, at last she said that their marriage would certainly be broken off.

Clearly, there is in the former case a clash between the durative or stative mental processes and the adjuncts indicating change in time, a clash not found in the translation, where the mental processes are changed into externalised speech acts, which are successive to, rather than simultaneous with, each other, a change that further undercuts the ironic effect.

To represent Mrs Bennet's speech in an apparent thought form is to tone down, to tranquillize her temper. Indeed, do we not have reason, in a situation like this, to take "disbelieving the whole of the matter" as understatement, a cover for some ruder remark like "It's sheer rubbish!" And do we not have reason to assume that the translator, if he had been in Austen's place, would have accorded to Mrs Bennet a stream of explicit abuse (note, among other things, the change of Austen's "on these two points she principally dwelt" into "she kept on cursing")?

It is clear that Jane Austen's passage is marked by multiple ironic gaps between the narrative style (appearance) and the purported fictional world (reality). And if "illogicality" is taken in a broad sense, any of these ironic gaps, each involving some shape of inconsistency, may be treated as a form of "illogicality." In the following chapter a distinction will be drawn between imitating and shaping reality. In the case of shaping reality, there is always a gap between the narrative style and the purported fictional reality, a gap that may also be taken as "illogical" in the broad sense.

The divergence between an appearance and a reality, the involvement of a double decoding (and their mutual conditioning) is what "illogical" gaps as such share in common. But as regards the reader's attitude towards the appearance involved, the "illogical" gaps in the present case differ fundamentally from those which will be discussed in the following chapter where, as we shall see, the appearance, which embodies the author's point of view, is to be accepted by the reader and where the appearance is seen positively to superimpose a meaning upon that of the fictional reality. In the present case, however, the appearance is to be rejected by the reader: the beguiling logical appearance is to be rejected as false; similarly, the apparent calmness is to be rejected as deceptive. If, in the other cases referred to, the emphasis is on "as if it were," here the emphasis falls, by contrast, on "actually it is not." It is through the tension between the appearance and the reality, through the reader's amusement in detecting the falsity and reconstructing the reality that there is conveyed the true reality subtly, ironically and penetratingly.

In Jane Austen's passage, there is, in effect, another kind of "illogical" gap, manifested in "Elizabeth was the real cause of all the mischief; and ... she herself had been barbarously used by them all": a gap between an appearance created by Mrs Bennet and the fictional reality that lies underneath; a gap which is marked by the fact that the appearance is to be attributed to a character rather than to the authorial narrator. In such cases, whether the appearance is to be accepted or rejected depends largely on the role of, and the author's attitude towards, the character. As shown above, the loci of the appearance in question: "all the mischief," "by them all" and the foregrounded "barbarously" are omitted in the translation where we find instead the more logical form "she blamed Elizabeth ... she regretted that she herself had been used by others": a change accompanied again by the notable loss of irony.

It may be noted that intentional "illogicality," either in the narrow or broad sense, is an element which I find characteristic of literary discourse. Unfortunately, in translation not only are the more strictly "illogical" elements often brought towards coherence with the loss of, say, irony or intensity, but also the broadly-speaking "illogical" gaps, which involve a divergent double-decoding, may suffer a similar fate due to the general inclination for coherence, plainness, or transparency.

Now, in arguing that the translator should capture the various gaps between the narrative style and the purported reality (in monologic fiction), I am committed, apart from a devotion to the original work, to the aesthetics which appreciates the ingenious implicit interference of the authorial narrator, the subtle superimposition of one point of view upon another, the paradoxical effect accompanying the divergent double-decoding, and the resultant textual intensity. One may object to this in favour of some opposing aesthetic principles such as "absolutely no interference from the author." But the point is that what motivates a translator's adaptation seems not so much a matter of different aesthetic principles as a lack of sensitivity towards the author's stylistic devices which, as we have seen and shall see, are very subtle: a play on referential equivalents, on syntactic rank or shape, on textual distance, on modes of speech or on the different roles of the narrator. Such subtlety, though prized in the original, poses a problem in the translating process where the subtle devices are often, since they do not really bear on the brute facts, overlooked. But, as borne out by Dong's translation of Jane Austen, failure to carry over the subtle stylistic devices may result in serious distortions of the original: in Dong's translation, there is no fusion of multiple "illogical" gaps and,

CHAPTER 6 ASPECTS OF LEXICAL EXPRESSION 119

therefore, no subtlety, irony, no author's implicit satirical humour, no source for the reader's mocking amusement, no secret communication between the author and the reader; in short, none of the features which, combined together, form the Austen savour or the determiner of Austen's style. Indeed, Dong's translation may serve to highlight, as a negative case, the necessity of applying stylistics to the translation of literary discourse as opposed to ordinary discourse.

We now turn to the translation from Chinese into English. In Chinese fiction, as in English fiction, one finds contradictory statements made by the author and intended for the discerning reader who can readily expose the seeming illogicality and reconstruct the author's true meanings and purposes. Such a case is found in Lu Xun's "The True Story of Ah Q" ("Ah Q Zheng Zhuan"): a case whose seeming illogicality is carried over by translation (A) but brought towards coherence by translation (B), as follows:

(A) However, the truth of the proverb "misfortune may be a blessing in disguise" was shown when Ah *Q was unfortunate* enough to win and almost suffered defeat in the end. (Trans. Yang and Yang 1956:86, my emphasis)

(B) But "who knows that it is not a blessing for the Tartar to have lost his horse?" The only occasion on which Ah Q did win, he came near to tasting defeat. (Trans. Chi-chen Wang 1941:85)

"The True Story of Ah Q" is a satire on the negative side of the Chinese character as embodied by the antihero, Ah Q, a figure who, though fundamentally tragic, is in a sense more comic than Mrs Bennet. Even from these few decontextualized lines, where the antithetical "unfortunate enough to win" forms one of the many ironic twists present in the story, the reader may get some flavour of the narrator's sustaining satirical humour. In terms of interpretation, the seemingly illogical "unfortunate enough to win," which utilizes, by way of reversing, the truth of the preceding proverb and which is followed by an illustrative context, does not really pose any problem. As regards literary effects, the term "unfortunate" seems to take on at once a ring of irony and tragedy. Throughout the story, underlying the narrator's scathing satire on the protagonist, one can sense the narrator's deploring sympathy for him, a figure who suffers from deep oppression and a tragic fate. In the present case, while one cannot miss the narrator's tone of mockery in the semantic clash between "unfortunate" and "win," the term "unfortunate" seems to point to the tragic side of the protagonist, to the narrator's underlying sympathy. The duality of the term seems to generate a paradoxical effect and textual intensity which fit perfectly well in this context. Given this, (B)'s omission of the seemingly illogical "unfortunate" is at once unnecessary and undesirable.

If the use of the seemingly illogical "unfortunate" marks Lu Xun's tone or style, the paradoxical effect or the divergent double-decoding is an element which I find, as noted above, characteristic of literary discourse and which I find often unappreciated by Chinese-English literary translators, many of whom are accomplished ones. This is to be accounted for primarily by the translator's persistence of logic, by their drive to make a text cohere. The translators' readiness to make things straightforward may again be brought out by a comparison between the following two translations of a passage in the same story:

> (A) (All Ah Q's scars turned scarlet. Flinging his jacket on the ground, he spat and Said, "Hairy worm!" "Mangy dog, who are you calling names?" Whiskers Wang looked up contemptuously) Although the relative respect accorded him in recent years had increased Ah Q's pride, *when confronted by loafers who were accustomed to fighting he remained rather timid. On this occasion, however, he was feeling exceptionally pugnacious.* How dare a hairycheeked creature like this insult him? (Trans. Yang and Yang 1956:89-90,

CHAPTER 6 ASPECTS OF LEXICAL EXPRESSION   121

> my emphasis)
>
> (B) *If* the challenge *had come* from one of the idlers in whose hands he had suffered ignominious defeat, Ah Q, in spite of the distinction that he had recently won and the pride that he took in it, *might have been* more cautious about taking it up. But he did not feel any need for caution on this occasion; he felt very brave. How dare the hairy face talk to him like that? (Trans. Chi-chen Wang 1941:88—89, my emphasis)

Translation (A) presents a close rendering of the original (except for the omission of "only" from "only on this occasion" ["duyou zhehui"] and the change from "valiant" ["wuyong"] into "pugnacious"[1]), against which (B)'s adaptation should be apparent. In the original, one finds some element of "illogicality":

> Ah Q was *timid* when confronted by idlers who were accustomed to fighting. Whiskers/Beard Wang was one of those idlers.
> Ah Q (however) was valiant on this occasion towards his challenge.

However, by changing the indicative mood into the subjunctive, coupled with other changes (including the change of "who were accustomed to fighting" into "in whose hands he had suffered ignominious defeat"), translation (B) excludes Whiskers Wang ("the hairy face") from those idlers whose fighting is expected to intimidate Ah Q. Thus, one finds in (B) the perfectly logical form:

> Ah Q was (only) afraid of those idlers ...
> Whiskers Wang was not one of those idlers.
> So Ah Q was not afraid of Whiskers Wang's challenge.

The picture that emerges from (B) is a plain or straightforward one of Ah Q's cowardice: his fearing the strong and bullying the weak. But the original picture, as reflected in (A), is a more complicated, twofold one of Ah Q's cowardice and conceit. In fact, Ah Q's conceit or self-deceiving "psychological victory" is the principal target of the author's satire in this story. Though the poorest in Wei village, "Ah Q was very proud and held all the inhabitants of Wei in contempt" (Wang 82). In the present case, Ah Q's contempt for Whiskers Wang, for whom he is no match and by whom he is readily defeated, serves to bring out satirically the absurdity of his conceit and the self-deceiving nature of his "psychological victory."

It seems that Ah Q's unexpected valiance in the present passage not only ironically reflects Ah Q's conceit but also, while by no means reducing Ah Q's cowardice, enables the author to depict Ah Q's cowardice more ironically: "Although Ah Q recently ... remained timid. Only on this occasion however he was *exceptionally* valiant" ("Ah Q jinlai suiran ... hai danqie. Duyou zhehui que feichang wuyongle"). Through the subtle fusion and driving tension between "timid" (cowardice) and "valiant" (conceit), both traits in Ah Q's character are ingeniously, paradoxically and sardonically conveyed *at once*.

6.1.2 "Illogicality" and Authenticity

In order to obtain a clearer picture, we shall, before going any further, attempt here a classification of "illogicality" in the light of the analysis above. Although one can easily think of borderline cases and subspecies, "illogicality" as employed in fictional art seems to fall basically into four types:

- (a) that which comes from mental activities prior to the state of complete awareness: a common phenomenon in stream-of-consciousness fiction;
- (b) that which is attributable to the absence or loss of normal reasoning power: as reflected in Mrs Bennet's inconsistency;
- (c) that which is to be accounted for by the complexity or change in a character's trait or mood or attitude or the like: as illustrated

CHAPTER 6 ASPECTS OF LEXICAL EXPRESSION

by the coward Ah Q's being valiant towards Beard Wang's challenge;

(d) that which is deliberately encoded by the author to achieve certain effects: as reflected in Austen's depiction of Mrs Bennet or Lu's "unfortunate to win."

Of these types, (a) to (c) pertain to the fictional reality that the novelist has chosen to describe or create; the last type is, by contrast, a matter of the novelist's formal operations over and above the experience depicted. The demarcation between the two levels is, though, sometimes problematic. In Jane Austen's passage, for example, there is seen an interplay between the existential and the formal operations. Even in Lu's "unfortunate enough to win," to attribute the use of "unfortunate" exclusively to the formal principle is perhaps to neglect the character's immediate loss as well as his tragic fate.

In what follows, attention will be directed to all of these four types of "illogicality." In terms of the correlation between "illogicality and authenticity," we now examine a case taken from Lu Xun's "The New Year's Sacrifice" ("Zhufu"), which displays the (c) type of "illogicality":

(A) Of all the people I had seen this time at Luchen none had changed as much as she: her hair, which had been streaked with white five years before, was now completely white, quite unlike someone in her forties. Her face was fearfully thin and dark in its sallowness, and *had moreover lost its former expression of sadness, looking as if carved out of wood.* Only an occasional flicker of her eyes showed she was still a living creature. ... (Trans. Yang and Yang 1956:152, my emphasis)

(B) Although other folk I used to know in Lo Ching have apparently changed little, Hsiang-lin Sao was no longer the same. Her hair was all white, her face was alarmingly lean, hollow, and burnt a dark yellow. She looked completely exhausted, not at all like a woman not yet forty, but like a wooden thing *with an expression of tragic sadness carved into it*. Only the movement of her lustreless eyes showed that she still lived. ... (Trans. Snow and Yao 1936: 53, my emphasis)

Lu's "The New Year's Sacrifice" is a depiction of the tragic life of a twice-widowed country woman, who represents a typical victim of feudal ethics (which discriminates against women and according to which it is immoral for a widow to marry again). The present passage occurs when the protagonist has been reduced to the most miserable state, that of a sheer beggar. What is striking in translation (B) is the replacement of Lu's "her face ... had moreover completely lost its former expression of sadness, as if carved out of wood" ("lianshang ... erqie xiao jinle xianqian beiaide shense, fangfu shi muke shide") with "she looked ... like a wooden thing with an expression of tragic sadness carved into it." What underlies this adaptation seems to be the normal reasoning that the more miserable a state in which one finds oneself, the sadder one would appear.

Now, the seemingly illogical element—losing completely the expression of sadness in a saddest state—forms a typical case of the (c) type of "illogicality" which is to be accounted for by complexity or change in a character's trait or disposition or the like. The phrase "the former expression of sadness" in Lu refers to the expression that the protagonist wears after the death of her second husband and her son. But her subsequent tragic experience, chief among which is the scorn or discrimination to which she as a remarried widow is subjected, breaks, so to speak, her spirit and reduces her to a state of complete apathy. It is precisely through this change from deep sorrow to complete apathy that is emphatically conveyed the extreme tragedy of the protagonist, which forms a strong indictment against feudal ethics. Seen in this

CHAPTER 6   ASPECTS OF LEXICAL EXPRESSION   125

light, (B)'s adaptation in question is very regrettable.

It should be noted that this passage actually appears prior to the I-narrator's retrospective account of the protagonist's experience. As the first introduction to the protagonist, this passage, which in a sense outlines the outcome of her life, is psychologically prominent. Furthermore, due to the absence of any preceding substantiating context, the statement "her face ... had moreover completely lost its former expression of sadness" is quite puzzling, giving rise to an element of suspense: why does this woman, now a sheer beggar, no longer appear sad? This arouses the reader's interest, impelling the reader to find out the grim reality that lies underneath. Clearly, the effect of suspense, coupled with the psychologically prominent position, adds to the importance of the faithful transference of Lu's seeming illogicality, through which is authentically brought out the protagonist's tragic change to complete apathy.

Before turning to the discussion of illogicality and the effect of intensity, we now look into a case from Lao She's *Rickshaw Boy* (*Luotuo Xiangzi*), a case where the seeming illogicality involved seems to be associated with both authenticity and intensity:

(Lao)... ta fangfu bu shi lazhe liang che, ershi lazhe kou
　　... as if he was not pulling a rickshaw, but was pulling
guancai shide. Zai zheliang cheshang, ta shishi kanjian yixie
a coffin. In this rickshaw, he constantly saw some shadows
guiying, fangfu shi. (157)
of ghosts, as if they were really there.

(A) (... He was always apprehensive, as if he didn't know when trouble would turn up. Sometimes he would suddenly think about Ch'iang and all his hard luck.) It was as if he was pulling a coffin, not a rickshaw. Now and then he saw ghosts riding in it, or thought he did. (Trans. James 1979:167)

(B) ... It seemed to him that he was constantly seeing the shadowy

spirits of the dead riding for nothing in this rickshaw of his.
(Trans. King 1946:175)

(C) ... Often he seemed to see shadows of ghosts around it.
(Trans. Shi 1981:171)

Clearly, the seeming illogicality occurs in the clause "In this rickshaw, he constantly saw some shadows of ghosts," which violates the commonsensical conviction that ghosts do not materially exist and which is immediately corrected, as it were, by the hypothetical "as if." Now, the "illogicality" involved here, though ostensibly straightforward, is subjected to two contrastive interpretations. On the one hand, it may be treated as belonging to what I classified as type (a) illogicality that comes from mental activities prior to the state of complete awareness. In this light, the protagonist is seen to perceive the shadows of ghosts in a preconscious, hallucinatory state; but when he becomes fully conscious, the perception as such is rationalized into a hypothetical "as if." The resulting effect is of course that of authenticity in the shape of a faithful recording of the movement from preconscious hallucination to a conscious realization.

In contrast to this, the seeming illogicality may be taken as belonging to type (d), a type that is deliberately encoded by the author to achieve certain effects. From this perspective, the case is one in which the author purposefully chooses the form "he constantly saw..., as if they were really there" in place of "as if he constantly saw..." with the former functioning or, rather, passing off as a referential equivalent to the latter. What accompanies this splitting of one statement into two complementary ones is the effect of intensity: the assertion "... he constantly saw some shadows of ghosts" is, by virtue of its impossibility, at once striking and shocking, an effect that seems only partially cancelled out by the following "as if." The author, that is to say, is playing on the presentational sequence, on the linear progression of language.

Further complication arises with yet another possible, though less likely, interpretation. Perhaps "he constantly saw..." is an authentic report of the character's whole perception (he sees or believes that he sees). But since the perception goes against common sense, the narrator, in order to make the narrative acceptable or himself reliable, modulates it by "as if."

The potential coexistence of these contrastive interpretations results in a paradoxical effect and textual intensity characteristic of literary discourse. It should be stressed that, as Lao's work is a well-formed one, the "illogicality" involved which occurs on the narrative plane seems far from fortuitous. But, as shown above, Lao's "illogicality" is captured only by translation (A) which produces the similar effects of authenticity and intensity; both effects are undercut in (B) and (C) where Lao's two "complementary" statements are unfortunately combined into a logical, coherent whole.

6.1.3 "Illogicality" and Intensity

In terms of the correlation between "illogicality" and intensity, a most common phenomenon is found in the narrator's own seemingly contradictory statements, with the antinomy functioning to intensify the effect. Attention will be directed here to two illustrative cases. The first is taken from Lu Xun's "Medicine" ("Yao"), in which the "illogicality" involved is purely a matter of rhetorical form:

> (A) It was autumn, in the small hours of the morning. The moon had gone down, but the sun had not yet risen, and the sky appeared a sheet of darkling blue. *Apart from night-prowlers, all was asleep. Old Chuan suddenly sat up in bed.* He struck a match... (Trans. Yang and Yang 1956:29; my emphasis)
>
> (B) ... Everything still sleeps, *except those who wander in the night, and Hua Lao-shuan.* He sits up suddenly in his bed...

(Trans. Chi-chen Wang 1941:30; my emphasis)

This is the beginning of the story. The protagonist gets up in the small hours to get some medicine for his only son who is dying from pulmonary tuberculosis. The unexpectedness of the protagonist's getting up is dramatically intensified in Lu through the contradiction between "except for those creatures who wander in the night, all was asleep" ("chule yeyoude dongxi, shenme dou shuizhe") and the immediately following "Hua Laoshuan suddenly sat up in bed" ("Hua Laoshuan huran zuoqi shen"): the former, contradicted by the latter, functions as a rhetorical form of exaggeration or emphasis, which, by purposefully misleading the reader, enables the latter to defeat the reader's expectation so as to appear more striking.

This seeming illogicality, which is captured by (A), is completely dissipated in (B)'s coherent form "Everything still sleeps, except those who wander in the night, and Hua Lao-shuan," an adaptation with the possible implication of treating the contradiction in Lu as a reflection against the author. But clearly, Lu's seeming contradiction is an artistic device rather than a mistake resulting from carelessness. (B)'s adaptation, which involves the loss of the dramatized intensity, seems at once unnecessary and undesirable. The second illustrative case comes from Mao Dun's "Spring Silkworms" ("Chun Can"). In contrast with the preceding example, here is found a subtle interplay between the existential and the formal operations:

(Mao) "Keshi na dasuan tou shangde miao que dangzhen
"But that garlic really had only grown three or four shoots!"
zhiyou san si jingya!" Lao Tong Bao zi xinli zheme xiang,
Old Tong Bao thought so,
juede qiantu zhishi yin'an.   Kebushi, chile xuduo
felt that the future was only gloomy. Indeed, it did often
yequ, yizhi luotai dou henhao, ran'er shangle shan que

CHAPTER 6　ASPECTS OF LEXICAL EXPRESSION　　　　129

happen that having eaten a good deal of leaves and having gone

ganjianglede shi, yeshi changyoude.
well all the way, the silkworms still dried up and died when ready to spin their cocoons.

Buguo Lao Tong Bao wulun ruhe bugan xiangdao
But Old Tong Bao did not on any account dare let himself think

zheshangtouqu; ta yiwei jishi shi duzili xiang, yeshi bu jili.
of this; he took it that even to think of it in the secret recesses of the mind, would still be inviting bad luck. (my emphasis)

(A) Old Tung Pao recalled gloomily that the garlic had only put forth three or four shoots. He thought the future looked dark. Hadn't there been times before when the silkworms ate great quantities of leaves and seemed to be growing well, yet dried up and died just when they were ready to spin their cocoons? Yes, often! *But Old Tung Pao didn't dare let himself think of such a possibility.* To entertain a thought like that, even in the most secret recesses of the mind, would only be inviting bad luck!
(Trans. Shapiro 1956:31—32; my emphasis)

(B) The obsession of bad luck gradually took root in his old heart. Everything might go properly with the silkworms all the way as it should be. But who could tell, he reasoned further, that at the last minute the worms would not suddenly turn stiff? *The more he thought the more he became afraid, afraid that the thoughts might come true.* (Trans. Yeh 1946:22; my emphasis)

(C) Tung Pao became full of misgivings about the future. *He knew well that* it was possible for everything to go well all along the way only to have the worms die on the trees. But he did not dare to think of that possibility, for just to think of it was enough to bring ill luck. (Trans. Chi-chen Wang 1944:155; my emphasis)

It is clear that Mao's sentence "Indeed, it did often happen that ..." can be taken as free indirect thought. Seen in this light, the following narratorial statement constitutes an obvious contradiction to the fact with the contradictory element intensified by the emphatic "on any account." This heightened illogicality is attributable either to the fictional reality or to the level of the narrative discourse.

As a matter pertaining to fictional reality, the clause headed by the adversative "but" can be said to reflect the character's self-deceiving conception. In his extreme fear, the character seems to go so far as to escape reality, that is, to evade by way of forcibly contra-dieting (in his consciousness) the fact that he has actually thought about "this." The narrator, seen in this way, is giving an account of the character's contradictory and "escaping" state of mind.

However, if this is the case, the narrator is expected by convention to depict it in a way like "But Old Tong Bao would not on any account admit that he had thought (or: was thinking) about this. He didn't dare let himself think of it for he took it that. ..." Significantly, the point is that if the narrator had given such a representation, the contradiction between the free indirect thought and the following narratorial statement as found in Mao would have dissipated. In this light, the "illogicality" involved could be regarded as a matter of rhetorical form.

What underlies this heightened contradiction, which occurs at the level of narrative report, seems to be an effort at intensifying the character's fearfulness. If the contradiction between the actual thought act and the character's denial of the act functions to put across the character's extreme apprehension, the narrator's commitment to the contradiction produces a shock effect which renders the contradiction at once more driving and penetrating. Indeed, the narrator may be seen at

CHAPTER 6   ASPECTS OF LEXICAL EXPRESSION   131

this moment to be suspending his judgement and fully empathizing with the character's "escaping" state of mind. This naturally promotes a deeper sympathetic identification on the part of the reader, thus making the character's fear more keenly felt.

The case is in effect more subtle than it appears. A factor which fails to show up in all three translations is that the sentence in Mao "Indeed, ... " ("Kebushi, ... ") could perhaps also be taken as the narrator's intruding explanation, with an effect analogous to the offscreen voice in theatre. In this light, the narrator is extricated from any representational contradiction. The point to notice is that, as one possible interpretation which makes for subtlety, it does not cancel out the other possible interpretations; more relevantly, it does not cancel out the given contradiction and the resultant intensifying effect.

Now, how is Mao's "Illogicality" represented by the translations? In (A), the illogicality and the correlated intensifying effect is toned down through (i) the omission of the emphatic adjunct "on any account," (ii) the addition of the temporal adjunct "before" coupled with the choice of the past perfect tense ("hadn't there been") which, by distancing the happenings into the past, reduces their present relevance; and, closely related to (ii), (iii) the choice of "such a possibility" which has a relatively less direct referential connection with the preceding free indirect thought (compare (C)'s "it was possible ... But he did not dare to think of *that* possibility").

If (A) only reduces Mao's "illogicality," (B) has completely eliminated it. The narrator's contradictory assertion in Mao is simply rendered by (B) into the opposite and the perfectly logical form "the more he thought." It is obvious that the picture that emerges in (13) departs dramatically from the one depicted in the original. What one sees in Mao's description "But Old Tong Bao did not *on any account dare* let himself think of this; he took it that *even* to think of it in the secret recesses of the mind, *would still be* inviting bad luck" are not only the character's escaping state of mind but also his exceeding caution and simplistic superstition, all serving to underline his extreme apprehension as well as to characterize very tellingly his particular consciousness. These individual qualities are not at all reflected in (B)'s "The more he thought the more he became afraid, afraid that the thoughts might come true" which presents a colourless mind, one that is relatively less scared, for at least it dares admit its thoughts.

A less blunt adaptation is found in (C) where Mao's active and actual process of thinking (in the form of free indirect thought) is presented as the phenomenon of the more inert cognitive verb "know" and is consequently made to appear as information acquired in the past and not necessarily thought about at present. Thus, the following statement no longer involves any contradiction. It is apparent that this plain or straightforward version reduces, relative to the paradoxical and tension driven Mao, the intensity of the character's fear.

The fact that Mao's "contradiction," which forms an ingenious stylistic device, is either undercut or totally eliminated in the translations brings out the necessity of emphasizing the aesthetic function of "illogicality" as such and points to the importance of guarding consciously against one's inclination for coherence or plainness in the process of *literary* translation (otherwise one can easily produce "deceptive equivalence" as such). Although both Mao and (B) or (C) serve to represent a mental state possible under such circumstances, perhaps only Mao, with its ambiguity, paradox/double-decoding, tension and textual intensity, could be said to be characteristic of literary as opposed to ordinary discourse.

6.1.4 "Illogicality" and Suspense

The effect of suspense gives a manifest expression to the privilege of the authorial or, possibly, the dramatized narrator, in whose hands information is stored up and at whose will it is released or held back.[2]

This privilege is clearly demonstrated by the passage taken from Lu's "The New Year's Sacrifice": "... her face ... had moreover completely lost its former expression of sadness ... it was clear that she had become a sheer beggar," where, as already noted, the I-narrator presents this description prior to his retrospective account of the protagonist's life. Because of the absence of any preceding substantiating context, the statement in question, which is in a sense "illogical" and quite puzzling in the immediate context, gives rise to suspense, an effect that would not have arisen if the presentational sequence had been chronological.

Interestingly, the correlation between "illogicality" and suspense is seen to bring to the fore not only the privilege of the author/narrator but also a particular kind of illogicality which I consider as conceptual as opposed to representational. As distinct from the antithetical "unfortunate to win" or the literally contradictory "everything was still asleep except for those creatures who wander in the night. Hua Laoshuan suddenly sat up in bed," the description "... her face ... had moreover completely lost its former expression of sadness, it was clear that she had become a sheer beggar" does not, as a synthetically true statement (true to the purported fictional reality of course), involve any violation of logic on the level of discourse in terms of, say, truth conditions; but it violates instead the relevant stereotypic conceptual frame in the reader's mind concerning human characteristics or behaviour under given circumstances—to the effect that the sadder a situation in which one finds oneself, the sadder one would appear. The same applies to the coward Ah Q's being valiant towards Beard Wang's challenge, where, whatever "illogicality" is involved, it arises not from the narrator's representation but from the violation of the reader's conceptual expectation.

Of the four types of illogicality classified above, type (c) may be treated as exclusively conceptual, a type which is to be accounted for by the complexity or change in a character's disposition or mood or the like and which clearly differs from other types in that it is to be attributed not to the violation of logic, unconscious or purposeful, on the part of the speaker/character or reporter/narrator but to the gap between the purported reality (which in itself has significantly no relationship to logicality) and the reader's stereotypic conceptual frames. But, of course, the narrator's holding back information or refraining from comment may have here a key role to play.

The way in which such conceptual illogicality functions to give rise to suspense may be further brought out by the following case taken from Lu's "Medicine":

(A) In the darkness nothing could be seen but the grey roadway. The lantern light fell on his pacing feet. Here and there he came across dogs, but none of them barked. It was much colder than indoors, *yet* Old Chuan's spirits rose, *as if* he had grown suddenly younger and possessed some miraculous life-giving power. He had lengthened his stride. And the road became increasingly clear, the sky increasingly bright. (Trans. Yang and Yang 1956:29—30; my emphasis)

(B) In the blackness nothing is at first visible save a grey ribbon of path. The lantern illumines only his two feet, which move rhythmically. Dogs appear here and there, then sidle off again. None even barks. Outside the air is cold, *and it refreshes* Laoshuan, *so that* it seems to him that he is all at once a youth, and possesses the miraculous power of touching men into life. He takes longer strides ... (Trans. Chi-chen Wang 1941:31; my emphasis)

What comes in between this passage and the beginning of the story (which was looked into in the last section) is fully quoted in note 3, from which it can be clearly seen that the story so far is marked by an air of mystery and suspense, leaving the reader with a series of questions: Why does the protagonist suddenly get up in the small hours? What is the money for? Why is he going out? Where is he going? In the present passage, what is most puzzling is the change in the mood of the protagonist who feels "as if he had suddenly become a youth and acquired some miraculous life-giving power" ("fangfu yidan bianle shaonian, dele shentong, you gel ren sheng-mingde benling shide"). The cause underlying this change is in this immediate context left unstated but just one page later, it comes, implicitly yet unmistakably, to light:

> "Whose sickness is this for?" Old Chuan seemed to hear someone ask; but he made no reply. His whole mind was on the package, which he carried as carefully as if it were the sole heir to an ancient house. Nothing else mattered now. *He was about to transplant this new life to his own home, and reap much happiness.* (Trans. Yang and Yang, my emphasis)

Clearly, it is the thought of the medicine which the protagonist is going to buy for his dying son that has caused the change in the protagonist's mood. By holding back the cause (a device that fits well in the overall suspenseful context), the effect, which is highly puzzling in the immediate context, gives rise to suspense which impels the reader to find out the unspecified cause and which therefore makes the cause, once revealed, all the more prominent. In effect, the mysterious change in the protagonist's mood forms part of a dramatically built-up thematic pattern which has on the one hand the firmly-believed-in magical curing power of the "medicine" (that is, steamed bread soaked with the blood of a decapited person) and on the other hand the death of the patient being treated: the stark and shocking contrast between the two pathetically reveals the deeply-rooted ignorance and superstition involved, which constitutes a strong indictment of the dark social conditions.

As shown above, the effect of suspense is dissipated and the thematic pattern impaired in translation (B) where the change in the protagonist's mood is ascribed to the fresh air rather than the thought of the medicine. What motivates this change is apparently a desire to correct the conceptual "illogicality" found in Lu: with the cause held back, the seemingly un-aroused change in mood violates the stereotypic conceptual frame that there must be a cause underlying a notable change in one's mood. While the existence of this conceptual frame enables the narrator to create suspense by withholding the cause, this conceptual frame leads the translator, who has ap-parently failed to capture the true purpose of the conceptual "illogicality" involved, to assume that the fresh air, which is the only potential cause available in the immediate context, is the cause of the protagonist's change in mood.

Now, since conceptual "illogicality" as such seems to have attracted scant critical attention, I wish to emphasize two points here. First, the translator's "corrections" of such conceptual illogicality in the three cases shown above serve to bring out the fact that the various stereotypic conceptual frames have an important role to play in the decoding process. Indeed, we are very much expectation-based parsers of texts (cf. Brown & Yule 1983:236ff. ; Culler 1975:230—238; Perry 1979). Significantly, such conceptual expectations may, as borne out by the translators' "corrections," go so far as to override one's actual reading experience. In the three cases concerned, the original statements subjected to alteration are linguistically valid and readily comprehensible. Clearly, they are altered simply because they violate the conceptual expectations of the translators, who, that is to say, carry out the changes simply to bring the texts into line with their given stereotypic conceptual frames. By this is meant that, as a reader in general and as a translator in particular, one has to guard consciously against being misled by one's conceptual expectations so as to avoid distortions of the literary text. Furthermore, in terms of the encoder/

author, the cases of conceptual illogicality shown above, which are consciously encoded to generate desirable values, point to the fact that the author may play not only upon linguistic conventions but also upon stereotypic conceptual expectations; the violation of either can be used to good effects. Indeed, like linguistic deviation, conceptual deviation seems to form a fruitful area for stylistic investigation.

6.2 OBJECTIVITY

In this section, attention will be directed to the translator's objectivity, an issue related to the preceding discussion on conceptual illogicality. As shown above, stereotypic conceptual frames of human behaviour may lead to subjective renderings of the original and should therefore be consciously guarded against in the process of translation. But most essential to the translator's objective reproduction of the original seem to be the following two frequently related qualities; a) neutrality toward conflicting ideologies, toward opposed religious beliefs or other kinds of social and/or political differences; b) detachment from emotional involvement and any resulting biases. In this section, I shall only slightly touch on the former and focus sharply on the translator's emotional involvement, particularly as regards the characters in a narrative.

The translator's emotional involvement in this respect may find its typical expression in what Wayne Booth defines as "practical interests":

> We have, or can be made to have, a strong desire for the success or failure of those we love or hate, admire or detest; or we can be made to hope for or fear a change in the quality of a character. (1961:125)

The fictional reality may nonetheless be found at odds with such practical interests: in the former case, a loved one may end up in disaster and a hated one may get the upper band; in the latter case similarly, the implied author may choose at any time to bring to light the wickedness of an otherwise virtuous man. At such points where the translator's expectation or desire is contradicted, there may arise, with more than usual likelihood, the danger of his or her being oversympathetic or over-contemptuous toward the character(s) involved and, consequently, the danger of his or her toning down the vice and highlighting the virtue.

It is important, therefore, if the original is to be faithfully carried over, that the translator maintains a certain measure of detachment and impartiality. As far as the translator is concerned, the socalled "practical interests" are clearly to be guarded against, since it is not the reader's position that the translator should put himself or herself in but that of the original author. Whatever his or her own inclinations, he or she should bring himself or herself to come to terms with what the original author presents.[4]

To narrow down the issue to the latter kind of "practical interests." Despite one's fear of change in the quality of a character, it is not all that rare that a character is partly formed by traits "which are necessarily opposed in ways that produce tension and ambiguity" (Culler 1975:237; see also Allen 1974:329; Leggett 1934:103—107). If a character is to be treated as an organic whole, as the meeting place of various qualities gathered from throughout the text, to portray a character with "equal" intricacy or richness in the target language would require the objective reproduction of the original tension and ambiguity.

The translator's objectivity seems to call for particular emphasis in the transference of non-contextual commentary by the authorial narrator on a character or characters: non-contextual in the significant sense that the commentary is not based on or substantiated by dramatized facts. As the reader tends to take on trust the judgement of the God-like author and, further, as judgement in such a case cannot be measured against dramatized facts, any notable change by the translator in authorial

CHAPTER 6 ASPECTS OF LEXICAL EXPRESSION   139

evaluation may have a significant hearing on characterization. A case in point is the following passage taken from Cao's A *Dream of Red Mansions* (*Honglou Meng*):

(Cao) ... Sui caigan youchang,   weimian
... Although his ability was excellent, it must be admitted

tan ku;   qie shi cai wu shang,
that he was grasping and ruthless; moreover he was conceited

           na tongyin jie cemu er shi,
(because of his ability) and was insolent to his superiors, his

                   bu shang yi nian,
fellow-officials all looked askance at him with anger, in less

           bian bei shangsi canle yi ben.
than a year, he was impeached by his superiors with a written report ... (chapter two)

(A) (Yu-tsun, after receiving Shih-yin's gift of silver that year, had left on the sixteenth for the capital. He did so well in the examinations that he became a Palace Graduate and was given a provincial appointment. He had now been promoted to this prefectship.) But although a capable administrator Yu-tsun was *grasping* and *ruthless*, while his *arrogance* and *insolence* to his superiors made them view him with disfavour. In less than two years they found a chance to impeach him. (Trans. Yang and Yang; emphasis mine)

(B) But although his intelligence and ability were outstanding, these qualities were *unfortunately offset* by *a certain* cupidity and *harshness* and a *tendency* to use his intelligence in order to *outwit* his superiors; all of which caused his fellow-officials to cast *envious* glances in his direction, with the result that in less than a year an unfavourable report was sent in by a senior official stating that ... (Trans. Hawkes, emphasis mine)

(C)... but, in spite of the excellence and sufficiency of his accomplishments and abilities, he *could not escape being ambitious and overbearing*. He failed besides, *confident* as he was in his own merits, *in respect toward* his superiors, with the result that these officials looked upon him scornfully with the corner of the eye. A year had hardly elapsed, when he was readily denounced in a memorial to the Throne by the High Provincial authorities, who represented that... (Trans. Joly, emphasis mine)

This passage, which is fully self-contained, forms a typical case of what I just referred to as "non-contextual" authorial commentary. The character involved is first dramatized in chapter one as a highly intelligent, ambitious and handsome scholar and then, in the immediately preceding context (the beginning of chapter two) presented as a compassionate and grateful administrator. The authorial commentary here "it must be admitted that he was grasping and ruthless; moreover he was conceited (because of his ability) and was insolent to his superiors" is at once unsubstantiated and unexpected. But clearly, the reader can only take on trust the author's words. Thus the qualities "grasping," "ruthless," "conceited," "insolent," which though have little or no dramatized facts to rest on, invariably figure as inherent traits in the character, giving to the character complexity as well as tension and ambiguity.

In rendering the narrator's commentary, the three translations shown above seem to form a cline of increasing subjectivity. Translation (A) presents a fairly objective rendering of the original.[5] Translation (B), however, displays a tendency both to tone down the vice and to highlight the virtue. If the added interpersonal adjunct "unfortunately," which conveys the narrator's empathy, only serves to shorten the narrative distance, the additions "a certain" and "a tendency" apparently function to undercut the demerits involved, while the demerit "harshness" in itself seems to occupy a point lower or weaker than "ruthlessness" on the given linguistic scale (see Levinson 1983:133 — 135). Even more notable is the change from the derogatory "he was conceited (because of his ability) and was insolent to his superiors" to the fairly neutral "to use his intelligence in order to outwit his superiors." It seems arguable that, on a more general scale, (B)'s making the virtues and vices, which are actually not in direct conflict, cancel each other by the lexical choice "offset" also functions to keep the character neutral. Furthermore, (B)'s choice of the singular and indefinite "a senior official," instead of "his senior officials," seems to imply personal prejudice (compare C's choice of "the High Provincial authorities"), while (B)'s selection of tile epithet "envious" seems to suggest more merits than defects on the part of the character concerned.

When it comes to translation (C), the character is shown in a more favourable light. On the one hand the strong points are unduly highlighted and, on the other, the translator seems to disguise purposefully the vices by translating, say, "conceited" into "confident," or "grasping" (primarily for money) into "ambitious" (primarily for honour or achievement)—a quality of the character which was prominently and quite positively dramatized in the preceding context. It should be apparent that the other lexical choices in italics all function to tone down or to trans form the disparaging qualities depicted in the original.

It is true that the various changes involved in both (B) and (C) could well be explained in terms of the so-called "practical interests" discussed above. But to attribute these changes to "practical interests" alone could be, at the very least, one-sided. To gain a fuller and clearer picture, we need to look into the matter in the light of what is called, by psychologists and critics, the "primacy effect," that is, the crucial effect of information situated at the beginning of a message (see Perry 1979; also Rimmon-Kenan 1983). In determining the overall impressions of personality, the functions of the "primacy effect" as brought out by some psychological experiments are summarized by Perry as follows (The subjects may be given just a series of personality-trait adjectives, e. g. "intelligent—industrious—impulsive—critical—stubborn—envious." The overall impressions thus formed are compared with the impressions formed by subjects who are given the same series but in *reverse* order.):

(a) assimilative change of meaning: the later adjectives change their meanings as a function of the initial adjectives ... ;

(b) *active* discounting process: later words change only in their importance or weight; they are given less weight because of their inconsistency with the initial words without new meanings being activated in them;

(c) *passive* attention decrement: the subjects pay more attention to words at the beginning of the list while they are first attempting to form some impression, but once a first impression has been formed, they pay less attention to the rest of the list. According to this explanation, there is no interaction between the meanings of initial words and those occurring at the end of the list.

According to Perry, only the "assimilative changes of meaning" (a) and the "active discountings" (b) are operative in the literary text which is, though, based on the tension between the forces resulting from the primacy effect and the material at the *present* point of reading, rather than being constructed according to the dictates of its initial material (57). However, translations (B) and (C) seem interestingly to exemplify all the three functions of the primacy effect. Most of the changes made by (B) and (C), such as the relatively positive interpretations of "shi cai wu shang" ("he was conceited [because of his ability] and was insolent to his superiors"), can be seen as a function of assimilative change of meaning, while (B)'s additions "a certain" and "a tendency" seem typically to illustrate the active discounting process. The remaining function— "passive attention decrement" whose applicability to literary texts is ruled out by Perry (for a reader of literature "expects the sequel to enrich, modify, surprise")— also finds exemplification in (C)'s replacement of "grasping" (for money) by "ambitious" (for honour/ achievement), where the new information is overlooked and superseded by the impression which the translator got in the preceding context.

It may be worth noting that, in the study of "primacy effect" in impression formation, it seems misleading to focus on the order of the information structure alone. The fact that subjects who are given the series "intelligent—industrious—impulsive—critical—stubborn—envious" form far more favourable impressions than those who are given instead "envious—stubborn—critical—impulsive—industrious—intelligent" should be accounted for, apart from the sheer order of the message, in terms of the relevant conventions or stereotypic situations. In introducing or depicting a person (under normal or neutral circumstances), one usually mentions first the traits which are most prominent in or representative of the person. It is therefore not surprising that the traits which are placed on top of the list are crucial in determining the overall impressions of personality. Quite similarly, in a narrative text, the reader usually expects the narrator to give, at the first introduction of a character, a representative picture. In the present case, the character Jia Yucun is first presented as a highly intelligent and ambitious scholar; and it is natural for the reader to take these traits as being the most representative of the character.

Now, my purpose in bringing in the "primacy effect" as a theoretical framework is basically to show that the subjectivity of the translators involved, is not a sheer matter of emotional involvement (which is what Booth's "practical interests" seem to be exclusively concerned with). The translator's subjective changes are also attributable to the relevant conventions, to the relevant stereotypic perceptual characteristics.

The changes made by the translators here do seem to bring us back to what was defined above as "conceptual illogicality." The incompatibility between the newly introduced negative traits and the positive traits previously presented seems to amount to violation of the relevant stereotypic conceptual frame(s). The changes made by (B) and (C) to reconcile the incompatibility could be seen, in a way, as efforts to reduce the "conceptual illogicality" involved (the picture presented by C: "very competent—ambitious and overbearing—confident—disrespect towards his superiors" is apparently more consistent than the picture in the original). Perhaps the best way to account for these changes is to see them as a joint function of the relevant "practical interests," "primacy effects" and stereotypic conceptual frames.

This is another way of saying that, in making these changes, the translators are subjectively, though not necessarily consciously, making the text conform to their expectations, which is no doubt a regrettable act. As it is, literary effects are typically generated through deviation from, rather than conformation to, conventions or expectations. In the present case, the authorial commentary "Although ... he was grasping and ruthless; moreover he was conceited (because of his ability) and was insolent to his superiors" serves to frustrate the reader's expectations, thereby giving rise to contrast, tension and complexity. In fact, the character involved is of a highly dubious or ambiguous nature: he is both grateful (see ch. 2) and ungrateful (see ch. 4), both compassionate (see ch. 2) and ruthless (see ch. 48). Semiotically and structurally, he is symbolic of the worldly and is set in direct contrast with another character Zhen Shi-yin who stands aloof from worldly affairs. Seen in this light, the character, who is marked by such worldly qualities as "careerism" and "greed", plays a role which is more negative than positive.

Indeed, whatever the role or function of the character, it is reasonable to argue that the translator should objectively carry over all the traits depicted by the original author. Ideally, a translator may treat a character as an art object and assume that significance inheres in precisely those traits, compatible or incompatible, which the author reveals, otherwise subjective colouring or "deceptive equivalence" might be unavoidable.

An important, though perhaps obvious, point to notice is that the translator's subjective colouring of one part of the text may affect the reader's response to the related subsequent parts, consequently giving rise to further distortions of the original. In the present case, shortly after the authorial commentary, a mention is made of "the money accumulated during his years in office" ("linian suo ji huan nang"). This is translated by (A) into "the capital accumulated during his years in office;" by (B) into "the loot he had accumulated during his years of office;" and by (C) into "the savings which he had accumulated during the several years he had been in office." The term "capital" in (A) indicates large possessions while (B)'s choice of "loot" is derogatory, suggesting illicit gains or pillage. Both choices are partly determined by context, i.e. associated with the character's cupidity or grasping nature as revealed by the authorial commentary (such an association between the character's avarice and the phrase in question will also be naturally made by a reader of the original). Clearly, a quite different picture is offered by version (C). Given (C)'s preceding replacement of "grasping/ cupidity" by "ambitious" which, conditioned by the previous context, is to be taken as a matter of thirsting after honour or achievement, (C)'s present choice of "the savings..." seems to invite a positive interpretation, as money saved through the honest exercise of economy. This points to the particular need to be objective in the transference of non-contextual authorial commentary. Had the present commentary been based on facts of the character's greed for money,

(C)'s replacing "grasping" by "ambitious" would not, indeed, have had any significant bearing on characterization.

Now, in the fictional world, the author's point of view tends to be taken as authoritative, against which other points of view are evaluated. The translator's alteration in authorial commentary is therefore likely to bear on the reliability of the words of the dramatized narrator or of a character. This point is well reflected in the present case where the changes made by (B) and (C) in the authorial commentary—particularly in the quality "ruthlessness"—function to reduce the reliability of the following related speech of a character:

> "It's all the fault of that upstart Chia Yu-tsun—the bastard deserves to starve to death!" fumed Ping-er, grinding her teeth. "In the less than ten years that we've known him he's stirred up endless trouble. This spring Lord Sheh happened to see a few old fans somewhere, which made him so dissatisfied with all our best fans at home that he sent men out at once to search for better ones. A wretched crank they call the Stone Idiot had twenty old fans as it happened, but though so poor that he'd hardly a bite to eat, he'd sooner die than part with them. ... "Then that black-hearted scoundrel Chia Yu-tsun heard about it and hatched a scheme. He had the idiot taken to his Yamen on a charge of owing the government some money, and ordered the default to be made good by the sale of his property. So the fans were seized, paid for at the official price and brought to our house. As for that Stone Idiot, who knows whether he's alive or dead? ..." (Trans. Yang and Yang, chapter 48)

The cruel action attributed to Jia Yucun, the character concerned, is not presented in the first-line narrative (i. e. not directly described by the narrator); the reader can only rely on Ping-er's words for information. In the context of the original and (A) where Jia Yucun is bluntly assessed by the authorial narrator as "ruthless," the reader may take

Ping-er's description as quite reliable. In (B) and (C), however, due to the relatively favourable commentary by the authorial narrator who regards Jia Yucun only as somewhat "harsh" or "overbearing," the reader is more likely to doubt about the truth of Ping-er's account.

In the discussion of the translator's subjective colouring so far, I have been emphasizing the possibility of distorting the purported fictional reality, a possibility which is brought to the fore in the transference of "non-contextual" authorial commentary. To gain a fuller picture, attention will now be directed contrastively to the following "contextual" authorial commentary where the translator's subjectivity (see B) leads to a quite different kind of distortion which likewise seems very regrettable:

(A) ... So Yu-tsun twisted the law to suit his own purpose and passed arbitrary judgement. The Fengs received a large sum for funeral expenses and made no further objections. ... (chapter 4)

(B) ... *By a judicious bending of the law to suit the circumstances, Yu-cun managed to arrive at some sort of judgement* whereby the plaintiffs received substantial compensation and went off *tolerably well satisfied*. ... (emphasis mine)

(C) ... Following readily the bent of his feelings, Yu-ts'un disregarded the laws, and adjudicated this suit in a random way; and as the Feng family came in for a considerable sum, with which to meet the expense for incense and the funeral, they had, after all, not very much to say (in the way of objections). ...

What Yucun, the character has done is readily inferable from the context: in short, letting the person who has committed manslaughter go unpunished simply because of his powerful relations who are helpful to Yucun's career and whom Yucun cannot afford to offend. This unjust act can be viewed in two different ways. On the one hand, one may attribute the unjustness wholly to the circumstances. In fact, at the beginning, Yucun does intend to bring the criminal to justice. But given the criminal's powerful relations, if he had attempted to do so, he may not only have failed to punish the criminal but also may have put his own life in danger. From this perspective, what he finally decides to do can be regarded literally—rather than ironically—as "judicious." Nevertheless, if one sticks to the moral standard, one will still treat Yucun's act as dishonourable. This is the viewpoint adopted by the authorial narrator who assesses Yucun's act as "perverting the law out of his personal considerations" ("xunqing wangfa"), an assessment which is objectively put across by translations (A) and (C) but is notably distorted by version (B).

In effect, given the relevant dramatized facts upon which the authorial commentary is based, whether the narrator says "Yu-tsun twisted the law to suit his own purpose..." or "by a judicious bending of the law to suit the circumstances..." does not have any bearing on the purported fictional reality but it does make a great difference in terms of authorial tone and stance and, not least, the reader's empathy. If in the original (see A & C), the authorial narrator is, as indicated by his disparaging tone, morally opposed to the character's act, in version (B), by virtue of the translator's subjective colouring, the authorial narrator is made to appear to share the character's moral standard or point of view. This switch is in turn expected to bear, in varying degrees, on the reader's empathy since it is significantly conditioned by that of the authorial narrator. This is just another way of saying that even if the translator's subjective colouring does not involve any distortion of the fictional reality, it may lead to distortion of such important stylistic values as authorial stance or tone and may thereby mislead the reader.

CHAPTER 6 ASPECTS OF LEXICAL EXPRESSION   149

Now, the element of sympathetic identification which underlies (B)'s subjective colouring above is most frequently seen in the case of first-person narrative. Before ending this section, attention will now be directed to a passage from such a narrative, where the translator's subjectivity (see B) seems to stem typically from sympathetic identification:

(Lu) ... Wo zhidao wo jinlaide chaoguo tade lengmo,
   ... I realized that my greater coldness to her recently

yijing yinqi tade youyilai. ... (1963:120)
had aroused in her worry and uncertainty . ...

(A) The cold weather and her cold looks made it impossible for me to be comfortable at home ... Finally I found a haven in the public library ... it was closing time. I had to go back to Chichao Street, to expose myself to that icy look. Of late I had sometimes been met with warmth, but this only upset me more. I remember one evening, from Tzu-chun's eyes flashed the childlike look I had not seen for so long, as she reminded me with a smile of something that had happened at the hostel. But there was a constant look of fear in her eyes too. *The fact that I had treated her more coldly recently than she had me worried her.* Sometimes I forced myself to talk and laugh to comfort her.
(Trans. Yang and Yang 1956:252; my emphasis)

(B) ... I remember that one evening her eyes suddenly sparkled with childlike innocence as she talked about the days at the Guild. I detected, however, a note of fear and anxiety in her cheerfulness and I *realized that I had become indifferent to her indifference and this, in turn, had aroused in her fear and uncertainty.* I tried to smile and to give her some measure of comfort. (Trans. Chi-chen Wang 1941:173)

This passage comes from Lu Xun's "Remorse for the Past" ("Shangshi") in which the narrator/protagonist depicts regretfully his ill-fated love affair which leads to the tragic death of his girlfriend. The author's impersonation in this story is marked by sympathetic identification and the reader is strongly invited to share the same point of view. The present passage takes place when a wide rift has been found between the protagonist and his girlfriend. The coming into being of this rift is attributed by "I" entirely to "her," to "her" failure of understanding under the new pressure of life and to "her" other limitations. The sentence quoted above is, in fact, the first time "I" makes a mention of his coldness to "her": so far the reader has been given the impression that "she" has become unfairly and unilaterally cold towards "I" (see A). What is striking about this first mention is that "I" reveals not only his recent coldness but also his even greater coldness to "her." At this late revelation, the reader may feel somewhat misled so far, which could seriously affect the I-narrator's reliability, a quality which is most susceptible to doubt in the first-person narrative mode (cf. Goldknopf 1972). This could go so far as to condition the reader's overall response to the story.

As shown above, the sentence in question is subjectively coloured in (B): the fact that "I had treated her more coldly" is modified or toned down into "I had become indifferent to her indifference." Furthermore, the fact that the I-narrator had kept his own coldness or indifference in the dark is completely glossed over by a change in the object of the cognitive verb "realize": in Lu, the object contains a piece of information previously known to the narrator but kept from the reader, i.e. "my greater coldness to her recently," whose modified form is, however, presented by (B) in the shape of new information "I realized that I had become indifferent to her indifference." This change from "given" to "new" apparently functions to preserve the narrator's reliability or, in more precise terms, apparently constitutes a subjective colouring of the narrator's reliability.

While the translator's alteration is almost certainly motivated by sympathetic identification, one must not overlook the possible function of the so-called "primacy effect." The impression up to that point that "she" had become unfairly and unilaterally cold towards "I" could in itself make it difficult for the translator to accept the fact that "I" had actually treated "her" more coldly recently. Again, the translator's alteration could be seen as a matter of making the text conform to his expectations.

From the discussion in this section, it is, I hope, clear that in order to avoid distortion of the original, a translator has to guard consciously against being misled by his to her emotional involvement as a reader (i. e. sympathetic identification or, on a wider scale, "practical interests") and against being misled by various perceptual or conceptual characteristics, such as the "primacy effect." Otherwise subjective colouring or "deceptive equivalence" may be unavoidable.

6.3 UNRELIABILITY AND CHARACTERIZATION

Fictional unreliability forms an essential aspect of narrative style. Though of a complex nature, it is primarily a question of the source of the narration: is it narrated from the point of view of the authorial narrator, a dramatized narrator, or a certain character? Insofar as traditional novels are concerned, the implied author or his/her unequivocal spokesman enjoys, by convention, absolute reliability (see Booth 1961). A dramatized narrator, though, is fallible and greater unreliability may arise when it comes to a character.

It seems that, in discussing unreliability, critical attention tends to focus on the communication model, that is, on the unreliability of the narrator or narratee (see Booth 1961; Chatman 1978; Yacobi 1981;

Rimmon-Kenan 1983). In this section, however, much emphasis is placed on the unreliability of the character as a reflecting versus a speaking entity. Stanzel argues that the concept of (un)reliability should be limited to "characters who make verbal statements and thereby address or intend to address an audience" (1986: 152). But I would like to follow Wayne Booth and some other critics (chiefly Anglo-American) who apply the criterion of reliability to both teller-characters and reflector-characters. It is true that the distinction between teller and reflector, or between the overt and covert mediation of narrative, is an important one. But the criterion of reliability/unreliability—if taken in the sense of objective/subjective, unbiased/biased, or valid/invalid—can surely be applied to both categories. Whether spoken out or not, the unreliable perceptions and judgments of a given character may play a significant role in characterizing this particular consciousness. Like a narrator's unreliability, a character's unreliability may stem from a whole host of causes, including personal experience, an unacceptable value-scheme (especially when the role is unsympathetic or negative) or sheer ignorance.

In fictional discourse, different kinds or degrees of (un)reliability are appropriate to different purposes of characterization, to the revelation of authorial stance or attitude, to the regulation of the reader's distance or empathy and, not least, to the secret communication between the author and the reader.

Because of the neglect of the correlation between unreliability and characterization in Chinese-English translation of fiction, some translators tend to objectify, consciously or unconsciously, the perceptions and judgements of characters. Such processes to increase reliability are often accompanied by the loss of the character's individuality as found in the source text. One such process is marked by a change from free indirect thought to authorial narrative report, a process which typically takes place when the free indirect thought

CHAPTER 6   ASPECTS OF LEXICAL EXPRESSION   153

embodies a viewpoint agreeable to the translator, who does not therefore hesitate to use the mode of reliable authorial statement. Compare the following translation (C) with (A) and (B):

> (Lao) Zheme dade ren, lashang name meide che,   ta zijide
> Such a big man, pulling such a beautiful rickshaw, his own
>
> che,   gongzi ruande chanyou chanyoude,   lian
> rickshaw, the springs were so flexible that they bounced, even
>
> cheba dou weiweide dongtan; chexiang shi name liang, dianzi
> the shafts slightly wavered; the body was so shiny, the cushion
>
> shi name bai, laba shi name xiang;   paode bu kuai zenneng
> was so white, the horn was so loud; if he didn't run fast how
>
> duideqi zijine,   zenneng duideqi na liang chene?
> could he face himself, how could he face this rickshaw [of his]?
> (Lao She, *Rickshaw Boy*, 11)

(A) How could a man so tall, pulling such a gorgeous rickshaw, his own rickshaw too, with such gently rebounding springs and shafts that barely wavered, *such a gleaming body*, *such a white cushion*, *such a sonorous horn*, face himself if he did not run hard? How could he face his rickshaw? (Trans. James 1979:11; my emphasis)

(B) A fellow as big as that, pulling a rickshaw as beautiful as his rickshaw was—his own rickshaw, with soft springs bouncing as he went along, so that even the shafts shook a little in his hands, with the back of the seat *so brightly polished*, *the cushion so white*, *and the horn so loud*—if he just dragged along and didn't run fast, how could he face himself? How could he face his rickshaw? (Trans. King 1964:13; my emphasis)

(C) (Everytime he had to duck through a low street-gate or door, his heart would swell with silent satisfaction at the knowledge that he was still growing. It tickled him to feel already an adult and yet still a child.)

With his brawn and his beautiful rickshaw—springs so flexible that the shafts seemed to vibrate; *bright chassis, clean, white cushion and loud horn*—he owed it to them both to run really fast. (This was not out of vanity but a sense of duty. For after six months this lovable rickshaw of his seemed alive to what he was doing ...)

(Trans. Shi 1981:18; my emphasis)

Both (A) and (B) convey well the original presentational mode of free indirect thought, with (B) approximating closer to the original syntax. In (C), however, there is found a shift in mode to that of authorial statement, a shift reflected in the removal of all the positive features of thought, including the replacement of the interrogative forms by the statement "he owed it to them both to run really fast," and a shift backed up by the fact that both the preceding and following contexts of (C) contain authorial statement.

The contrast between Lao (A, B) and (C) thus formed is in fact of a most significant kind in narrative fiction. In a third-person novel like the present one, the authorial narrator and the characters present, by convention, the two opposite poles of fictional objectivity (reliability) and subjectivity (potential or actual unreliability). The distinction between Lao's "such a big man, pulling such a beautiful rickshaw" (emotional free indirect thought) and (C)'s "with his brawn and his beautiful rickshaw" (calm authorial statement) could be assumed as one between subjective evaluation and objective description. Seen in this light, it is no accident that Lao's emotively charged "the body was so shiny, the cushion was so white, the horn was so loud" is rendered by (C) into the fairly neutral "bright chassis, clean white cushion and loud horn" which indicates a sober objectivity of presentation.

This process of objectification is, not surprisingly, accompanied by a negative effect on characterization. In fictional discourse, a character's particular point of view is frequently and most effectively brought out through his/her unreliable evaluation or interpretation. In the present case, the protagonist's perception of his rickshaw, which is to him his very life, is undoubtedly partial. The intensified "so shiny, ... so white, ... so loud" points to the protagonist's extreme love for his own rickshaw, which has cost him at least three or four years of hard toil and on which he pins all his hope.

As is clear from the present case, the mode of free indirect speech/thought offers a congenial vehicle for putting across such unreliable evaluation. Given the mode of authorial statement chosen by (C), if (C) had tried to convey Lao's intensifiers by a version like "very bright chassis, extremely clean white cushion and very loud horn," it might still be taken as a reliable description (from a perspective shared by the narrator and the character). Indeed, what underlies (C)'s suppression of the intensifiers may well be an awareness of the partiality/unreliability involved in the character's evaluation. But unfortunately (C) does not seem to be aware that such unreliability forms a locus of the character's feelings and has a significant part to play in characterization.

The potential unreliability inherent in free indirect speech/thought as a mode in itself also bears on characterization (cf. 8.5). If "with his brawn and his beautiful rickshaw" appeared in this mode, it would immediately lose its factual status, since the propositional content of free indirect speech/thought is no more than "an assertion or presupposition of a fallible or unreliable SELF" (Banfield 1982:218; see also Pascal 1977:50). The reader would perhaps discern in this then potentially unreliable assertion or reflection the character's self-confidence, self-complacency or even vanity. The effect is much more obvious in Lao and (A, B) where the lexical and syntactic choices (e.g. the repeated intensifiers and rhetorical questions) argue a stronger SELF of the character, thus making for a potentially greater unreliability and thus arousing in the reader a stronger sense of the character's confidence, pride or complacency. These feelings are in effect pertinent to a larger thematic pattern which has on the one hand the character's overestimation of, or blind faith in, his own strength and will and, on the other, the futility of all his efforts in a ruthless social environment, with a tragic note struck in the stark contrast between the two. It is clear that (C)'s rendering reliable/factual the propositional content concerned is regrettable; it leads to the suppression of the character's particular point of view, to the suppression of the unstated yet discernible feelings of the unreliable SELF.

Given that unreliability as such is ascribable to the particularity of the SELF, the more unreliable a judgement is, the more effectively it may function to characterize the individual consciousness involved. In the following translation (A), which faithfully conveys the original, the character's opinion departs drastically from the norm to the point of bordering on absurdity. This deviation or unreliability, which has an important role to play in characterization, is unfortunately undermined by version (B):

(A) Hsiang Tzu seemed to have forgotten the farmer's life he once led. He didn't much care if the fighting ruined the crops and didn't pay much attention to the presence or absence of spring rain. All he was concerned about was his rickshaw; his rickshaw could produce wheat cakes and everything else he ate. *It was an all-powerful field which followed obediently after him, a piece of animated, precious earth.* (Trans. James 1979:12—13; my emphasis)

(B) Xiangzi seemed to have forgotten that he had once tilled the fields and did not much care if war devastated the crops or if there were no spring rain. His sole concern was his rickshaw. This could *provide* griddle cakes and all sorts of food; *it was a horn of plenty which followed him meekly around.* (Trans.

Shi 1981:19; my emphasis)

In (A) and in the original, the far-fetched comparison of the rickshaw to a powerful living field tellingly brings out the unique mentality of the protagonist, a country boy marked by a lovable simplicity. The somewhat redundant "[it was] a piece of animated, precious earth" which occupies the prominent end-focus position puts an emphasis on this simple farmer's mentality. Interestingly, the preceding statement only functions to reinforce the peculiarity of the mind thus revealed: he may have forgotten the farmer's life he once led, he may no longer be concerned with farming, yet deep in his brain there remains firmly unaltered his farmer's outlook. This is not stubbornness but simplicity, simplicity to such an extreme that it leads not only to the choice of a piece of earth as the focus of the metaphor but also to its naive animation.

This far-fetched and therefore unreliable metaphor is to a great extent normalized by (B). In fact, normalization begins in the earlier replacement of "produce" (suggestive of farmland) by "provide." The highly personal focus of the metaphor is rendered by (B) into the much more conventional "a horn of plenty." Given that a horn is, in sharp contrast with a field, literally movable, (B)'s "which followed him meekly around" also becomes much more sensible than its counterpart in (A) and the original. As a result, not only does the metaphor fail to convey the character's naive-farmer's view, the preceding statement also takes on a function contrary to that intended by the original: it now serves merely to emphasize that the character's world-view is no longer a farmer's. This is a distortion. It is particularly regrettable in the light of the fact that, despite the frequent reference to the protagonist's having come from the countryside, this is the only occasion which directly reveals his mentality as characteristic of a farmer.

Now, like many other issues discussed in this book, the issue of reliability may be further complicated by linguistic and stylistic differences between Chinese and English. A most relevant difference is the frequent omission of subjects and determiners in Chinese, which may give rise to ambiguity as regards who functions as the reflector at a given point of the narration. Since reliability has primarily to do with point of view, the translator's alteration in the perceiving source, which is likely to occur given ambiguity as such, may have a significant bearing on reliability. This point finds its telling illustration in the following passage taken from Cao's *A Dream of Red Mansions*:

(Cao) Zhou Rui jiade cai chuqu lingle tamen jinlai.
1. Zhou Rui's wife accordingly went out to lead them [Granny

       Shangle zhengfang taijie,
Liu and her grandson] in. 2. [They] mounted the steps to the

     xiao yatou daqi xinghong zhan lian,
main reception room, 3. a little maid lifted up a scarlet felt

    cai ru tangwu,   zhi weng
portiere, 4. soon as [they] entered the room, [they] just

yizhen xiang pule lianlai,
smelled a waft of perfume [which] greeted [their] faces,

jing bu zhi shi he qiwei,
5. [Granny Liu] even did not know what odour it was,

shenzi jiu xiangzai yunduanli yiban,
6. [her] body just seemed to be high in the clouds,

man wulide dongxi dou shi yaoyan zhengguang,
7. [to her] everything in the room was dazzling and glittering,

shi ren touyun muxuan, Liu laolao cishi
making one feel dizzy and dazzled, 8. Granny Liu at this

zhiyou diantou,   zazui nianfo eryi.
moment could only nod her head, smack her lips and pray to

CHAPTER 6   ASPECTS OF LEXICAL EXPRESSION   159

Buddha. (chapter 6)

(A) 1. accordingly Mrs. Chou went out to fetch them. 2. As they mounted the steps to the main reception room, 3. a young maid raised a red wool portiere 4. and a waft of perfume greeted them as they entered. 5. Granny Liu did not know what it was 6. but felt she was walking on air. 7. And she was so dazzled by everything in the room that her head began to swim. 8. She could only nod, smack her lips and cry "Gracious Buddha!" (Trans. Yang and Yang)

(B) 1. Zhou Rui's wife went off again to fetch her charges. 2. As they ascended the steps to the main reception room, 3. a little maid lifted up the red carpet which served as a portiere for them to enter. 4. & 5. A *strange*, delicious fragrance seemed to reach forward and enfold them as they entered, 6. producing in Grannie Liu the momentary sensation that she had been transported bodily to one of the celestial paradises. 7. *Their* eyes, too, were dazzled by the bright and glittering things that filled the room. 8. Temporarily speechless with wonder, Grannie Liu stood wagging her head, alternating clicks of admiration with pious ejaculations. (Trans. Hawkes, my emphasis)

(C) 1. Chou Jui's wife thereupon went out and led them in. 2. When they ascended the steps of the main apartment, 3. a young waiting-maid raised a red woollen portiere, 4. and as soon as they entered the hall, they smelt a whiff of perfume as it came wafted into their faces: 5. what the scent was *they* could not discriminate; 6. but *their* persons felt as if *they* were among the clouds. 7. The articles of furniture and ornaments in the whole room were all so brilliant to the sight, and so vying in splendor that they made the head to swim and the eyes to blink, 8. and old goody Liu did nothing else the while than nod her head, smack her lips and invoke Buddha. (Trans. Joly, my emphasis)

This passage depicts one scene from the first visit by Granny Liu, a country bumpkin, to the magnificent Rongguo Mansion in the capital. From these few lines one may get a sense of the well-intentioned authorial irony directed at the ignorance of Granny Liu, which is brought out almost caricaturally through her unreliable perception coupled with bizarre reaction, an unreliability which in turn reflects the huge gap in living standards between the city rich and the country poor.

As illustrated here, the frequent subject and determiner omission allowable in Chinese can add much subtlety to the change from a reliable to an unreliable point of view. The fact that from clause 5 the point of view is shifted exclusively to that of Granny Liu is not spelt out but to be inferred by the reader from the narrative content. Of the three persons who entered the reception room—Zhou Rui's wife, Granny Liu and her grandson—the first is a high-rank servant in the Rong Mansion and so the experience depicted in 5—7 does not apply to her (notice the concessive adjunct "even" which conveys the narrator's surprise at or emphasis on the ignorance involved). Given that the five-year old boy's point of view is consistently suppressed, what is presented in 5—7 should be exclusively the viewpoint of Granny Liu.

The most notable effect of this exclusion is dramatic irony. The superior narrator and the competent reader share their amusement at the coloured perception of this country bumpkin and derive even greater fun from her bizarre reactions. Although the irony ultimately depends on the distance that separates Granny Liu from the narrator/reader, in the immediate narrative context, it stems from the gap between Granny Liu and the excluded potential reflector Mrs Zhou who comes much closer to the author's norms. Now, Cao's keeping implicit the exclusion in question seems to generate not only subtlety but also textual tension and a shock effect which accompanies the reader's realization of the dramatic irony involved.

In translating into English, however, not only cannot such subtlety and shock effect be preserved (in that the omitted subjects and determiners have to be spelt out), but also the very implicitness of the exclusion lays a trap for the translators. Of the three translations of Cao, only (A) emerges free from the trap while (B) partially escapes it and (C) fully falls into it. In terms of (A) it should be noted that, since the butt of the irony lies in the interaction between Liu's coloured perception and her bizarre reaction, (A)'s omission of the earlier part of Cao's 7 which exhibits the former Seems to involve some loss of irony (cf. C's treatment of Cao's 7).

As for (B), it preserves well the dramatic irony in 6 by limiting the bizarre reaction to Liu, but it fails to do so in treating Cao's 5 and 7. The former is transformed by (B) into the epithet "strange" which is made to appear as a reliable evaluation shared by the narrator and the characters rather than as a locus of Liu's own ignorance. No less regrettable is (B)'s choice of the plural determiner "their" in 7 which bridges the intended gap between Liu and Zhou thereby leading to another partial loss of the dramatic irony.

In version (C), the consistent choice of the plural anaphoric "they/their" leaves in 5—6 no perceptual or responsive distance between Mrs Zhou (one of the Mansion's household) and Granny Liu (a country bumpkin on her first visit to the Mansion). As a result, what is depicted in 7 (where no personal pronoun appears) no longer takes on Liu's subjective colouring but figures as a reliable description by the narrator. It seems worth noting that in translating into English, subjective colouring of this kind which is implicit yet discernible in Chinese may have to be explicitly signalled by means like "to her."[6] Interestingly, as the preceding perception and response are made to appear as plausible or natural, Liu's reaction presented in 8 also seems to lose its bizarre nature, thus making for a further departure from the ironic effect of Cao. The point to stress here is that in specifying the implicit subjects and determiners, the translator has to take into account not only the participants superficially involved but also the given degree of reliability pertaining to each participant and its bearing on characterization. Only in this way can the translator in circumstances like the present one succeed in picking out the actual experiencing source and in preserving the narrative distance created by the original narrator.

Now, to add a new dimension to the present discussion of the correlation between unreliability and characterization, I would like to bring in a case from a first person retrospective narration where the issue of reliability typically centres round the twofold perspective of the same person: the unreliable point of view of the experiencing self and the relatively reliable point of view of the narrating self.

The case is taken from Lu Xun's "Remorse for the Past" ("Shangshi") which depicts a tragic love affair:

(Lu)... Anning he xingfu shi yao ninggude,　　yongjiu
... Tranquillity and happiness would solidify, it

shi zheyang de anning he xingfu. ...
would forever be so tranquil and happy. ... (113)

(A) As the days passed, Tzu-chun became more lively. However, she didn't like flowers. ... She had a liking for animals, though, which she may have picked up from the official's wife; and in less than a month our household was greatly increased. ... there was a spotted dog, bought at the fair. I believe he had a name to begin with, but Tzu-chun gave him a new one—Ahsui. And I called him Ahsui too, though I didn't like the name.

It is true that love must be constantly renewed, must grow and create. When I spoke of this to Tzu-chun, she nodded understandingly.

Ah, what peaceful, happy evenings those were!

Tranquillity and happiness must be consolidated, so that

they may last forever. When we were in the hostel, we had occasional differences of opinion or misunderstandings; but after we moved into Chichao Street even these slight differences vanished. We just sat opposite each other in the lamplight, reminiscing, savouring again the joy of the new harmony which followed our disputes.

(Trans, Yang and Yang 1956:244; my emphasis)

(B) ... This is true: Love must be renewed, must be made to grow, must be creative. When I told Tzu-chun this, she nodded understandingly.

Ah, what quiet, happy nights those were!

But peace and happiness have a way of stagnating and becoming monotonous. When we were at the Provincial Guild we used to have occasional differences and misunderstandings, but since we had come to Chi-chao Hutung there was not even this. We merely sat facing each other by the lamp and ruminated over the joy of reconciliation after those clashes.

(Trans. Chi-chen Wang 1941:164—165; my emphasis)

The parts marked by italics in (A) and (B) have been translated from the same statement in Lu. The notable antithetical element between the two different renderings, which may puzzle the reader, stems from the unreliability associated with the original. The assertive "Tranquillity and happiness would solidify, it would forever be so tranquil and happy" does not tally with the tragic death of their love which comes to light later on. What is shown in this assertion is most plausibly the experiencing self's false hope at the height of their love. Its unqualified form seems to indicate that the narrator has at this moment abandoned his external/retrospective focalization in favour of the internal/experiencing one (compare: "at that time I falsely believed that ... ").

As this shift in focalization is kept implicit so that the earlier illusion passes off as a sincere assertion by the narrating self, which is therefore easily taken on trust by the reader, the shift rhetorically heightens the tragic contrast between illusion and disillusion about love by luring the reader deeper into the illusion. However this shift is not necessarily purposeful: perhaps the narrator is for the moment unconsciously indulging himself in the false hope he once cherished, an illusion typical of this idealistic intellectual who is constantly immersed in impractical dreams. In this connection, it may be noted that the present passage (see A) seems to be the least coherent and most spontaneous of the narrative text (notice the lack of logical link between paragraphs one, two, and three). But no matter whether we take this shift as intentional or unconscious, the rhetorical effect of deepening the tragedy in virtue of temporarily misleading the reader remains unaltered.

Interestingly, the past illusion in question is not totally uncoloured by later reality. An ominous shadow may be discerned in the dubious nature of the term "solidify" ("ninggu"), especially in the light of the preceding emphasis on the renewal and growth of love. This contrastive emphasis seems to foreground the narrator's retrospective understanding, with the retrospective nature highlighted in both translations by the switch to the present tense. It is true that the past experiencing self did acquire such an understanding, but it is not surprising that during the height of their love he also hoped that the existing peace and happiness would last forever.

The contradiction between the experiencing self's beliefs, the possibly unconscious shift from the external/reliable to the internal/unreliable focalization and the opposition between the positive and ominous sides of "solidify" combine to add to the text much authenticity. For such multiple contrasts with their tension, ambiguity and complexity are just characteristic of the fallible and indeterminate self, which the text seeks to lay bare.

Such contrasts are suppressed in both translations. If Lu's

"Tranquility and happiness *would* solidify, it *would* forever be so tranquil and happy" is contradicted by reality, the unreliability pertaining to the illusion is discarded by (A) through the modal auxiliaries "must" and "may" coupled with the subordinator "so that," which operate to transform the illusion into a general truth: "Tranquillity and happiness *must* be consolidated, *so that* they *may* last forever" (my emphasis). Even more radical changes are found in (B)'s "But peace and happiness have a way of stagnating and becoming monotonous," where only the gloomy side of Lu's "solidify" is preserved and elaborated into "stagnating and becoming monotonous" with the negative nature underlined by the added adversative "but." Further, Lu's unreliable "it would forever be so tranquil and happy" is simply omitted. Indeed, both (A) and (B) seem to have turned the experiencing self's illusion into a general truth, realized particularly if not exclusively by the narrating self. If (A)'s rendering merely leads to the loss of the rhetorical effect of deepening the tragedy as referred to above, (B)'s rendering goes even further to the point of weakening the tragic contrast between illusion and disillusion by untimely preparing the reader for the latter. In fact, this untimely warning in (B) has, as a side effect, cast a shadow on the immediately following context, with the pleasing occasion depicted in the original now made to exemplify, though not quite fittingly, the monotony of love.

But what suffers most is the picture of the SELF. The indeterminate and idealistic SELF, who even seems to indulge in the already dashed hope, is made by (B) to appear as a consistent and rational being who soberly faces the reality. The distortion is of course only local. But given that a literary text is an organic whole, local distortions inevitably bear on the overall effect.

Interestingly, if in first-person narration the author can make use of the contrast between the narrating self and the experiencing self, in third-person narration, characterizing effects may be created by the "identity" of the narrating self and the experiencing self. Conventionally or traditionally, the primary narration in a third-person novel conveys the view of the authorial narrator in contradistinction to the views of fictional characters. In some modern English novels, however, primary narration is used, for shorter or longer stretches of the text, to dramatize the viewpoint of a character to the extent of suppressing the authorial narrator's view and of fusing the narrating self and the experiencing self. A most telling case is the well-known Lok's language found in primary narration in William Golding's *The Inheritors*, a language which embodies the conceptualization of the prehistoric character Lok in stark contrast with that of the modern authorial narrator, for example:

> Lok's feet were clever. They saw. They threw him round the displayed roots of the beeches ... (chapter 1)
>
> A stick rose upright and there was a lump of bone in the middle. ... The stick began to grow shorter at both ends. Then it shot out to full length again. The dead tree by Lok's ear acquired a voice. "Clop!" (chapter 5)

Compare the latter with a more reliable description that a modern man may offer: "The man raised his bow and arrow. ... He drew the bow and shot at Lok. The arrow hit the tree near Lok with a 'Clop!'." Clearly, it is the prehistoric Lok who 'narrates' the story as he experiences it. Such unconventional fusing of the narrating self and the experiencing self enables the author to reveal the character's mind with striking immediacy, vividness, and authenticity. Apparently, the strong characterizing effect would be lost if the translator tries to make canonical or reliable the narrating discourse.

In conclusion, I would like to stress that, when a character's opinion is seen as primitive, partial, exaggerating or weird; when contradictory beliefs of the same self are found at close range; or when an assertion is belied by reality, the translator should, before making any alteration in reliability, carefully consider the underlying reasons or motivations, consider the immediate effects in relation to the work's larger functional design. As illustrated above, deviations in terms of reliability may have a significant role to play in revealing or reinforcing authorial stance, in characterizing a particular consciousness or, in more general terms, in fulfilling the work's thematic and aesthetic goals.

6.4 "REDUNDANT" ENCODING

Having examined how "illogical" or unreliable elements function to generate literary effects, we now come to the correlation between "redundant" encoding and the literary effects it produces. The redundancy in question is of course not that which is conventionalized in the use of language but that which deviates from the conventional norm.

6.4.1 Encoding a Normally Presupposed Process

Conventions about the use of language often seem to operate on the basis of presupposition. Given a clause "he saw John over there", it is very probable that this perception process presupposes a process of identification from, say, "a man" to "John." In fact, in depicting a perception process, the process of identification entailed in it is normally not spelt out. This may shed some light on the interpretation of the following case from Conrad's *The Secret Agent*:

> She saw there an object. That object was the gallows. She was afraid of the gallows (chapter 12).

The case is quoted by Leech and Short to illustrate occasions where "simple sentences are just what is needed." They write,

> These three sentences occur at the climactic point in the novel where Mrs Verloc realizes the full consequence of her action in murdering her husband. They record with brutal simplicity and clarity the three separate impressions (perception of object—

identification of object—fear of object) which pass through Mrs Verloc's mind in logical progression, dramatising the mounting horror of her discovery. The dramatic force of this step-by-step revelation would be dissipated in a complex sentence such as "She saw there an object she was afraid of—the gallows" or "The object she saw there—the gallows—frightened her." (1981:219—220)

But I would like to suggest, from a different perspective, that the stylistic effect generated comes from "redundant" encoding and would be dissipated once the "redundant" part were omitted:

She saw there the gallows. She was afraid of the gallows.

The amount of information conveyed remains the same, the mode of narration unchanged (still "showing"), the sentence structure is as simple and the psychological sequencing unaltered, but the dramatising effect has evaporated. Perhaps my suggestion could be further backed up by the fact that Leech and Short's alternatives, whose complex structure is deemed responsible for the dissipation of the dramatic effect, no longer exhibit redundant encoding. Compare a similar set of statements:

(a) She saw there the thing she was looking for—her pen.
(b) The thing she saw there—her pen—was what she was looking for.
(c) She saw there a thing. That thing was her pen. She was looking for her pen.
(d) She saw there her pen. She was looking for her pen.

Of these, only (c) displays "redundant" encoding. For the process of identification recorded in (c) is presupposed in its alternatives. Clearly, "the thing" in "the thing she was looking for" (or, similarly, "an object" in "an object she was afraid of") is already identified, though unnamed. As the *process* of identification is normally presupposed by this or that form, its being recorded in Conrad appears to be foregounded:[7]

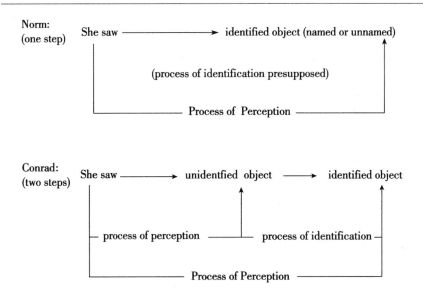

Against the norm, the description in Conrad takes on the notable effect of *slowing down* the perception process, which helps to reveal, gradually and emphatically, the mounting horror of Mrs Verloc's discovery. Closely related to this, but distinct from this, is the effect of suspense. As the reader expects, by convention, an identified object after the perception verb, the appearance of an unidentified object naturally leads to suspense. The uncertainty is then contradicted by the *marked* demonstrative "that" (note the difference that would obtain if the unmarked anaphoric "it" or "the" were used instead). The paradox thus generated makes the reader all the more eager to identify *that* object. The revelation of "the gallows" thereby becomes psychologically much more prominent or, in more precise terms, much more shocking. In terms of syntax, the use of three independent sentences lends support not only to the slowing down of the perception process but also to the heightening of suspense. For the full stop after "object" has the effect of making "She saw there an object." appear as a self-contained perception process, thereby giving rise to great suspense concerning the identity of the object. Notice the difference obtained if the syntax is changed into:

She saw there an object which was the gallows ...

This apparently undercuts the effect of suspense.

It seems arguable that, in terms of modes of narration, "She saw there an object. That object was the gallows" could be given a different interpretation. We may take "she saw there an object" as Mrs Verloc's whole perception process and "that object was the gallows" as the narrator's explanation rather than Mrs Verloc's mental impression. In that case, the whole focus would fall on the use of referring expression, that is, on the narrator's deliberately using "an object" instead of "the gallows" so as to create momentarily the effect of suspense. The deviation would then be a matter of "flouting" the Gricean maxim of quantity (the situation clearly requires the referring expression to be as informative as "the gallows"). And here we come back to "redundant" encoding: it takes the form of elaborating a perception process ("She saw there the gallows") into a perception process ("She saw there an object") plus an explanation ("That object was the gallows") without adding any information, but with desirable stylistic effects. The message for the translator is clear, namely, to try and preserve the deviant two-step encoding with its simple sentence structure and its marked deictic "that."

6.4.2 Encoding Entailed Quantity Predicates

When it comes to quantity (or scalar) predicates, redundancy becomes relatively easy to determine. If a quantity predicate is asserted, the assertion of a less informative one is regarded, by convention, as redundant (e.g. "he spent ten days on it" renders "he spent eight days on it" redundant; similarly, "he loves her" renders "he likes her" redundant). If, as shown above, the encoding of a usually presupposed process can help to create aesthetic effects, the encoding of entailed quantity predicates may also function to produce thematically-related stylistic values. At the beginning of Lao She's *Rickshaw Boy* is found a case which displays the latter kind of "redundancy." This case is faithfully carried over by the following translation (A) but is regrettably edited by version (B):

> (A) Becoming independent was not a simple matter at all. *It took one year, two years, at least three or four years, and one drop of sweat, two drops of sweat, who knows how many millions of drops of sweat,* until the struggle produced a rickshaw. By gritting his teeth through wind and rain, depriving himself of good food and good tea, he finally saved enough for that rickshaw. That rickshaw was the total result, the entire reward, of all his struggle and suffering. (Trans. James 1979; my emphasis)
>
> (B) But this was certainly not easy to come by. *It had taken him at least three or four years and untold tens of thousands of drops of sweat* to acquire that rickshaw of his. He had earned it by gritting his teeth in the wind and rain ... (Trans. Shi 1981:10; my emphasis)

As indicated here, Lao's novel centres round the symbol "rickshaw," the gaining of which forms the protagonist's purpose in life and the losing of which leads him to despair. Indeed, his whole tragic life may be encapsulated in "the gaining—losing—gaining—losing of a rickshaw". The present passage depicts the process of his obtaining a rickshaw. It is narrated with retrospective distance and in the mode of "telling." As shown by (A), the authorial narrator tries to achieve an iconic matching of form and meaning, an attempt usually excluded from "telling," by means of "redundant" encoding. Clearly, the progression from the entailed quantity predicates to the full amount seeks to enact, up to a point and relative to (B), the process of time passing or sweating. The choice of the simple past tense "took," as opposed to "had taken" (see B), seems to lend support to the iconic effect.

Iconicity, however, is far from the sum of the stylistic effect generated by the entailed quantity predicates, the encoding of which also makes for contrast and subtlety. What is notable is the contrast between the plodding rhythm "one year, two years" and the quick, smooth rhythm "at least three of four years," the former pointing to the stow passing of each long, hard, toiling year while the latter to the flying away of the years before he earned enough to buy a rickshaw. The effect is even more striking where "sweat" is involved. As distinct from years, drops of sweat do not come out in strict successive order and, moreover, they are usually uncountable. Thus, while "he had only one drop of sweat" would be impossible, "he had ten drops of sweat" would be metaphorical. By counting what is in a sense uncountable and by recording literally what is in a sense metaphorical: "one drop of sweat, two drops of sweat," the narrator succeeds in magnifying the significance of each drop of sweat.

More subtlety or paradox arises when time and sweat are viewed in relation to each other. Particularly notable is the paradoxical semantic relation obtaining between "one year, two years" and "one drop of sweat, two drops of sweat." The two are in a sense similar, both being relatively minor in comparison to what follows. But viewed in their own right, they are, to a great extent, contrastive to each other. Surely, "one drop of sweat, two drops of sweat" is more compatible with, say, "one minute, two minutes" than with "one year, two years." In the present context, however, the semantic contrast between the two in terms of amount is obscured both by the structural and by the situational parallelism, to the point of establishing an element of semantic similarity between them. As a result, the semantic strength pertaining to "one year, two years" serves to underline the magnification of "one drop of sweat, two drops of sweat."

It is clear that much, if not all, of the stylistic effect referred to is lost in version (B) where the basic sense conveyed remains the same but the semantic organization is quite different. By virtue of (B)'s omission of the entailed quantity predicates, the effect generated is brought towards singleness (versus contrast or paradox) and towards plainness (versus subtlety) or, in more general terms, towards that which is produced by ordinary discourse as opposed to literary discourse.

In this chapter, the discussion is centered on various kinds of deviation, both conceptual and formal. This emphasis is determined in part by the nature of literary discourse where aesthetic effects are often generated through violation of conventional rules or expectations and in part by the fact that, because of the general human inclination for coherence or straightforwardness, deviant elements are most frequently made to undergo losses in translation. Many aspects of deviation, such as the "illogical," "unreliable," or "redundant" elements singled out for the present discussion, are ostensibly undesirable, and thus tend to bear the brunt of the translator's alterations. Through an effort to reveal their true meanings and purposes, the analysis above may operate to help the translator to preserve the aesthetically-motivated deviant choices. In effect, as a reader, one may find it much easier to come to terms with deviant elements. For one is after all reading a work done by someone else. It is particularly when one functions as a translator—when the work is subjected to one's own reproduction—that one's reasoning processes are likely to collide with those of the original author. The discussion above also reveals that the forces militating against a successful representation of the original may take the form not only of conventional expectations or stereotypic conceptual or perceptual characteristics, but also of emotional involvement such as sympathetic identification or "practical interests," all of which need to be guarded against in the process of translation. Indeed, one may have to suppress consciously one's own liking in favour of that of the author, based on a full awareness of the aesthetic functions of the original choices involved, otherwise distortion or "deceptive equivalence" might be unavoidable.

CHAPTER 7
ASPECTS OF SYNTAX

In translating traditional realistic fiction, the translator tends to take syntax for granted, without being fully aware that syntax is often chosen or manipulated to generate literary significance. The present chapter seeks to throw light on how aesthetic losses can result from the translator's failure to take full account of the literary functions of syntax. As already touched on, in contrast to the translation of ordinary discourse where critical attention is focused on syntactic errors, syntactic stylistics in literary translation typically goes beyond questions of mere grammaticality. The translations compared below frequently constitute what could in a broad sense be called "referential equivalents," which convey approximately the same propositional content but which, primarily because of differences in syntactic structure, give rise to quite different effects.

Although stylistic investigation of syntactic form, no matter whether intra-lingual or inter-lingual, is always comparative in nature, the comparison in intra-lingual analysis is made between the actual choice and other *potential* choices (that could have been chosen by the *same* author), whereas the comparison in inter-lingual analysis is characteristically between *actual* choices (translations compared with the original and/or with each other). While in intra-lingual analysis one can take for granted the same lexical choice, in inter-lingual investigation sufficient room has to be left for synonyms in the form of different lexical choices made by the author and the translator(s). As the difference in (even though synonymous) lexical choice often bears on syntax, the boundary (already sometimes unclear) between syntactic

CHAPTER 7 ASPECTS OF SYNTAX 175

choice and lexical choice tends to become even more problematic. The case is further complicated by the fact that stylistic values generated in the source language by syntactic means may be conveyed in the target language, to a certain extent, by lexis or, similarly, that SL lexical means might find their correspondence in TL syntatic features (a phenomenon more frequently found in translating from the paratactic Chinese into the hypotactic English). This is hardly surprising since linguistic choices are made often only half consciously and seldom in isolation from each other. For this reason, relevant linguistic features other than syntax but bearing on a centrally syntactic question are also freely discussed in what follows.

Now, because of the radical differences in syntactic structure between the paratactic Chinese and the hypotactic English, fictional translation between the two languages seems frequently to pose various kinds of dilemma for the translator. We shall pay special attention to certain of the peculiar ways in which syntax functions to convey literary effects in Chinese and to the methods used by the translators to achieve functional correspondence in English. Again the limitation of space permits me to deal with only a few aspects, whose discussion will nevertheless have implications for narrative translation between Chinese and English in particular and for literary translation or interpretation in general.

7.1 SYNTAX AND PACE

In narrative fiction, a world built up solely through linguistic means, syntactic organization may act in various ways upon the pace of the experience depicted. As syntax is largely responsible for the connection between events, the association between syntax and pace tends to come to the fore in the presentation of a sequence of happenings. The different ways in which the syntactic units are connected seem frequently to have a role to play in determining the pace of the processes involved.

Interestingly, in Hemingway's "A Very Short Story" (a sketch of an ill-fated love affair in his *In Our Time*), there occurs a case where the tempo is notably quickened by omitting commas. On one occasion at the front, the protagonist Nick receives a large number of letters from his lover:

> Fifteen came in a bunch to the front and he sorted them by the dates and read them all straight through.

The processes "come," "sort," "read" are made here, by virtue of the absence of commas, to appear to happen in rapid succession, which obliquely suggests Nick's anxiousness and his intense feeling towards his lover, an effect reinforced by the emphatic adjunct "straight through."

Now, attention will be directed to a case in Cao Xueqin's *A Dream of Red Mansions* (*Honglou Meng*), where the authorial narrator uses "covert changing of the subject"—a device peculiar to Chinese—to quicken psychologically the pace at which one event follows another:

(Cao) Jiemeimen yizhao xiangjian,   beixi jiaoji,
1. The two sisters were now reunited, needless to say,

zi bubi shuo;   xule yifan qikuo,
joy and sorrow mingled together; 2. ( ) talked for a while

                                       you yinzhe baijian Jia mu,
about the years of separation, 3. and ( ) took (them) in to

                                       jiang renqing tuwu
pay respects to the Lady Dowager, 4. ( ) presented the

gezhong chouxianle,   hejia ju sijianguo;
various kinds of gifts of Nanking produce, 5. the whole family

                                       you zhixi jiefeng.

CHAPTER 7 ASPECTS OF SYNTAX   177

were introduced to one another, 6. and ( ) spread a feast of welcome for the guests.

(chapter 4, "( )" indicates the omission of the subject)

(A) 1. The sudden reunion of the two sisters was, it goes without saying, an affecting one in which joy and sorrow mingled. 2. *After* an exchange of information about the years of separation, 3. *and after* they had been taken to see Grandmother Jia and made their reverence to her, 4. *and after* the gifts of Nanking produce had been produced 5. and everyone had been introduced to everyone else, 6. there was a family party to welcome the new arrivals. (Trans. Hawkes; emphasis mine)

(B) 1. The two sisters were now reunited, at an advanced period of their lives, so that mixed feelings of sorrow and joy thronged together, but on these it is, of course, needless to dilate. 2. After conversing for a time on what had occurred, subsequent to their separation, 3. Madame Wang took them to pay their obeisance to dowager lady Chia. 4. They then handed over the various kinds of presents and indigenous articles, 5. and after the whole family had been introduced, 6. a banquet was also spread to greet the guests. (Trans. Joly)

In the presentational mode of narrative summary and with the 'synopses' kept to a minimum, pace in Cao's text is accelerated by means of "covert changing of the subject." The sentence begins with the subject "the two sisters" (Lady Wang and Aunt Xue), a subject that the following clause 2 implicitly sticks to. When it comes to clause 3, the omitted subject is understood to be shifted to "Lady Wang" alone, which is covertly and immediately changed in 4 to the other of the two sisters "Aunt Xue" (possibly and her children). After the explicit subject "the whole family" in 5, the subject is again in the following clause 6 implicitly shifted to a different entity "the hostesses (and the hosts)." Now, although "covert changing of the subject" forms a conventional rhetorical device in Chinese, it usually occurs no more than once in a sentence. Such constant shifts within the compass of a single sentence are indeed quite uncommon. If, according to normal practice, some of the omitted subjects were supplied (in 3 and 4 and, possibly, 6), the original might naturally be broken into a few separate sentences: a change that would visually as well as audibly mark the events more strikingly off from each other, thereby slowing down the psychological speed with which the events follow one another in sequence:

> ... talked for a while about the years of separation, and Lady Wang took them in to pay respects to the Lady Dowager. Aunt Xue (or the Xues) presented the various kinds of gifts of Nanking produce. The whole family were introduced to one another. Then the Jias spread a feast of welcome for the guests.

Compare the original: [1]

> ... talked for a while about the years of separation, and took them in to pay respects to the Lady Dowager, presented the various kinds of gifts of Nanking produce, the whole family were introduced to one another, and spread a feast of welcome for the guests.

This would be a regrettable change. For the psychological hastening of pace by virtue of the unexpectedly frequent use of covert changing of the subject is seen to be of thematic significance. The description of the Xue's arrival (at the central scene of the fiction), synthesized into a single sentence, in fact forms a stark contrast to the preceding description of the arrival of Lin Daiyu which is depicted in elaborate detail, going on for pages. Now one of the Xues: Xue Baochai (Aunt Xue's daughter) and Lin Daiyu, being the two female protagonists in the novel, represent two contending forces: anti-feudalist versus feudalist; their symbolic contention for the love of the hero forms one of the major themes of the novel. With a strong anti-feudalist tendency, the implied author takes a stand for Lin Daiyu, the one with democratic ideas. Never once, though, is this stand explicitly stated, but it is to be detected, among other things, in the subtle stylistic choices. The radical difference in attention accorded to their respective arrivals at the central scene serves to bring out the implied author's partiality for Lin Daiyu over Xue Baochai, the latter being, significantly, kept obscure in the already inconspicuous description. The author's indifference towards Xue Baochai, as indicated by his merely touching on her arrival, is underlined by the psychological hastening of pace which generates a rapid continuity that adds a good deal to the tone of customariness or predictability underlying the bald summary (which only serves as a necessary connective framework). This goes towards reducing the psychological prominence or, more to the point, the significance of the affair.

Cao's psychological hastening of pace is well captured by translation (A) where the corresponding means chosen for Cao's constant covert changing of the subject (unavailable in English) takes the form of the consistent "after ... and after ... and after. ..." The continuous downward shifts in rank in the clauses concerned (from a main clause to a prep. phrase [2] or to a subordinate clause [3, 4, 5]) operate to lump the events involved together into a circumstantial whole, as a background to "a family party." As the reader expects the main clause to follow the first "after ... ," the appearance of "and after" generates an element of suspense, pressing the mind forward to find the main clause, an expectation only to be defeated by the subsequent "and after ... ," thus further pressing the mind forward. The resulting effect is that the circumstantial whole is seen to progress with speedy continuity, perceptibly accelerating the pace of the processes involved. We may note that the three subsidiary instances of "after," being considerably parallel in situation and function and with a strong undertone of monotony and predictability, interact to render each other obscure, helping to quicken the processing speed and, related to that, to hasten the psychological pace. As if to strengthen the effect, specification of the omitted subjects, which is often called for in Chinese-to-English transfer, is avoided by means of either nominalization "an exchange of information" (2), or passivatization (3, 4), or an existential clause (6). All this amounts to the fact that version (A) runs on at a fairly quick speed with the events, marked by psychological obscurity, closely following one another, which matches well the effect of the original.

By contrast, Cao's psychological hastening of pace is not al all reflected in version (B). Although two of Cao's main clauses (2, 5) are subordinated in (B), it goes no further than what is normally expected in coping with the much less syntactic Chinese. While no effort is made to correspond to the unexpectedly frequent covert changing of the subject, Cao's quickly run-on narrative flow (2—6) is broken into 3 somewhat separate units (2—3, 4, 5—6), with the consequence that the pace is notably slowed down.

Having seen how syntax can be manipulated to quicken the pace at which a sequence of summarized events follow one another, we now turn to another case in Cao which exhibits the opposite narrative mode, that is, showing or scenic description:

(Cao) Gang shuodao zheli,　　zhiting ermenshang
Granny Liu had got no further, (when) the pages by the

　　xiaosimen huishuo: "Dongfuli xiaodaye jinlaile."
second gate announced: "The young master from the East

　　　　Feng Jie mang he Liu laolao bai shou dao:
Mansion is here." Xifeng *promptly* gestured to Granny Liu:

"Bubi shuole." Yimian bian wen: "Ni Rong daye zai
"That's enough." She *at the same time* asked: "Where is

naline?"

CHAPTER 7 ASPECTS OF SYNTAX   181

Master Rong?" (chapter 6; my emphasis)

(A) Just then pages by the second gate called out, "The young master from the East Mansion is here." Cutting Granny Liu short Hsi-feng asked, "Where is Master Jung?"
(Trans. Yang and Yang)

(B) She had got no further when the pages from the outer gate announced the arrival of "the young master from the Ning mansion" and Xi-feng gestured to her to stop. "It's all right. There is no need to tell me." She turned to the pages. "Where is Master Rong, then?" (Trans. Hawkes)

The rhetorical or psychological[2] hastening of pace is realized in Cao mainly by lexical means. In response to the unexpected announcement, Xifeng promptly silences Granny Liu and *"at the same time"*—an adjunct that imposes *simultaneity* on two obviously successive events—asks "Where is Master Rong?" This prompt reaction points to a prominent trait in Xifeng, namely, her extraordinary adaptability; and more significantly, it serves to bring out, in a subtle and oblique way, Xifeng's dubious relationship with Master Rong, her husband's nephew (a scandalous affair is suspected to be going on between the two).

Cao's rhetorical hastening of pace is well matched by (A) through the choice of "cutting Granny Liu short." Now except for existential ones, the present participial clause is often used to indicate accompanying circumstances, with the implication of incomplete happening with limited duration. Given the sentence "Crossing the street, he ...," it is to be understood as *"While* crossing ..." rather than "After crossing ..." or "Having crossed. ..."Despite its instantaneous nature, "cutting short" in (A) seems, by association with the paradigmatically related durative verbs, to pass off, up to a point, as accompanying circumstances. By this is meant a measure of pseudo-simultaneity between "cut short" and "ask." Moreover, the fact that Xifeng's first speech act is reduced to a "circumstantial" position hastens the psychological appearance of her second speech act. The reader seems to get the impression that "The young master from the East Mansion is here" is in a way directly responded to by the utterance "Where is Master Jung?" Notice the difference obtained if the participial clause is promoted to an independent sentence:

... called out, "..."
Hsi-feng cut Granny Liu short. She (then) asked, "Where is ..."

Here the syntactic structure accords Xifeng's two speech acts equal prominence, and the syntactic boundary marks the case that the announcement is responded to first by Xifeng's cutting Granny Liu "at short and only then, as distinct from Cao's "at the same time," by her inquiry. The pseudo-simultaneity generated by Cao's lexis and conveyed by (A)'s syntax fails to appear in version (B) where the pace is perceptibly slowed down. This is attributable in part to the omission of "promptly" and "at the same time" and in part to the elaboration of the curt speech act "That's enough." as well as to the addition of the process of turning to the pages. The elaboration in question makes Xifeng's first speech act attract more attention, which, coupled with the addition, delays the appearance of Xifeng's inquiry (as a result, the addition of "then" is called for by naturalness of expression). In (B) one is not made to feel the promptness of the reaction or the eagerness of the inquiry; instead one is given the impression that Xifeng's response may well be a normal one and the arrival may well be a normal guest rather than the very Master Rong in whom Xifeng is particularly interested.

The differences in pace shown above point to a fundamental issue that lies underneath. In a fictional world, one that is in a sense "dissociated from the immediate social context" (Widdowson 1975:54), the reader can only take on trust the written medium. As indicated here, in describing the same events, different syntactic choices, because of the different psychological effects they create, may result in different

CHAPTER 7 ASPECTS OF SYNTAX   183

decoding processes which, consequently, may vary psychologically the pace of the events involved. This, in turn, may bear on authorial stance, on characterization, or on the relationship between the characters concerned, among other things. In the preceding case, Cao's rhetorical hastening of pace leads the run-on events to tail off into inconsequence, implicitly bringing out the implied author's attitude towards the characters. In the present case, though no mention is made of Xifeng's extraordinary adaptability or her dubious relationship with Master Rong, it is however subtly hinted at by her quick reaction, particularly, by the pseudo-simultaneity.

It is arguable that stylistic values as such are functional only in a literary context. Found in a non-literary work whose purpose is to convey information, such differences could well be overlooked by the translator since they do not, broadly speaking, affect the basic propositional content. The same holds true for the rhetorical or psychological slowing down of pace. To look at a brief example from the same novel by Cao:

(Cao) Laodaole banri,
He chattered for quite a while (half-of-the-day),
fang chou shen qule.
(before) finally tearing himself away. (chapter 9)

(A) He chatted with her for quite a bit longer before finally tearing himself away. (Trans. Hawkes)

(B) After chatting for a while he turned to leave. (Trans. Yang and Yang)

This takes place before the hero goes to school in the morning. He hurries to the heroine's room to say good-bye to her. Judging from the context, the chatting can only have lasted for a short while. If what is required is a neutral description, version (B) would be sufficient (e. g. in answering the question "What happened that morning?"). In this literary context, however, (B) falls short in that it fails to convey Cao's rhetorical slowing down of pace. The slowing down of pace is realized in Cao through lexical choice. The first predicate "chatter" connotes unhurriedness and lengthiness which is reinforced by the metaphorical "half-of-the-day." The effect is further strengthened by the interpersonal adjunct "finally" as well as by the dragging force in "tearing himself away." Thus a short time span is stretched to take on a greater length, subtly revealing the hero's unwillingness to part with the heroine, with whom he has apparently fallen in love.

The rhetorical slowing down of pace is well transferred by (A) whose syntactic structure makes prominent the act of "chatting" (the predicate of the main clause) modified by "for quite a bit longer." The conjunction "before," allied to "finally," delays the act of "tearing himself away." This forms a contrast to (B) where the emphasis is shifted, with the backgrounding of the act of chatting, to "turned to leave" (which occupies the prominent position of the predicate of the main clause) and where the neutral description drops no hint of the hero's unwillingness to part with the object of his affections.

From these few examples it will have emerged that rhetorical or psychological hastening or slowing down of pace forms a stylistic device which is to be taken into account by a literary translator so as to avoid deceptive equivalence and to recapture the full range of responses produced by the original text. And it is the syntactic aspect that seems to deserve particular attention, since it may be more easily overlooked in translation.

7.2 SYNTAX AND PROMINENCE

A most crucial function of the syntactic hierarchy is to represent different degrees of importance attached to different parts of the message. In a hypotactic language like English, syntax plays a vital role in highlighting or backgrounding information and in distinguishing new information from what is given. In the paratactic Chinese, though, differentiation of prominence or givenness is not so much a role of syntax but rather, to a great extent, a function of the reader's contextual inference. In translating from Chinese into English, then, not only does naturalness of expression call for frequent subordinating or rankshifting by the translator, but also the difference in syntactic function between the two languages makes it necessary for the translator to signal differentials of importance or givenness by means of the syntactic hierarchy so as to cater for a readership much more dependent in this respect on syntax. The success of the translator's task in this aspect rests essentially on his or her correct contextual inference and on finding the appropriate syntactic choice. In the following case, taken again from Cao's *A Dream of Red Mansions*, translation (A) presents a successful rendering while (B) seems to fall short:

> (Cao) ... Liu laolao bugan guoqu,   dandan yifu,
> ... Granny Liu did not dare to go over, [she] dusted down
>
>   you jiaole Ban'er jijuhua,
> her clothes, and taught Ban'er again a few appropriate words,
>
> ranhou liudao jiaomen qian ...
> after that [she] sidled up to the side entrance ... (chapter 6)

(A) There, at each side of the stone lions which flanked the gates of the Rong Mansion, she saw a cluster of horses and palanquins. *Not daring to go straight up, she first dusted down her clothes and rehearsed Ban-er's little repertoire of phrases before sidling up to one of the side entrances* ... (Trans. Hawkes; my emphasis)

(B) But Granny Liu was too overawed by the crowd of sedanchairs and horses there to venture near the stone lions which flanked the Jung Mansion's main gate. *Having dusted off her clothes and given Pan-erh fresh instructions, she timidly approached the side entrance* where some arrogant, corpulent servants were sunning themselves on long benches, engaged in a lively discussion. (Trans. Yang and Yang; my emphasis)

This passage depicts one scene of the first visit by Granny Liu—a country bumpkin—to the Rong Mansion in the capital. In the last but one case discussed in 6.3, we were given, it will be recalled, a glimpse into the character's ignorance and bizarre reactions. This country bumpkin, with her grandson Ban'er, is now at the entrance to the Rong Mansion. Wanting to but not daring to enter, she displays two preparatory actions "dust down her clothes" and "teach Ban'er again a few appropriate words" which are characteristic of her as an overawed country woman. As the Chinese critic Jiang Hesen says, "just by seizing upon these two distinctive details, the author succeeds in bringing out vividly and thoroughly the country bumpkin's hesitation, humbleness and timidity" (1982:18).

These two distinctive details are given due emphasis in (A) where they are foregrounded through the position of two coordinated main clauses and are further set off by the preceding and following participial ones. This treatment by (A) of Cao's four coordinate clauses fits well the logical relationships between the processes involved. The use of a participial clause to render "not dare to go over" suits perfectly the nature of the mental process as an accompanying state of mind and as a reason underlying the following actions. The choice of "before sidling up to one of the side entrances" on the other hand conveys well the fact that this is an intended act which is due to follow the two preparatory actions. It may be worth noting that the lexical addition "first" serves to strengthen the signal of new information and to reinforce the role of the two highlighted actions in characterization.

When it comes to version (B), the descriptive focus is regrettably shifted to "she timidly approached the side entrance" which occupies the prominent position of the only main clause in the sentence while the two "distinctive details" concerned are translated through two participial clauses headed by the auxiliary "have." Because of the backgrounding effect arising from the subsidiary structure coupled with the associated strong undertone of predictability, the two preparatory actions seem to lose their distinctiveness, consequently playing a much weaker role in revealing the character's hesitation, humbleness or timidity.

The comparison between (A) and (B) may shed some light on how meaning arises from within the mechanisms of syntax in fiction, a world in which the reader can only take on trust the written medium. In a hypotactic language like English, the reader seems to be heavily reliant on syntax. As we see here, the surface structure in version (A) focuses the reader's attention on the two "distinctive details," allowing the reader room to appreciate fully their role in characterization. In version (B), however, the reader's attention is directed by surface structure to concentrate on two different points: (1) Granny Liu was too overawed to venture near the main gate, (2) so she timidly approached the side entrance. The two actions in between are made by syntax to appear obscure and expected, and are therefore made somewhat dissociated from the feelings they are intended by the narrator to convey. Given the significant role of English syntax in directing the reader's differentiation of prominence or givenness, the translator has to see to it that his/her syntactic choices match the intended logical relationships between the processes involved.

In the following case taken from Lu Xun's "Remorse for the Past" ("Shangshi"), translation (B) exhibits, due to an inappropriate surface syntactic choice, a notable distortion of the original emphasis:

(Lu) ... Zhe yanguan shexiang sichu, zhengru haizi zai
... She looked all around,   just like a hungry

jikezhong xunqiuzhe ci' aide muqin, dan zhi zaikongzhong
child looking for its kind mother, but only looked into

xunqiu, kongbude huibizhe wode yan. Wo buneng
space, [she] fearfully avoided my eyes. I could not bear the

kanxiaqule . . .

sight any more . . .

(A) To clinch the matter, I said firmly: ". . . Well, to tell the truth—it's because I don't love you any more! Actually, this makes it better for you, because it'll be easier for you to work without any regret. . . . " I was expecting a scene, but all that followed was silence. Her face turned ashy pale, like a corpse; but in a moment her colour came back, and that childlike look darted from her eyes. She looked all around, like a hungry child searching for its mother, but only looked into space. *She fearfully avoided my eyes.* The sight was more than I could stand. . . . (Trans. Yang and Yang 1956: 254; my emphasis)

(B) . . . I had expected violent reaction to this, but there was only silence. Her face turned deathly pale and yellowed, but she recovered almost immediately. Her eyes sparkled with their childlike innocence, *and while trying to avoid my eyes, flitted about the room like those of a hungry child looking for its mother.* I could bear it no longer. . . . (Trans. Chi-chen Wang 1941: 175; my emphasis)

Coming from a story which depicts a tragic love affair, the passage presents a scene where the narrator/protagonist finally plucks up his courage and tells his girlfriend the truth that he does not love her any more, a truth which eventually leads to her premature death in a loveless world. Clearly, her reaction to his words diverges from his expectations not only in the sense that she reacts quietly rather than violently but also, as indicated by the adversative "but" coupled with the interpersonal adjunct "only," in the fact that she fearfully avoids his eyes. And it is no doubt the latter unexpected fact that he finds particularly difficult to stand. This fact of her fearfully avoiding his eyes argues her disillusionment about their love and points to the cruelty of his words, forming a prelude, as it were, to his everlasting guilt. The very night his girlfriend leaves him.

> In the darkness I seemed to see a pile of food, then the sallow, pale face of Tzu-chun, *looking at me imploringly with her childlike eyes*. When my gaze steadied, I could see nothing. My heart again grew heavy. Why could I not have endured it a few days longer? Why must I have so impulsively told her the truth? (from translation B,178; my emphasis)

It is no accident that the only reaction of his girlfriend in his hallucination is one of her looking at him imploringly, which forms such a stark contrast to the reality that she fearfully avoids his eyes. In Lu, this real reaction of hers is marked by descriptive emphasis: realized through its final position in the sentential climactic progression—particularly through the use of "but only looked into space" which operates to make the final clause emphatic and prominent. Notice the difference that would obtain if the sentence were to appear in a form like:

> She looked all around, just like a hungry child looking for its kind mother, and she fearfully avoided my eyes.

Although the information conveyed remains the same (so far as her reaction is concerned), the alteration in linguistic form brings about a significant change in the viewpoint of the I-narrator who is now seen to take her reaction in the last clause as somewhat expected, a change which would in turn bear on the response of the reader. In this altered form, the last clause appears no more than parallel to the preceding one, in no way forming a sentential climax. In Lu, however, with the adversative "but" signalling unexpectedness, the assertion "only looked into space" creates an element of suspense, which heightens the effect of shock and, related to it, the prominence of the climactic final clause which discloses the grim reality that "she fearfully avoided my eyes."

This climactic progression formed by the two coordinate clauses headed by the adversative "but" is in fact peculiar to Chinese where the characteristic paratactic structure allied to the distinctive omission of subject enables the two clauses to function closely together—in a way somewhat like two successive predicates in one clause:

... but only looked into space, fearfully avoided my eyes.

Clearly, the subject of the last clause has to be spelt out in English:

... but [she] only looked into space, she fearfully avoided my eyes.

In the hypotactic English, such a form appears loose and unacceptable. If one translates it into the following acceptable form:

... but [she] only looked into space: she fearfully avoided my eyes.

it would involve a partial loss of the effect of unexpectedness and shock associated with the last clause since the climactic progression in Lu is now changed into a statement plus an explanation.

As shown above, the means that version (A) chooses to get round the dilemma is to translate Lu's last clause into an independent sentence. The short, separate graphic unit renders the process involved very emphatic and psychologically prominent: Despite the separating force inherent in the full stop, the strong semantic link, or rather the complementary function, between this sentence and the preceding clause enables the "disjoined" (A) to represent, up to a point, the climactic progression in Lu. Indeed, the full stop in between seems to function to heighten the element of suspense as well as to deepen the shock effect produced by what follows.

In contrast with (A), Lu's descriptive emphasis is seriously distorted by (B) where the fact of her avoiding his eyes is backgrounded in the shape of a participial clause and made to appear as an accompanying circumstance, to serve merely a modifying role and to take on a strong tone of predictability. As the syntax focuses the reader's attention on the two main clauses which overshadow the participial one, the "it" in "I could bear it no longer" seems to have little to do with her "trying to avoid my eyes," which originally forms its crucial referent. Consequently, much of the tragic contrast between the reality of her "fearfully avoiding my eyes" and the hallucination of her "looking at me imploringly" is lost in (B). What underlies (B)'s distortion is most probably inadequate contextual inference by the translator, who seems to take the fact of her avoiding his eyes as an inessential detail, an attitude reflected not only in the use of the subsidiary structure but also in the omission of the adjunct "fearfully." Another factor which may partly account for the distortion is the constraint of naturalness of expression. In translating from Chinese into English, one is always ready to carry out subordinating or rankshifting so as to make the text appear natural in the hypotactic target language. As illustrated above, the clause "..., [she] fearfully avoided my eyes" appears in English as a trailing element, rendering the sentence unacceptably loose. (B)'s subordinating it and sandwiching it in between two main clauses may be seen as an effort to tighten up the syntactic structure. The result is a neat, well-balanced sentence with distorted emphasis.

In effect, in translating from Chinese into English, the concern with naturalness of expression quite frequently leads to distortions in terms of prominence (of which the following case is another example). As the contrast between prominence and obscurity or between "new" and "given" plays an essential part in revealing or conveying the viewpoint of the authorial or dramatized narrator, and/or a character (which significantly conditions the reader's decoding process), it should be stressed that, in making syntactic choices, one needs to consider carefully the communicative emphasis or the logical relationship obtaining in the original text and try to reflect or underline it, with naturalness where applicable by appropriate syntactic choices in the target language.

Now in the two cases examined above, the distortions of prominence involved seem to be locally clear. But in many others, the distortion of prominence becomes clear only in the light of a larger context, most typically, in the light of a pertinent motif. For convenience of discussion, I have chosen here an illustrative case from the same story by Lu:

(Lu) (Jiuzai zheyang yige hunheide wanshang, wo zhaochang
(Just on such a dark evening, I came back home listlessly as

meijing-dacaide huilai ...) Wo sihu bei zhouwei suo
usual, ...) I felt as if I was being squeezed out by the

paiji,   bendao yuanzi zhongjian,
surroundings, [I] rushed out to the middle of the courtyard,

you hunhei zai wode zhouwei; zhengwude zhichuangshang
there was darkness around me; on the window paper of the

yingchu mingliangde dengguang, ...
central room there was shining bright lamplight, ... (my emphasis)

(A) (One dark evening, I came home listlessly as usual ... It was dark inside, and as I groped for the matches to strike a light, the place seemed extraordinarily quiet and empty. I was standing there in bewilderment, when the official's wife called to me through the window. "Tzu-chun's father came today," she said simply, "and took her away." This was not what I had expected. I felt as if hit on the back of the head, and stood speechless. ...) Feeling my surroundings pressing in on me, I hurried out to the middle of the courtyard, *where all around was dark*. Bright lamplight showed on the window paper of the central rooms, (where they were teasing the baby to make

CHAPTER 7   ASPECTS OF SYNTAX   193

her laugh. My heart grew calmer, and I began to glimpse a way out of this heavy oppression ...) (256, my emphasis)

(B) (It was after dark when I came home. ...) I felt oppressed and *rushed out into the darkness of the courtyard*. The landlady's room was bright (and resounded with children's laughter. My heart calmed down and there gradually emerged out of the oppressiveness of my situation a path into life ...) (176—178, my emphasis)

This passage depicts the I-narrator's reaction to his girlfriend's leaving him after he has told her the truth. As far as the immediate context (say, the graphic sentence) is concerned, (B)'s nominalization of Lu's "there was darkness around me" is perfectly acceptable since it not only does not bear on the denotative meaning but also does not seem to affect the logical relationships between the constituent parts of the message. But when viewed in relation to a larger context, it will be found that (B)'s rendering falls short in terms of prominence.

In this story, "dark" or "darkness" is almost consistently used with figurative significance, serving to stand for despair, disillusion, death or sinister social forces. For example:

All around was a great void, quiet as death. I seemed to see the darkness before the eyes of every single person who died unloved ... (A, 259)

Sometimes the road to life appeared like a long white snake, wriggling and rushing towards me. I waited and waited but it disappeared into the darkness when it came close. (B, 182)

The figurative references to darkness combine to form a thematic motif which is set in striking contrast with the motif formed by figurative references to light or brightness, used to symbolize happiness, hope or a promising future. The following is a case in point:

In the public library I often got glimpses of light, of a new road to life ahead of me. (B, 176)

Given the pertinent thematic patterns, the contrastive references to darkness and brightness in the present passage are seen to take on symbolic significance (see A and B for the causal relation between the bright lamplight and the rising of his hope). The I-narrator is fully aware that the returning of his cohabitant to her father's home would only end in her destruction since there is "nothing for her to look forward to" but harshness, chilly glances and emptiness and, worst of all, "a tomb without even a tombstone!" The term "darkness" here points to the hopeless situation of his girlfriend and to the I-narrator's own disillusion and despair, as well as to the dark social forces underlying the tragedy. In view of the larger structural function, we can understand better Lu's use of "there was darkness around me" ("you hunhei zai wode zhouwei"), which exhibits structurally deviant and semantically redundant elements. The use of the existential form to depict the colour of the sky is deviant in Chinese and also, perhaps to a lesser extent, in English. Compared with the more usual expression "it was dark in the courtyard" ("yuanzili heiheide"), the existential form "there was darkness around me" has the function of highlighting the bearing of "darkness" on "me."

In fact, given the preceding reference to the setting "one dark evening," the reference to darkness here is semantically redundant. What matters, though, is not the redundancy itself but the fact that the existential form makes the redundancy consciously felt. Compare:

(1) It was dark inside the room. I went into the darkness of the room.

(2) It was dark inside the room. I went into the room. There was darkness around me.

In (2) the existential form seems to foreground the redundancy by virtue of the fact that the redundant element is treated as new information and asserted by a separate clause. As a result, the "darkness around me" is made psychologically more prominent and is more consciously felt on the part of both encoder and decoder. The latter, if attentive, would surely be alerted to whatever motivation there is underlying the deviant assertion and, in Lu's case, be alerted to the symbolic significance involved, a significance that could perhaps be best preserved in English through the existential form allied to the prominent position of an independent sentence:

(A) Feeling my surroundings pressing on me. I hurried out to the middle of the courtyard. There was darkness around me. Bright lamplight showed on the window paper of the ...

(B) I felt oppressed and rushed out into the courtyard. There was darkness around me. The landlady's room was bright ...

But what one actually finds in (A) is the subordinated form:

... I hurried out to the middle of the courtyard, where all around [me] was dark.

Interestingly, despite the subordination, the term "dark" takes on considerable prominence partly through its end-focus position and partly from the fact that the preceding comma marks the adverbial clause as a relatively independent information unit, making it appear less presupposed and consequently rendering the semantic redundancy involved more consciously felt, which in turn functions to alert the reader to the figurative meanings involved. Moreover, the choice of "around [me] was dark" approximates to the function of the existential form in terms of stressing the bearing of darkness on the protagonist, while the addition of the adjunct "all" serves to underline the sinister potency of darkness, contributing to the preservation of the figurative significance concerned.

The symbolic significance of darkness is drastically undercut by (B)'s:

I felt oppressed and rushed out into the darkness of the courtyard.

where Lu's main clause "there was darkness around me" is reduced to the obscure position of the head of an embedded nominal group and made to function as part of a locative adjunct. As a result, "darkness" appears to be totally presupposed, which makes for cancelling the unconventional redundancy. What is more, the presentation of darkness as part of the locative adjunct functions to render darkness into a refuge, as it were, for the protagonist, who rushes into it to avoid oppression. This forms a contrast to Lu and (A) where the protagonist is seen to seek refuge in the courtyard where, for a good reason, he feels and asserts the existence of darkness and its hearing on him. It is apparent that the sinister potency of darkness, which one senses in Lu's "there was darkness around me" or A's "all around [me] was dark" is totally suppressed in (B) where there is virtually no linguistic signal left to alert the reader to any significance of "darkness" over and above its literal meaning.

This is seen to be all the more regrettable given that the local effacement of the symbolic significance of "darkness" would necessarily impair the echoing effect of the pertinent motif. Indeed, what underlies the local effacement is surely, among other things, a failure to realize the function of the present reference to darkness in the larger symbolic pattern. The point to stress is that, in order to represent adequately the differentials of prominence or givenness obtaining in the original, the translator needs to be aware of the function of a given structure in a larger pattern, in addition to an adequate awareness of the logical relationships involved in the immediate context.

7.3 SYNTAX AND THE IMITATION OF PROCESS

This section will direct attention to two specific areas: premodification and sequencing. In these areas, among many others, there may occur the artistically-motivated iconic matching of syntactic form with the processes involved, either within or outside the consciousness. The examples below have been chosen invariably for the reason that the iconic schemata found in the original are peculiar to Chinese and are difficult to transfer into English.

7.3.1 Premodification

In Chinese, the head of a nominal group is, as a rule, only premodified, with the premodification possibly containing a complex of rankshifted groups and clauses. This restricted positioning of the modifying element and, related to it, the allowance for heavy premodification are of course just conventional features of the arbitrary organization of the language. But these features may be consciously exploited by the writer in an effort to imitate the process(es) involved. The following passage, taken from Mao Dun's "Spring Silkworms," is a good case in point:

> (Mao) Zheshi yige longzhongde yishi! Qianbai nian
> This was a solemn ceremony! A ceremony handed down
>
> xiangchuande yishi! Na haobishi shishi dianli,
> through the ages!   It was like an oath-taking ceremony,
>
> yihou jiuyao kaishile yige yue guangjingde he eliede tianqi he
> from now on would begin an about-a-month-long's-
>
> eyun yiji he buzhishenmede lianrilianye wu xiuxide da juezhan!
> against-bad-weather-and-bad-luck-and-against-goodness-knows-what-else's-without-rest-for-days-and-nights-running's-big decisive combat!

> (A) A solemn ceremony! One that had been handed down through the ages! Like warriors taking an oath before going into battle! Old Tung Pao and family now had ahead of them a month of fierce combat, with no rest day or night, against bad weather, bad luck and anything else that might come along (Trans. Shapiro 1956:25)

(B) It was solemn ceremony, one that had been observed for hundreds and hundreds of years. It was as solemn an occasion as the sacrifice before a military campaign, for it was to inaugurate a month of relentless struggle against bad weather and ill luck during which there would be no rest day or night. (Trans. Chi-chen Wang 1944:12)

(C) The ceremony was holy, and as old as China. Beginning from this day a battle against bad weather and bad luck started. And this battle had to be continued for a whole month. (Trans. Yeh 1946:18)

Mao's "Spring Silkworms" is about the arduous struggle of Old Tong Bao and family, among their fellow villagers, to raise a crop of spring silkworms under the joint depredation of imperialism and feudalism. This passage comments on the ceremony involved on the day when newly-hatched silkworms are harvested, which marks the beginning of one month of toil before the spinning of cocoons. What is striking in Mao is the heavy premodification in the last nominal group, which may be analysed in terms of the notion "arrest" (see Sinclair 1982). Although the first modifying element "about a month long's" may be taken as quite natural, the following rankshifted prepositional group headed by "against" surely functions to arrest the expected progression to the head noun, an effect which is reinforced by the coordinate "against goodness knows what else's" and is further strengthened by the juxtaposed "without rest for days and nights running's." The effect is very remarkable in English and even in Chinese, where heavy premodification is commonplace, the premodification occurring in this inverted clause is felt to be too heavy with arrest. The heaviness emerges with the extending element "and against goodness knows what else's" and is significantly underlined by the subsequent "without rest for days and nights running's," the former appearing to have been deliberately added to lengthen the arrest and the latter, which could have been more naturally presented in surface structure as the predicate of another clause,[3] seeming to have been purposefully juxtaposed here to reinforce the ponderousness of the arrest.

The literary effect thus produced is not so much one of building up a phrasal climax (to emphasize the head noun "decisive-combat" ["juezhan"]) as one of dramatically imitating, through the physical properties associated with the exceptional arrest, the relevant traits of the process concerned. It is notable that the ponderous arrest sets a great burden upon the memory, building up a mental strain which imitates and interacts with the psychological tension that one feels in decoding the meaning of the premodifying elements, thereby iconically reinforcing the strenuousness and laboriousness of the process. In this particular context, the juxtaposition of the premodifying elements in itself seems, in addition to making for their mutual intensification, to serve to underline, merely through placing these elements side by side, the multiplicity of the hardships involved. Also of interest is the fact that, in decoding the premodification in Chinese, when reading aloud, one's breath may be about to run out at the end of "buzhishenmede" ("goodness knows what else's") and, if seeking to decode on the same breath "lianrilianye wu xiuxide" ("without rest for days and nights running's"), one may have to stretch the breath very hard, dramatically enacting the tension and restlessness involved. Quite similarly, in silent reading, the mental strain arising from the burden on the short-term memory caused by the arrest is particularly keenly felt when one reaches "without rest for days and nights running's." Furthermore, in this particular context, the very length of the premodification seems to make for an imitation of the lengthiness of the given process. What we have here then, is a multi-dimensional matching of the physical shape of the structure and the content conveyed, with the former operating to intensify the latter. What underlies this intensification by way of imitation is, among other things, the authorial narrator's deep empathy, which is also shown graphologically by the recurrent use of "!" as well as being semantically reflected in the metaphorical expressions. The narrator's keen sympathy towards the hardship involved—as one is sure to sense in decoding the heavy premodification as such—operates to promote effectively the reader's emotional involvement, heightening, as a result, the affective force of the message.

In translating into English, postmodification, or rather heavy postmodification, offers one, and perhaps the only, way open to a translator who attempts to represent the iconic matching in question. Not surprisingly, both (A) and (B) exhibit considerable postmodification, replacing Mao's premodifying arrests by postmodifying extensions, thereby managing to capture to some extent the iconic effects referred to. A better representation, though, could be achieved if we combine the virtues of (A) and (B) to form a rendering like:

> A solemn ceremony! One that had been handed down through the ages! Like warriors taking an oath before going into battle! Old Tong Bao and family now began a month of fierce combat against bad weather, ill luck and goodness knows what else during which there would be no rest day or night!

Marked by an emotive force as strong as that in the original, this version seems to capture more fully Mao's iconic matching of form and meaning through the joined function of (i) the representation of the extending element "and against goodness knows what else" and (ii) the preservation of the original order of the modifying elements. The former serves to heighten, by making more ponderous the extension as a whole, the imitative effect of burdensomeness or laboriousness. Associated with the latter, on the other hand, is the interesting fact that "during which there would be no rest day or night" is made to occur at a period where the mental strain or, in reading aloud, the exertion of the breath, may be most keenly felt, making for a dramatic enactment of the content. However, given that postmodifying extension does not involve nearly so much suspense or progressive burden on the memory as is found in premodifying arrest, the imitative effects referred to are relatively weaker in English.

Now, compared with the Chinese original or with the English versions just mentioned, translation (C) notably falls short, completely failing to make the syntactic form reinforce the propositional content. With the use of two simple sentences to render the clause under discussion coupled with the omission of the juxtaposed "without rest for days and nights running's," (C) totally dissolves the syntactic tension created by Mao, resulting in a version marked by relative plainness, faintness or easiness. The reader is given the impression that the narrator is much more detached, an impression also ascribable to, among other things, (C)'s suppression of the exclamation marks. Clearly, in (C), the hardship facing the characters is toned down and the affective or the rhetorical force of the message is drastically reduced.

It should be noted that, in translating from Chinese into English, the use of a simple sentence to render a certain part of the heavy premodification in the original is by no means a rare practice. But in those cases, the heaviness of the premodification usually does not take on aesthetic effects or may not even lead to any notable syntactic tension. The decomposition, as it were, of the premodification by means of simple sentences in such cases does not therefore involve any loss of stylistic values. This general practice may well account for (C)'s regrettable use of two simple sentences to decompose Mao's heavy premodification. The problem is that (C) seems to have failed to notice the literary effects associated with Mao's case and to have treated it unjustifiably on a par with those cases which are not artistically motivated and which are no other than natural uses of the language. In fictional translation, it has to be stressed, one must guard against being misled by the general practice in dealing with the peculiarities of a given language. The novelist may consciously exploit some of those peculiarities to create artistic or rhetorical effects; and in such cases, optimal corresponding means are demanded from the translator so as to achieve functional equivalence.

Before ending this section, it may be of interest to note that we have already touched on three different modes of the literary function of syntax, namely, (a) exploiting the conventional values; (b) extending the conventional values; and (c) creating an illusion of similarity. In the discussion of prominence above, the positive renderings shown in the first two examples present successful exploitation of the conventional values inherent in the forms concerned. In the immediately preceding case, Lu's use of the existential form to alert the reader, through foregrounding the semantic redundancy involved, to the symbolic significance of "darkness" could be taken as an exemplification of mode (b). There is, though, no clear-cut boundary between modes (a) and (b), which are frequently overlapping. Mode (c) was reflected in 7.1 in Cao's rhetorical use of the covert changing of the subject where the fast continuity generated in the decoding process creates the impression that the events depicted follow one another at a great speed. This mode is more tellingly illustrated by the present case where Mao's heavy premodification dramatically imitates, by virtue of certain superficial similarity, the relevant traits of the process concerned.

7.3.2 Sequencing

Interestingly, linguistic mimesis always rests on some form of "parallel" which exists between the linguistic fact and the content mimed. This is obviously the case when it comes to sequencing. The linear progression of syntax, which is analogous to the progression of processes, offers a possibility of miming, apart from the sequence of phenomena occurring in the fictional reality, the sequential inner thoughts or ideas. It is understood that the normal syntactic order is often in keeping with the

CHAPTER 7   ASPECTS OF SYNTAX   203

sequence of the represented phenomena (see Bolinger 1980:20; Leech &. Short 1981:234—235). Such iconicity, though, being conventionalized or automatized, usually does not take on artistic function. This points to the fact that aesthetically-motivated iconic sequencing is typically marked by deviation from the normal or neutral syntactic order. In fictional translation, that is to say, one needs to bear in mind that deviant syntactic sequence, particularly in a well-formed text, may be associated with desirable literary effects. And if such is the case, the deviation should be preserved rather than normalized. Relevant here is an example from Lao She's *Rickshaw Boy* (*Luotuo Xiangzi*), which exhibits an instance of artistically-motivated deviant sequencing:

(Lao) ... ta zhen xiang yixiazi tiao xiaqu,
... he really wanted to all of a sudden jump off the bridge,

tou chaoxia, zapole bing,   chen xiaqu,
head first, break[ing] through the ice, sink[ing] down,

xiang ge siyushide dong zaibingli.
like a dead fish freez[ing] in the ice.

(A) ... he wanted to jump off the bridge, right now, head first, break through the ice, and be frozen into it, like some great dead fish. (Trans. King 1946:85)

(B) He actually thought about jumping off the bridge all of a sudden. His head would hit and crack the ice and he'd sink down and freeze there like a dead fish. (Trans. James 1979:83)

(C) What he really wanted was to dive off the bridge, smashing through the ice and sinking down to the bottom to freeze there like a dead fish. (Trans. Shi 1981:90)

Two preliminary points must be made here. First, in Chinese, a language which is not inflected, the word-order is, generally speaking, more strict than in English; second, in Chinese, manner adjuncts normally precede the verbs they modify. In the light of the latter, it is clear that, in Lao's case, the sequencing is marked by deviation, since what conventionally precedes the verb—the manner adjunct "tou chaoxia" ("head first")—is now positioned unexpectedly after the verb, with a comma in between; and the thoughts appear to be somewhat disordered. What underlies this deviant sequencing is surely the desperation of the protagonist who is seen to be seized by an impulse to (all of a sudden) jump off the bridge and only then to come to think about the manner of jumping "head first." By this is meant that apart from authenticity, immediacy or vividness—the virtues usually associated with the presentation of impromptu thoughts—the iconic sequencing here effectively heightens the mood of desperation, an effectiveness partly attributable to the fact that in this novel the presented thoughts are normally well-formed, against which this disorder is foregrounded.

Given the differences in linguistic conventions between Chinese and English, the deviation involved in Lao's sequencing cannot be directly carried over into English. But its effect of heightening desperation can be conveyed by some functionally corresponding linguistic features, as one can see from (A). In this version, two commas are added (after "bridge" and "it"), which, allied to the choice of the adjunct "right now" as well as the use of the infinitive verbal form, make the thoughts appear psychologically immediate, structurally terse and emphatic, semantically incoherent and emotionally impulsive, all contributing to the mood of utmost desperation. No attempt, though, is found in (B) and (C) to convey the effect generated by Lao's deviant sequencing. In (B), the thoughts are presented by two independent sentences, with the sentence boundary marking a transition from the (intended) action to its (imagined) consequences, which constitutes a perfectly normal sequence. This, coupled with the replacement of the volitional "want" by the volitionally neutral "think about," leads to a perceptible reduction in impulsiveness and dramatic urgency. This regrettable loss

CHAPTER 7 ASPECTS OF SYNTAX   205

is shared by (C), a version marked by coherence and normal sequence. The point to stress is that deviant linguistic features in the source language may not be found deviant in the target language. It follows that, to preserve the iconic value or other kinds of stylistic values generated, the translator needs to use some other linguistic features in the target language which are functionally equivalent to those involved in the source language.

7.4 THE TRANSFERENCE OF PARALLELISM

In Chinese prose fiction, parallelism, in various forms, constitutes one of the most frequently found rhetorical devices. What underlies this frequency is, at the very basic level, Chinese as a language: its monosyllabic structure and its tonal system which cooperate to provide ideal soil for such a symmetrical structure as parallelism. While parallelism is used in European poetry, it occupies a much more prominent place in Chinese poetry where, instead of being a purely stylistic device, it often forms a semi-prosodic feature, required or expected in certain forms of poem, e.g. *lüshi*. In terms of Chinese prose, its early development was characterized for some long periods of time by the domination of *pianwen* which, literally translated, means parallel-composition. Tradition as such can however be overly or misleadingly stressed. In fact, Chinese prose fiction is usually written in *santi*, a prose style which does not require parallelism. What should be stressed, though, is that in Chinese narrative fiction, by virtue of the language combined with the tradition, parallelism appears to be more natural and to be more frequently employed than in English.

One of the novels that we are mainly concerned with, Cao's *A Dream of Red Mansions*, was written in the 18th century when *pianwen* (parallel-composition), though waning, was still an influential prose style. And it was adopted by Cao for, among other things, the description of the appearance of some characters. This style, marked by consistent rhythmical parallel structure and ornate figures of speech, is most certainly unfamiliar to, if not out of place in, 20th-century English fiction. Translation (A) therefore finds it necessary to render the description into poetic form, for example:

(A) As to his person, he had:
 a face like the moon of Mid-Autumn,
 a complexion like flowers at dawn,
 a hairline straight as a knife-cut,
 eyebrows that might have been painted by an artist's brush,
 a shapely nose, and
 eyes clear as limpid pools,
 that even in anger seemed to smile,
 and, as they glared, beamed tenderness the while.
 (Trans. Hawkes 1973:100—101)

Compare:

(B) His face was as radiant as the mid-autumn moon, his complexion fresh as spring flowers at dawn. The hair above his temples was as sharply outlined as if cut with a knife. His eyebrows were as black as if painted with ink, his cheeks as red as peach-blossom, his eyes bright as autumn ripples. Even when angry he seemed to smile, and there was warmth in his glance even when he frowned. (Trans. Yang and Yang 1978:46)

The layout of (A) forms a visual signal of poetry towards which the reader has a different set of expectations and in which Cao's ornate parallel figurative description, which is deviant in relation not only to English fiction but also to modern Chinese fiction, finds congenial accomodation. It may be worth noting that this change by (A) in genre-form constitutes part of a larger strategy to naturalize Cao, involving, among other things, the replacement of "Buddha" by "God," while no such effort is made by (B), whose aim is rather to introduce the differences in culture as well as in literary conventions. Each approach has of course its own justifications. The point to notice is that (A)'s choice of poetic form may be regarded as being a functionally equivalent form. As a means of 'naturalization,' it points to the possibility of neutralizing, up to a point, the differences in literary convention by resorting to genre-associated expectations. Adaptation of form may, nevertheless, sometimes lead to a regrettable loss of content, as is shown by the following case:

(A) (When they saw the pure translucent Stone which had shrunk to the size of a fan-pendant, the monk took it up on the palm of his hand and said to it with a smile: "You look like a precious object, but you still lack real value. I must engrave some characters on you so that people can see at a glance that you're something special.) Then we can take you to some civilized and prosperous *realm*, to a cultured *family* of official status, a *place* where flowers and willows flourish, the *home* of pleasure and luxury where you can settle down in comfort."
(Trans. Yang and Yang 1978:2; my emphasis)

(B) (...) After that I shall take you to a certain

                brilliant

                successful

                poetical

                cultivated

                aristocratic

                elegant

                delectable

                luxurious

                opulent

locality on a little trip.
(Trans. Hawkes 1973:48)

First, some contextual information needs to be given. The origin of Cao's novel (entitled by some versions *The Story of the Stone*) is attributed to a magic stone which is brought by a monk and a Taoist into the human world and whose account of its experience there constitutes the rudimentary version of the novel. The present passage (see A) depicts the monk's and Taoist's discovery of the magic stone and the monk's promise to take it to the human world. In the light of the context, it will have emerged that (A)'s "realm," "family," "place" and "home," which are closely translated from Cao, combine to refer to the major scene of the novel. As the first mention of the scene which is not gradually unfolded until some pages later, the four nominal groups (which are, in the original, strictly parallel to each other) take on psychological prominence, contextual importance, and, further, arouse in the reader a measure of suspense.

In version (B), Cao's four parallel nominal groups are rendered into a single one by means of the superordinate term "locality." It is not clear whether this substitution is motivated by a desire to use the quasi-poetic layout or whether the layout is necessitated by the substitution. If we assume that the latter is the case, the quasi-poetic layout certainly helps to make acceptable what is otherwise unacceptable. Compare the prose form:

> "... After that I shall take you to a certain brilliant, successful, poetical, cultivated, aristocratic, elegant, delectable, luxurious and opulent locality on a little trip."

In adopting the deviant layout, what (B) resorts to is perhaps not only conventional expectations associated with poetry but also those associated with such a register as advertisement, in which we frequently find the enumeration of attributes vertically set out. Now if we reverse the hypothesis and assume that the superordinate "locality" is used to pave the way for the deviant layout, the translator's purpose would then be seen as one of highlighting these epithets and, possibly, of giving the monk's utterance some supernatural flavour as well as of adding to this certain "locality" some mystical colour, which helps to heighten the reader's interest and, significantly, suspense.

These are desirable stylistic effects but seem to have been achieved at the expense of some content. According to an authoritative commentary (see the *Qi* version 4), Cao's four nominal groups refer to four different yet closely associated scenes: "bang" ("realm")—the capital city, "zu" ("family")—the Rong Mansion, "di" ("place")—the Grand View Garden, "xiang" ("home")—the Orchid Studio, with the latter three scenes situated in the first. Each nominal group—at least of the latter three—is in a sense used synecdochically and each therefore takes on a general reference superimposed on the specific. Because of the parallelism obtaining between the nominal groups (a feature more notable in Cao than in A), the general reference receives emphasis whereas the specific reference persists. Thus the reader is on the one hand given the impression that the four parallel nominal groups refer to (different aspects of) the same general locality while, on the other, being aware that each may refer to a different specific locality. The ambiguity or the interplay of the general and the specific, coupled with the interaction between the parallel general or specific references, gives rise to interest, suspense and, not least, a good deal of subtlety. Apparently, these multilayered stylistic effects are brought towards singleness in version (B), where the subtle interplay of the general and the specific is brought towards generality only. By this is meant that (B)'s adaptation of form involves not only a partial loss of content (the specific references) but also a loss of some desirable stylistic values.

Interestingly, parallelism is often characterized by circularity. It is true that, unless associated with desirable stylistic values, circularity as a feature in itself does not really deserve reproduction. But in cases where the circularity involved is consciously worked out to generate aesthetic or thematic effects, it may have a strong claim to preservation.

Such is the case with the following example taken from Lao She's *Rickshaw Boy*, where circularity plays an important part in artistically shaping the character's emotions:

(Lao) Youshihou *xinxi*, youshihou *zhaoji*, youshihou
/sometimes *happy*, sometimes *anxious*, sometimes

fanmen, youshihou wei *xinxi* er youyao cankui,
glum, sometimes for *happy*(iness) would feel ashamed,

youshihou wei *zhaoji* er youyao ziwei, youshihou
sometimes for *anxious*(ness) would console himself, sometimes

wei *fanmen* er youyao *xinxi*. Ganqing zai ta xinzhong
for *glum* (ness) would feel *happy*. /Emotions were *circling* in

raozhe yuanquan, ba ge zui jiandande ren naode bu zhidaole
his heart, which made this simplest of men unable

dong-nan-xi-bei.
to tell east from west or south from north. (chapter 19, emphasis mine; within// basically word-for-word translation)

(A) (She wouldn't let him work at night and wouldn't let him get a good night's sleep either. He was in a daze all day long, hadn't a thought in his head, and didn't know what to do.) Sometimes he was *happy*, sometimes he was *anxious*, sometimes he was *glum*. Sometimes he was *happy* and then ashamed of himself for being happy. Sometimes be was *anxious* and had to comfort himself because he was anxious. Sometimes he was *glum* and then had to *cheer himself up* because he was glum. Emotions revolved in his heart in circles and made this simplest of men so upset he couldn't tell east from west or south from north. (Trans. James 1979: 191; emphasis mine)

Compare:

(B) (...) He felt pleased, anxious and annoyed by turns, with sometimes a sense of guilt over his pleasure or of consolation in his anxiety. And being such a simple soul, these conflicting emotions made him lose his balance. (Trans. Shi 1981:192)

This passage (see the parentheses in A) depicts an impossible situation in which the protagonist, a poor rickshaw puller, finds himself. His wife is about to give birth to a child and becomes more demanding of both money and attention. After a day's hard toil, he only finds himself deprived of a good night's sleep by a trying wife. Thus the feeling of happiness at the prospect of becoming a father is mingled with financial worries, anxiousness and glumness. In Lao (and A), two sets of parallel clauses are used to form a circle ("happy"—"glum"—"happy"), a circle marked by ambiguity or paradox that comes largely from the consistent use of the adjunct "sometimes" and from the final parallel clause. Compare the following two alternatives:

(i) "sometimes" in the first set $>$ "sometimes" in the second
    "happy" (1) $>$ "happy" (2)   "happy" (1) $\neq$ "happy" (3)

(ii) "sometimes" in the first set $=$ "sometimes" in the second
    "happy" (1) $=$ "happy" (2) $=$ "happy" (3)

If the occurrences of "sometimes" in the first set of parallel clauses do not correspond to those in the second and if the first "happy" only partially overlaps the third (see i), the description is one of conflicting emotions. But if the instances of "sometimes" in the two sets share the same temporal references and if the first, second and the third "happy" can be equated with each other (see ii), "happy(iness)" would always be a result of glumness and always be accompanied by shame, in which case, the overall circle ostensibly displaying "happy(iness)" at the beginning, middle and end would be a combination of similarly unhappy feelings (notice Lao's use of "circling" versus B's "conflicting").

While one's experience of the world inclines one to adopt the former interpretation, the linguistic form—the lexical identity coupled with the structural parallelism—slants one towards the latter. Thus one decoding is superimposed on another, making for an impressionistic "as if": as if the protagonist's happiness were always caused by glumness and accompanied by shame and, further, as if the happy and unhappy feelings were all on the unhappy side. By virtue of subtly undermining "happiness" through the latter decoding, this well-wrought circle foreshadows the tragic birth (which involves the death of both mother and child) and, further, points to the underlying theme, namely, the disintegration of a rickshaw puller who "has to take the lowest place in the human world and wait for the blows from every person, every law and every hardship" (Lao 108).

It is surely regrettable that this artistic circle is lost in version (B) which not only leaves out the last parallel clause (one that plays a key role in forming the circle) but also combines the first set of parallel clauses into one clause while reducing the second to the position of adjunct. What results from this is a straightforward or transparent description. The reader is given the impression that the protagonist's happiness (or "pleasure") is no longer caused by any unhappy feeling and is definitely not always, though sometimes, accompanied by a sense of guilt. Notice the different effect achieved by version (A)[4] where the paired clauses leave room for ambiguity and make for the double decoding which subtly contributes to the underlying theme.

7.5 JUXTAPOSITION AND PSEUDO-SIMULTANEITY

In this section, attention will be directed to an interesting case in Lao She's *Rickshaw Boy*, where the writer uses deviantly close juxtaposition of verbs to generate pseudo-simultaneity:

(Lao) Zou,   dei kangzhe lazhe huo tuizhe bingmende
When marching, he had to carry pull or push the soldiers'

dongxi; zhanzhu,   ta dei qutiaoshui shaohuo wei
stuff; when they halted, he had to fetch water light fires feed

shengkou.
the pack animals.

(A) (He had been following the troops for days with sweat running down to his heels.) He was forced to carry or pull or push their stuff when they marched. He had to carry water, light fires, and feed the pack animals when they halted. (Trans. King 1946:85)

(B) When they were marching, he was either pulling or toting or pushing the property of the soldiers. When they halted, he had to carry water, make fires, and feed the animals. (Trans. James 1979:18)

What is conveyed here is the nonstop toil of the protagonist after he is seized by the warlord soldiers. The means used in Lao to heighten the effect is the deviant omission of punctuation marks: "carry pull" or "fetch water light fires feed the pack animals," whereby the successive or alternative processes are closely linked together, to the point of appearing somewhat like a single process. Thus there is found a paradox between singleness (one process) and diversity (different successive or alternative processes), with the former imposing a measure of pseudo-simultaneity on the latter. If the medium were film, a similar effect could be achieved by showing the successive or alternative processes simultaneously—each occupying a certain part of the screen (i.e. "split screen"), which, by virtue of the same paradox: singleness (one screen scene) versus diversity (with more than one scene on the screen), could generate, perhaps in a more striking manner, pseudo-simultaneity. It may be of interest to note that the paradox obtaining between the artistically generated simultaneity and the actual successiveness or alternativeness makes for a metaphorical "as if"—as if he were doing both or all of the things at the same time; and it is by virtue of the practical impossibility that the excessiveness of the toil is paradoxically intensified.

Lao's deviantly close juxtaposition fails to appear in the translations. What underlies this failure seems to be, among other things, the lack of precedent in English. Although the deviantly close juxtaposition is in a sense untranslatable, it seems worthwhile to present it here. The conventionalized association between textual distance and psychological distance is a feature shared by both (perhaps all) languages and is therefore an area that can be exploited for stylistic effects not only in Chinese but also in English (cf. Bolinger 1980:20; Leech & Short 1981:239—242).

In effect, insofar as intelligibility is concerned, the absence of punctuation marks does not, whether in Chinese or in English, pose a problem. But by convention, there have to be some textual gaps (in the shape of punctuation marks or conjunctions) to mark the boundaries between the juxtaposed processes; and the conventionalized reader automatically expects the presence of the gaps. That the omission of these markers or gaps results in a pseudo 'singleness' argues the fundamental fact that the psychological distance (in the reader) between the processes is in a sense contingent upon the textual distance between them. By this is meant that, over and above one's experience of the world, the text contains certain conventions which (or, more precisely, the subversion of which) may act on the reader's interpretative process. Given the following two sentences:

(i) He had to fetch water, light fires, and feed the pack animals

(ii) He had to fetch water light fires feed the pack animals

the experience conveyed remains the same, but in (ii) the textual convention suggests that "fetch water light fires feed the pack animals" be interpreted as one process while the reader's world-experience says otherwise. It is this double decoding that produces subtle stylistic effects (compare the single decoding in (i) where the role of textual distance does not come into play). As distinct from the more central kinds of grammatical deviation, the matter here is a straightforward correspondence between the reduction of the textual distance and the reduction of the psychological distance. But the strategy in this kind of deviation is primarily the same as that employed elsewhere, which is to defeat, in the first place, the reader's conventional expectations.

Now, summarizing the above analyses of syntax and lexis (only the "formal" cases or cases marked by an interaction between the formal and the existential principles), I would like to discuss briefly the relation between linguistic form and fictional reality.

7.6 LINGUISTIC FORM AND FICTIONAL REALITY

The relation between linguistic form and fictional reality in narrative is essentially a relation between the narrative discourse and the narrated story. This relation is composed of similarity and of contrast: the similarity, if involving conscious manipulation, is usually embodied by the deliberate use of linguistic form to imitate the fictional reality, while the contrast typically displays an effort to exploit linguistic form to shape the experience depicted.

7.6.1 Imitating the Fictional Reality

Representing "linguistic mimesis" in the narrow sense, the schema involved in this aspect is basically one of matching, such as the use of the heavy premodification to enact the laborious and lengthy nature of the process involved (7.3.1). The stylistic effect here comes from the author's deliberately manipulating linguistic form to achieve such a correspondence and from the reader's realization of the existence of such a correspondence, which may lead to a new awareness of the iconic potential in language.

The correspondence between syntax and reality which we have been examining is fairly straightforward. This is to be attributed largely to the fact that the reality against which the syntax is judged is in itself readily comprehensible. When the reality involved becomes more elusive, the syntactic schemata used to enact the reality may become highly subtle or highly complex. This is in general more typical of poetry than of prose fiction (with, of course, the exception of such experimental novelists as Woolf or Joyce).

7.6.2 Shaping the Fictional Reality

As indicated by the analyses above, in literary discourse, linguistic form may go beyond the point of matching the reality to the point of shaping the reality. In 7.1, it was shown how pace could, for this or that thematic purpose, be rhetorically hastened or slowed down. Even more striking is the pseudo-simultaneity discussed in 7.5 where the deviantly close juxtaposition "fetch water light fires feed the pack animals" results in a metaphorical "as if": as if he were doing all of the things at the same time. No less interesting is the last example discussed under 7.4 where we saw how circularity generated by parallelism, coupled with semantic ambiguity, operates subtly to undermine the protagonist's happiness.

In the preceding chapter, attention was also drawn to certain of the ways in which lexical form could be used to shape the reality. If the antithetical "unfortunate enough to win" functions somehow to alter the nature of the winning process as such (6.1.1), the contradictory "except for those creatures who wander in the night, all was asleep. Hua Laoshuan suddenly sat up in bed" is seen dramatically to intensify the unexpectedness of the character's action (6.1.3), while, more interestingly, the use of the complementary "he constantly saw some shadows of ghosts, as if they were really there," in place of "as if he constantly saw some shadows of ghosts," seems to go some way towards objectifying the character's hallucination (6.1.2).

As distinct from imitating, in cases of shaping the reality, what is conveyed by the linguistic form is a meaning over and above that of fictional events as such. It is worth stressing that the relation obtaining between the linguistic form and the fictional reality here is, instead of one of correspondence, one of divergence or contrast. If, both in imitating and in shaping the reality, the reader has a double decoding, the nature of the double decoding in imitating is seen to differ fundamentally from that in shaping. In the former case, the decoding of form reinforces the decoding of the experience depicted (e. g. the heavy premodification reinforces the laborious nature of the process concerned) whereas in the latter case, the decoding of form conditions the decoding of the reality involved (e. g. the pseudo-simultaneity implied by syntax conditions the reader's interpretation of successive events). The typical effect which comes from the latter double decoding is paradox, due to the fact that, say, one's world experience suggests successiveness whereas the linguistic form makes for simultaneity. The correlation between the two decodings often, if not always, results in a paradoxical "as if," say, as if the successive events were happening at the same time. And it is through the paradoxical "as if" that the immediate thesis or the underlying theme is subtly yet emphatically conveyed.

Now in other kinds of representational art such as film, painting or photography, various techniques are available in terms of shaping versus imitating reality. In film, for instance, there exist such devices as special shot, trick shot or slow motion. Within the linguistic domain, the means used to shape reality can take the form of deviations from various conventions (which, though, may also be used as means of imitating the reality). In the lexical cases just referred to, the effects are ascribable to the violation of the relevant rules, i. e., to contradiction, exaggeration or the splitting of one statement into two complementary ones. In this chapter, I have tried to draw attention particularly to the deviation that operates on the syntactic shape and to the way that such deviation acts, by virtue of the resulting psychological effects, upon the reality depicted.

The point to notice is that, whatever the linguistic form involved, it is used here to colour the represented phenomenon by creating an additional decoding with which the phenomenon is not usually associable. It is this artistically produced, superimposed decoding that in particular embodies the authorial point of view (either directly or derivatively—as in the case of first-person narration), that takes on thematic significance and that accounts for stylistic values.

7.6.3 Imitating or Shaping?

In interpreting a realistic novel (which forms my major concern), one can normally assume that the fictional world is in a sense isomorphic with the real world and one is therefore able to use one's experience of the world as a criterion. Indeed, it would make little sense to draw a dichotomy between "the fictional reality" and "the value suggested by linguistic form" in such a case like:

> I am the enemy you killed, my friend... (Owen)

where it also makes no sense to draw a distinction between imitating and shaping the reality: a distinction that can, though, be drawn hypothetically without difficulty in the case of realistic prose fiction. But this is only a hypothesis. Even in realistic fiction, the borderline between imitating and shaping is frequently covered up by different degrees of overlap found between the two. Take the case of "redundant encoding" discussed in 6.4.2 for an example:

> It took one year, two years, at least three or four years, and one drop of sweat, two drops of sweat, who knows how many millions of drops of sweat, until the struggle produced a rickshaw.

On the face of it, the writer is trying to represent faithfully the process of time passing or sweating. But is there no effort made to shape the reality? I have already discussed the way that the significance of each drop of sweat is magnified—not only by counting what is in a sense uncountable or by recording literally what is in a sense metaphorical but also by borrowing semantic strength from "one year, two years." It is easy to imagine that the same effect can be achieved in film or photography by a close-up.

In effect, apart from the magnification, the semantic contrast obtaining between "one drop of sweat, two drops of sweat" and "who knows how many millions of drops of sweat" also makes for subtly shaping the reality, since the abrupt switch from a close-up of the initial process to an overall summary involves presenting the reality from a specific angle and directing the reader's interpretation in a particular way. Here it seems worth stressing once again that the whole matter is in essence one of convention. If the switch from a description of the initial process to an overall summary were a way of presentation that is conventionalized, then there would be no element of shaping involved. For the interpretative process would then be automatized. The point may become more apparent if we have another look at Conrad's:

> She saw there an object. That object was the gallows. She was afraid of the gallows.

If the presentational mode always went as, say, "He saw there a man. That man was John" or "He saw there an animal. That animal was a cat," it would make no sense to talk in Conrad's case about the effect of *slowing down* the perception process (see 6.4.1). Indeed, such is the working of language and such is the relationship between language and reality. Simply by spelling out what is normally or conventionally presupposed, the automatized interpretative process may be disturbed, which in turn may bear on the reality depicted. It is worth stressing that, in narrative fiction, the shaping effects of linguistic form, which are usually thematically-motivated and which directly or derivatively embody the authorial point of view, are of great artistic significance and have therefore a strong claim to preservation in translation.

CHAPTER 8

SPEECH AND THOUGHT PRESENTATION

In narrative fiction, a character's speech/thought may appear in a range of reporting modes, through which "language reveals its different functions" (Banfield 1982: 23). The contrast between these modes primarily in terms of the communicative and expressive functions enables these paradigmatically-related forms to provide effective means for the novelist to vary point of view, tone and distance. Because of the differences of linguistic and literary conventions between languages, the interlingual conveyance of the character's speech/ thought may at times be subjected to the constraint that no equivalent mode in the target language is available—or if available, the resulting literary effect may be quite different. The demand upon the translator is therefore not only that of acquiring a full awareness of the different functions or effects taken on by the reporting modes, but also that of being ready to make contextual adjustments when called for.

In contrast to the sustained investigation made of intralingual speech/thought presentation, no critical attention seems to have been paid to its interlingual transference. The discussion here seeks to offer some fresh insights into the contrastive functions or effects associated with the different reporting modes and into the relevant literary conventions which condition the writer/translator's choice; and, in a more general sense, into the way in which fictional discourse is organized. Given the special need of translation, attention will also be directed to some more basic problems of style, such as the functional correspondence between reporting verbs.

8.1 BASIC MODES IN ENGLISH

In English, the traditional dichotomy: direct speech (DS) versus indirect speech (IS) has been found inadequate to give a satisfactory coverage of the diversified types of speech presentation. Free direct speech (FDS) and free indirect speech (FIS), which have been developing in English fiction at least since the 19th century, were added around the 1960's (following the earlier practice of French stylisticians) to the categorical framework (cf. Banfield 1982:228ff. ; Gregory 1965: 43; Jones 1968:163). Further systematic subdivision and expansion are made by Page (1973:35) who offers a framework composed of eight types: from DS to "slipping." A neater, though less elaborate, distinction is found in Leech and Short (1981:344) where five basic modes are presented as follows:

		NORM			
Speech presentation:	NRSA	IS	FIS	DS	FDS
Thought presentation:	NRTA	IT	FIT	DT	FDT
		NORM			

(NRSA = Narrative report of speech act, T = Thought; for exemplification, see note 1)

As distinct from Page's analysis, this arrangement from NRSA to FDS forms a neat cline with a gradual decrease in the narrator's interference and a progressive increase in immediacy. I shall adopt this categorization made by Leech and Short, but meanwhile, for the sake of economy, follow Page in treating speech and thought presentation together (referred to as "S" and "T" respectively when necessary).

It should be made clear that I do not wish, by adopting Leech and Short's classification, to commit myself to their underlying criterion for determining free indirect speech—"that features from any of the three major linguistic levels might be instrumental in indicating that a

CHAPTER 8 SPEECH AND THOUGHT PRESENTATION 223

particular sentence is in FIS" (1981:331). They offer two examples to illustrate their contention:

(1) He said that the bloody train had been late.
(2) He told her to leave him alone!

Here, the only features which show that we are dealing with FIS are the swear word in the first sentence and the exclamation mark in the second. Neither of these forms are normally used by narrators in novels, and so inevitably evoke the character's manner of expression.

I would prefer to follow Page (1973) and call such sentences "coloured" indirect speech. For the application of FIS to (1) and (2) which exhibit subordination is somewhat misleading, since it is the suppression of subordination that, as systematically investigated and linguistically formalized by Banfield, enables FIS to "develop as a form distinct from either indirect or direct speech" (1982:233).

Interestingly, " coloured " indirect speech, whose subordinate clause retains certain embeddable lexical or graphological features expressive of the quoted speaker's subjectivity or viewpoint, is frequently found in both English and Chinese narrative fiction.[2] But unfortunately, this reporting mode lies outside Banfield's generalization of 1E/1 SELF (1982:93), which is, though, supposed to cover all reporting modes. According to Banfield, a sentence of indirect speech constitutes a single E (to be understood as expression), with the quoted clause forming an embedded S. "Since the SELF is related to the node E," Banfield asserts, "indirect speech may not introduce in its quoted S a new SELF" (93 — 94). In other words, if embeddable expressive lexical items, like "bloody" in the present case, occur in indirect speech, "the attitude they express is ascribed to the speaker of the entire E and not to the quoted speaker" (55). It seems to me that this point only holds good for an interactive communicative context; and in narrative in particular, holds good for a context in which the quoting speaker is in himself or herself a character or a dramatized narrator. It does not apply to the narrative context in which the quoting speaker is an impersonal authorial narrator since the quoting speaker as such is unlikely to call a train in the fictional world "bloody" or to call a character "the idiot of a doctor" or "a peach of a girl" (compare Banfield, 52—57). If the authorial narrator reports:

(a) John said that the idiot of a doctor was impossible.
(b) Oedipus said that his Momma was beautiful.

"the idiot of a doctor" in (a) and "Momma" in (b) can only be said, in such a narrative context, to express the viewpoint of "John" and "Oedipus" respectively. The two sentences can be seen as typical examples of what we call "coloured" indirect speech, where a new SELF is introduced in the quoted S. It is clear that there are in every reporting mode two potential SELVES: the SELF of the reported/original speaker and the SELF of the reporting speaker. In indirect speech, the reported SELF is usually suppressed due, among other things, to the subordination (which excludes non-embeddable expressive elements) and the conventionalized neutral reporting style. But if the reporting speaker forsakes the neutral reporting style and retains certain lexical or graphological features expressive of the quoted speaker's subjectivity, a new SELF may naturally appear in the quoted S. [3]

8.2 BASIC MODES IN CHINESE

In Chinese narrative fiction, not only exist all the basic modes appearing in western narrative fiction, but also there are found certain modes lying between or outside western classifications. A most notable feature of Chinese is that it is free from verbal tense indicators. In this language, that is to say, there is no "backshift" in tense when the mode shifts from a direct to an indirect one, nor is the subordinating conjunction "that" or capitalization used. So except for the personal pronoun, which is sometimes left out in Chinese, a language characterized by frequent subject and determiner omission, there can be no perceivable linguistic difference between indirect speech and the speech in quotation marks. This means that indirect speech can sometimes pass for free direct speech (i.e. the type which differs from direct speech only in terms of being free from quotation marks), or vice versa.[4] To avoid confusion, such a peculiar mode of speech, one that is liable to two or more interpretations, requires a new name which I consider proper to call BLEND (see Shen 1991:397).

It should be noted that blend also occurs in English, where, however, it seems to be limited to two particular cases. One is that of a moodless clause (or a clause with a tenseless modal verb) which may be liable to the interpretation of either free indirect speech or free direct speech (especially when immediately preceded by free indirect speech). The other case involves the ambiguity between authorial statement and free indirect speech: when the tense and the pronoun selection are appropriate to either, both interpretations become possible (see Leech & Short 1981:338—340). In Chinese, these two kinds of English blend have their counterparts which, nevertheless, do not in themselves present any difficulty for the translator and are therefore to be left aside.[5] What concerns us here are the 'finite' Chinese sentences which, by virtue of being free from verbal tense indicators, frequently give rise to a two-ways or three-ways ambiguous mode. But of course the ambiguity arises only when other formal discriminating features are absent, particularly, when the pronoun is omitted, for example:

Ta youyule yi xia. Ta dui ziji shuo kanlai gao cuole.
He hesitated for a moment. He said to himself (I/he) seem/seemed to be wrong.

(see Shen 1991:396—397)

This can be seen as a blend of Indirect Speech and Free Direct Speech (free from quotation marks). In Chinese, blend is not only frequent in occurrence but also rich in variety. It mainly falls into three types: Indirect Speech/Free Indirect Speech; Free Indirect Speech/Free Direct Speech; Narrative Report/Free Indirect Thought/Free Direct Thought (for their exemplification and transference, see below).

8.3 THE TRANSFERENCE OF BLEND

In the case of a Chinese blend, the reported speech is integrated into the narration while being free from positive features of the narrator's interference (i. e., can be quoted), for the simple fact that it can be taken to be both in the direct and the indirect mode. The Chinese blends, that is to say, have the advantage of taking on immediacy without hindering the smooth narrative flow. In translating into English, however, the absent tense indicators have to be supplied by the translator, who is often placed in a dilemma. To preserve the immediacy of speech (or thought) by translating a blend into the present tense is to raise it immediately out of the narrative plane which is normally translated into the past tense. To keep a blend on the narrative plane by using the past tense means on the other hand the loss of vividness and immediacy. Things are sometimes made more awkward as the omitted subjects, objects or determiners have to be spelled out in English either as the first/second person (hence away from the narrator's reporting voice) or the third-person (possibly away from the character's voice). That is to say, while both voices are potentially contained in the original by virtue of being indistinguishable in terms of formal linguistic criteria, one voice has to be favoured in English at the expense of the other.

8.3.1 The Transference of the Blend of Indirect Speech and Free Direct Speech (Without Quotation Marks)

In Lu Xun's "The True Story of Ah Q," there are twenty-three instances of this kind of blend, which are dealt with in different ways by its two translations.[6]

	IS	FIS	DS
Version (A):	14	2	7
Version (B):	18	4	1

What strikes one here is the absence of Free Direct Speech (free from quotation marks), which is one of the two modes potentially contained in the original. Clearly this is not because the translator always finds the alternative Indirect Speech more satisfactory; rather, if s/he finds Indirect Speech unsatisfactory, s/he would choose Direct Speech or Free Indirect Speech instead. Such treatment in effect commonly occurs in translations. This may be accounted for in part by the fact that this kind of blend forms a norm of presentation in Chinese, while the type of Free Direct Speech in question, which differs from Direct Speech only in terms of the omission of inverted commas, seems to be of much rarer occurrence in English. Thus in terms of norm for norm, it is not surprising that the translator prefers the more normal Direct Speech or Free Indirect Speech. Equally important, in the interest of smooth narrative flow, the translator usually will not choose a direct form unless immediacy and vividness are seen to deserve priority. And if such priority arises, Direct Speech, with its inverted commas serving as invitations to an auditory experience, certainly offers more emphasis and impact than the type of Free Direct Speech concerned.

Although Indirect Speech is frequently chosen by both translations, (A) differs from (B) in that if there is more than one reported clause, (A) tends to omit the subordinator "that" (especially after the first clause), thus letting the mode slip from Indirect Speech into Free Indirect Speech. Compare for instance the following:

> (A) All who heard of this said Ah Q was a great fool to ask for a beating like that. Even if his surname *were* Chao—which wasn't likely—he should have known better than to boast like that when there was a Mr. Chao living in the village. (79)

(B) All those who heard about this incident agreed that Ah Q had invited the thrashing by his own impudence, that his surname was probably not Chao, and that even if it had been, he should not have been so presumptuous as to talk the way he did. (79)

By virtue of the omission and the slipping in question, (A) notably reduces the narrator's interference, thereby enabling the speech to gain briskness and vividness (which is of course also attributable to the colloquial lexical forms). (A)'s treatment is, in effect, more in line with the original mode which starts in the blend Indirect Speech/Free Direct Speech and then slips, due to the fact that in Chinese there is no subordinator to indicate parallel subordination, into a blend of Free Indirect Speech/Free Direct Speech, a mode that carries even less potential interference from the narrator. The omission of "that" seems to point to a larger issue in dealing with the Chinese blends, namely, when an indirect form is chosen, how to keep the narrator's interference to the minimum. This results because in all Chinese blends, as far as the reported speech is con-cerned, the narrator's interference is only of *potential* existence (no "that," no visible back-shift in tense or remote-shift in person), which normally does not affect the vividness and immediacy typical of the direct mode. Thus, if the translation can take on the virtues of the indirect as well as, to some extent, the direct form, it can offer a better representation of the peculiar mode in the original.

8.3.2 The Transference of the Blend of Free Indirect and Free Direct Speech/Thought

This kind of blend is more frequently found in thought presentation. In translation, one of the potentially contained modes, the free indirect one, is constantly given priority over the other. For instance, in Mao Dun's short story "The Shop of the Lin Family," fourteen cases of this kind of blend are found, which are translated by Shapiro invariably into the free indirect mode. This preference may be accounted for in part by the virtues of the free indirect mode, one that "offers the novelist the opportunity to combine some of the separate advantages of both the direct and the indirect form" (Page 1973:36); and in part by the consequences of raising the speech/thought out of the narrative plane, an act that, apart from breaking the narrative flow, may, by clearly marking off the character's voice from that of the narrator's, involve the loss of subtlety:

(Mao): Lin xiansheng xinli yi tiao, zanshi huida bu chulai.
Mr Lin's heart gave a leap, for the moment he couldn't answer.

Suiran shi qiba nian de lao huoji,
Although Shousheng has/had been my/his salesman for seven or eight years

yixiang meiyou chuguo chazi,
and has/had never made a slip,

dan shui neng bao daodi ne!
still, there is/was no absolute guarantee!

Both the free indirect and the free direct mode can be derived with equal probability from the original. The choice facing the translator is clearly one between subtlety (free indirect) and immediacy (free direct). In the former case, the absence of manifest features of thought presentation[7] enables the narrator to slip inconspicuously from narrative statement to interior portrayal, while in the latter case the reader is given direct access to the character's consciousness. By the latter is meant the narrator's complete detachment from the character's thought, which may not be desirable in this particular context where the narrator deeply empathizes with the character. In Shapiro's choice of the free indirect form, through remote-shift in person and back-shift in tense, the distance between the narrator and the character is, compared with the free direct form, perceptibly shortened. "The tinting of the narrator's speech with the character's language also promotes an empathetic identification on the part of the reader" (Rimmon-Kenan 1983:114). The effect which results from this is, notably, the heightening of suspense. For here the worried party is not only the character (the self-centred "my") but also the interpreting narrator and, probably, the reader.

Although the free indirect mode presents some advantages, in certain contexts, the free direct mode seems to be a more suitable choice. This is especially so when the speech or thought, typically containing exclamations or rhetorical questions, is emotively charged and when the pronoun or deictic selection is appropriate to both modes (where therefore the immediacy of the free direct form can be gained with less cumbrous "gear-shifting"). Under such circumstances, whichever mode is chosen, the impulsive voice of the character is marked off from that of the narrator, so there is none of that subtlety which comes from the merging of the two voices involved, while on the other hand the immediacy of the free direct form is particularly desirable, as in the following (taken from Mao's "Spring Silkworms"):

Mao: Dan dang lao Tong Bao qiaoqiaode ba nage "mingyun" de
But when Old Tong Bao secretly took another look at his

da suantou na qilai kan shi, tade lianse like bianle! Da
"luck" garlic, he immediately turned pale! It had

suantou shanghai zhi de sansi jing nenya! Tian na!
grown only three or four tender shoots! Heavens!

Nandao you tong qunian yiyang?
Will/Would this year be like last year all over again? (italics indicate its being rhetorical and emphatic)

Shapiro: But when the old man secretly took another look at his garlic, he turned pale! It had grown only four measly shoots! Ah! Would this year be like last year all over again?

Mao's passage strikes one as being highly dramatized. Apart from the

CHAPTER 8   SPEECH AND THOUGHT PRESENTATION   231

outward tokens of emotive involvement ("!"s, "heavens" etc.), the dramatic impact is ascribable to the order in which information is presented. More specifically, the cause ("It had grown ...") is held back and given after part of the effect:

| Part of the effect→ | Cause→ | Part of the effect |
| ("he immediately turned pale") | ("It had grown only ...) | ("Heavens! Will/Would ...) |

What results from this presentational sequencing is on the one hand suspense and, on the other hand, the simultaneity of the effects: the blend appears to be uttered at the same time as the face turns pale, which hastens psychologically the appearance of the already impulsive blend. The narrator is, at this moment, a highly involved witness, who seems little prepared to interfere and who thus lets the character's words burst out, interrupting the flow of narrative. This is only another way of saying that, in this context, the free direct mode, where the switch to the present tense may not appear unnatural, seems to form a more suitable choice.

8.3.3 The Transference of the Blend: Narrative Report/Free Indirect Thought/Free Direct Thought

The three-way ambiguity makes the blend take on the combined features of Free Indirect Thought/Free Direct Thought and the blend of Narrative Report/Free Indirect Thought. Like the blend of Narrative Report/Free Indirect Thought, it leaves it open whether it is made up of the narrator's statement or of the inner thoughts of a character. As regards the latter, there is, furthermore, no way of telling whether it consists of actual words spoken or reported by the narrator. The overall effect is one of indeterminacy and subtlety.

If the translator selects a tense (past), pronoun (third-person), and a style appropriate both to Narrative Report and Free Indirect Thought, the mode will remain two-way ambiguous, its virtue lying in its preservation of the subtle merging of the two voices, in providing an access to the character's mind without breaking the narrative flow. Given the same tense and pronoun selection, a relatively neutral or formal reporting style may incline the reader to take the mode as the narrator's statement instead of the blend Narrative Report/ Free Indirect Thought, which may involve some loss of subtlety (cf. A in the case below). The subtlety will be totally lost if the mode chosen is Free Direct Thought (with of course a gain in immediacy), or if the translator attributes the blend to the character concerned by means of a reporting clause, as (B) does in the following case:

(Cao) Zhengzai tingshang xuanzhuan,　　　zen de ge ren
1. He was pacing helplessly around the hall, 2. how to get
wang litou shao xin,
someone to take a message to the inner apartments, 3. (but)

pianpiande mei ge ren lai,　　　　　　　lian Pei-ming
it has to happen that nobody comes just now, 4. even Pei-ming
it had to happen that nobody came just then, even Pei-ming
it so happened that nobody came just then, even Pei-ming

ye buzhi zai nali. (chapter 33)
is nowhere to be found.
was nowhere to be found.
was nowhere to be found.

(A) 1. —and as he stood where his father had left him, he twisted and turned himself about, 2. anxiously looking for some passer-by who could take a message through to the womenfolk inside. 3. But no one came. 4. Even the omnipresent Tealeaf was on this occasion nowhere to be seen. (Trans. Hawkes)
(B) 1. There he still stood in the pavilion, 2. revolving in his mind how he could get some one to speed inside and deliver a message for him. 3. But, as it happened, not a soul appeared.

CHAPTER 8   SPEECH AND THOUGHT PRESENTATION   233

> 4. He was quite at a loss to know where even Pei Ming could be. (Trans. Joly)

In Cao's clause 2, the "wh-" question, whose implication is clearly on the lines of "he was wondering how to get ... ," leads one to infer that the narrator/focalizer has now penetrated into the inner life of the character. When it comes to 3 and 4, two possibilities emerge: on the one hand, the narrator/focalizer seems still within the consciousness of the focalized (Free Direct Thought/Free Indirect Thought); but on the other hand, 3 and 4 seem to form outer description (Narrative Report) perceived from a perspective shared by the empathetic narrator and the character. By the latter is meant that the narrator's spatial focalization is for the moment changed from the bird's-eye view to that of a limited observer which goes no further than the character's perception. The effect is twofold. As far as the narrator is concerned, the limited internal focalization makes him directly involved, which is reflected in the fretful tone underlying "it so happened" "even. ... " As for the reader, the narrator's limitation destroys momentarily his/her conventional security—the belief that the narrator is in the know (given, of course, the overall omniscient mode of narration), adding a good deal to the effect of suspense.

In translation (A), the narrator's voice dominates the scene, which becomes notable in 2 where Cao's Free Indirect Thought (how to get ...) is rendered through the mode of narratorial statement ("looking for some passer-by ... "). The reader is consequently taken out of the direct experience of the character's thought and is shown instead the state of the character's mind. This change somehow limits 3 and 4 to the single mode of Narrative Report (as opposed to Cao's blend), a mode confirmed by the fairly formal style ("omnipresent," "on this occasion"). It is worth noting that the single mode of Narrative Report offers a good chance to heighten suspense. In contrast with Cao, where the narrator's limitation is, after all, an alternative possibility,

(A)'s narrator is obviously adopting limited internal focalization, i. e., he is, like the character, clearly not in the know. However, this opportunity is not fully exploited by (A), where the emphatic "it so happened that" is omitted, making the narrator appear less involved.

In terms of suspense, (B)'s choice of Indirect Thought in rendering 4 seems quite unwise. The shared restricted perspective (Cao & A) is ascribed by (B) explicitly to the character alone ("he was quite at a loss to know where …"). This leads one to infer that the narrator's focalization is still external, i. e., the narrator is in the know. Such an inference may condition one's interpretation of the preceding clause, thereby failing to destroy the reader's conventional security in both places. Clearly what matters most in this case is not an access to the character's consciousness but the dramatic effect of suspense; and it is the empathetic narrator's voice that deserves emphasis. Indeed, as the cases discussed above also show, in translating a blend, priority, i. e., what to exploit, is largely determined by context; to some extent, by literary effects as such that go beyond a simple dichotomy between smoothness and immediacy.

8. 4 THE TRANSFERENCE OF DIRECT SPEECH

Direct Speech is "the most purely mimetic type of report" (McHale 1978: 259). Being "actual words spoken," this mode not only reproduces the communicative and expressive functions of the reported speech act but also enables the novelist to bring into full play the character's idiolectal features. It therefore contributes to characterization in a more distinctive and dramatic manner than Indirect Speech. Even when it is used mainly to advance plot, it takes on an immediacy and a direct impact not found in Indirect Speech (cf. Banfield 1982; Page 1973).

Interestingly, Direct Speech is almost exclusively used in classical

Chinese novels. This is ascribable to the fact that in classical Chinese fiction, there are no quotation marks, no comma or full stop, or punctuation of any kind. In addition, there is no paragraph division. The author usually uses a character's actual words to distinguish them from narrative report. To avoid confusion, a reporting clause ("X said") frequently has to be introduced before the reported speech. Because of the differences in linguistic and literary conventions between Chinese and English, coupled with the chronological differences, the translation of Direct Speech from those novels into modern or contemporary English calls for many necessary adaptations. In what follows, attention will be directed to the use of Direct Speech in a representative classical Chinese novel-Cao Xueqin's A *Dream of the Red Mansions* (*Honglou Meng*, written in the middle of the eighteenth century) and the corresponding modes chosen in its three translations: (A) (1973—1980), (B) (1978), (C) (1892—1893). [8]

8.4.1 From Direct Speech to Direct Speech

In Cao, the reader often can identify the characters by the words they utter, with the words playing an essential role in revealing the characters' inner selves or temperaments. And it is the mode of Direct Speech (as opposed to the less direct modes) that provides a full scope for the individual tone and expression. With a few exceptions, Cao's Direct Speech is rendered by the translations into Direct Speech. But some adaptations are necessary.

Specification of the Reporting Verb

In early Chinese prose, normally only one superordinate reporting verb "yue" is used, which can be rendered in English by "say," "ask," "reply," "exclaim" etc. Although by Cao's time the number of reporting verbs had increased, there were still many fewer than in English. And the term "dao"—an equivalent to the earlier "yue"—still takes on a superordinate function, thus calling for specification in English. In

Cao's Chapter Fifteen, forty one "dao"s are used, which are rendered by (A) into "put in," "observe," "inquire," "broach," "speak entreatingly," "mimick," "accede;" and by (B) into "remark," "answer," "whisper," "observe," "rejoin," "caution," "demur," "explain," "ask," "reply," "plead," "demand;" and by (C) into "explain," "observe," "reply," "expostulate," "remark," "ask," "rejoin," "exclaim," "suggest," "add," "hint," "remonstrate," "retort," "plead."

The specification provides stylistic variety. It should be noted that Cao's text is marked by ornate description and a dramatic tendency, against which the constant use of "say" in English where a large number of reporting verbs is available would appear very monotonous. Further, the specification facilitates the decoding process. As distinct from Cao's eighteenth-century Chinese readers, who had to be content with the superordinate "dao" (say), the English reader tends to lean more heavily on the reporting verb for information. More specific terms such as "demand," "explain," "expostulate" serve to direct the reader's interpretation, while "mimick," "whisper," "exclaim," etc. provide the reader with paralinguistic qualities of the speech. In addition, the more or less diatypicalized reporting verbs like "observe" (formal), "caution" (legal) may in certain contexts point to the social function of the interlocutors and to the nature of the speech.

Repositioning the Reporting Clause

In classical Chinese novels, the reporting clause invariably precedes the reported speech. This, if strictly rendered into English, where inversion is commonplace, would result in monotony and, possibly, incongruity. To achieve a functional correspondence, inversion is frequently adopted by Cao's three translators. Now, certain advantages of inversion seem to be worth mentioning. First, inversion lends itself to the effect of speech cutting into action or speech directly responding to speech, e. g. :

"In that case," said Xi-feng, "I'll send for her straight away."

"Please do," said Bao-yu. and started to go.

"Hey, come back," said Xi-feng. "I haven't finished with you yet."(A, vol. 2:50)

Thus, it is not surprising that such reporting verbs as "put in," "exclaim" are often accompanied by inversion, with the latter intensifying the abruptness or impulsiveness of the speech. Furthermore, by placing the comment clause[9] after the speech (or interrupting it), inversion enables the presentation to attain a higher degree of mimesis. For it is more natural to comment on something when it has oc curred than to give a comment before its appearance (unless on a hypothetical entity). Closely related to this is the reduction of the narrator's interference. As the reported speech has already been partially or totally presented, the comment clause, now having lost its reporting function (but retaining a commenting role), is made psychologically less prominent. Finally, in some contexts where there is more than one potential speaker, the fact that the speech appears before the speaker is identified may momentarily give rise to an element of suspense, which may heighten the reader's interest and add to the vividness of the description. Given these advantages, it is not surprising that inversion has come to be frequently used by many modern Chinese writers.

Paragraphing the Reported Speech

Paragraph division is not seen in Cao, as in classical Chinese prose in general. Although its modern editions are paragraphed, almost no paragraphing takes place within the inverted commas. Now, one's reluctance to paragraph speech is perhaps associated with mimesis. As paragraph division belongs typically to the written convention, its introduction into spoken words (though recorded on paper) may lead to artificiality. It is interesting to observe that in Cao's English contemporary, Fielding's Tom Jones, paragraphing occurs, though only occasionally, in speech. For instance, Mrs. Fitzpatrick's narrative speech is paragraphed (Book Ⅱ: chapters 4 & 5) and so is Mr. Allworthy's speech:

> Allworthy then gently squeezed his hand, and proceeded thus. "I am convinced, my child, that you have much goodness, generosity and honour in your temper; ...
> "One thousand pound I have given to you, Mr Thwackum; a sum, I am convinced, which greatly exceeds your desires, ...
> "A like sum, Mr Square, I have bequeathed to you. ..."
> (for the full version, see Penguin edition, 228)

where the paragraph division indicates the change of addressee and highlights the parallelism between the chunks of speech. It may also be possible that instead of a monologue, what is represented is actually a dialogue, with the intervening responses omitted and with the paragraph division marking the beginning of a new speech act.[10] But of course, paragraphing might be attributable to the publisher rather than to the author.

In Cao's translations, long speech is, with varying frequency, paragraphed. The paragraphed speech is either of a narrative or expository nature or just ordinary daily speech. Now, apart from its normal role of indicating topic shifts (cf. Brown & Yule, 1983:95— 100), paragraph division in speech seems to take on some additional function. In narrative (especially third-person) or expository (especially impersonal) speech, the intermittent inverted commas can serve to remind the reader that it is the character's voice as opposed to the narrator's. Thus paragraph division in speech which is, at least with reference to English, always accompanied by inverted commas may have the virtue of highlighting a different point of view, consequently helping the narrator to achieve, in a more striking manner, a measure of detachment. Furthermore, in ordinary daily speech, the intervening which usually indicates the beginning of a new speech act may give the reader something of the false impression that a new speech act is occurring (particularly so in a context where the reporting clause is frequently omitted). This may help to keep up or stimulate the reader's interest, hence serving as an effective remedy for any boredom that results from "the tendency to diffuseness inherent in the use of direct speech" (Page 1973:30).

8.4.2 From Direct Speech (DS) to Indirect Speech (IS) or Narrative Report of Speech Act (NRSA)

Having examined the direct transference from DS to DS, we turn to the more oblique transference from DS to IS or NRSA. It is important to note that Cao's text is written at a time (18th century) when the art of fiction, being far from technical maturity, still leans most heavily on the story-telling and the dramatic tradition (compare Page 1973: 25ff.). Being conceived very much in oral or dramatic terms, certain of Cao's DS appears somewhat out of place in late nineteenth-(C) and especially twentieth-(A, B) century English where the more developed fictional art tends to integrate such kinds of speech into the narrative.

Toning Down the Speech

If a character's utterance is recast in the words of the narrator, it necessarily loses both its communicative (in terms of its original addressor "I" —addressee "you" relationship) and expressive functions. Thus, IS contrasts with DS not only in immediacy but, closely related to it, in forcefulness or impact. Such contrast enables the novelist to control "the 'light and shade' of conversation, the high lighting and backgrounding of speech according to the role and attitude of characters" (Leech & Short 1981:335). Clearly, what is to be taken into account by the translator is not only immediacy, vividness or stylistic variety but also the association between the choice of modes and character's role and attitude.

In Cao, a text dominated by DS, little effort is made to control the light and shade of conversation. What interest us here therefore, and not surprisingly, are the translators' adaptations: in specific terms, the toning down or backgrounding of speech by way of left shifting the mode from DS to IS or NRSA. Perhaps the adaptations which are only local will be found slightly trivial. They may, nevertheless, from the particular angle of translation, throw some light on the contrastive force between DS and IS in terms of highlighting or backgrounding speech. Compare Cao with (A) and (B):

 (Cao) Liu Laolao zhide ceng shang lai
 Grannie Liu (could only) edge forward

wen: "Taiyemen nafu."   Zhongren daliangle
and said: "Greetings, gentlemen." The men looked her

yihui, bian wen: "Shi nali laide?" (chapter 6)
up and down, then asked: "Where have you come from?"

 (A) Grannie Liu waddled up to them and offered a respectful solutation. After looking her up and down for a moment or two, they asked her her business.
 (B) Granny Liu edged forward and said, "Greetings, gentlemen." The men surveyed her from head to foot before condescending to ask where she had come from.

Grannie Liu is a country woman who is coldly treated by the snobbish servants. The servants' snobbishness is best caught by (A) in the form of NRSA "they asked her her business," which does seem to carry a stronger cold undertone than Cao's DS. In (B), Granny Liu's speech is, as in Cao, accorded the direct form, the servants' speech is however reported through the narrator's indirect and impersonal voice. Thus the latter is notably distanced and backgrounded in contrast with the former. The effect is again one of toning down the speech so as to reflect the coldness and snobbishness of the speakers.

 Now, to highlight one speech act and background the other is a

CHAPTER 8   SPEECH AND THOUGHT PRESENTATION   241

technique that can be used to good effect in the presentation of one speaker's two consecutive speech/thought acts. This point will readily emerge by comparing Cao with (A) and (B):

    (Cao) Dai-yu bian cunduozhe: "Yin ta you yu, suoyi cai wen wode."
    Dai-yu speculated: "Because he has a jade himself, he asks me

                    Bian dadao: "Wo meiyou yu.
whether I have one or not." She answered: "I don't have a jade.
Ni nayu ye shi jian xihan wuer, qi neng renren jie you?"
Your jade is a rare object, how can everybody have one?"
(chapter 3)

(A) ... Dai-yu at once divined that he was asking her if she too had a jade like the one he was born with. "No," said Dai-yu. "That jade of yours is a very rare object. You can't expect everybody to have one."

(B) Imagining that he had his own jade in mind, she answered, "No, I haven't. I suppose it's too rare for everybody to have."

In Cao, the thought and the speech, both appearing in the direct form, are given equal prominence and equal auditory impact. In (A) and (B), however, the thought act (TA) is backgrounded by means of the indirect mode, which suppresses the verbal articulation of the TA and which enables the speech act (SA) to take on, by contrast, greater immediacy and auditory impact. This treatment is surely more in line with the nature of the T and S acts involved. The TA, a quiet speculation in Dai-yu's mind, does in a sense form a 'back ground' (see A & B) of the words said aloud which, containing a negative and a rhetorical question, call for strong emphasis. Indeed, against the indiscriminate treatment of Cao (which not only gives the TA 'undue' auditory impact but also detracts, due to the lack of contrast, from the prominence of the SA), the choice of the contrastive modes made by (A) and (B) can be fully appreciated.

It is of interest to note that the contrast between the direct and the indirect form is sometimes resorted to by the translators to vary the distance of a single speech act. In more specific terms, the translators sometimes choose to background (to render into IS) the beginning of Cao's DS so as to foreground the rest of the DS.

A Matter of the Speaker's Obscurity

If in the theatre the actor's physical presence always makes it natural for him to speak for himself, in the fictional world, where the symbol "someone" is quite different from the someone perceivable on the stage, the psychological obscurity of an imagined speaker may be found to conflict with the auditory immediacy of DS. Reconciliation can however be sought in the shape of IS or NRSA, a mode that enables the visual (mentally) or psychological distance between the reader and the character to be paralleled by the auditory distance, as shown by the following translations:

(Cao) Yin you ren hui Wang furen shuo: "Xi-rende gege
Then there was someone who reported to Lady Wang: Xi-ren's

Hua Zi-fang, zai waitou hui jinlai shuo,
elder brother Hua Zi-fang is outside and has sent in

ta muqin bingle ..." (chapter 51)
word that his mother was seriously ill ..."

(A) While they were there, a message arrived for Lady Wang to say that Aroma's brother, Hua Zi-fang, had come and was waiting outside in the front. "His mother is seriously ill ..."

(B) Then a maid reported to Lady Wang that Hsi-jen's brother Hua Chih-fang had brought word that their mother was ill ...

The abruptness involved in Cao's use of DS is largely attributable to the insufficiency of the verbal context concerning the speaker. Note the difference that would obtain if more information were brought in: "Then a servant came in, went up to Lady Wang and said: 'Xi-ren's ...'"

Obviously, the kind of information that serves to prepare the reader for the speaker's direct utterance will be within sight of an audience in a theatre. To get rid of the abruptness of the actual words spoken, the translators resort to the narrator's reporting voice, one that enables the speech proper, now *distanced* from the reader, to match the speaker's obscurity: "Then there was someone who reported to Lady Wang that Xi-ren's elder brother was outside ..." (but of course the speaker is well in sight and the speech well in hearing of the *intermediary narrator*). In (A), not only is the speech reported indirectly by the narrator, the speaker is also abstracted and impersonalized into the form of "a message." But after the initial reporting, the narrator allows the character to "speak for himself." Notably, this time, the use of DS is free from abruptness, for the reader is by now sufficiently acquainted, though only in an oblique way, with the voice and the presence of the messenger, rendering as a result the narrator's intermediary role unnecessary. In (B), apart from the shift from DS to IS, the obscure "someone" is specified as "a maid," thereby making it possible for the reader to conjure up a more definite mental image.

Now I would like to mention a relative obscurity of the speaker which concerns anonymous servants but who are, in this case, at least spelt out as definitely as "a servant," "a maid," or "the pages." Although the relative obscurity may not really necessitate the shift from DS to IS, it does seem to incline one to do so, as borne out by Cao's translations where the anonymous servants' DS is frequently translated into IS or NRSA. This may be accounted for by the following considerations, some of which will be found applicable to some speech of minor characters, especially when speaking together; or found applicable to some short conventionalized utterances of protagonists. First, the anonymous servants, as mere instruments in the plot, do not require DS in terms of characterization. Indeed, their utterances typically consist of conventionalized reports or inquiries which normally do not call for the emphasis or impact of DS, and which may find in the indirect mode equal efficiency as well as more pace and economy. Furthermore, the small number of shifts from DS, a mode that predominates throughout, to IS or NRSA serve to provide more stylistic variety. Equally important, given the relatively minor difference between DS and IS in Chinese, where therefore the "gear-shifting" is much less clumsy, it is not surprising that when translating into English, one is more ready, in the interest of smooth narrative flow, to integrate unimportant utterances into the narrative.

Pseudo-dramatization

Before concluding the discussion of DS, attention will now be directed to a case in Cao which exhibits pseudo-dramatization and whose deviant technique as well as the translator's solutions may shed some interesting light on the way in which fictional discourse is organized.

(Cao) ... ye zhuang chuxiaogong qu,　　　　　zou
... he also pretended that he wanted to be excused, and

zhihoumian,　　　　qiaoqiao ba gen Bao-yu shutong
walked to the back, quietly called over Bao-yu's page

Ming-yan jiao zhishenbian, ruci zheban,
Ming-yan, and (in such and such a way) made a few

tiaobo ta jiju.　　　　　Zhe Ming-yan nai shi Bao-yu
inflammatory remarks to him. This Ming-yan was Bao-yu's

di yige deyong qie you nianqing bu an shide,
most serviceable but very young and inexperienced page, now

jin ting Jia Qiang shuo: "Jin Rong ruci qifu Qin Zhong,
he (had) heard Jia Qiang say: "Jin Rong insults Qin Zhong in

　　　　　lian nimende ye Bao-yu dou ganlian
such a way, that even your master Bao-yu has come in for a

zainei, bu gei ta ge zhidao,　　　　　　　xiaci yuefa

CHAPTER 8 SPEECH AND THOUGHT PRESENTATION 245

share, if (we/you) don't take him down a peg, next time he is
kuangzong."　　　　　　　Zhe Ming-yan wu gu
going to be quite insufferable." This Ming-yan never needed
jiuyao qiya rende... (chapter 9)
any encouragement to pick a fight ... (trans. based on A. For what follows, see A)

(A) ... he pretended that he wanted to be excused, and slipping round to the back, quietly called over Bao-yu's little page Tealeaf and whispered a few inflammatory words in his ear. Tealeaf was the most willing but also the youngest and least sensible of Bao-yu's pages. Jia Qiang told him how Jokey Jin had been bullying Qin Zhong. "And even Bao-yu came in for a share," he said. "If we don't take this Jin fellow down a peg, next time he is going to be quite insufferable." Tealeaf never needed any encouragement to pick a fight, and now, inflamed by Jia Qiang's message and open incitement to action, he marched straight into the classroom to look for Jokey Jin.

(C) ... and in one way and another, he made use of several remarks to egg him on. This Ming Yen was the smartest of Pao-yu's attendants, but he was also young in years and lacked experience, so that he lent a patient ear to what Chia Se had to say about the way Chin Jung had insulted Ch'in Chung. "Even your own master, Pao-yu," (Chia Se added), "is involved, and if you don't let him know a bit of your mind, he will next time be still more arrogant." This Ming Yen was always ready ...

In Cao the NRSA ("made a few inflammatory remarks") and the DS share the same referent, i.e., reporting twice a single SA, a device that goes well beyond the capacity of a dramatist. Semantically the NRSA is kept general, which is in no way specified by the seemingly substantiating adjunct "in such and such a way." A notable effect that results from this is suspense which, though, is only to be dissipated in the actual words spoken.

Two things need to be noted here: one is that Cao's presentational sequence seems marked by deviation. Compare Cao with the more normal sequence-first showing the scene, then referring to it in more general terms:

> ... quietly called over Bao-yu's page Ming-yan and said to him: "Jin Rong insults Qin Zhong in such a way that even your ..." Ming-yan was Bao-yu's most serviceable page, but he was very young and inexperienced. Now he (had) heard these inflammatory remarks ...

Such reordering apparently involves the loss of the rhetorical build-up of suspense. The second point to note is that given the deviant presentational sequence, the use of DS is only minimally expected in the specification. Since the speech act has already been presented ("made a few inflammatory remarks to him"), what is offered here, following the authorial narrator's commentary, is the narrator's exposition which seems much more in line with the indirect mode ("now he (had) heard Jia Qiang say that ...").

In Cao, through the peculiar use of DS, there is created a pseudo-dramatic situation which, in addition to bringing into full play a distinctive speaking voice, makes it possible for the narrator's exposition to combine with the immediacy and vividness of the actual happening. Moreover, owing to the pseudo-dramatic situation that appears amidst the narrator's commentary, the distance between the actual speech event and the resulting action is made to appear shortened, which contributes to the dramatic effect of Jia's words immediately plunging Ming-yan into action. This pseudo-dramatization is very likely to be associated with Chinese story-tellers' general inclination to build up suspense and to imitate character's speech. Natural as it appears in Cao, it seems not to be a device used in English.

In translating into English, one possible way out is to turn the pseudo-dramatic situation into a 'true' scene. This is manifested in (C) where the 're-presentation' of the SA ("now he (had) heard Jia Qiang say: '...'" which is co-referential with, though not retrievable from, the preceding NRSA) is partially embedded in the form of NRSA into a piece of new information ("so that he *lent a patient ear to* what Chia Se had to say about... [NRSA]"). By bringing in the new information, (C) changes the mode from the narrator's exposition of what has already been presented into a pure description of the scene whereby a 'true' dramatic situation is established. Interestingly, this second NRSA, though derived from no more than the beginning of Cao's DS, is, for its potential coverage of more than one remark, made to fulfil the co-referential function of the whole, thus enabling the rest of Cao's DS to be separated in (C) from "several remarks" and to appear as new information, with the newness explicitly signaled by the reporting verb "added." The reader is thus, instead of Cao's expository 're-presentation' of the same speech act, given a continuation of the scene. A similar treatment is found in version (A). Both versions put across well, with naturalness, the effects of suspense, immediacy and vividness mainly by means of shifting the beginning of Cao's DS to the more general NRSA.

8.5 THE FUNCTIONS OF FIS AND THE NEED FOR ITS PRESERVATION

The purpose of this section is to emphasize, by way of shedding some light on the losses that a change from Free Indirect Speech into another mode might involve, the necessity of preserving, under certain circumstances, the mode of FIS in fictional translation. FIS is a semidirect mode, grammatically and mimetically intermediate between IS and DS. In particular novels, FIS can take on various thematic functions, "contributing or being analogous to the governing thematic principle(s) of the work under consideration" (Rimmon-Kenan 1983:113; see also

McHale 1978:274). This section, however, is not concerned with what McHale calls "second-order" functions, which are peculiar to specific texts, but with the more general "first-order" ones.

8.5.1 Common Function or Peculiar Function

It is essential to set the functions that are peculiar to Free Indirect Speech apart from the functions that are common to all modes of speech. Only in this way can the discussion be of true pragmatic value to the translator in his/her choice between modes of presentation. Of the five functions of FIS or FID (Free Indirect Discourse) presented by Rimmon-Kenan (1981:113—114), the first one seems to be shared, in a sense, by all modes of speech:

> The FID hypothesis (even if not thought of in these terms) is often necessary in order to identify speakers and assign given speech-features or attitudes to them. This enables the reader to make sense of "deviant" linguistic practices, unacceptable attitudes, or even lies, without undermining the credibility of the work or of the implied author. (Ron 1981:28—29)

Ron, in the pages referred to, is actually concerned with a general discussion of the Mimetic Cooperation Principle; or more relevantly, with a discussion of apparent violations of one particular maxim in Mimetic Language Game. His plain conclusion that "the author of a mimetic fiction may not lie to the reader directly (within the boundaries of the fictional world), but may use the lying of his characters to mislead the reader temporarily" is relevant to "mendacious character statements" in general (cf. van Dijk 1976:52), statements which can be in FIS and, equally probably, in FDS (also without a reporting clause), IS, DS etc. By this is meant that as regards the capacity for "violating the CP without violating the MCP" (Ron 1981), FIS is by no means unique. Nevertheless, what seems to be implied by Rimmon-Kenan (signaled by "hypothesis" and "identify") is the fact that FIS, with its possible "grammatical disguise of a narrated fact" (Hernadi 1972:194), enables the violation of the CP (vs. the MCP) to be carried out in a more subtle manner than other modes of speech. In the extreme case, a character's false words presented in FIS may be entirely mistaken as authorial statement until later on, by virtue of the "FID hypothesis," being re-attributed to the character (see Banfield 1982:218—219). And the reader, having been misled so far by the seemingly authorial statement, gains no grounds for doubting the reliability of the authorial narrator.

It should be noted that a character's "false" statements are not necessarily lies. In many cases, the "falsehood"—false in the sense of being at variance with the fictional reality—is to be accounted for by the limitation rather than dishonesty of the character concerned. In such a case, apparently no violation of the CP is involved but a violation of the MCP would occur if the "false" statements were attributable to the omniscient narrator. From what has been discussed above, the following conclusions can be drawn:

In translating a fiction:
(1) In order to avoid affecting the reliability of the authorial narrator, it is best not to raise the character's intentionally or unintentionally false statements (FIS, DS etc.) to the narrative plane (cf. the discussion of the narrator's commitment in 8.6).
(2) Given that "the view of a character, when presented in FIS, has only a qualified validity in respect to truth, wins from the reader only a qualified assent" (Pascal 1977:50), then, in order not to overly mislead the reader, it is better to preserve the linguistic features, if any, that signal FIS as opposed to seemingly authorial statement.
(3) If the grammatical disguise of a narrated fact that FIS takes on is used as a means of strategically or dramatically misleading

the reader, it is advisable not to remove the disguise by adding speech/thought features or changing the mode into the unequivocal IS, DS etc. ...

8.5.2 The Function of Conveying Irony

It has been pointed out by most critics that Free Indirect Speech is a vehicle for irony; yet, as a mode in itself, FIS cannot automatically produce irony. Irony arises only when the content or possibly the context of the speech/thought contains some element of absurdity or incongruity. But to attribute the ironic effect solely to the content or context is to deny unwarrantably the potentially greater usefulness of FIS in conveying irony and to put it on a par, in this respect, with other modes of speech. This is not my intention. My concern is, instead, the question: how and why FIS is more effective than other modes in terms of conveying or reinforcing the ironic effect?

The first point to be noted is that the *identity* in grammatical form between Free Indirect Speech and authorial statement may serve to highlight the *discrepancy* in opinion between the author and the character, for example:

(i) He said/thought,"I'll become the greatest man in the world."
(ii) He would become the greatest man in the world.

If accorded by the author to a common character, the speech/thought—both (i) and (ii)—will generate irony. But the ironic effect in (ii) is at once more subtle and striking. For on the one hand the substitution of the authorial narrator's voice for the character's makes the irony more implicit while, on the other hand, something of the impression that the narrator is saying (mimicking the sense of) what s/he apparently takes to be false adds to the speech/thought a ring of mockery and makes the irony all the more penetrating. As Cohn puts it, casting "the language of subjective mind into the grammar of objective narration" can "throw into ironic relief all false notes struck by a figural mind"(1978:117).

Moreover, the remote-shift in person and back-shift in tense in FIS helps to generate an ironic distance between the reader and the words of the character. In the example above, the first-person pronoun in(i) may promote, where applicable, a measure of sympathetic identification through acting at the subconscious level on one'a tendency towards, say, self-glorification or narcissism. In(ii), by contrast, the remote-shift in person coupled with the back-shift in tense generates a distancing effect, allowing the reader room to sense the absurdity of the speech and to feel or share the authorial narrator's implicit comment of irony or mockery. Furthermore, "the double-edged effect" characteristic of FIS (Rimmon-Kenan 1983: 113 — 114) enables the narrator, while preserving some flavour of the original speech, to edit or modify what is said in an ironic way, such as "juxtaposing the various excuses in a list" (Pascal 1977: 52) or chopping the speech so as to underline the speaker's inexhaustible store of eager reassurances(Leech & Short 1981:326).

It may also be noted that FIS makes it possible to bring into play the ironic attitude of the interlocutor (see Pascal 1977:55;Ron 1981:31; cf. Banfield 1973: 31; 1982: 130). In such a case, one is given the impression that, rather than the narrator, it is the listener himself or herself who is representing or registering what is said—with notable implicit ironic evaluation. And in such a case, as Pascal observes, "FIS shows itself to be an instrument of meanings that cannot be communicated by other narrative forms" (op cit). Furthermore, FIS forms a convenient vehicle for conveying the irony of register, an irony "that arises from the juxtaposition between the formal literary style of narration and the non-literary styles represented in FID" (McHale 1978: 275). Apparently, irony as such will more or less disappear in other modes of speech.

8.5.3 The Function of Conveying Empathy

In thought presentation, free indirect style is seen as more direct than the norm (Indirect Thought), hence as a move into the active mind of the character (Leech & Short 1981:344—345). By bringing the reader closer to the character (thus making the emotive concern of the character more immediately felt), by fusing the narrator's voice with the character's (thereby involving the narrator and derivatively the reader), and by preserving the emotive force of the original thought (syntax and some choices of words which are often sacrificed in Indirect Thought), the free indirect mode presents a powerful vehicle for sympathetic identification (see Pascal 1977:42—43; Short 1982:184; Cohn 1978: 112,123—124; Banfield 1973:29; Ullmann 1957:104,107,117—119; Hernadi 1972:192,194—195).

It is of interest to note that the two somewhat converse functions of irony and empathy can, in a single instance of FIS, either be coexistent (Pascal 1977:42) or be indistinguishable (McHale 1978:275).

8.5.4 Polyvocality and Semantic Density

It will have emerged by now that Free Indirect Speech forms a mode that brings into play a plurality of voices and attitudes: e.g. the character's and/or the narrator's, or the character's and the listener's and possibly the narrator's—if the narrator clearly shares the listener's judgement (for a comprehensive discussion, see McHale 1978:278—281). This clearly contributes to the semantic density of the text (see Rimmon-Kenan, op cit); and this therefore constitutes yet another reason for preserving FIS in literary translation.

8.6 THE TRANSFERENCE OF SLIPPING

The individual modes that we have been concerned with so far not infrequently slip into one another. Though a diversified phenomenon, slipping basically falls into two types: unobtrusive or striking. One kind of unobtrusive slipping was touched on in 8.3.1: from IS/FDS to FIS/

FDS in Chinese and correspondingly, from IS to FIS in English. Another kind presents a subtle change from authorial statement to interior portrayal (see Leech & Short 1981:340). As for slipping that is striking, it is typically marked by the abrupt introduction of inverted commas and/or by the sudden switch in tense and person, e. g.

(i) From indirect to direct discourse:
His personal decision would be given as soon as "it is fixed in my mind." (see Schuelke 1958:92)

(ii) From narrative report to direct speech:
Mrs. Verloc rose, and went into the kitchen to "stop that nonsense." (Conrad, *The Secret Agent*)

whether the translator is justified in omitting the inverted commas or in unifying the tense and person depends largely on context. But one may on a general level call for the preservation of slipping—not only to reflect the original style but also on the grounds that such a device often takes on important stylistic values. In Old Icelandic, for example, the shift from indirect to direct discourse (i) is seen to correspond to the shift in content; it therefore forms a useful means of emphasizing or foregrounding, in direct quotation, the climactic part of the speech (Schuelke 1958). The slipping from narrative report to direct speech (ii) on the other hand provides a potential scope for irony, and, further, for dissociating the narrator from the words between the quotation marks (Jones 1968:171—172). The contrast thus formed between the objectivity of narrative report and the subjectivity of the character's words within the boundary of a single sentence functions to yield subtlety and stylistic variety. In translation, such effects will be to some extent lost if the quotation marks are omitted, unless the words concerned in themselves suffice to contrast with the narrator's voice.

In transferring slipping, either unobtrusive or striking, two issues, among others, are likely to emerge. One is how to get rid of the incongruity that may arise in translation because of differences in languages and literary conventions. The other is, when translating a slipping between narrative report and speech/thought, how to preserve the two different planes; or whether it is justifiable to raise speech/thought to the narrative plane, or vice versa. Both issues seem to come to the fore in the following case taken from Cao Xueqin's *A Dream of Red Mansions*:

   (Cao) Daiyu tingle zhehua,　　　bujue you xi
     1. Daiyu heard such remarks, she could not help feeling

you jing,　　　　　　　you bei you tan.
both delighted and surprised, both sorrowful and regretful.

   Suoxizhe:　　　　　　　　Guoran ziji yanli
   2. With what she was delighted was: As expected my own

bucuo,　　　　　suri ren ta shi ge zhiji,
judgement is correct, I always have regarded him as an

            guoran shi ge zhiji.
understanding friend, he really is an understanding friend.

   Suojingzhe:　　　　　　　Ta zai renqian yipian
   3. At what she was surprised was: He in front of others with

sixin chengyang yu wo, qi qinrehoumi jing bubi xianyi.
all his heart praised me, its warmth affection intimacy go so far

           Suotanzhe:
as to not avoid suspicion. 4. For what she was regretful was:

Ni ji wei wode zhiji,　　　　ziran wo yi
Since you are my understanding friend, naturally I also can be

kewei nide zhiji,　　　ji ni wo wei zhiji,
your understanding friend, since you and I are understanding

      you hebi you "jinyu" zhi lun ne?
friends, why there should be the talk of "gold and jade"?

CHAPTER 8 SPEECH AND THOUGHT PRESENTATION

Ji you "jinyu" zhi lun,   ye gai ni wo you zhi,
Since there is that talk of "gold and jade," it should be you

    you hebi lai yi Baochai? ... (chapter 32)
and I who have them, but why should have come a Baochai?
...

(A) (... she heard Xiang-yun lecturing Bao-yu on his social obligations and Bao-yu telling Xiang-yun that "Cousin Lin never talked that sort of rubbish" and that if she did he would have "fallen out with her long ago.") Mingled emotions of happiness, alarm, sorrow and regret assailed her.

Happiness:

Because after all (she thought) I wasn't mistaken in my judgement of you. I always thought of you as a true friend, and I was right.

Alarm:

Because if you praise me so unreservedly in front of other people, your warmth and affection are sure, sooner or later, to excite suspicion and be misunderstood.

Regret:

Because if you are my true friend, then I am yours and the two of us are a perfect match. But in that case why did there have to be all this talk of "the gold and the jade"? Alternatively, if there had to be all this talk of gold and jade, why weren't we the two to have them? Why did there have to be a Bao-chai with her golden locket? ...
(Trans. Hawkes)

(B) This surprised and delighted Tai-yu but also distressed and grieved her. She was delighted to know she had not misjudged him, for he had now proved just as understanding as she had always thought. Surprised that he had been so indiscreet as to acknowledge his preference for her openly. Distressed because their mutual understanding ought to preclude all talk about gold matching jade, or she instead of Pao-chai should have the gold locket to match his jade amulet... (Trans. Yang and Yang)

(C) This language suddenly produced, in Lin Tai-yu'S mind, both surprise as well as delight; sadness as well as regret. Delight, at having indeed been so correct in her perception that he whom she had ever considered in the light of a true friend had actually turned out to be a true friend. Surprise, "because," she said to herself: "he has, in the presence of so many witnesses, displayed such partiality as to speak in my praise, and has shown such affection and friendliness for me as to make no attempt whatever to shirk suspicion." Regret, "for since," (she pondered), "you are my intimate friend, you could certainly well look upon me too as your intimate friend; and if you and I be real friends, why need there be any more talk about gold and jade? But since there be that question of gold and jade, you and I should have such things in our possession. Yet, why should this Pao-ch'ai step in again between us?"... (Trans. Joly)

In Cao, the several parallel slippings from narrative report to free direct thought, which have to do with the marked tendency to use parallelism in classical Chinese literature, are most certainly peculiar to the original. A strict transference into English is bound to result in incongruity. It seems that (A)'s neat and deviant lay-out is motivated by a consideration which is more than aesthetic. It may be designed to raise the authorial narrator's statement visually to a plane higher than and different from that of free direct thought, a device that serves to divide the reader's attention between the two modes and consequently makes the reader more ready to accept the contrast between them. To further play down the incongruity, (A) resorts to a subtle 'play on modes.' Behind the well-wrought, clear-cut boundary between narrative report and free direct thought, is hidden the displacement of "because" which, though we recognize it as unmistakably belonging to the narrator, is nevertheless unequivocally attributed to the character. Thus the role of narrator is imperceptibly forced upon the character, making her collaborate in the secondary speech situation with the narrator in the first (the effect is of course that of smoothing the narrative flow). Perhaps one can even take a step further and interpret it as an imperceptible switch towards the first-person narrative mode:

Third-person:

Happiness (she was happy) because: After all (she thought) I wasn't mistaken ...

First-person:

Happiness (I was happy): because after all I wasn't mistaken ...

We can see that (A)'s choices of the unmodified, non-deictic abstract nouns "happiness," "alarm" etc. lend themselves to the play on modes. Interestingly but not fortuitously, a 'play on modes' appears in almost the same form in version (C) where (A)'s deviant lay-out also finds its counterpart (in the sense of reducing incongruity) in the inverted commas. But of course, the most smooth and natural rendering, with a notable gain in narrative economy, is offered by (B), a version that, instead of reproducing, replaces Cao's slipping by the consistent mode of the authorial narrator's statement. There apparently occurs a loss of stylistic variety. And what else does this change involve?

In a third-person novel like the present one, the authorial narrator and the characters present the two opposite poles of fictional objectivity and subjectivity. The slipping in the original displays an artistic alternation between the narrator's neutral reporting voice and the protagonist's emotive inner thoughts. Translation (B)'s integration of the embedded thoughts into the narrative plane leads to the objectification of the former to a certain degree. It is arguable that the inner thoughts are presented by (B) in such a way that they take on the appearance of facts which impinge on the character and which are perceived and reported by the omniscient narrator ("she was delighted to know (the fact that) she had not misjudged him. ... Surprised (at the fact) that he had been so indiscreet as to ..."). By this is meant a shift in descriptive focus from interior portrayal to external report. As the originator of thoughts is now turned into a passive receiver of facts, the character's mind is made to appear much less active. It is notable that in the original the thoughts constitute integral processes of the emotive states (delighted, surprised, etc.) with the beginning of the thoughts marking the beginning of the emotive states; and it is the free direct thought that plays the essential role in directly revealing the complex feelings of the heroine. In (B), as the thoughts are made to appear as facts, the focus of interior portrayal falls back on the emotive states, of which the facts do not constitute an integral part but form the causes that exist prior to the emotive states. Compared with the free direct thought of Cao and (A), (B)'s facts have a much poorer or much less direct role to play in conveying the feelings of the heroine. They become associated with the feelings only by virtue of being perceived by the character.

(B)'s integration of the embedded thoughts into the narrative plane leads, moreover, to (at least a possible) commitment on the part of the authorial narrator. What is most regrettable is the narrator's commitment to "so indiscreet as to," since in the original the hero's deeds would not be regarded as too indiscreet but for the extreme sensitivity and sense of propriety of the heroine; and it is precisely through this unreliable evaluation that the heroine's disposition is subtly revealed.

Now, in both the primary and the embedded speech situations in a third-person narrative, there is theoretically no limitation on personal reference or modes of expression. The authorial narrator is free, as s/he occasionally does, to choose to address the reader or even a character as "you" and s/he can use the interrogative or exclamatory form. But the point is that if an embedded utterance is reported through the narrator in the primary speech situation (which inevitably involves a change in the addresser/addressee relationship), the first and second person in the reported speech or thought are necessarily switched to the third, and the emotive modes of expression are usually sacrificed. This brings us to some further consequences associated with (B)'s change in mode.

It will be clear that in the original, the "he" and "you" share the same referent, namely, Baoyu, the hero. By referring to the hero as "he" (2,3), the heroine treats him as one of the others. By addressing him as "you" (in the earlier part of 4), the heroine separates him from others and draws him near to herself; by referring to the two of them together as "you and I" (in the later part of 4), which is the natural equivalent of the inclusive "we," the heroine identifies herself with the hero as a component part of the implied "we." This *dynamic* change in reference within the *static* situation lends to the subtle bringing out of the complex feelings of the heroine. Being suspicious, the heroine is seldom sure of the hero's love for or understanding of her, so she is delighted with and surprised at "his" preference. Being deeply in love with him however, she cannot help subconsciously taking the two of them as being one. The term "subconsciously" might be descriptively inadequate, but the deviant conversational thought form (addressed to an absent interlocutor) that 4 presents does point to a rise in emotional key and an escape into unreality. One may regard the development from differentiation ("he") to identification ("you and I") as being of thematic importance for the growth of their mutual love and common struggle forms one of the major themes of the novel. This significant stylistic feature is lost in (B)'s authorial statement, a mode that does not permit the switch from "he" to "you" (compare version C). It is true that the switch also fails to appear in (A), but (A)'s failure is, importantly, not to be attributed to the limitation of the presentational mode.[11]

The adaptation made by (B) has yet another regrettable consequence, that is, limitation of modes of expression. In (B), there is no room left for representing the change in the original from the declarative mood to the interrogative. This, coupled with the related consequences referred to above, notably suppresses the character's SELF and leads to a fall in emotional key. Indeed, the uncertainty or puzzlement that underlies the character's reasoning is drastically undercut by (B)'s straightforward "their mutual understanding," an expression to which the narrator is clearly committed and thus unwittingly made factual. Perhaps against (B)'s edited, coordinate statements, the climactic progressive questioning well brought out in (A) and (C) could be better appreciated.

It is clear that once the embedded speech or thought is raised to the narrative plane, it becomes subjected to many limitations and is made to serve quite different functions (the rendering by (B) seems to form a typical case of "deceptive equivalence"). The discussion here may highlight the point that, in the transference of slipping, the problem confronting the translator goes beyond a simple matter of available modes. The slipping from narrative report to free direct thought is, abstractly speaking, not unavailable in English, but as we have seen, a strict reproduction of Cao's slippings in English is out of place. Indeed, differences in languages and literary conventions are more likely to come to the fore in the transference of slipping than in that of a single mode.

8.7 CONCLUSION

In this chapter, a fairly systematic examination is taken up in terms of the communicative and expressive functions of the modes of speech or thought presentation in Chinese and English, and in terms of the functional correspondence in this area between the two languages. From the evidence of both the negative and positive renderings presented above, it is clear that an adequate realization of the function of stylistic norms as well as the contextualized stylistic devices (in both languages) is crucial to the avoidance of "deceptive equivalence" and to the production of expressive identity.

As indicated by the cases of "deceptive equivalence" analysed above, translation of realist prose fiction is quite often marked by a lack of adequate awareness of the novelist's verbal artistry, an artistry which is much less obtrusive than that of the poet's. If Cluysenaar is reasonable in attributing C. D. Lewis's mistranslating of Paul Valery's poem "Les Pas" to "a failure in translation theory as applied to literature" (1976: 41), one surely has a good reason to ascribe the fictional translator's stylistic non-discrimination to the backwardness of studies of fictional translation, which have on the whole remained remarkably traditional and impressionistic. The remedy clearly resides in the introduction of the more precise and more penetrating stylistic analysis which, not only informed by modern linguistics but also taking literary competence or sensitivity as a prerequisite, can effectively help the translator to achieve functional equivalence.

It is to be hoped that more theorists and practitioners of literary translation would be interested in literary stylistics (based on an adequate knowledge of modern linguistics and literary criticism). For without adequate stylistic competence, a theorist cannot effectively help the literary translator to achieve functional correspondence or expressive identity. Similarly, without adequate stylistic competence, a literary translator seems to be in no position to convey successfully the aesthetic significance of the original.

It is likewise to be hoped that more stylisticians would come to the field of literary translation, a field not only offering a congenial area for demonstrating the practical potential of stylistics but also providing various opportunities for enriching the knowledge of stylistic properties (the same applies to literary translation in general). The problems and solutions that emerge in interlingual fictional transfer, as shown by the present analysis, serve to offer fresh insights into the workings of stylistic devices, and/or into the dialectical relation between linguistic form and fictional reality, and/or into the way that fictional discourse is organized. In this connection, I directed attention especially to certain of the peculiar ways in which language is manipulated to generate aesthetic significance in Chinese and to the methods used by the translators to achieve functional correspondence in English. The contrast in various forms between the peculiarities of the original and the contextual adjustments made by the translators often operates to shed light on the aesthetic function of the linguistic medium and on the underlying linguistic, literary, and cultural conventions, which tend to remain opaque within the boundary of a single language. Interestingly and significantly, in this field, instead of one actual choice and its hypothetical or potential alternatives, the analyst has the benefit of two or more actual choices made by two or more human beings with different expressive means in two, or possibly more, different languages (this seems to be a most natural kind of material for stylistic analysis). The contrast or conflict between the consciousnesses, as well as that between the linguistic, literary, and cultural conventions involved, functions to offer stylistic insights and to provide opportunities for enriching stylistic resources both in the source language and in the target language.

NOTES

CHAPTER 1

1. In the sense as used by Pearce (see chapter 3) but not in the sense as used by Ronald Carter who contrasts linguistic stylistics with practical stylistics (1982) or with literary stylistics (Carter and Simpson 1989). This intermediary discipline is also quite frequently referred to as "literary linguistics." Interestingly but not surprisingly, it is referred to by M. H. Short (1982) as "literary linguistic stylistics."
2. The romanization used in this book is basically the pinyin system; but for the convenience of the reader, I adhere to the romanization used in the translations concerned. All literal translation is mine.

CHAPTER 2

1. I think mental characteristics are something quite different from distinctive ways of perceiving and organizing experience since the former refers primarily to one's 'inner' temperament and mental make-up (i.e. mental characteristics such as "weak," "dominating," or "agitated"), while the latter refers to one's perception of external entities. Compare: "his terse syntax points to his dominating nature" with "he sees things as closely associated with one another, which is reflected in the interconnection of his syntax."
2. Of course with the exception of modern experimental fiction and the like, where the medium tends to attract attention in its own right and where the reader's reconstruction of fictional reality is frequently frustrated by violations of normal linguistic usages or rules.
3. It is, though, understood that many narrators use what is referred to as "speech allusion," that is, the selective imitation by the narrator of a character's or some characters' style of speech in primary narration (see Leech & Short 1981: 349 —

350). But speech allusion is usually very short and intermittent in narrative discourse. Further, it may be noted that, to save space and to avoid complications. I shall not discuss the case of a dramatized narrator (or dramatized narrators).

4. As alternative expressions of the same fictional event, their difference can be regarded as a matter of linguistic form. But they differ at the level of phrase structure, and could not, in any logical sense, be taken as paraphrases of one another (see Leech & Short 1981:31ff.).

CHAPTER 3

1. I made a full analysis of Fish's criticism of Halliday in my Ph. D. dissertation but due to the limitation of space, I have not presented it here.
2. Thorne's article "Generative grammar and stylistic analysis" falls basically into three parts: first, a discussion of the relation between general subjectively-stated impressions of style (such as "complex" "terse") and identifiable structural properties; secondly, a study of the relation between syntax and literary significance; thirdly, a discussion of linguistic structures characteristic of poetry and of how to give them an adequate grammatical description.

CHAPTER 4

1. The point is that the symbolic system need not have any natural relation with what is symbolized, though the two may sometimes coincide with each other (such as a similarity between natural order and syntactic order or pictographic characters).
2. Readers Who are as yet uninitiated into the institution of literature or, put another way, who are as yet unfamiliar with the system of literary conventions are not in a position to produce acceptable interpretations.

CHAPTER 5

1. A "homologue" refers to a feature which corresponds to the original in form but not in function, while an "analogue" stands for a feature which corresponds to the SL feature in function but not in form. The presence of the choice between the two, which is attributable to the differences in literary conventions and in the formal possibilities contained in the specific languages involved, often poses a dilemma to

the translator (see Holmes 1978:75).
2. The choice of blank verse instead of the rhymed couplet, for instance, confounds correspondence at the phonic level and makes correspondence on the endstop/enjambment axis for all practical purposes impossible. (Holmes 1978:76)
3. In the case of a dramatized narrator in particular, if the narrator's viewpoint is found to be unreliable, it will be rejected by the reader. But the very unreliability here is in itself of aesthetic significance, playing an important role in characterizing the narrating consciousness.

CHAPTER 6

1. (A) would have done better if it had preserved the original lexical choice "valiant" ("wuyong") which forms a direct contrast to "timid" ("danqie").
2. However, the authorial or, more frequently, the dramatized narrator may take on only a limited perspective and be as "unprivileged" as the reader, a limitation that could readily help to generate the effect of suspense (see 8.3.3).
3. The preceding text goes as follows:

MEDICINE

It was autumn, in the small hours of the morning. The moon had gone down, but the sun had not yet risen, and the sky appeared a sheet of darkling blue. Apart from night-prowlers, all was asleep. Old Chuan suddenly sat up in bed. He struck a match and lit the grease-covered oil-lamp, which shed a ghostly light over the two rooms of the tea-house. "Are you going, now, dad?" queried an old woman's voice. And from the small inner room a fit of coughing was heard. "H'm." Old Chuan listened as he fastened his clothes, then stretching out his hand said, "Let's have it." After some fumbling under the pillow his wife produced a packet of silver dollars which she handed over. Old Chuan pocketed it nervously, patted his pocket twice, then lighting a paper lantern and blowing out the lamp went into the inner room. A rustling was heard, and then more coughing. When all was quiet again Old Chuan called softly: "Son! ... Don't you get up! ... Your mother will see to the shop." Receiving no answer, Old Chuan assumed his son must be sound asleep again; so he went out into the street. In the darkness nothing could be seen but the grey roadway. (Trans. Yang and Yang)
4. It is important to note that to empathize fully with the author, the translator may need to be emotionally involved, needing to love or hate the characters as the author

does. What is argued against in this section is in fact the translator's emotional involvement as a reader versus as an imitator of the author (see the discussion below).
5. (A)'s "in less than two years" instead of "in less than one year" is due to a difference between the original versions (A is based on a manuscript version different from the one presented above).
6. The following emphasized parts have been translated from Cao's "had no comparison elsewhere" ("fei bie chu ke bi") and "were different from elsewhere" ("yu bie chu bu tong") respectively:
   (A) Peeping through the gauze panel which served as a window, she could see streets and buildings *more* rich and elegant and throngs of people *more* lively and numerous *than she had ever seen in her life before*. (Trans. Hawkes, 87)
   (B) As she was carried into the city she peeped out through the gauze window of the chair at the bustle in the streets and the crowds of people, the like of *which she had never seen before*. (Trans. Yang and Yang, 35)
7. This only applies to cases where the object is more or less readily identifiable and where the identification does not involve any other process(es) or act(s).

CHAPTER 7

1. Given the difference in the relevant linguistic conventions, the contrast between the two different renderings is more striking in English than in Chinese. Indeed, apart from the difference in terms of omitting structural elements, it would be clear from the examples we have seen and shall see that, in Chinese, the distinction between "," and "." or between ";" and "." is less strict than in English.
2. Whether we take it as "rhetorical" or "psychological" depends on whether we are focusing on the means (which is rhetorical) or on the effect (which is psychological): rhetoric functions by way of producing psychological effects.
3. Literally translated, "lianrilianye wu xiuxi" would take the following shape: "for days and nights there would be no rest," which usually functions in Chinese as the predicate or adjunct of a clause and is rarely used as a premodifying element. The sentence in question would have been more natural if "lianrilianye wu xiuxi" had been presented in surface structure as the predicate of a following clause, in a form like "zai zhege guochengzhong, jiang lianrilianye debudao xiuxi" ("during this

process, there would be no rest for days and nights running").
4. (A) would, I believe, have done better if "be (or become) happy" had been used in place of "cheer himself up" since lexical identity helps to achieve the effect referred to.

CHAPTER 8

1. (a) DS: He said, "I'll come back here to see you again tomorrow."
   (b) IS: He said that he would return there to see her the following day.
   (c) FDS: (i) He said I'll come back here to see you again tomorrow.
         (ii) "I'll come back here to see you again tomorrow."
         (iii) I'll come back here to see you again tomorrow.
   (d) FIS: (i) He would return there to see her again tomorrow.
         (ii) He would come back there to see her again tomorrow.
   (e) NRSA: He promised to return/He promised to visit her again.
2. For exemplification, see for instance Page 1973:31,34; McDowell 1973; Jones 1986; Leech & Short 1981:330; also Cao 1979:284 ; W. Zhou 1979:50; Mao 1966:300.
3. In narrative report of speech act, the quoted SELF is, more frequently than in indirect speech, suppressed. But even here, the quoted SELF may come into play. Given the sentence "He kept complaining about the *bloody* train," if it is reported by an authorial narrator who is understood to be unlikely to call the train "bloody," the epithet "bloody" cannot but be expressive of the subjectivity of the quoted speaker.
4. Idiolectal or tonal features can also function as differentiating criteria, but many reported speech acts do not display those features (see Shen 1991:396—397).
5. In the former case, by "counterpart" I refer to utterances composed of nominal or adverbial phrases interjections (compare Page 1973:37—38), which can be readily transferred from Chinese into English without losing their ambiguity. In the latter case, since the tense and pronoun selection are appropriate to either, there is no choice involved. The same applies to the reverse process of translating from English into Chinese.
6. (A): Trans. Yang & Yang, 1956:76—135. (B): Trans. Wang, 1941:77—129.
7. The narrator is emotively involved in this story where the exclamation mark is sometimes used on the narrative plane and therefore somewhat loses its value in

determining speech/thought.
8. Version (A) is translated by David Hawkes; (B) translated by Hsien-yi Yang and Gladys Yang; (C) translated by H. Bencraft Joly.
9. See McHale 1978:252; also Quirk *et al* 1972:11. 73.
10. It is also arguable that paragraphing is just another "literary" feature of *Tom Jones*, where speech is, on occasion, metrical (making up lines of blank verse) or is found with ornate poetic diction, and so on. Or alternatively, one may say that, as a verbal will, the speech here is made to follow the convention of the written will in terms of paragraphing.
11. Clearly, given the mode of free direct thought chosen by (A), the switch in question can be put across without difficulty. (A)'s consistent use of the second person "you" is, I believe, due to a personal preference for the deviant conversational thought form which presents a gain in immediacy, in verbal articulation and, not least, in emotionality. But one needs to be aware that this deviant form in Cao achieves particular prominence and striking effect only by standing out against the more objective, placid thoughts that precede, and this contrast is seen to be functional and important.

BIBLIOGRAPHY

PRIMARY SOURCES

Austen, Jane. *Pride and Prejudice*. Penguin, 1972.

Cao, Xueqin. *A Dream of Red Mansions (Honglou Meng)*. 4 vols. Beijing: People's Literature Press, 1979.

Cao, Xueqin. *The Story of the Stone*: Prefaced by Qi Liaosheng (*Qi Liaosheng Xuben Shitou Ji*). 3 vols. Beijing: People's Literature Press, 1975.

Dong, Liu, trans. *Pride and Prejudice*. By Jane Austen. Taipei: Dadong Publishing Company.

Fielding, Henry. *Tom Jones*. Harmondsworth: Penguin, 1966.

Fowles, John. *The Collectors*. London: Pan Books, 1963.

Golding, William. *The Inheritors*. Boston: Faber, 1955.

Hawkes, David, trans. *The Story of the Stone*. 3 vols. By Cao Xueqin. Harmondsworth: Penguin, 1973—1980.

Hemingway, Ernest. "A Very Short Story" in *In Our Time*. New York: C. Scribner's Sons, 1955, 83—85.

James, Jean M., trans. *Rickshaw*. By Lao She. Honolulu: University of Hawaii Press, 1979.

Joly, H. Bencraft, trans. *Hung Lou Meng*. 2 vols. By Cao Xueqin. Hong Kong, 1982, 1893.

King, Evan, trans. *Rickshaw Boy*. By Lao She. London: Michael Joseph, 1964.

Lao, She. *Rickshaw Boy (Luotuo Xiangzi)*. Beijing: People's Literature Press, 1978.

Lu, Xun. *The Complete Works of Lu Xun (Lu Xun Quanji)*. vols. 1—2. Beijing: People's Literature Press, 1963.

Mao, Dun. *Selected works of Mao Dun (Mao Dun Wenji)*. Vol. 7. Hong Kong: Contemporary Book Publishing Company, 1966.

Shapiro, S. trans. *Spring Silkworms and Other Stories*. By Mao Dun. Peking: Foreign Languages Press, 1956.

Shi, Xiaoqing, trans. *Camel Xiangzi*. By Lao She. Beijing: Foreign Languages Press, 1981.

Snow, Edgar and Yao Hsin-nung, trans. "Benediction" in Edgar Snow, ed. *Living China: Modern Chinese Short Stories*. London: George G. Harrap, 1936, 51—74.

Wang, Chi-chen, trans. *Ah Q and Others: Selected Stories of* Lusin. New York: Columbia Univ. Press, 1941.

Wang, Chi-chen, trans. "Spring Silkworms." By Mao Dun, in Wang Chi-chen, trans. *Contemporary Chinese Stories*. New York: Columbia Univ. Press, 1944, 143—158.

Wang, Keyi, trans. *Pride and Prejudice*. By Jane Austen. Hong Kong: Zhongliu Publishing Company, 1969.

Yang, Hsien-yi and Gladys Yang, trans. *Selected Works of Lu Hsun*. vol. 1. Peking: Foreign Languages Press, 1956.

Yang, Hsienyi and Gladys Yang, trans. *A Dream of Red Mansions*. 3 vols. By Cao Xueqin. Beijing: Foreign Languages Press, 1978.

Yeh, Chun-chan, trans. "Spring Silkworms" by Mao Dun, in Yeh Chun-chan, trans. *Three Seasons and Other Stories*. London: Staples Press, 1946, 9—26.

Zhou, Wen. *Selected and Annotated Stories by Lu Xun (Lu Xun Xiaoshuo Xuan Zhu)*. Hong Kong: Shanghai Book Co. ,1979.

SELECTED SECONDARY SOURCES

Adams, R. *Proteus, His Lies, His Truth: Discussions on Literary Translation*. New York: Norton, 1973.

Allen, J. P. B. and S. Pit. Corder, eds. *The Edinburgh Course in Applied Linguistics Vol 3: Techniques in Applied Linguistics*. London: Oxford Univ. Press, 1974.

Allen, W. "Narrative distance, tone, and character," in J. Halperin (1974), 323—337.

Arrowsmith, W. and R. Shattuch, eds. *The Craft and Context of Translation*. Austin, Texas: Univ. of Texas Press, 1961.

Attridge, D. *The Rhythms of English Poetry*. London & New York: Longman, 1982.

Austin, J. L. *How to Do Things with Words*. London: Oxford Univ. Press, 1962.

Bakhtin, M. *Problems of Dostoevsky's Poetics*. trans. R. W. Rotsel. U. S. A. : Ardis, 1973.

Bakhtin, M. "The word in the novel." trans. A. Shukman, in E. S. Shaffer (1980), 213—220.

Bakhtin, M. *The Dialogic Imagination*. Austin & London: Univ. of Texas Press, 1981, 259—422.

Bailey, R. W. "Stylistics today." *Foundations of Language* 2 (1974), 115—139.

Bal, M. *Narratology*. Univ. of Toronto Press, 1985.

Banfield, A. "Narrative style and the grammar of direct and indirect speech." *Foundations of Language* 10 (1973), 1—39.

Banfield, A. *Unspeakable Sentences: Narration and Representation in the Language of Fiction*. Boston: Routledge, 1982.

Barthes, R. "Style and its image," in S. Chatman (1971), 3—15.

Bassnett-McGuire, S. *Translation Studies*. London & New York: Methuen, 1980.

Beaugrande, R. de. *Factors in a Theory of Poetic Translating*. The Netherlands: Van Gorcum, 1978.

Bernstein, B. "Social class, language and socialisation," in P. P. Giglioli, ed. *Language and Social Context*. Penguin, 1972, 157—178.

Berry, M. *Introduction to Systemic Linguistics*. 2 vols. London: Batsford, 1975.

Boase-Beier, J. "Stylistics and Translation," in *The Oxford Handbook of Translation Studies*. Oxford: Oxford Univ. Press, 2011, 71—82.

Bolinger, D. *Language—the Loaded Weapon*. London: Longman, 1980.

Booth, A. D. et al. *Aspects of Translation*. London: Secker & Warburg, 1958.

Booth, W. C. *The Rhetoric of Fiction*. Chicago & London: Chicago Univ. Press, 1961.

Booth, W. C. "Distance and point-of-view: an essay in classification," in P. Stevick (1967), 87—107.

Booth, W. C. *A Rhetoric of Irony*. Chicago & London: Chicago Univ. Press, 1974.

Boulton, M. *The Anatomy of the Novel*. London: Routledge, 1975.

Brislin, R. W., ed. *Translation: Applications and Research*. New York: Gardener Press, 1976.

Brook, G. L. *The Language of Dickens*. London: Deutsch, 1970.

Broeck, R. van den. "The concept of equivalence in translation theory: some critical reflections" in J. S. Holmes et al. (1978), 29—47.

Brower, R. A., ed. *On Translation*. New York: Oxford Univ. Press, reprinted 1966.

Brown, G. and G. Yule. *Discourse Analysis*. Cambridge: Cambridge Univ. Press, 1983.

Burgess, A. *Joysprick: An Introduction to the Language of James Joyce*. 1973, London: Andre Deutsch, reprinted 1979.

Burke, M., ed. *The Routledge Handbook of Stylistics*. London: Routledge, 2014.

Burton, D. "Through glass darkly: through dark glasses," in R. Carter (1982), 195—214.

Cantrall, W. R. "The artistic use of seeming contradiction," in B. Kachru & H. Stahlke (1972), 217—230.

Carne-Ross, D. S. "Translation and transposition," in W. Arrow-smith & R. Shattuck (1961), 3—21.

Carter, R., ed. *Language and Literature*. London: George Allen & Unwin, 1982.

Carter, R. and D. Burton, eds. *Literary Text and Language Study*. London: Arnold, 1982.

Carter, R. and Paul Simpson, eds. *Language, Discourse and Literature*, London: Unwin Hyman, 1989.

Casparis, C. P. *Tense Without Time: The Present Tense in Narration*. Bern: Francke, 1975.

Catford, J. C. *A Linguistic Theory of Translation*. London: Oxford Univ. Press, 1965.

Chapman, R. *Linguistics and Literature*. London: Arnold, 1973.

Chapman, R. *The Language of English Literature*. London: Arnold, 1982.

Chatman, S., ed. *Literary Style: A Symposium*. London: Oxford Univ. Press, 1971.

Chatman, S. *Story and Discourse*. Ithaca & London: Cornell Univ. Press, 1978.

Chatman, S. and S. R. Levin, eds. *Essays on the Language of Literature*, Boston: Houghton Mifflin Company, 1967.

Chomsky, N. *Syntactic Structures*. The Hague: Mouton, 1957.

Cluysenaar, A. *Introduction to Literary Stylistics*. London: Batsford, 1976.

Cohn, D. *Transparent Minds: Narrative Modes for Presenting Consciousness in Fiction*. Princeton: Princeton Univ. Press, 1978.

Culler, J. *Structuralist Poetics*. London: Routledge, 1975.

Culler, J. *On Deconstruction*. New York: Cornell Univ. Press, 1982.

Cummings, M. and S. R. Simmons, *The Language of Literature*. Oxford: Pergamon Press, 1983.

Darbyshire, A. E. *A Grammar of Style*. 1971. London: Andre Deutsch, reprinted 1979.

Davie, D. *Articulate Energy: An Inquiry into the Syntax of English Poetry.* London: Routledge, 1955.

Dijk, T. A. van, ed. *Pragmatics of Language and Literature.* North-Holland Studies in Theoretical Poetics, vol. 2. Amsterdam: North-Holland, 1976.

Dijk, T. A. van, *Text and Context: Explorations in the Semantics and Pragmatics of Discourse.* London: Longman, reprinted, 1980.

Dillon. G. L. *Constructing Texts.* Bloomington: Indiana Univ. Press, 1981.

Duff, A. *The Third Language: Recurrent Problems of Translating into English.* Oxford: Pergamon Press, 1981.

Empson, W. *Seven Types of Ambiguity.* London: Chatto & Windus, 1949.

Enkvist, N. E. "On defining style" in N. E. Enkvist, J. Spencer and M. J. Gregory (1964), 1—56.

Enkvist, N. E. *Linguistic Stylistics.* The Hague: Mouton, 1973.

Enkvist, N. E. , J. Spencer and M. J. Gregory. *Linguistics and Style.* London: Oxford Univ. Press, 1964.

Epstein, E. L. "The self-reflexive artefact: the function of mimesis in an approach to a theory of value for literature" in R. Fowler (1975), 40—78. Reprinted in D. C. Freeman (1981), 166—199.

Epstein, E. L. *Language and Style.* London: Methuen, 1978.

Erlich, V. *Russian Formalism—History-Doctrine.* The Hague: Mouton, 1969.

Fillmore, C. J. "The case for case," in E. Bach and R. Harms, eds. *Universals in Linguistic Theory.* New York: Holt, Rinehart Winston, 1968, 1—88.

Fish, S. "Literature in the reader: affective stylistics." *New Literary History* 2 (Autumn, 1970), 123—162.

Fish, S. *Self-Consuming Artifacts: The Experience of Seventeenth-Century Literature.* Berkeley: Univ. of California Press, 1972.

Fish, S. "What is stylistics and why are they saying such terrible things about it?" in S. Chatman, ed. *Approaches to Poetics.* New York: Columbia Univ. Press, 1973. Reprinted in D. C. Freeman (1981), 53—78.

Fish, S. *Is There a Text in This Class?* Harvard Univ. Press, 1980.

Fowler, R. , ed. *Essays on Style and Language.* London: Routledge, 1966.

Fowler, R. *The Language of Literature.* London: Routledge, 1971.

Fowler, R. , ed. *Style and Structure in Literature.* Oxford: Blackwell, 1975.

Fowler, R. *Linguistics and the Novel.* London: Methuen, 1977.

Fowler, R. *Literature as Social Discourse.* London: Batsford, 1981.

Fowler, R. *Linguistic Criticism*. London: Oxford Univ. Press, 1986.

Freeman, D. C. *Linguistics and Literary Style*. New York: Holt, Rinehart & Winston, 1970.

Freeman, D. C., ed. *Essays in Modern Stylistics*. London: Methuen, 1981.

Friedman, N. "Point of view in fiction: the development of a critical concept," in Philip Stevick (1967), 108—137.

Garvin, P. L., ed. & trans. *A Prague School Reader on Esthetics, Literary Structure and Style*. 1958. Washington D. C.: Georgetown Univ. Press, reprinted 1964.

Genette, G. *Narrative Discourse*. Oxford: Blackwell, 1980.

Goldknopf, D. *The Life of the Novel*. Chicago & London: Chicago Univ. Press, 1972.

Goodman, P. *Structure of Literature*. Chicago: Chicago Univ. Press, 1954.

Graham, J. F. "Theory for translation," in M. Rose (1981), 23—30.

Gray, B. *Style: The Problem and Its Solution*. The Hague: Mouton, 1969.

Gregory, M. "Old Bailey speech in *A Tale of Two Cities*." *A Review of English Literature* 6 (1965), 42—55.

Gregory, M. "Aspects of varieties differentiation." *Journal of Linguistics* 3 (1967), 177—198.

Gregory, M. and S. Carroll, *Language and Situation*. London: Routledge, 1978.

Halliday, M. A. K. "Categories of the theory of grammar." *Word* 17 (1961), 241—292.

Halliday, M. A. K. "Descriptive linguistics in literary studies," in M. A. K. Halliday & A. McIntosh. *Patterns of Language, Papers in General, Descriptive and Applied Linguistics*. London: Longman, 1966, 56—69.

Halliday, M. A. K. "The linguistic study of literary texts," in S. Chatman & S. R. Levin (1967), 217—223.

Halliday, M. A. K. "Notes on transitivity and theme in English: Part I." *Journal of Linguistics* 3 (1967), 37—82.

Halliday, M. A. K. "Notes on transitivity and theme in English: Part II." *Journal of Linguistics* 3 (1968), 199—244.

Halliday, M. A. K. "Language structure and language function," in J. Lyons (1970), 140—165.

Halliday, M. A. K. "Linguistic function and literary style: an inquiry into the language of William Golding's *The Inheritors*," in S. Chatman (1971),

330—365.

Halliday, M. A. K. *Explorations in the Functions of Language.* London: Arnold, 1973.

Halliday, M. A. K. *System and Function in Language;* Selected Papers Ed. by G. R. Kress. London: Oxford Univ. Press, 1976.

Halliday, M. A. K. *Language as Social Semiotic.* London: Arnold, 1978.

Halliday, M. A. K. "Modes of meaning and modes of expression: types of grammatical structure, and their determination by different semantic functions," in D. J. Allerton, E. Carney & D. Holdcroft, eds. *Function and Context in Linguistic Analysis.* Cambridge Univ. Press, 1979, 57—80.

Halliday, M. A. K. and R. Hasan, *Cohesion in English.* London: Longman, 1976.

Halperin, J., ed. *The Theory of the Novel: New Essays.* London: Oxford Univ. Press, 1974.

Hasan, R. "Rime and reason in literature," in S. Chatman (1971), 299—329.

Hawkes, T. *Structuralism and Semiotics.* London: Methuen, 1977.

Heyes, C. W. "A study in prose style: Edward Gibbon and Ernest Hemingway," in D. C. Freeman (1970), 279—296.

Hernadi, P. *Beyond Genre: New Directions in Literary Classification.* Cornell Univ. Press, 1972.

Hirsch, E. D. *The Aims of Interpretation,* Univ. of Chicago Press, 1976.

Hollander, J. "Versions, interpretations, and performances," in E. A. Brower (1966), 205—231.

Holmes, J. S., ed. *The Nature of Translation.* The Hague: Slovak Academy of Science, 1970.

Holmes, J. S. "Forms of verse translation and the translation of verse form," in J. S. Holmes (1970), 91—105.

Holmes, J. S. "Describing literary translation: models and methods," in J. S. Holmes, J. Lambert & R. van den Rroeck (1978), 69—82.

Holmes, J. S., J. Lambert & R. van den Broeck, eds. *Literature and Translation.* Leuven: acco, 1978.

Horton, D. "Linguistic structure, stylistic value, and translation strategy: introducing Thomas Mann's Aschenbach in English," in *Translation and Literature* 19 (2010), 42—71.

Honnighausen, L. "'Point of view' and its background in intellectual history," in E. S. Shaffer (1980), 151—166.

Hough, G. *Style and Stylistics*. London: Routledge, 1969.

Huang, L. *Style in Translation: A Corpus-Based Perspective*. Shanghai and New York: Shanghai Jiao Tong Univ. Press and Springer, 2015.

Huddleston, R. *An Introduction to English Transformational Syntax*. London: Longman, 1976.

Iser, W. *The Act of Reading*. London: Longman, 1978.

Jakobson, R. "Closing statement: linguistics and poetics," in T. A. Sebeok (1960), 350—377.

Jiang, Hesen, "The artistic traits and achievements of *Honglou Meng*" in New Critical Essays on Honglou Meng. Heilong Jiang People's Publishing Company, 1982, 1—38.

Jones, C. "Varieties of speech presentation in Conrad's *The Secret Agent*." *Lingua* 20 (1986), 162—176.

Juhl, P. D. "Stanley Fish's interpretive communities and the status of critical interpretation," in E. S. Shaffer (1983), 47—58.

Kachru, B. B. and F. W. Stahlke, eds. *Current Trends in Stylistics*. Champaign: Champaign Linguistic Research, 1972.

Kelly, L. G. *The True Interpreter*. Oxford: Blackwell, 1979.

Kennedy, C. "Systemic grammar and its use in literary analysis," in R. Carter (1982), 83—99.

Keyser, S. J. "Wallace Stevens: form and meaning in four poems," in D. C. Freeman (1981), 100—122.

Knox, N. *The Word, Irony and Its Context*, 1500—1755. Duke Univ. Press, 1961.

Kroeber, K. *Styles in Fictional Structure*. Princeton: Princeton Univ. Press, 1971.

Lambrou, M. and P. Stockwell, eds. *Contemporary Stylistics*. London: Continuum, 2007.

Leavis, F. R. *The Great Tradition*. London: Chatto & Windus, 1948.

Leech, G. N. *A Linguistic Guide to English Poetry*. London: Longman, 1969.

Leech, G. N. *Meaning and the English Verb*. Essex: Longman, 1971.

Leech, G. N. *Semantics*. Harmondsworth: Penguin, 1974.

Leech, G. N. *Principles of Pragmatics*. London: Longman, 1983.

Leech, G. N. and M. Short, *Style in Fiction*. London: Longman, 1981.

Leech, G. N. and J. Svartvik, *A Communicative Grammar of English*. London: Longman, 1975.

Lefevere, A. *Translating Poetry, Seven Strategies and a Blueprint*. Amsterdam:

Van Gorcum, 1975.

Lefevere, A. "Beyond the process: literary translation in literature and literary theory," in M. G. Rose (1981), 52—59.

Leggett, H. W. *The Idea in Fiction*. London: George Allen & Unwin, 1934.

Levin, S. R. "Poetry and grammaticalness," in S. Chatman and S. R. Levin (1967), 224—230.

Levinson, S. C. *Pragmatics*. Cambridge Univ. Press, 1983.

Lodge, D. *Language of Fiction*. New York: Columbia Univ. Press, 1966.

Lodge, D. The *Modes of Modern Writing*. London: Arnold, 1977.

Lutwack, L. "Mixed and uniform prose styles in the novel," in P. Stevick (1967), 208—219.

Lyons, J. *Introduction to Theoretical Linguistics*. Cambridge Univ. Press, 1968.

Lyons, J., ed. *New Horizons in Linguistics*. Harmondsworth: Penguin, 1970.

Lyons, J. *Semantics*. 2 vols. Cambridge Univ. Press, 1977.

Macleod, N. "This familiar regressive series: aspects of style in the novels of Kingsley Amis," in A. J. Aitken *et al.*, eds. *Edinburgh Studies in English and Scots*. London: Longman, 1971, 121—143.

Macleod, N. "The stylistic analysis of poetic texts: Owen's 'Futility' and Davie's 'The Garden Party'," in J. Anderson, ed. *Language Form and Linguistic Variation*. Amsterdam: John Benjamins, 1982.

Macleod, N. "'This strange, rather sad story': the reflexive design of Graham Greene's *The Third Man*." *Dalhousie Review* 63 (1983), 217—241.

Macleod, N. "How to talk about prose style: an example from Golding's *Lord of the Flies*." *Revista Canaria de Estudios Ingleses* 10 (April, 1985), 119—140.

Malla, K. P. *A Study of Contemporary Models of Stylistic Analysis, Literary and Linguistic, and their Pedagogic Relevance*. Unpublished Ph. D. dissertation, Univ. of Edinburgh, 1974.

Malmkjær, K. "Translational stylistics: Dulcken's translations of Hans Christian Andersen," in *Language and Literature* 13 (2004), 13—24.

McDowell, A. "Fielding's rendering of speech in *Joseph Andrews* and *Tom Jones*." *Language and Style* 6 (1973), 83—96.

McHale, B. "Free indirect discourse: a survey of recent accounts." *Poetics and the Theory of Literature* 3 (1978), 249—287.

McIntyre, D. and B. Busse, eds. *Language and Style*. New York: Palgrave Macmillan, 2010.

Milic, L. T. *A Quantitative Approach to the Style of Jonathan Swift*. The Hague: Mouton, 1967.

Milic, L. T. "Rhetorical choice and stylistic option: the conscious and unconscious poles," in S. Chatman (1971), 77—88.

Miller, J. H. *Fiction and Repetition*. Oxford: Blackwell, 1982.

Muecke, D. C. *Irony and the Ironic*. London & New York: Methuen, 1970.

Mukařovský J. "Standard language and poetic language," in P. L. Garvin (1964), 17—30.

Nash, N. "Lawrence's 'Odour of Chrysanthemums'," in R. Carter (1982), 101—120.

Newmark, P. *Approaches to Translation*. Oxford: Pergamon Press, 1981.

Nida, E. A. *Towards a Science of Translating*. Leiden: Brill, 1964.

Nida, E. A. *Translating Meaning*. English Language Institute, 1982.

Nida, E. A. and C. R. Taber, *The Theory and Practice of Translation*. Leiden: Brill, 1969.

Nida, E. A. et al. *Style and Discourse*. Bible Society, 1983.

Ohmann, R. "Generative grammar and the concept of literary style." *Word* 20 (1964), 423—439; reprinted in D. C. Freeman (1970), 258—278.

Ohmann, R. "Literature as sentences." *College English* 27 (1966), 261—267.

Ohmann, R. "Prolegomena to the analysis of prose style," in P. Stevick (1967), 190—208.

Ohmann, R. "Speech, action and style," in S. Chatman (1971), 241—254.

Ohmann, R. "Speech, Literature and the space between," in D. C. Freeman (1981), 361—376.

Olshewsky, T. M, ed. *Problems in the Philosophy of Language*. New York: Holt, Rinehart & Winston, 1969.

Osgood, C. E. "Some effects of motivation on style of encoding," in T. A. Sebeok (1960), 293—306.

Page, N. "Categories of speech in *Persuasion*." *Modern Language Review* 64 (1969), 734—741.

Page, N. *Speech in the English Novel*. London: Longman, 1973.

Pascal, R. *The Dual Voice*. Manchester Univ. Press, 1977.

Pearce, R. *Literary Texts*. Discourse Analysis Monographs no. 3. University of Birmingham, English Language Research, 1977.

Perry, M. "Literary dynamics: how the order of a text creates its meaning." *Poetics*

Today1: 1 (1979), 35—64 and 311—361.

Popovič, A. "The concept 'shift of expression' in translation analysis," in J. S. Holmes (1970), 78—87.

Postgate, J. P. *Translation and Translations*. London: G. Bell & Sons, 1922.

Pratt, M. L. *Towards a Speech Act Theory of Literary Discourse*. Bloomington: Indiana Univ. Press, 1977.

Prince, G. *Narratology: the Form and Functioning of Narrative*. New York: Mouton, 1982.

Procházka, V. "Notes on translating technique," in P. L. Garvin (1964), 93—112.

Quirk, R. et al. *A Grammar of Contemporary English*. London: Longman, 1972.

Rabin, C. "The linguistics of translation," in A. D. Booth (1958), 123—145.

Rabin, J. *The Technique of Modern Fiction*. London: Arnold, 1968.

Radford, A. *Transformational Syntax*. Cambridge Univ. Press, 1981.

Raffel, B. *The Forked Tongue*. The Hague: Mouton, 1971.

Rahv, P. "Fiction and the criticism of fiction." *The Kenyon Review* 18 (Winter, 1956), 276—299.

Ray, L. "Multi-dimension translation: poetry," in R. W. Brislin (1976), 261—278.

Richards, I. A. *Practical Criticism*. London: Kegan Paul, 1929.

Richards I. A. "Towards a theory of translating," in T. M. Olshewsky (1969), 490—504.

Rieu, E. V. "Translation," in *Cassell's Encyclopedia of Literature*, vol. 1. London: Cassell, 1953, 554—559.

Riffaterre, M. "Criteria for style analysis." *Word* 15 (1959), 154—174.

Rimmon-Kenan, S. *Narrative Fiction: Contemporary Poetics*. London: Metheun, 1983.

Ron, M. "Free indirect discourse, mimetic language games and the subject of fiction." *Poetics Today* 2: 2 (1981), 17—39.

Rose, M. G., ed. *Translation Spectrum: Essays in Theory and Practice*. Albany: State Univ. of New York Press, 1981.

Ross, S. D. "Translation and similarity," in M. G. Rose (1981), 8—22.

Savory, T. *The Art of Translation*. London: Jonathan Cape, 1957. New and enlarged edition 1968.

Schorer, M. "Technique as discovery," in P. Stevick (1967), 65—84.

Scholes, R. and R. Kellogg, *The Nature of Narrative*. London: Oxford Univ. Press, 1966.

Schuelke, G. L. "'Slipping' in indirect discourse." *American Speech* 33 (1958), 90—98.

Searle, J. R. *Speech Acts*. Cambridge Univ. Press, 1969.

Sebeok. T. A., ed. *Style in Language*. Mass: MIT Press, 1960.

Shaffer, E. S., ed. *Comparative Criticism: A Yearbook*. vol. 1. Cambridge Univ. Press, 1979.

Shen, D. "Fidelity versus pragmatism." *Babel* 31 (1985), 134—137.

Shen, D. "Literalism: NON 'formal-equivalence'." in *Babel* 35 (1989), 219—235.

Shen, D. "On the transference of modes of speech (or thought) from Chinese narrative fiction into English." *Comparative Literature Studies*. 28 (1991), 395—415.

Shen, D. "Review: The Routledge Handbook of Stylistics," in *Style* 49 (2015), 565—569.

Shen, D. "Review: The Cambridge Handbook of Stylistics," in *Style* 49 (2015), 569—573.

Shen, D. "Review: The Bloomsbury Companion to Stylistics," in *Style* 51(2017), 88—100.

Short, M. H. "'Prelude' to a literary linguistic stylistics," in R. Carter (1982), 55—62.

Shukman, A. *Literature and Semiotics*. Amsterdam: North-Holland, 1977.

Sinclair. J. McH. "Taking a poem to pieces," in R. Fowler (1966), 68—81.

Sinclair, J. McH. "A technique of stylistic description." *Language and Style* 4 (1968), 215—242.

Sinclair, J. McH. "Lines about 'Lines'," in R. Carter (1982), 163—176.

Sotirova, V. ed. *The Bloomsbury Companion to Stylistics*. London: Bloomsbury, 2016.

Stanzel, F. K. A *Theory of Narrative*. Cambridge Univ. Press, 1986.

Steiner, G. *After Babel*. London: Oxford Univ. Press, 1975.

Steiner, T. R. *English Translation Theory*. Amsterdam: Van Gorcum, 1975.

Stevick, P., ed. *The Theory of the Novel*. New York: The Free Press, 1967.

Stockwell, P. and S. Whiteley. eds. *The Cambridge Handbook of Stylistics*. Cambridge: Cambridge Univ. Press, 2014.

Thorne, J. P. "Stylistics and generative grammars." *Journal of Linguistics* 1 (1965), 49—59.

Thorne, J. P. "Poetry, stylistics and imaginary grammars." *Journal of Linguistics* 5 (1969), 147—150.

Thorne, J. P. "Generative grammar and stylistic analysis," in J. Lyons (1970), 185—197.
Thorne, J. P. "The grammar of jealousy: a note on the character of Leontes," in A. J. Aitken *et al.*, eds. *Edinburgh Studies in English and Scots*. London: Longman, 1971, 55—65.
Todorov, T. "The place of style in the structure of the text," in S. Chatman (1971), 29—44.
Toolan, M. J. *The Stylistics of Fiction*. London: Routledge, 1990.
Toury, G. "The nature and role of norms in literary translation," in J. S. Holmes, J. Lambert & R. van den Roeck (1978), 83—100.
Toury, G. "Translation, literary translation and pseudo-translation," in E. S. Shaffer (1984), 73—85.
Traugott, E. C. and M. L. Pratt. *Linguistics for Students of Literature*. New York: Harcourt Brace Jovanovich, 1980.
Turner, G. W. *Stylistics*. Harmondsworth: Penguin, reprinted, 1975.
Tytler, A. F. *Essays on the Principles of Translation*. London: J. M. Dent, 1979.
Ullmann, S. *Style in the French Novel*. Cambridge Univ. Press, 1957.
Ullmann, S. *Language and Style*. Oxford: Blackwell, 1964.
Ullmann, S. "Style and personality." *A Review of English Literature* 6 (April, 1965), 21—31.
Ullmann, S. *Meaning and Style*. Oxford: Blackwell, 1973.
Vachek, J. *The Linguistic School of Prague*. Bloomington & London: Indiana Univ. Press, 1966.
Wang, Zuoliang. *Essays on English Stylistics*. Beijing: Foreign Languages Teaching and Research, 1980.
Watt, I. *The Rise of the Novel*. Great Britain: Cox & Wyman, 1957.
Weber, J. J. ed. *The Stylistics Reader*. London: Arnold, 1996.
Wellek, R. "Stylistics, poetics, and criticism," in S. Chatman (1971), 65—76.
Wetherill, P. M. *The Literary Text: An Examination of Critical Methods*. Oxford: Blackwell, 1974.
Whitehall, H. "From linguistics to criticism." *Kenyon Review* 13 (Autumn, 1951), 710—714.
Widdowson, H. G. "Stylistic analysis and literary interpretation." *Use of English* 24 (1972a), 28—33.

Widdowson, H. G. "On the deviance of literary discourse." *Style* 6 (1972b), 294—308.

Widdowson, H. G. "Stylistics," in J. P. B. Allen and S. Pit. Corder (1974), 202—231.

Widdowson, H. G. *Stylistics and the Teaching of Literature*. London: Longman, 1975.

Widdowson, H. G. "The conditional presence of Mr. Bleaney," in R. Carter (1982), 19—26.

Wilss, W. "Methodological aspects of the translation process." *AILA Bulletin* 2 (1982), 1—13.

Winter, W. "Translatability and synonymity," in T. M. Olshewsky (1969), 460—464.

Winter, W. "Impossibilities of translation," in T. M. Olshewsky (1969), 477—490.

Yacobi, T. "Fictional reliability as a communicative problem." *Poetics Today* 2: 2 (1981), 113—126.